# You Can
# RUN...

## BOOK II OF THE
### Thompson Family Trilogy

## GLORIA ANTYPOWICH

outskirtspress
DENVER, COLORADO

You Can Run...
Book II of the Thompson Family Trilogy
All Rights Reserved.
Copyright © 2012 Gloria Antypowich
v3.0

Cover Photo © 2012 JupiterImages Corporation. All rights reserved - used with permission.

Outskirts Press, Inc.
http://www.outskirtspress.com

ISBN: 978-1-4327-9082-0

Outskirts Press and the "OP" logo are trademarks belonging to Outskirts Press, Inc.

PRINTED IN THE UNITED STATES OF AMERICA

This book is dedicated to my blue eyed granddaughters:
Lydia and Annie.
I love you both and am so happy that you have come into my life.
I will save signed copies of my books to give you
when you are old enough to read
the "naughty" things your grandma writes!
Hello to "Karma"; Jason and Sarah's little toy Havanese puppy who
gets honourable mention in this book

Thank You, to Sharron Hynes for becoming my "new set of eyes"
and helping me with the final edit.

# CHAPTER ONE

*S*hauna Lee Holt stared unseeingly out the window in her office. A knot of frustration formed in her gut. She sighed as she looked back at her desk, her eyes resting on the folder in front of her. *Thompson Land and Cattle Company.* She flicked a loose staple with her long, brightly coloured finger nail. Then she absently tapped the keys on her computer key board.

C O L T  T H O M P S O N—the name popped up on her screen. She stared at the door he had just walked out of. "*Damn!*" she breathed. "*Why did I let him go so easily?*"

But she knew why. When he had asked her to marry him four years ago, neither one of them had professed to be in love. No unrealistic, romantic notions. They were mature adults…friends, companions. He was the only son of a moneyed, respected family in the area. He was good looking and treated her like someone special when they went out: a great dinner companion, someone to go to high profile events with. They had even gone to Mexico once, even though he was totally out of his element there. And he was great in bed.

"*Yeah—he was great in bed,*" she thought, as she pushed her chair back and stood up. She scooped up the file on her desk and carried it down the hall to the junior accountant that the client had been assigned too.

Then she walked back to her office and grabbed her jacket. Stopping at the reception desk she told Christina, that she was leaving early. As she pushed through the door, she took out her cell phone and quickly dialed a familiar number. She smiled when the deep masculine voice answered. She knew he had read his call display when he said, "Hi sexy, how about dinner tonight?"

"Why did it take you so long to ask? I'm available, willing and ready!"

Josh Kendall laughed. "Okay sweet cheeks! But if you're available, willing and ready, I'm definitely going to need some nourishment first. If it's alright with you, we could grab a bite at the Steakhouse on George Street. Then we can head on over to your place."

She gave a throaty laugh. "That works for me; I'll meet you there."

Shauna Lee pulled up in front of the restaurant and parked. She surveyed the lot, but didn't see Josh's car. She hesitated for a minute, running her fingers through her blonde hair which was cut in a stylish bob. Then she looked in the rear view mirror. The big blue eyes, which were her most notable feature, reflected back at her. They were wide and luxuriously fringed with sweeping dark lashes that she had inherited from her mother.

A quick glance showed that her mascara and subtle application of eye shadow were still in place. She took a slim stick out of her purse and applied fresh lipstick. Josh still hadn't shown up, so she decided to go inside and get a table for them. She could order a glass of wine for herself.

She picked a table, midway down the dining room, against the wall. After ordering a glass of wine at the bar, she carried it to the table. She smoothed her stylish dress as she sat down and stretched her legs in front of her, admiring her high heeled shoes. She sipped her wine as she looked around the room.

People were coming and going. She watched them idly. Suddenly, she heard a familiar laugh. She sat up, alert. It was Colt! He came into the dining room with another man; someone she didn't recognise. Her heart leapt. What was he doing there? She thought he would have been back in his happy home by now. He had left her office an hour and a half ago. He hadn't said anything about staying in town.

She watched him intently, willing him to look at her. At one time he would have instantly been aware of her, but today he sat down at a table, absorbed in conversation with his companion.

Irrationally, she felt slighted. If she went to the washroom, she could go right past his table. She got up and walked by, tossing her hair and swaying her hips. He didn't notice her. Neither did his companion.

She went into the washroom, fluffed her hair and retouched her lipstick. Then she sashayed out and up to his table. She feigned surprise when she stopped by him. "Colt," she purred. "You didn't mention that you would be in town tonight."

He looked up at her, surprised. "Shawna Lee! I didn't expect to see you here." He didn't ask her to join them or give her any indication that she was welcome.

"I thought you'd be home by now."

He motioned to his companion. "We're going to an agriculture seminar at the Best Western tonight. We stopped here for a bite to eat before we wandered over there. Have you two met?"

Both of them shook their heads, so Colt introduced them. "Shauna Lee Holt, this is Brad Johnson. Brad has set up shop here in Swift Current: *Windspeer Wind Turbines*. He's giving a presentation about small wind energy generated turbines at the tonight's seminar."

He looked at his companion. "Shauna Lee owns *Swift Current Accounting and Bookkeeping Services*. Her firm has managed our accounting for years."

She looked at Colt's companion: tall, well toned, dark brown hair, grey eyes. Actually he was a good looking guy: long legs encased in blue jeans, a soft shirt, a western cut denim jacket, cowboy boots and a Stetson that sat on the table: a real country boy.

She gave him an intimate smile and she didn't miss the spark of interest that flashed in his eyes. "How nice to meet you, Brad. Are you new to the area?"

"Yes. I'm from British Columbia; Dawson Creek, to be exact."

"If you need someone to show you around, I'm free and over twenty one." She flashed him a smile as reached into her purse for a business card and handed it to him. "My number is on the card.

"If you need accounting services, my firm is the best." She winked. "And, I'm good company too, aren't I Colt?"

Colt had been watching the exchange with amusement. Her question startled him. What the hell was she up too? "Oh...yeah...I guess you are."

"Colt," she chided him. "You guess? Have you forgotten already?"

Just then Josh Kendall walked in. He sauntered up to them.

"What's this Sweet Cheeks? I'm late, so you're checking out the competition already?" He winked at Brad. "She's mine for tonight, so you're out of luck this time buddy." He slid his hand familiarly around her waist, letting it rest on her hip, with his fingers trailing down toward her pelvic bone. "Sorry I'm late babe, but I got hung up at the last minute."

She felt heat rise in her face. *I'll get even with you for that remark Josh Kendall,* she fumed as she turned away; *you're out of luck this time buddy!...as if I'm up for grabs.* Josh tightened his arm around her waist and suggestively rubbed against her. She was suddenly embarrassed and wondered what Colt and his friend had thought.

Brad looked at Colt and raised an eyebrow. Colt just shrugged and said nothing. They resumed their former conversation.

Shauna Lee suddenly lost her appetite. She had initiated the evening; it had been a knee jerk reaction to Colt's indifference to her. Josh was primed and ready for a night of sex, but his words rankled. *He made me sound like a prostitute....or a common whore.* Anger surged through her; she would show him who was out of luck!

She set her wine glass on the table. "Josh, I'm sorry. Suddenly I don't feel very good. I think I'm going to have to pass on tonight. I'm just not up to it."

He looked at her in surprise. "What do you mean you're not up to it? You're always up to it." Then he laughed. "Are you playing hard to get?"

He reached across the table to caress her hand. He raised an eyebrow as she pulled away. "Come on sweet cheeks. We both know that you are never hard to get. In fact I'll bet you're hot and wet right now and I'm ready to go." He reached for her hand.

"I'm serious Josh." She stood up, avoiding his touch. "I shouldn't have called you. I'm going home now: alone."

"The hell you are! You think you can tease me and get away with it? I'll be at your door, right behind you." He grabbed her arm, trying to pull her with him.

"Josh Kendall," she raised her voice and heads turned. "Take your hands off me. I said NO."

His face turned red and he let go of her arm. He swore as he turned and went to pay his bill. Then he strode outside angrily.

Shauna Lee finished her glass of wine. She looked out the window and saw that Josh was still standing outside, waiting for her. *Damn him!* She cringed when she saw Colt look at her and decided to escape to the washroom. She avoided his table on her way.

Ten minutes later she thought it would be safe to leave, certain that Josh would have left by then. Colt and Brad Thompson were paying at the till when she slipped out the door. She had just started toward her car when Josh stepped around the corner of the building.

"Thought you'd ditched me eh? Not so easy babe." He grabbed her arm. "What the hell's gotten into you? I don't appreciate being embarrassed in public."

"And I don't like having you talk about me like I'm a common whore."

"Funny, you never seemed to mind acting like one before. What's got you so high and mighty now?"

"You bastard!" She slapped his face.

Colt and Brad witnessed the interaction as they came outside. Colt quickly realized that the situation could get ugly. In an instant he made a decision and stepped into the angry tableau.

"All right you two; it's time for both of you to dial this back and cool off." He looked at Josh. "It's none of my business, but whatever is going on between you, she quite plainly said *No* when you were inside. You'd better take off now. Both of you need time to rethink things."

Josh's face flushed. "Damn right it's none of your business. And aren't you one to talk! How many years did she screw the balls off you?" He laughed harshly. "Why aren't you home with that wife of yours instead of here defending her? Don't tell me you've still got the hots for our Shauna Lee."

"That's enough!" Colt spoke with steely calm. He reached into his pocket, took out his cell phone and flipped it open. He pushed a bottom and waited while it rang. Then he spoke. "I'm calling to report a problem brewing in the parking lot at The Steakhouse on George Street. I'd appreciate it if you would send someone down here to diffuse this situation before it gets out of hand."

He waited for a couple of seconds. "My name is Colt Thompson. Yes, I'll wait here to fill you in and I'll give you a statement."

His hard, green eyes pinned Josh as he closed the phone and put it back in his pocket. "Don't ever question my love and loyalty to my wife. Shauna Lee is my business associate, and I still view her as a friend; *that's it: period.*

"But I won't stand by and watch you or anyone else force himself on any woman. The fact that she and I had a relationship in the past makes no difference now; *that is in the past.*"

They heard a siren blip twice and the flash of red and blue lights could be seen coming down the street. Josh swore violently as he turned to his truck. "You'll pay for calling the cops on me. I know people in high places."

He laughed. "Hell, I know a guy at the cop shop that's screwin' her too. Good luck bitch!" He slid into his truck, started the engine and gave Colt 'the finger' as he eased past the patrol car that was pulling into the parking lot.

Shauna Lee covered her face; she wished she could disappear. She had been insulted by Josh's attitude; his lack of respect for her. But now she was humiliated. Colt had come to her rescue, but he hadn't defended her honour. In fact he had left no doubt about where she fit in his life. There were no lingering feelings of attraction there. What a fool she was; and now she had to go through all of this hassle with the police.

Two officers stepped out of the patrol car. Colt stepped toward the one nearest to him. He extended his hand. "Colt Thompson, sir. I made the call." He introduced Shauna Lee and then briefly sketched out what had happened.

Brad Johnson stood back, not wanting to get involved. He was grateful that Colt had not drawn him into the situation, even though

6

they were together. He was surprised by this steely, calm side of Colt Thompson. Clearly he was a man who didn't stand for much bull shit. He thought about the way he had made that call, knowing it would involve him in an awkward situation.

His eyes moved to the woman standing by Colt. She was clearly someone out of his past; he had left no doubt about that. She was good looking. It sounded like she was pretty hot, too. Josh Kendal was probably ten years younger than her, and he had left little doubt that their relationship was all about sex. She was definitely trouble; the kind of woman a smart man would steer clear of.

Colt walked over to Brad. "Sorry about this mess. Go ahead; you need to get set up. I'll get there as soon as I get finished here." Brad nodded and walked across the street to the Best Western.

Twenty minutes later, Colt came into the small meeting room, followed by a subdued Shauna Lee. Brad had saved a seat at the front for him and he looked at Colt with dismay when he ushered Shauna Lee into it. "The place is pretty full. I'll find a spot against the wall at the back," Colt said softly as he stepped away.

Brad scarcely looked at Shauna Lee, but he couldn't miss the tension in her body as she sat next to him. Shauna Lee shifted uncomfortably in her seat, and he couldn't help but notice the way the slim skirt of her dress rode up on her thigh, or the curve of her ankles, and the slender length of her legs. She was petite and delicate looking.

He had set up his laptop and slide presenter when he had first gotten there, so all he had to do now was turn it on and start his power point presentation. He fidgeted, waiting for his turn; wanting to get up and move away from her. He was uncomfortably aware of her.

He had been an onlooker, but he couldn't totally push aside everything that had happened; like the way she had smiled at him when Colt had introduced them. He had recognized the invitation. Then she had baited Colt. That had thrown him. Colt's cool, disinterested response had piqued his interest. Then Josh Kendall had shown up and the whole picture had deteriorated after that.

Brad gave his presentation about the innovation of wind energy and its potential for use in agriculture. He didn't miss the change in Shauna Lee's demeanour as he spoke. She became alert with unfeigned interest. She watched the slides and listened to the questions from the audience and paid attention to his answers.

The seminar broke for coffee after he finished and everyone started circulating around the room. He fielded several questions about his company's wind energy program. Eventually he noticed Shauna Lee standing at the edge of the group listening and talking with the others. He noticed the professionalism in her manner as she conversed with the people and the respect that she was greeted with. She was all business; there was no coquette there now.

He had to wonder; who was the real Shauna Lee Holt?

After the meeting Colt joined Brad and helped him pack up his presentation. He looked directly at Brad when they were finished. "I need to ask a favour of you."

"OK."

"The cop said that Shauna Lee shouldn't go home immediately. He wanted to have a talk with Josh and tell him to back off, but he wasn't sure if Josh would show up at her place before he tracked him down.

"I suggested that she come here with me. I told him that I'd make sure she got home all right after the meeting. I hate to ask you, but would you come with me? I'd rather not go there on my own. Do you understand?"

Brad sensed the tension in Colt. "Yeah—I guess I can."

"It won't take long. She doesn't live too far from here. I just want to make sure that she gets in the house all right: then I'll bring you right back here to your pickup and I'll head home to my wife and kids.

Shauna Lee sank onto the couch in her living room. Colt had been the perfect gentleman. He'd followed her home in his truck, walked her to the door, made sure she'd gotten safely inside, and waited until he'd heard the sound of her turning the dead bolt. Then he'd hurried back to his truck and left.

She couldn't ignore the emptiness in her gut. What the hell was wrong with her? She couldn't get Colt out of her mind. It was insane. He was married and nauseatingly happy with the family he never thought he'd have until Frankie came along.

Shauna Lee sighed heavily. She and Colt had seen each other on and off over a four year period before he had proposed to her. Truthfully she had never seen him exclusively, although she had never actually admitted that to him.

She had been surprised when he'd suggested they should get married, but to her amazement he had been persistent. He had even agreed to live in Swift Current and commute to the farm, because his parents had been living there and had no thought of moving.

At first she had hesitated. He loved kids and she had known he would probably want them. That was the last thing she wanted. And in spite of all his finer points, he worked too damn hard. He was a farmer and a rancher at heart and she'd had *zero* interest in that lifestyle. She had already spent too many years on a farm and she had smelled enough cow shit and breathed enough grain dust to last her a life time.

Colt had wanted to announce their engagement at the annual barbecue for his birthday. By the time she had agreed, the ring she had picked out could not be resized in time; but the announcement had been made anyway.

At first he had been almost feverish about getting married, wanting it to happen quickly. She finally had gotten into the idea of planning the wedding, when she had started to notice sadness in him. His excitement had faded and she had known something was wrong. She hadn't been in love with him, but she had loved him as a friend. He was probably the only person she had gotten close to since her life had fallen apart twenty years previously.

He had come to her just before Christmas, anguish plain in his demeanour. She had tried to talk to him, to find out what was going on. His pain was obvious and when she had tried to distract him by making love, he hadn't wanted to. He had left early that night.

He had came back to the office the next day and asked her if they could go to her place. Once they arrived there he had sat on the couch, hanging his head and wringing his hands. When she had firmly told him he had to tell her what was going on, his shoulders had began to shake.

He had sobbed as he told her he couldn't marry her. He was in love with Frankie and he was miserable without her. He had apologised over and over for asking her to marry him.

Shauna Lee sat, remembering the whole scene. She hadn't really been upset. Marriage had been his idea, not hers. Relationships had never worked for her; not even childhood ones. Marriage certainly hadn't been on her 'to do' list.

Colt had always sworn he would never fall in love again. If he cared that much about Frankie, she had decided she wouldn't stand in his way: there were other guys.

And over the past three years there had been several. She had thrived on the variety. What did they say? It was the spice of life? But gradually, as she had observed the warm, loving, attentive man that Colt had become with his family and his adoration for Frankie, or *Fran* as he lovingly called her, a little voice in the back of her mind had began to tell her that could have been her life. She had been a fool to give him up so easily. She should have fought to keep him. He couldn't have truly forgotten how good they were together. She could win him back.

She winced. She had made several subtle advances to him throughout the past year, but he was so involved in his own happiness he hadn't even seemed to notice.

And tonight…She cringed remembering how he had made it very plain to Josh that she was part of his *past*.

She stood up and walked into her bedroom. She threw her purse on the chair, stripped out of her clothes and went into the bathroom. She turned on the shower and let uncomfortably warm water sluice over her, feeling the burn, wanting to wash away the humiliation that Josh's words had left with her.

She stepped out on the mat and gave herself a brisk rubdown, then quickly blew her hair dry. She didn't look too closely at her reflection in the mirror, unwilling to meet her own eyes.

As she turned to step back into her bedroom she muttered *Screw him*, as she flipped the switch to turn off the bathroom light. Her eyes lit on the bed. She laughed with irony. That's exactly what he planned to be doing; right there on that bed, just like they'd done how many times before?"

She felt a flush of disgust. She wasn't certain how many times they had wrinkled the sheets there.

She sat on the edge of the bed, thinking. He'd been a voracious sexual companion. She hadn't asked for love. But he didn't respect her. *"What do you mean, you're not up to it? You're always up to it."* His word played a loop in her mind. *"We both know you're never hard to get."*

She cringed remembering his response when she had told him she didn't like having him talk about her like she was a common whore. *Funny, you never seemed to mind acting like one before. What's got you so high and mighty now?*

Anger washed through her, followed by embarrassment. *Hell, I know a guy at the cop shop that's screwin' her too.* Cripes…he had to have meant Jim Wiley. She had been with him a couple of times. Had they compared notes? Revulsion washed over her.

She buried her face in her hands. "How did I get to this place?" she groaned.

She turned back the covers and shut off the light on her night table. She lay down, pulling the sheets up under her chin. She tried to force the tension out of her body and relax, but her mind would not shut off. She could hear Josh's voice saying *"She's mine for tonight, so you're out of luck this time buddy."*

What had Colt and his friend thought? Not that it mattered; but damn it, it did matter to her. She turned the light back on, then went to her dresser and pulled out a pair of cotton pyjamas. Usually she didn't wear anything to bed, but tonight she felt naked and she needed something; as if the pyjamas would cover her humiliation.

She went to the bathroom. She opened the medicine chest and took a sleeping pill, then after a hesitation, swallowed a second one to ensure the oblivion of sleep; a respite from the devil that beleaguered her mind.

# CHAPTER TWO

*F*rankie Thompson tiptoed into the nursery to peek at the three year old twins who were sleeping soundly in their beds. Selena's dark curls were tousled on her pillow. Her 'blankey' was clutched tightly in her fingers, tucked up under her chin and pulled up against her cheek.

She was a combination of both her mother and father. She had Colt's dark curly hair, and Frankie's dark brown eyes. Her cupid bow lips were parted softly and a slurp of drool ran out of the corner of her mouth and onto the pillow. She was a wisp of a child; pixie like, but determined and feisty.

Sam was curled up in the other bed, his back to her, moonlight spilling softly over his sheets. She could hear the slurping sounds he made as he sucked his thumb. He was as sturdy as a linebacker; quiet and unexcitable. He had inherited his mother's auburn hair with the same fiery glints, but his eyes were calm blue ponds like those of his namesake; her grandfather, Frank Samuel Lamonte.

Her hand moved to the subtle roundness of her tummy. "I hope you have your daddy's green eyes," she whispered as she turned and eased out of the room silently, closing the door gently behind her as she went.

She went down stairs and into the living room and walked over to the bay window. Pushing aside the ruffle of the gauzy white Priscilla curtain, she looked out past the veranda, her eyes travelling down the tree lined driveway that lead up to the farm yard from the gravel road.

She glanced at her watch, noting that it was nine thirty. Colt should be getting home any moment. He had gone to Swift Current earlier in the day. He'd had an earlier appointment at the accountants and then later in the evening he was attending a meeting that the District Agriculturist was hosting at the Best Western Hotel.

Restless, she wandered over and turned on the electric fire place, then sank into a deep arm chair and watched the artificial flames flicker in the darkness.

She sighed contentedly. Four years ago she had never imagined she could be so happy. She smiled. *Colt*, she thought. *It's amusing to think about how we fought against our love.* She closed her eyes remembering. The clashes; the way they had wanted each other, but were too afraid to take the risk because neither of them wanted to get their heart broken again.

Colt had been so determined, that he had become engaged to Shauna Lee. He had imagined that getting engaged to her would give him protection from his true feelings. For him, Shauna Lee had been safe; a friend, not a love. She couldn't have hurt his heart. But eventually his love had overcome his fear and he'd gone to Shauna Lee with the truth.

Frankie groaned. *And Shauna Lee was so gracious, releasing Colt from the engagement without a fuss so he could feel free to come to me. I can't ever imagine letting Colt go. How did she do it?*

She reached out and picked up the wedding album from the end table. As she slowly turned the pages, her fingers brushed the pictures. Once Colt had found her, he had been relentless in his insistence that they have a real wedding. She and her mom had gone to Red Deer and found a wedding gown of simple design with an empire waistline that skimmed over her bulging midriff.

Colt had been handsome in his tux. Her childhood friend, Becky Freemont, had been her bridesmaid and Ollie, the ranch foreman, had been Colt's best man.

Ollie had been so proud, he had even shaved his beard off and cut his hair, revealing a much younger looking man than she had believed him to be. "A handsome man," she thought touching a photo of Colt and him.

The wedding had been small; the only guests had been their parents, Becky and her husband, Russ, and Ollie. They had said their vows in the church she had attended from childhood; in front of the pastor she had known all of her life. There were flowers and candles and a photographer who took pictures from positions and angles that were incredibly flattering in spite of her burgeoning belly.

There had been no honeymoon. They had stayed in Alberta, living in her apartment in Stettler until the end of January. Then they had returned to Saskatchewan, to live here on the farm at Cantaur.

Colt's mom and dad had decided to move into an apartment in Regina, leaving the farm house available for Colt and Frankie. Everything had fallen into place so quickly it had hardly seemed real. Colt had been delighted that his dad had chosen to step out of the business, knowing it was best for his health. And it had quickly solved the housing crisis for Colt and her.

They had barely gotten settled into the house, before the twins had made their appearance two weeks early! Chaos had reined for a while. Fortunately she had a lot of support. Colt had been such a proud, hands-on dad. She smiled, remembering the love that had flowed out of him. The man who had vowed he would never fall in love again, had fallen hook, line and sinker!

She closed the photo album and stared at the flickering light in the fireplace. A few minutes later she heard the crunch of tires on the driveway.

Colt bounded up the steps onto the veranda and was opening the screen door as Frankie opened the inside one to meet him.

"You had a long meeting!" she said with a smile, as she clasped his hand and pulled him inside. She shut the door behind him as he pulled her into a warm embrace.

"Yeah, it was an interesting evening. Not just the meeting!" He released her, took off his hat and put it on the rack, and then turned to her.

"What else happened?"

"Oh, Shauna Lee..." He shook his head. She was at the restaurant where Brad and I went for an early supper before the meeting. She came by and said hello and made a hit on Brad right off the bat!" He grinned and shook his head. "That girl never changes. Then Josh Kendall came in. I don't know if you know him."

Frankie shook her head.

"Well, he's a young high roller that works in the oil business. He's got an office in town. I guess they had arranged to meet there. When he got there she was talking to us. He got real territorial and let Brad know that she was *his* for the night.

"I think she was a little embarrassed by the way he said it. She got pretty red. Any way, they went to a table and I have no idea what happened but obviously the evening didn't go the way it was planned to. They got into a disagreement and she told him 'no' loud enough for the whole restaurant to hear. He was pissed off. He paid his bill and stormed out.

"She stayed at the table until he went outside. She waited a few minutes and then she went to the washroom. I think she was giving him time to get out of there. She must have slipped outside while Brad and I were paying for our meal.

"When we went outside Josh was still there and they were going at it again. She slapped his face and he grabbed her. It was getting ugly. I thought I could diffuse the situation if I just stepped in and got them both to back off."

He looked at her sheepishly. "It didn't work. He just got uglier and made her sound like the town tramp. Then he got personal about it with me; bringing up the fact that she and I had been together in the past and suggesting that I still had a thing for her.

"I set him straight on that score, but his attitude really put me off. I called the cops. Then, he was really pissed off. He threw some more insults at Shauna Lee and sped out of the parking lot just as the cop car arrived."

"Colt!"

"He won't be a problem. He was embarrassed as much as anything. I suspect he was planning to spend the night at her place; but she had plainly told him 'no' and he was trying to force her into a situation against her will. Anyway, when the cops came I told them what I'd seen and they talked to Shauna Lee."

"Where was Brad when all this happened?"

"He just stood back and watched the whole damn mess unfold. After I called the cops, I told him to go set up for the meeting and I'd meet him over at the meeting room when I was finished. He left right away. I'm sure he was relieved not to be drawn into the situation."

"I wonder what he thought."

"He didn't comment. But after Shauna Lee talked to the police, they said she should wait for a while before she went home so they had a chance to track Josh down and warn him to leave her alone.

"I ended up taking her to the meeting with me. After it was over I asked Brad to come with me and we followed her as she drove home. I made sure she got into the house and heard her turn the dead bolt. Then I took Brad back to his truck and came home. That's why I'm so late."

He put his arm around her and pulled her back into his embrace, kissing her deeply. "I love you," he whispered. "I am so glad you came into my life."

She nibbled on his bottom lip. "Let's go to bed." They turned off the lights as they moved through the house and up the stairs, stopping at the nursery to check on the twins.

"Little angels," Colt whispered as he looked at them, smiling.

"Well they look like angels when they are sleeping," she whispered with a chuckle. "But sometimes the halo needs a little polishing when they are awake."

He led her into the bedroom, where he began to unbutton her blouse as he kissed the corner of her lips. His fingers gently brushed her skin as they slid down to undo the tiny clasp between her breasts, releasing her bra. His mouth followed the same path, dropping little kisses all the way down her throat, across her shoulder to where the bra strap had lain, then down along her breast, coming to rest on her full nipple.

She moaned and pushed against him. Three years of marriage and the birth of the twins had not dimmed the fire that his touch stirred in her. The flames leapt hungrily as they helped each other get rid of the rest of their clothes. They tumbled on the bed and lost themselves in ageless ritual of sexual fulfillment.

Exhausted and satiated they dozed, Frankie lying in the circle of Colt's arm, her cheek against his chest. An hour later they stirred, and moved to pull back the sheets and get into bed. Colt was quiet.

"What are you thinking?" Frankie whispered.

"Oh…about life; you and me, how wonderful our life is…the twins, and in a few months our new baby arriving." He reached over and rested his hand on her belly. "I am so lucky to have all of you in my life. When I think about where I was stuck before, in my anger and bitterness; and all I would have missed, it gives me the chills."

"That goes for me too, Colt. When you told me what happened with Shauna Lee tonight, I had to feel sorry for her. I wonder if she'll ever find what we have."

"You know, I'm not sure what she's doing now. But if any of the crap Josh was rattling off is true, I'm concerned for her. He gave the impression that she is pretty promiscuous. When I was with her, she was definite about not wanting to get into a real relationship. We spent a lot of time together over the four years when we were seeing each other, but when I asked her to marry me, she wasn't very keen on it. If I hadn't been so desperate to 'save myself from you' and hadn't been so insistent, I doubt if she would agreed."

"What is she running from, Colt? Obviously, it's not sex because she seems to gravitate to that. So what has hurt her so much?"

Colt sighed. "I know her dad was an alcoholic. Shawna Lee had a brother quite a bit younger than her and she worshiped him. He died in an accident on the farm when he was three or four."

Frankie groaned. "It makes me sick to think of that. How could any of them deal with it?"

"I think that is part of her problem. It was like the straw that broke the camel's back. From what she told me, her dad just buried himself deeper in the bottle. He mother slid into depression. Shawna Lee was thirteen, or somewhere around that age, when it happened. She really had no support at home.

"She moved in with a local guy when she was really young. I don't know if they ever actually got married. He was a farmer and from what she told me, the guy was a damn poor one. Eventually he took off and left her and she had to make a life for herself. But she's got guts; she pulled herself together, finished her education and got her CA."

"I feel sorry for her. I wish she could meet someone special; like you. Someone she would truly be happy with."

"I doubt if she'll meet that kind of guy doing what she seems to be doing now."

"Do you think it would help if you talked to her, Colt?"

He frowned. "I'd really have to think about that. It bothered me to hear the insinuations that Josh made tonight. That's why I asked Brad to go with me when I followed her to her place. I don't want to do anything that could be misinterpreted. I don't want to put us at risk."

Frankie snuggled close. "I'm not worried about that. We are solid."

The phone rang at six thirty the next morning. Frankie was pouring coffee for them when Colt answered it. The conversation was brief.

"That was Ollie. He is wondering when we going to move the cows and calves in from the lease."

"I want to go with you this year. I'd enjoy a few days in the saddle again!"

Colt frowned. "Will that be OK? You know; for the baby and all?"

"Colt, I'm not sick! I'm pregnant. That's the oldest condition in the world and I'm as strong as a horse!" Her smile was radiant. "I was riding out there when I was carrying the twins and it didn't hurt me. I've missed being on the round up for the past three years, but I really couldn't go with the twins being so small.

"They are old enough to leave with your mom now, if she'll look after them. It would be great if your mom and dad would come out to the ranch and watch them there. Then we could give them a kiss goodnight and tuck them in. What do you think?" Excitement sparkled in her eyes.

Colt thought for a moment. "Well, Ollie would sure be happy to have you there. He still swears you are the best ranch hand he has ever had." He reached out and took her hand, pulling her onto his lap. He nuzzled the curve of her neck. "And I'd love to have you out there with me. We made some wonderful memories there."

She turned her face to settle her lips on his. Their kiss deepened and she could feel him harden as she rested against him. He shifted and turned her to face him, his hand moving to her breast. Fire leapt in her groin.

"Do we have time?" he whispered. She nodded and he swept her up in his arms and carried her up to their bedroom. They both tore their clothes off and fell onto the unmade bed that they had left little more than an hour earlier.

Fifteen minutes later they lay together, panting and sweaty. Colt ran his fingers through the tips of her hair. "Wowee. That was good!" He curled his arm, drawing her tight against him and nibbled at the corner of her lips. "You're still so hot woman! I don't think I'll ever get enough of you."

"And you're still so horny!" she said with a laugh. "We'd better get up and have breakfast now. The coffee will be cold and the twins should wake up in half an hour. Quickie time is over!"

He sighed. "You're right. While you make breakfast, I'll call mom and see if they will come out to the ranch and watch the kids."

Colt came back to the kitchen with a frown on his face. "Mom can't come; she and dad have already made plans. But she suggested someone that one of her friends knows. This woman's husband died ten years ago. Her family was grown up and she was an elementary teacher. She retired and the last couple of years she's been a nanny for this Mrs. Chapman's daughter. Mom says she comes highly recommended. We could check her out. What do you think?"

"I don't know. We don't know her and the twins don't know her. I'm not sure if…"

"We could meet her and see how we feel about her. If it feels right, we can bring her out here and see how it works with her and the kids. I've been thinking for awhile…I'd like to get someone who could help you out. You handle it all so well, but sometimes I'm just blown away by what all you do. I see how much work the twins are, and now with you being pregnant again, I'd like to get someone to give you a hand."

"Colt, I don't need help…"

He laid two fingers across her lips. "There is a selfish motive in this for me too. I'd like it if you could come to a meeting with me; like last night, or go to a horse race with me when I go, and you could come out to the ranch for a day with me. You should have a bit of time for yourself. I didn't marry you to keep you barefoot and pregnant. I wanted you to be my companion as well!"

"I…well…all right, we can check her out. When are you moving cows?"

"Ollie and I decided next week will work best, so we had better get on this nanny thing right away. I want you to be on the round-up this year."

"Did your mom tell you her name?"

"She is going to call me back with her phone number. Her name is Ellie Raines."

"Does she know if she's available now…" Suddenly she heard a whimper from up stairs. "That's Selena! The kids are awake!" Frankie whirled and went flying up the stairs to the nursery. Colt shook his head slightly. She was so in tune with the twins that it amazed him.

He could hear her crooning to their daughter. Selena would be rubbing her eyes with her little fists, her face all scrunched up on the verge of tears, protesting grumpily as she shed the drowsiness of sleep. Sam would be sitting his bed, calm and wide eyed. They were as different as night and day.

The phone rang. Colt picked it up and answered it, ignoring the call display. He didn't recognise the callers' voice.

"Could I speak to Colt Thompson?" a youthful sounding female voice asked.

"Speaking."

"This is Ellie Raines. Connie Chapman talked to your mother this morning. She said you are looking for a babysitter next week."

"We could be. Of course, we need to meet you first."

"I could drop by your place anytime today."

"That would be a great idea. Do you know where we live?"

"Not exactly; Connie said you live on a farm near Cantuar, but I don't know your exact address."

Colt gave her directions to the farm and she said she would be there around eleven that morning. Then he bounded up the stairs to tell Frankie and the twins.

Ellie Raines was punctual. She drove down the tree lined driveway and parked her silver coloured compact car in front of the old two story house. She noted how well kept the house and grounds were. As she stepped out of her car, she looked through the tall trees that formed a dividing line between the lawn around the house and the equipment yard.

She looked with interest at the huge, modern combines parked in front of a large machine shed. Experience told her that harvesting was finished. It had been a good fall for the farmers. She noted the large metal grain bins lined up. The little tell-tale piles of grain on the ground in front of each one told her that grain had been augured into them and they were probably all full.

She turned as she heard the house door open. Her eyes met a tall, good looking man with the greenest eyes she had ever seen. She decided he was probably in his late thirties or early forties. She smiled as she sized him up.

"Hi. I'm Ellie Raines. I was just looking at the combines and the grain bins. My husband and I had a mixed farm near Chitek Lake. Our kids weren't interested in the farm and it was too much for me to handle, so I sold it after he died. But I've always loved harvest time."

Colt smiled as he watched her walk up the sidewalk. She was dressed in comfortable brown chino slacks and a fresh looking pink blouse. She was petite. She was probably about five foot four, pleasantly rounded and motherly looking; not fat but definitely not thin. He guessed that she was in her early sixties. Her hair was a warm brown with golden high lights and a few threads of silver showing up in the temples. It was cut in a smart style that suited her well. Her eyes were a cool grey; warm, open and friendly. His first instinct was to like her. He reached out to shake her hand and invited her in.

"Fran," he called, "Ellie Raines is here."

He heard her answer from upstairs. "I'll be right there. I'm changing Selena's clothes. She spilled a glass of milk on herself. Will you make a fresh pot of coffee? Oh, and watch where you step by the table. I didn't get the milk all wiped up."

Colt motioned for Ellie to follow him into the kitchen. He pulled some paper towel from the roll and turned toward the table. Ellie reached to take it from his hand. "Let me clean up the spill while you make the coffee. I'm dying for a cup." She smiled as she took the paper towel from his hand and nimbly bent down to wipe up the spill.

Frankie and the twins came down the stairs and smiles of unfeigned delight wreathed Ellie's face. Colt introduced her to Frankie and each child in turn. Selena ran to Ellie, open and accepting and Ellie stooped and picked her up. Frankie and Colt watched the immediate connection between them and looked at each other with understanding.

Ellie moved slowly toward Sam, speaking to him softly as she knelt down in front of him. She gently stood Selena on the floor beside her, cradling her close to her as she held her hand out to Sam. She spoke to both of the children, letting Sam make the next move. At first he clung firmly to his mother's legs but gradually he relaxed as Ellie gained his confidence and reached out to touch her fingers.

She looked up at Colt. "Well daddy, is that cup of coffee ready?" She took both children by the hand and followed Frankie and Colt to the kitchen table. As they drank coffee, Ellie produced her credentials and references and phone numbers of people she had worked for.

She told them she was looking for full time work and asked them to phone her past employers, particularly the family where she had last worked. She was no longer needed there because the mother had been laid off, but she had been sad to leave. She said she loved working with small children.

She left, giving them time to make a decision and assuring them that she could be available immediately. That evening, after they had checked out her references and talked to her former employers, Colt phoned Ellie and confirmed that they wanted to hire her for two weeks. If the five of them worked well together, he assured her there was a good possibility that they would want her to stay on full time.

She was thrilled and agreed to be there the next day.

"Where is she going to stay?" Frankie asked.

"Well she could stay in the spare room."

Frankie wrinkled her nose. "Not enough privacy. That cuts out early morning activities like this morning." She grinned as she arched her eyebrow.

"We can't have that! What else can we do? We don't have a cottage or anywhere else to put her."

"Could we buy a mobile home; something that's not too big, yet enough room for her to be comfortable? Then she would have her own place to do whatever she wants to in and we'll have our privacy too."

"That is a good idea. We'd have to figure out how to get power and water and sewer in for it right away."

# CHAPTER THREE

*S*hauna Lee struggled to consciousness. Her thinking was fuzzy, still affected by the extra sleeping pill. She stretched out and rolled over onto her back, pushing the covers away from her face. She squinted against the light that streamed in through the bedroom window and then looked at the clock on her night table. "Ten o'clock. Jeeze, I simply died!"

She rolled her legs out of the bed and sat up. Her pyjamas twisted around her slender frame uncomfortably. Her head was still foggy. She rubbed her eyes and yawned, thinking that a cup of coffee would bring her back to the world of the living.

She pushed herself off the bed and wandered into the kitchen. After she set up the coffee pot, she wandered over to the front window and looked outside. Idly she watched a couple strolling down the street, hand in hand, enjoying the beautiful September morning. Another family came into sight; a husband and wife and two small children.

The little girl swung on her father's hand. The little boy was about four years old. He was running ahead, then spinning back and charging toward his mother. He stopped just beyond her reach, eluding her as she smiled and leaned forward to catch him. Then he ran back up the street again, laughing as he went.

Shauna Lee's eyes fastened on the little boy. She bit her lip as she watched him. Feelings she had buried twenty-one years ago bubbled to the surface. She shook her head, pushing them away; but she couldn't seem to tear her focus away from the child. Tears filled her eyes, blurring her vision, then escaping down her cheeks. She turned away from the window, dashing them away with back of her hand.

She stumbled to the table and sat on a chair. Sobs racked her body and she cried uncontrollably until she was exhausted and drained. Then she just sat there, staring out the kitchen window, her emotions numb.

Ben would have been twenty two now. The son she had loved with all her being; the son whose father wouldn't accept him because he had been born with a physical deformity; a deformity that had revolted him.

Shauna Lee couldn't hold on any more. She ran to the bathroom and vomited the bitter acid that roiled in her stomach. It burned her throat and lay sour in her mouth. She hadn't eaten anything since late the afternoon before. The coffee she had made sat in the thermal carafe on the counter.

She was cold and sick. She filled a glass with water and rinsed her mouth, then crawled back into bed and huddled under the sheets, willing her thoughts to still. Gradually the exhaustion of her emotions claimed her in sleep.

She woke up later in the day. Her watch said it was four thirty. Her head hurt and she knew she needed to eat. She went to the kitchen and poured herself a cup of coffee. The carafe had kept it lukewarm. She sipped it mindlessly and opened the fridge to look inside. Nothing looked appetizing. She closed the door, uncertain what she would do. She knew she needed something, but what? She looked like hell and she definitely was not going out. Pizza? She could order in. She reached for the phone and then hesitated.

In her mind, pizza was meant to be shared. Suddenly she realized that she couldn't think of anyone she could call to share one with. At one time she would have called Colt. In the years since then…well she'd seldom had lonely weekends. Men like Josh hadn't been hard to find for company.

What the hell had happened this time? It was as if Josh had opened Pandora's Box with his crude remarks and things just kept tumbling out. She had been forced to look at her life, like Scrooge at Christmas time; but she wasn't Scrooge and it wasn't Christmas. However, as it had been for Scrooge, it was difficult for her to realize what her life had become.

She picked up the phone and ordered a pizza. She decided to have a shower while she waited for it to be delivered. She would eat it by herself while she watched TV and escape reality until she got back on track.

Shauna Lee woke up crying at four thirty on Sunday morning. She had been dreaming about the night Ben had died. The horror of it clung to her as she fought off the cloud of sleep. Dave's rage hung in the room, so real she could feel it.

She lay there thinking about that time in her life, wondering why those images had come back now. She had managed to close that part of her memory off for years, burying it so deep that she had been able to pretend that none of it had happened. She hadn't told anyone about Ben; not even Colt. What had triggered the memory, making it come to the surface yesterday?

She got up and went to the bathroom. She was still wearing her pyjamas from the day before and they were creased and damp with sweat and tears. Glancing at the clock she noted that it was only five in the morning.

*What day is it?* she wondered. She went into the kitchen and turned on the soft light under the microwave that was installed above the stove. Automatically she emptied the thermal coffee carafe and set up a new pot of coffee. She poured herself a bowl of dry cereal, splashed some milk over it and added a sprinkle of sugar.

Then she sat down at the table. She ate mindlessly, purposely pushing her clamouring thoughts aside. *It has to be Sunday…it'll be another long day to get through. What am I going to do? I can't just sit here and drown in my memories.*

She sighed and got up to pour herself a cup of coffee. "Maybe I should go for a drive or something; but where?" She wandered over to the couch and turned on the TV, but there wasn't much that interested her at six in the morning.

She surfed through the channels and clicked on a program about small wind turbines. She listened with idle interest as the spokesman explained to the interviewer how the new small wind turbines were

27

helping the environment by replacing dirty grid power with free, clean, green, wind energy that was economical and affordable too.

When he introduced their newest dealer, her senses sprang alert. She recognized Brad Johnson. She heard him say, "Years ago the landscape of western Canada was dotted with windmills that were mainly used to pump water out of the ground."

But what really caught her attention was the rich timbre of his voice and the smooth way he delivered his words with a cadence that captured her. She watched his expressions and the way he moved his hands as he talked, shifting slightly on his feet from time to time. He was confident and sincere; an earthy, unpretentious, very real person. She had been aware of that on Friday night, but now she was really struck by it.

She picked up his words again…"and eventually I can see this type of landscape recreated again with our small power-generating wind turbines popping up on farms and ranches across the country. They are highly efficient, and they require very little maintenance. And they are simple to put in place; a truck or a tractor will easily pull the assembled tower into place."

The sound of his voice washed over her. She studied his physique. He was tall; over six feet she was certain. And she'd bet he didn't get those muscles pumping iron in a gym. He probably got them from throwing bales or wrestling calves.

He was wearing blue jeans again and a western shirt that accentuated the grey of his eyes. He wasn't wearing a Stetson today, and his rich brown hair was ruffled by the breeze. Did he have cowboy boots on? She watched closely as the camera moved back. "Yes!" she murmured "And nice ones, too. He is a hunk!" She watched him dreamily, until the camera shifted away to show a wind turbine being installed.

Then reality hit her like a punch. "And…I'm sure he thinks I'm the town tramp….he probably wouldn't come near me."

Discontent washed over her as she surfed through the channels a few more times, then stood up and turned off the TV. She dropped the remote on the coffee table and glanced at her watch again, debating what she should do. *It's only eight thirty.* She sighed deeply. *This is going to be a long day. Well, I have laundry to do. That will take up some of my time.*

As she gathered her laundry from the hamper in her bedroom, she wondered what had happened to her. *Why haven't I made friends? Right now I wish I had someone to talk to—maybe a girlfriend. But I've never had a real girlfriend,* she thought as she dropped a load of whites in the washing machine.

The phone rang as she was closing the lid. She turned the machine on and ran to answer it. Glancing at the call display she hesitated, trying to recognise the name. It was from the Country Lane Inn in town.

*Who the heck?* she thought as she answered. "Hello?"

"Shauna Lee, this is Mitch here…."

"Mitch…?" There was a question in the word. *Who…?*

"Mitch Wagner; from Saskatoon."

"Oh, Mitch. I'm sorry. You caught me off guard. I was thinking about something else."

"I'm in town. I have a meeting tomorrow, but I was wondering if you wanted to get together today. We could go for a drive, or I think the Eliminators Car Club is having its show and shine at Riverside Park. We could stop in there and check it out if you like."

"Hey, I'd love to get together. I'm just sort of kicking around here on my own!"

"All right, I'll drop over in an hour or so to pick you up. It'll be great to see you again!"

"I'll be waiting," she said with a smile. *Mitch, you're a wish come true. You've rescued me from myself. Thank you! Thank you!* She quickly shut off the washing machine and ran to the bedroom. She opened a dresser drawer and selected a sexy, lacy set of matching panties and bra. She dashed into the bathroom and turned on the shower.

She washed her hair and lathered her body quickly and then reached for her razor and shaved her under arms and her legs. As she rinsed off, she ran her hands down her legs. *Smooth as silk,* she thought with a smile.

She blew her hair dry, applied her make-up and added a light spray of seductive perfume. Then she slipped into her bra and panties and flew to the closet to decide what to wear. After some thought she picked out a silky, bayou blue top that closed with a crossover tie and showed a lot of cleavage. It brought out the colour of her eyes.

She picked out a pair of stretchy jeans that fit her like a glove and grabbed a long tweedy blue sweater. She riffled through her sock drawer and grabbed a pair of white ones. Then she slid her feet into a pair of running shoes and she was ready. She went into the kitchen and tossed her purse and house keys on the table. She poured herself a cup of coffee, just as the doorbell rang.

She had totally slipped into predator mode without even thinking about it. She waited a minute, and then strolled to the door. "Can't appear too eager," she mused as she opened it. She smiled coyly at the tall blonde man that stood in front of her.

"Mitch, imagine seeing you again!" She stood aside and let him step in, then closed the door behind him. She looked him over from top to bottom, then slid her arms around his neck and pulled him to her.

He smiled as he bent his head to kiss her gently. "It's been a long time," he said softly.

She nestled her head against his shoulder. "It has," she breathed on a sigh. She slipped her hand into his and led him into the living room, pulling him down onto the couch beside her. Her hand slid to rest on his thigh. "You're looking too handsome," she said, smiling into his admiring eyes.

"And you're still gorgeous! You never change. What's it been; three or four years? What's been going on in your life? I heard once that you were engaged to a farmer. That surprised me!"

"What surprised you; that I was engaged or that I was engaged to a farmer?"

He laughed and raised her hand to his lips, nibbling on her fingers. "Both. I couldn't picture you with a farmer; or for that matter one guy. You always said you'd never get married."

She gently pulled her hand away. "And I didn't."

"I heard something to that effect. That's why I decided to call you when I was in town this time."

She stood up. "So what are we going to do?"

He raised his eyebrows and looked at her quizzically.

"Hey man; I just made the bed. And we've got the whole day ahead of us." She playfully punched him in the shoulder. "Have some class! I at least expect a nice dinner and a good glass of wine," she said, laughing as she walked to the table and picked up her keys and purse.

"It's just that you're looking so hot...."

"I'm sure I heard you say something about going to the Eliminators Show and Shine." She walked to the door, and stood waiting for him. "I thought they usually had that in August."

"There was some kind of a change in schedule this year." He grinned as he pushed himself up off the couch and walked over to join her. He pushed the door closed and pulled her against him, kissing her deeply, his tongue slipping into her mouth, dancing with hers.

She could feel the bulge in his crotch as he rubbed against her and fire leapt in her groin. She moaned as he ravaged her mouth. Then he swung the door open, pushing her out in front of him. He grabbed her hand and pushed it into his straining hardness. He groaned. "We'll do it your way for now; then we'll do it my way tonight!"

It was beautiful, warm fall day and there was a large crowd at the show. Shauna Lee really smiled for the first time in two days. She loved looking at the hotrods and old classic cars. She knew a lot of the people that were there; several of them were her clients. She stopped and chatted with them as she moved through the rows of cars with Mitch.

Mitch met someone he knew and stopped to talk business, so she kept wandering down the line. A hopped up old truck caught her eye. She wandered closer to look it over. "Sweet!" she said softly as she trailed her finger along the polished grill.

"It's well done," a deep rich voice commented from behind her. Shauna Lee jumped and whirled around, almost losing her balance. She stared into a pair of warm grey eyes that widened in surprise. Brad Johnson was standing there.

Her heart stood still momentarily. "Oh…you…I didn't hear you come up behind me." She looked so shocked, so defenceless, he couldn't help but smile. He reached out and touched her shoulder, a gesture meant to steady her.

"The grass muffles the sound. I didn't realise it was you."

She flushed. *Or you probably have gone the other way,* she thought. "Isn't this a cool old truck," she babbled, trying to hide the fact that seeing him had thrown her off balance. She slid a caressing hand along the bright red fender. "I think it says it's a 1949 model!"

"It's custom built. These guys rebuild old cars and trucks for a hobby." He touched his toe against the spokes of the chrome tire rim. "It's all rodded up; did you notice the chrome stacks behind the cab?" He rubbed his hand along the top edge of the box. "This baby never looked so good; even when it was new."

They fell into step and moved along the line to the next vehicle.

"Oh! I saw you on TV this morning."

He looked puzzled and shook his head.

"Yes; you were being interviewed about the wind turbines."

"Oh, I see." He smiled and her heart missed a beat. "They recorded that last week. So you saw it this morning?"

"I don't know what station it was on. I was channel surfing and I happened to hear a guy talking about the wind turbines. And then, there you were. Actually, it was pretty interesting. Listening to you today, and having seen your presentation the other night; I can see where there is a lot of potential, especially in the outlying areas for farmers and ranchers."

"The potential is incredible. And not just in the rural areas. You know hydro isn't as expensive here as it is in other parts of the world. The manufacturer is really a forward thinking guy and most of his market is overseas now. But hydro costs will eventually go up here in Canada, too. Then people will be looking for the opportunity we offer. It's just a matter of time."

"I can see where a few of my clients could be interested in them; especially ranchers and farmers. So many of the smaller places have amalgamated into the larger ones; some places you travel miles without seeing an active home site."

Brad looked at her, seeing the intelligent business woman he had gotten a glimpse of on Friday night. They stopped and inspected a bright yellow Ford Fairlane. Brad ran his hand along a front fender. "My dad owned one of these fifty years ago."

Conversation was easy between them, and neither of them noticed that an hour had passed before Mitch caught up with them. He came up behind Shauna Lee and slid an arm over her shoulder.

"Sorry for leaving you on your own. I didn't expect to meet him here. He is a client and I needed to talk to him"

"Not a problem. I ran into Brad. He markets small wind powered turbines. He gave a power-point presentation on them the other night at a seminar that the DA put on. They are a fascinating concept."

She turned to Brad; she could see the speculation in his eyes. *Damn* she thought fiercely. *What must he be thinking?* "Brad Johnson, this is Mitch Wagner. I've known him for several years. He's from Saskatoon and he's in town for a meeting tomorrow so he looked me up this morning."

The two men shook hands and made small talk for a few seconds, before Mitch reached in his pocket for his cell phone. She saw him frown as he turned away and answered. His face blanched. "I'll be right home. No; forget about the meeting. I'll reschedule. You just hang in there; I'm on my way."

He turned to Shauna Lee. "I have to go home."

"Is something wrong?" she asked with genuine concern.

"M..my son, Kyle. He was playing baseball and got nailed in the head with a bat. They're taking him to the hospital right now."

*Your son?* "How old is he?" she asked, her voice choked.

"Eleven…I've got to go." He looked at Brad. "Look, I'm sorry to do this, but could you give Shauna Lee a lift home?"

"Don't worry about me, Mitch. Just go…your son needs you and you should get home as soon as possible. I'll catch a ride with someone. I know a lot of people here."

"I'll give her a ride home," Brad said. "Just get on the road, man! I hope your boy is OK."

"Thanks guys. I'm out of here."

Shauna Lee watched him run through the cars. *That bastard! He's married and has a family. Five hours ago he was trying to get in my pants.*

Brad touched her arm, mistaking the reason for the troubled expression on her face. "All we can do is hope that everything is all right. Getting hit in the head with a baseball bat is tough. It's hard to say how bad it is until the doctors examine him."

"Poor kid." *You have no idea!*

"Look it is four o'clock. Are you in a hurry to go home?"

"Brad, you don't have to worry about me. I'm a big girl. I'll get myself home."

"Hey, your friend asked me…and honestly," he chuckled as he looked her over from head to foot, "you don't look like a very *big* girl to me. If you're in a hurry to get home, I'll take you straight there. If you're relaxed about it, we could go have supper somewhere and then I'll take you home."

"Well…"

"Look, we both need to eat some time. Company with supper would be a nice change for me."

"Well, when you put it that way, I have to admit you're right. We can go anytime you like."

"We could swing by the steakhouse and eat. Then I'll take you home; how about it?"

She nodded. They turned and walked back to the parking lot. She felt disappointed when he didn't reach for her hand, or curl his arm around her waist and draw her close against his side. *It would feel so good to snuggle against his shoulder.*

The restaurant was busy, but they found a table in the corner where it was a little quieter. Brad asked her what she would like to drink. She opted for red wine; he ordered a rum and coke and when their drinks came they slipped into easy conversation.

"How long have you lived in Swift Current?" Brad was looking down as his drink, swirling amber liquid over the ice as he asked.

"I've been here for thirteen years. After I got my CA, I came here to work for the previous owner. I worked for him for three years. He had a good cliental, and I had worked with him long enough to earn their confidence. He wanted to retire so I bought the business from him."

She caught her bottom lip in her teeth, then sighed as she released it. "I'd worked hard through the years; in fact I did little else but work and study." She twirled the stem of her glass between her thumb and her index finger. Then she looked up to find him watching her intently. "I had saved enough to buy the business. He did give me a break though; he was happy to have me take it over. It's done well over the past ten years."

"You can be proud of what you've accomplished. What about your family? Didn't you have support from them?"

"I don't have any family." She decided she needed to shift the conversation away herself. "Now tell me about you? The other night you said you were from B.C.?"

"Yes, from Dawson Creek."

"Where is that?"

"More northern; if you drew a line from North Battleford across to Dawson Creek, you would find that they are pretty close in latitude. I took the Wind Turbine Maintenance Program at Northern Lights College there. That got my toe in the door. Experience got me here."

The waitress came to take their food order and Brad ordered another drink for each of them, checking with her to make sure that it was all right.

"So were you born there?"

"Yeah, my dad owns a bulk station in town; he handles diesel and gas and oil and grease. Mom's retired now, but she was a teacher."

"Brothers or sisters?"

"The perfect family; there are two of each of us."

She smiled. "So what did you do for fun—Hockey? Football?"

"The truth? Neither one; but I like to watch both. As far as football goes, I'm a Saskatchewan Rough Rider fan now, but it's hard for me if they are playing the B.C. Lions. I still cheer for the Vancouver Canucks when they play hockey. But I like junior league hockey as much as I do NHL. They are young and full of piss and vinegar. They usually put on a good game. Are you a hockey fan?"

Shauna Lee shrugged. "Not really, but I can't say for sure. I've never actually checked it out. I've seen games on TV in the bar, but I wasn't actually concentrating on them. But tell me more; what do you do for R&R. Somehow, I don't think you're a couch potato."

He grinned. "No; I'm an outdoors guy. I like to hike in the mountains. And Dad and I hunted together from the time I was a kid; we used to pack in with horses. We would go away back into the mountains where you seldom saw anyone else. I rode bareback too; high school rodeo stuff."

Her eyes sparkled. "Wow! A real cowboy; sexy."

"Don't get carried away there. I wasn't big time or anything like that. But I loved to ride; I still do. Give me a horse and turn me loose and I'll be happy for days."

"You are Colt's kind of guy; cows and horses."

"I like Colt. I think we have a lot in common."

"So," she said leaning across the table toward him. "Are there any women in your life?"

He raised an eyebrow. "Are you always so direct?"

"Well, you're a good looking man; I'm just curious."

"How many guys are there in your life?"

She blushed. "Touché"

The waitress brought their meals and they ate in silence.

When he was finished, Brad put his utensils onto the plate and pushed it aside. "Are you ready for coffee?"

"I am stuffed. You could take me home and stop for a coffee. It would give me half an hour to digest the steak."

He looked at her for a long moment. She heart accelerated, wondering what he was thinking. "If you'd like to do that, we could," he said soberly.

"Sure, let's go. I might even offer you some dessert."

Brad paid for their meal, and then held the door open for her to step outside. His hand touched the small of her back as they walked to his truck. His touch sent a hot tightening into her belly and down into the core of her femininity. He opened the door and helped her up onto her seat in the truck. He was smiling when he got in on his side. "These trucks are so high. It's quite a stretch for a shortie like you to get your little tush up onto the seat."

"Now, a gentleman wouldn't have noticed," she said with a sexy little giggle.

"I guess I'm not a gentleman then, because I noticed."

When they pulled up in front of her house, he got out and came around to open her door so he could help her out. Shauna Lee felt giddy with anticipation. She smiled as she opened her front door and stepped inside, standing aside to let him in.

"You can leave those beautiful boots on the mat," she spoke over her shoulder, as she moved into the kitchen and tossed her keys and her purse on the table. "Just grab a spot to sit and I'll put on the coffee."

Brad looked around the open kitchen and living room area. It was beautifully decorated, but he noted the lack of personal things; no pictures of family or friends and no books, just a top of the line TV and stereo.

He eased his long frame down on a kitchen chair. "Nice place."

"It works for me," she said with a warm smile. "Do you want a tour of the rest of the place while the coffee pot does its magic?" She smiled at him, raising an eyebrow. "There is a laundry room and a bathroom and the bedroom with a queen sized bed."

"I just got settled here. Why don't we just sit down and chat until the coffee is ready." The way he said it wasn't a rebuff. It struck her as meaning that there would be plenty of time later. As they talked her eyes registered an unspoken invitation, her inherent sexual essence oozing out.

Brad smiled, accepting the coffee cup that she gave him, her fingers brushing his softly, lingering with promise. When their coffee cups were drained, he leaned back in his chair and looked at her, his grey eyes cool and intent.

"Shauna, I told you I'm a hunter. I have hunted cougars in the wild. That is where I like to keep them: in the wild; with me doing the stalking."

Her face went scarlet. "Are you calling me a cougar?" she asked, indignantly.

"I'd say that description fits you pretty accurately. You're no tee-ny bopper getting her first hormone flushes. If you were looking for a wedding ring you'd have one. You're successful, and I'm not blind; you're so hot looking you sizzle.

"I'm not stupid either; you are on the prowl for sex. You've been stalking me all evening. I'm no eunuch. I could take you to that queen sized bed that you so coyly mentioned earlier and do it justice. But I seldom hunt where everyone else has been hunting."

He stood up. "I enjoyed your company today. I enjoyed having supper with you. But I'm not into playing *this* game. I'm not willing to be another one of your boy-toys." He walked to the door and opened it.

"I'm sure you don't want my advice, but I'll throw it out there any-way. Figure out who you are Shauna Lee, before it's too late. You've got a lot more to offer than sex, but you'll never find that out if you keep running from real intimacy.

"Bed hopping with your nothing serious, no strings attached, no risk attitude is never going get you there. One day you'll wake up and find yourself old and alone."

He stepped out and closed the door.

She stood immobile for a second, stunned. She grabbed his coffee cup off the table and flung it against the door. It shattered in a million pieces, but she didn't even flinch. "Who the hell do you think you are Brad Johnson?" she raged. "A shrink? Well I don't need one."

She kicked the leg of the chair he'd been sitting on. "I've got news for you. I know just who I am and I've been old and alone since I was eighteen years old."

# CHAPTER FOUR

*I*t was seven thirty in the evening when Colt made the turn off the main road and followed the long driveway to the ranch house. As they crossed the bridge over Belanger Creek, his eyes met Frankie's in the dim light of the cab and he winked. She reached her hand across the seat to squeeze his. They were both remembering the night they had struggled to save the bridge during a heavy rain four years ago when she had been working on the ranch as a ranch hand.

She had twisted her ankle and Colt had carried her to the truck and then into the house. As much as they had tried to deny it, the sparks flew and a fire had ignited. They had made love for the first time that night. Hot and passionate; it was possible the twins had been conceived then—or most certainly the next day.

Colt brought the truck to a halt in front of the old ranch house. "We are here, Ellie"

Colt opened the backdoor on the driver's side and Selena, who was first out of her car seat, scrambled over Sam into her father's arms. He gave her little hug and then stood her on the ground.

Sam was waiting patiently for his father to take him. Colt looked at his son. He was so laid back and mild mannered; a complete opposite of his sister. "Come on little man," he said softly as he lifted him out of the truck and held him in his arms.

Ollie's face was wreathed with smiles. He squatted down to catch Selena as she catapulted into his arms. "Ollie, Ollie," she yelled as he hugged her. Colt put a squirming Sam down and he followed her. Colt and Frankie were right behind the children. Ollie shook hands with Colt, and then enfolded Frankie in a big bear hug. "So you're goin' ridin' with us this year; I can't tell you how good it will be to have you here, back in the saddle again."

"Ollie, I'm so excited. You can't imagine," Frankie exclaimed. She turned back to look for Ellie who was standing by the fender on the far side of the truck. She walked back and reached out her hand. "Ellie, this is Ollie Little. He's been the ranch foreman for so many years he's considered to be a member of the Thompson clan now."

Ollie's attention perked up. "Ollie, this is Ellie Raines. She is our nanny now. She gives me a huge break and makes the twins keep in line."

Ollie reached to shake her hand, his eyes gleaming with interest. Ellie didn't seem to notice, but Frankie did. *Interesting* she thought. *There might be snow on the roof, but Ollie's still got a fire in the stove! I've never seen him with that look in his eye before!*

"Come in, come in. Watch your step here. There are shadows from the yard light here. Patch is inside too and you'll want to meet him."

"Patch?" Frankie queried.

"That's the new ranch hand, isn't it Ollie?" Colt asked.

"Yes, he got here a couple of weeks ago. Nice guy. I think he'll work out well."

Everyone followed Ollie into the house. A short, slender, white haired man was standing at the sink drying dishes. When he turned to look at them, the first thing Frankie noticed was the weary lines around his sad hazel eyes. His smile was friendly and he had the look of a tried and true ranch hand; bowed legs and all.

Ollie motioned to Colt. "Patch this is Colt Thompson. He owns the ranch. And this is his lovely wife, Frankie and their twins, Selena and Sam." He turned to Ellie. "And this good looking lady is Ellie Raines. It sounds like she is keeping these two little monkeys in line."

Patch nodded to them all. Colt shook his hand. "I missed your last name, Patch."

Ollie apologized. "Sorry guys, this is Patch Bergeron. He worked on the Gang Ranch in central British Columbia for fifteen years before he came here."

"I've heard of the Gang Ranch many times," Colt replied. "There's a lot of history there."

"That there is. I'm happy to meet you all," Patch responded.

Colt turned to Ollie. "It's getting to be bedtime for the kids. Any special room you want to put them in?"

"There are three single beds in the room at the back. Will that work?

Ellie responded quickly. "They will be fine in twin beds. I'll sleep in the room with them."

Frankie shepherded the twins and Ellie to their room and helped everyone get settled. When she came back to the kitchen she found Colt, Ollie and Patch talking about the round up the next day. She went over to stand by Colt.

Ollie looked at them and grinned as he said, "You two can sleep in your old room."

"You mean my old room, don't you?" Frankie refuted.

"Yeah, well it was officially your room." He winked at her. "You know I might be old, but I'm not dumb. So I think I'm not far wrong when I say *yours*."

Frankie blushed, and Colt slipped his arm around her shoulder and pulled her against him. "It's about four years too late to deny it, Fran," he said, dropping a light kiss on her cheek. "Come on. It's time to go try that bed out again."

Frankie's face went scarlet. "Colt!"

"Get your mind out of the gutter!" He laughed as he turned her around to lead her down the hall. "I simply meant it's late. It's time to go to bed."

As the bedroom door closed behind them, she turned and landed a playful punch onto his shoulder. "You're bad!"

He pulled her into his arms and kissed her soundly. "And that's good isn't it?"

He reached for the hem of her tee shirt, and slipped it up over her breasts. He leaned in and planted a kiss in the exposed cleavage. "Lift your arms up," he whispered as he bit gently at the nipple that protruded against the lace of her bra.

She squirmed and lifted her arms up. He slid the tee up over her head, pushing it higher, stopping at the elbows as he pushed her against the wall, trapping her there, her arms imprisoned. He leaned against her, nibbling at her lips. He slipped his tongue between them and started a sensuous mating dance with hers.

Fire leapt in both of them. Colt pushed his hardness against her and heat settled in the core of her femininity, leaving her swollen, moist and aching. She jerked her arms down out of the sleeves that had pinned her and slipped her hands between them, her fingers working the button on his jeans open.

He shifted his hips back to allow her room to slide the zipper down. She pushed his jeans as far as she could past his hips. Then she hooked her fingers into the elastic of his jockey shorts and tugged down. The tee shirt fell out of his grasp to the floor.

"Oh god," he moaned against her lips. His hand moved up to unhook her bra and slipped it off, letting it fall to the floor. His finger deftly undid the button on her jeans, jerked down the zipper and pushed her jeans and panties down in one swoop. He let them fall down to her feet, lifted her up and left them in a puddle on the floor.

He carried her to the bed and laid her down, then hurriedly shoved his jeans down and kicked them off as he lowered himself on top of her. There was no need for more foreplay; it had started when they had looked at each other with a knowing smile as they had crossed the bridge over Belanger Creek on the drive in.

The passion of the memories they had made in this house four years ago had simmered just beneath the surface all evening, building the tension that had mounted as it lead them to this moment.

He took her hard and fast; it was over quickly, and he felt her contracting around him as he exploded inside her. He slumped onto his side, pulling her over with him. They lay there drained, panting and slick with perspiration. After a few minutes Frankie stirred. "I have to clean up," she whispered.

He helped her roll over and slide off the bed. He watched her as she slipped into the ensuite, smiling at her naked form. Even after having the twins she had maintained her sexy, slender shape.

When she came back to the bed he held the sheet up, waiting for her to slide under it. Then he held her close. "This is where it all started," he murmured, kissing her hair as she slid her arm across his waist. "You, me, the twins. Right here in this bed."

She nestled her cheek against his chest. "Yes. Remember that first time?"

"Are you kidding? I'll never forget. I was so horny and out of control; I forgot that I thought I didn't like you! All I could think about was you, and making love to you over and over."

"Yeah," she sighed. "For about 36 hours and then you couldn't get away fast enough." She gave him a little pinch.

"Ouch!" He flinched. "You know that's not fair. I knew how I felt about you and I knew how much you would mean to me. I was scared to death."

She reached up and laid a finger against his lips, silencing his defence. "I know, I know. I just had to make you grovel a bit now!" She smiled as she snuggled closer. "We have to get to sleep. Tomorrow is going to be a busy day!"

The next morning the sky was clear, the air crisp. Colt went out to check on the horses, while Frankie slipped down to check in on the twins and Ellie. Selena and Sam were still asleep. Ellie wasn't there, so Frankie wandered back to the kitchen.

As she got closer she could hear the murmur of voices and then laughter. She recognised it was Ollie and Ellie. She walked quietly to the kitchen door and peeked in. To her surprise, Ollie and Ellie were working together, making breakfast. *Interesting—he usually doesn't like to have any one messing around in his kitchen.*

But he was happy to have company now. They were working side by side, sharing tasks. He asked her to turn the pancakes, while he cracked the eggs. Then she busied herself making coffee. They were working in close proximity, even brushing each other as they moved around. She was surprised at the ease with which they interacted.

"Good morning, you two. I see you are hard at it! I just checked in on the twins. They are still both off in dreamland."

Ellie smiled. "They were really played out last night. They may not wake up before you are ready to leave." She smiled at Ollie. "I'm going to cook supper tonight so it'll be ready when you all get in."

"That sounds wonderful. It's so nice to come in and find a warm meal waiting." Frankie looked at Ollie. "She's a good cook too."

Frankie turned as she heard the entry door open. She smiled as she heard Colt speak. She realized that Patch had to have been out doing chores with him. They came up the steps from the entry, engaged in companionable conversation.

Colt smiled when he saw her. He walked over and slid his hands around the back of her neck, under her collar. She jumped away. "Ohh! Get away from me. Your hands are cold."

Colt looked at her with a grin. He leaned forward to kiss her cheek and whispered; "Now that's not what you told me last night."

She wrinkled her nose as her laughing eyes met his. "That was then," she murmured quietly. She added in a louder voice, "Brrrr…It must be chilly out there."

"There's a bit of frost this morning. It's time to bring those cows in."

Ollie announced that breakfast was ready, and he and Ellie were busy putting the food on the table. They all helped themselves to the pancakes, eggs and bacon, while Ellie went to check on the twins. She announced that they were still sleeping when she came back and joined them.

After breakfast Ellie chased Ollie out of his own kitchen, assuring him that she would clean up the dishes and put the roast in the oven when it was time. He smirked as she ordered him out, but to Frankie's amazement he went without an argument.

Frankie was making more coffee to fill the thermoses for the day, when both she and Ellie alerted to the sound of the twins waking up. Ellie was gone to get them before Frankie could finish filling the first thermos. She had barely set up the second pot for the other thermos, when the three of them wandered into the kitchen.

Their faces lit up when they saw Frankie and they charged toward her with cries of "Mommy, mommy." Frankie cuddled them both while Ellie fixed breakfast for them.

Colt came in just as they were ready to eat, so he gave them both hugs and said, "OK, you guys. You be good for Mrs Raines. Mommy and I are going out riding with Ollie and we'll be gone all day. We'll see you at supper time." Colt turned to Ellie. "Keep them in line."

She laughed. "Don't you worry; I wasn't a school teacher all those years for nothing! We'll do just fine. Besides, these two are angels compared to some that I've seen."

As Frankie went outside with Colt, she chuckled. "She'll be OK with the twins. Did you notice that she has Ollie eating out of her hand already?"

Colt looked at her and raised an eyebrow. "You're joking?"

"No...Didn't you notice? They were making breakfast together like they'd done it every day for years! And you know how Ollie is about his kitchen."

Colt smirked. "It's got to be something in that house. Look at what happened to you and me." He reached out and took her hand. "It feels so good to have you along for the roundup. I've missed having you with us."

She hugged his arm. "It was a great idea you had; getting a nanny. At first I wasn't sure, but she is so good with the twins and I'm really beginning to appreciate the freedom she gives me."

He led her to the pickup. "We'll catch up with Ollie and Patch. They left with the horses in the trailer just after I came inside. They won't be far ahead of us."

Colt opened the door on the driver's side and motioned for her to get in. She looked up at him, questioningly. "I want my girl to sit close to me." She grinned and slid in, moving over until the gearshift rested between her legs.

He got in and rested his hand on her thigh as he grinned at her. "Do you realize that we've never really did this. We never actually had a courtship. By the time I accepted that I couldn't live without you and found you in Stettler, you were so pregnant..."

"I was huge. And after the twins were born, I really had my hands full. Not much time for anything that couldn't happen between feedings and diaper changes and exhaustion."

He started the truck and backed up so he could turn onto the drive way. They caught up to Ollie and Patch on the road through the Gap. Colt followed them to the corrals where Frankie had spent the summer in the travel trailer when she had ridden the range. Frankie looked around wide eyed. "WOW! You've made big changes here. How did I miss hearing about this?"

"Ollie hired a contractor to build the new corrals the first summer after we were married. The District Ag. and Ollie laid them out. Ollie showed me the plans and brought me out to get a look at how they'd fit here. It looked good so I gave the project my OK.

"If you remember, we had lousy harvesting weather that fall, so Ollie hired a crew to help with the roundup, but he was happy with the corrals. They've worked well the past couple of years too. It simplifies the whole job."

Colt opened the door and helped her out. She took a few steps, and then stood spread-eagle, her arms and legs spread wide. She threw her head back and took a deep breath. "This feels so good. I didn't realize how much I've missed this!"

They unloaded the horses and saddled up, then decided on a plan of attack. Ollie and Patch had driven around through the pastures for the past two days, so they had a good idea where the cattle were. They headed out on horseback travelling familiar trails. Frankie was flooded with memories of the summer she had spent riding the range.

Time went quickly with the four of them riding hard. At the end of the day they had brought over half of the cows and calves in. They arrived back at the ranch after seven. The twins were already in their pyjamas waiting for Frankie and Colt to come home. The aroma of the meal that was waiting wafted out to greet them when they stepped into the entry.

"It smells like heaven, Ellie," Colt called out. His voice was an instant trigger for the twins who came screaming down the hall. "Daddy, Daddy."

Ollie stepped around Frankie, as she stood watching her happy family hunkered down in the hallway; a tangle of giggles and arms and legs piled on Colt, all squirming in a knot. He walked into the kitchen with a spring in his step. The table was set.

He lifted the lids on the pots on the stove; mashed potatoes. He sniffed. Not just mashed potatoes; garlic mashed potatoes. The next pot was filled with peas and carrots in cream sauce. He found a pot of rich beef gravy. When he opened the oven he was greeted by the sight of a beef roast that looked like it was cooked to perfection.

Ellie was watching with a smile on her face. "Well, does it meet your approval?"

"Hump…" He reached in to pull the roaster pan out and took it over to the cutting board. He lifted the roast out and carved a couple of slices. It was pink and juicy; perfect."

"Hump: damn you woman."

Ellie flinched and lost her smile. "What's wrong?"

"You're going to ruin my reputation for home cooking." He looked at her and grinned. "You did a perfect job. You're too damn good!" He walked over and rested a hand on her shoulder, looking in her eyes. "If you were looking for a job, I'd hire you any day!"

"Knock it off, Ollie," Frankie protested. "She's already got a full time job; I'm pulling rank on you."

Ellie's smile had returned. She preened as she turned to the fridge and took out a salad to put on the table. Ollie spotted desert inside before she closed the fridge door.

While they ate supper they talked about the day's accomplishment, acknowledging that it would be more difficult the next day. The remaining cattle would be more scattered and take longer to bring in. Colt and Ollie went into the office after supper and talked about shipping dates and when they should haul the calves to market.

Colt stretched out his long legs and leaned back in the chair. "I've been thinking Ollie; I was at seminar that the DA put on ten days ago. A guy named Brad Johnson was there. I'd met him before a couple of times at farm equipment promotional days. He's a nice guy; we hit it off good.

"Anyway, he's selling and installing small wind generated turbines. I need to look into it a little more, but I think they have real potential here. I was thinking about putting up two or three; maybe even four. Two right here on the ranch and one at each of the water tanks on the range."

"Don't know anything about them. Just as long as they don't make more work…"

"Brad says they are pretty much maintenance free. I want to discuss it with Fran first before…"

"What do you want to discuss with me?" Frankie asked as she stepped through the door.

"I've been thinking about putting up some wind generated turbines out here at the ranch. But I wanted to talk it over with you before I did anything definite."

Frankie smiled at him. "You've always made those decisions, Colt."

"I know, but now that you have help with the twins and you're not so crazy busy with them all the time, I'd like your input too." He reached out and took her hand, pulling her close to him. "You're an intelligent woman; I want us to make decisions as partners."

She ruffled his hair with her fingers. She looked across at Ollie and words from the past echoed in her mind. *What he needs is someone who cares about the business and is willing to work with him.*

Ollie was playing with a pencil on the desk, acting disinterested, but Frankie was sure he was thinking the same thing now, waiting for her response.

"I…I appreciate you wanting my input. So, tell me what you are thinking."

"I was talking to Ollie about the wind turbines; but right now I'm thinking it's been a long hard day and we need to get to bed. When we go back to the farm I'll call Brad and have him come out one day and he can go over everything with both of us. Then we'll decide what to do."

He reached out a hand to her. "Help an old man up. I'm sore in places I forgot existed after all that riding today."

Ollie smiled as he watched Frankie take both of Colt's hands and tug to help him stand. *True love* he thought wistfully.

"Good night Ollie; we'll see you in the morning."

Ollie shut off the light in his office and stood in the hall watching the two of them go to their bedroom. *Somehow, I let that pass me by.* The thought was tinged with regret. He went to the kitchen to have a shot of Jack Daniels before he went to bed.

To his surprise he found Ellie bustling around at the sink. Warm pleasure flooded through him. "What are you doin', girl? I thought you'd be gone to bed."

She glanced at the clock on the wall. "It's getting time. Frankie helped me clean up and put the twins to bed. Maybe I should have checked with you first..." She hesitated. "But I thought if I made lunch for everyone now, it would simplify things in the morning. Did I step out of line?"

Ollie looked around the room, then back to her. "Don't see no line anywhere that you could have stepped out of."

She threw a tea towel at him.

He caught it in mid air and advanced toward her, mischief in his eyes. A light hearted feeling washed over him, something that he had experienced so long ago he'd forgotten what it was like.

He stopped. His heart did a little flip as he looked into her grey eyes; warm, open and friendly, twinkling with laughter. He wanted to reach for her, but pulled himself up short. *Old fool*, he thought. *It's watchin' those two young 'uns puttin' ideas in my head.*

He tossed the tea towel on to the counter. "Want to have a night cap with me?"

"That depends on what you've got."

"I'm having a shot of Jack Daniels. What would you like?"

"Rum and coke?" she asked with a smile.

"It's a done deal." Ollie mixed a drink and handed it to her. "Grab a chair," he said sitting down. "It's been a long day. It must have been long for you too; doing all that cooking and looking after the kids too."

"I had a wonderful day," she said with a smile. "Sam and Selena are great kids. They were so good today. And the cooking…honestly, it felt good to be part of everything going on; sort of like belonging again. I've missed that."

"Do you have any kids?"

"Yes, but they both ended up at the opposite ends of Canada; my son is in Toronto and my daughter is in Vancouver. And they are so busy with their own lives that I seldom see them. My husband, Eric, has been gone for ten years, but I still get lonely.

"One thing I have to say—I haven't been at Colt and Fran's for very long but they include me like family; they are wonderful." She smiled. "Do you have a family, Ollie?"

"No, I've been a rolling stone most of my life; until I came to work here. Now, the Thompson's are my family."

Colt and Frankie fell into bed, exhausted from the days ride. Colt spooned Frankie and slid his arm across her waist, dropping a kiss on the nape of her neck. They snuggled in silence for a few moments.

Then Frankie spoke softly. "Colt, I'm sorry; I haven't been much of a partner as far as the business goes. I know you have a heavy load, but I've just been so involved with the twins that I just assumed…I mean you've done it all for years. Have I disappointed you?"

"Are you kidding? I've felt damn guilty about the load you've been carrying. That's why I wanted a nanny; to give you a break from the kids. And yeah; I want days like today with you. I want to be able to share ideas with you without demanding too much of your time. But you have never, ever disappointed me. I'm almost in awe of you."

She turned in his arms and laid her cheek against his chest. "But now we're going to have another baby. I won't be able to just pick up and go with you after it comes."

He kissed her forehead. "That's true, for a couple of years anyway. But it will be easier than it would have been without Ellie's help. And hey! I'm looking forward to having this new little guy…or gal, in our family; possibly another one, sometime later too."

The roundup took three days of hard riding. Then it took another three days to haul the cattle from the pasture corrals to the ranch. After the last load on the stock liner arrived at the ranch, Colt and Frankie sat on the top plank of the corrals and looked at the herd.

"They look good Colt," Frankie commented.

"Yes and the prices have been steadily coming up. We should do well this year. We'll have to wean calves and sort for the next couple of days. How are you holding up? You're not used to riding like this. You're not getting overtired or anything? It's not too much for you and the baby is it?"

"I'm tired, but it's a good tired. I have to admit I'm sore; I haven't used some of these muscles for almost four years, but I've loved being back in the saddle again. I love it out here on the ranch."

"Let's go for a short ride. I want to run something past you."

Frankie tilted her head and looked at him questioningly. "What are you up to now?"

"Just get up in the saddle and come with me, woman."

She gave him a jab in the ribs. "All right, man."

They both swung up into their saddles and Colt led the way up a wide draw to a level plateau just above the ranch buildings. He turned his horse so they could overlook the scene below; the old house, the barns, corals, the shop. "Nice, eh?" he asked.

"Beautiful. What are you thinking? Wind turbines?"

"No; they'd do better at the top of the ridge behind here. Could you imagine a sprawling ranch style house here?"

"You...you mean for ...."

He reached out and took her hand. "For us?"

"But how can we do that; what about the farm? We can't live all the way out here and have you go back to run the farm. We'd be apart most of the time."

"Well, we need to talk about this; you and I. I love it out here; you love it out here. It's a great place to raise the kids. I could see us having an arena down there by the barns in that open spot. You can teach the kids how to team rope. I might even teach Sam how to bulldog steers."

"Sounds like a dream, but what about the farm?"

Colt swung down from his horse, and Frankie joined him. They stood there, reins in hand, side by side, overlooking the view around them. "I've been thinking that we should look for a farm manager. This is the life that both of us love; it's what I want for us and our family. What do you think?"

She smiled up at him. "I'd be here in a heartbeat, even if we lived in the old ranch house. But we can't let the farm go downhill. That's your family inheritance, your dad's life work."

He squeezed her shoulders. "No, no. I'm thinking I should have Shauna Lee work through a head-hunter to find someone with the right background and credentials to manage the farm. There are guys out there who are very capable.

"In the meantime, we could start looking at house plans, and we could start building the house out here in the early spring. Hopefully, we could be living out here by this time next year. Imagine it; Christmas on the ranch next year! The five of us—make that six with Ellie."

"And Ollie?"

"He'll stay where he is. He's part of the family. But he's in his sixties; soon he is going to need extra help."

"Can we really do all this? I mean, can we afford to build a house, hire a manager and all that?"

He looked at her with a smile. "I think so, hon; between the ranch and the farm, we've got a pretty big holding. We've done well the past few years, and I've invested with pretty good returns."

"Oh…I've never really thought about the money; it just seems to be there. Dumb of me."

"And you've never asked for a lot, hon. But we've worked hard; my dad and I. I don't care about traveling around the world when I'm old. I look at Dad. He worked himself into the ground and now they don't travel very much anyway; they hardly even come out to the farm anymore.

"What do they say? Life is the journey, not just the destination. I want us to *live* our whole life, enjoying what we do as we go; not just marking time until we retire." He kissed her lightly and then smiled. "So, what do you think? Do you like this spot for the house? Or do you want to look at other places."

"No, I love this. There's shelter from behind, full sun, we can see the creek winding through the field below, and it overlooks the ranch. There are just enough trees around to make it nice." She kicked at the grass with the toe of her boot. "And it's not bad soil for a yard—maybe a bit of garden. It's perfect."

"I've been thinking something else too. If you want to, we could set up a small vet clinic for you here. We're away out in the country, but there are ranchers and hobby farms around. Word of mouth travels fast. You probably wouldn't want a major surgery facility, but big enough to do emergency stuff. What do you think?"

Frankie's eyes were sparkling. "Colt, this sounds too good to be true. It's like a dream world; you and I out here on the ranch with the kids, a new house and a vet clinic too! But let's take it one step at a time, OK? We can start looking at house plans; that sounds like fun. But we have to find a manager for the farm."

She patted her tummy with a smile. "And we have to get this little one on terra firma and give it a year or two to grow, before I get into a vet clinic." She turned to hug him. "This is so exciting."

# CHAPTER FIVE

*M*onday morning Shauna Lee sat at her desk and looked at her calendar. Things looked pretty slow today; she liked it better when she was busy.

She looked out the window, focusing on the street outside. She was thinking about the weekend. She hadn't been able to push Brad's parting words of unsolicited advice away, even though he had infuriated her. *Figure out who you are, Shauna Lee, before it's too late. You've got a lot more to offer than sex, but you'll never find that out if you keep running from real intimacy. Bed hopping—with your nothing serious, no strings attached, no risk attitude, is not going get you there.*

She had spent Friday night at home watching TV. Boring! Saturday she had changed the sheets, done laundry and cleaned house but the evening had loomed ahead of her like a lonely prison sentence. *To hell with him,* she'd thought. *I'm not sitting here all by myself. I'm going to the bar and I'll see what happens!*

She'd showered, shaved her legs, styled her hair and dressed in one of her sexiest mini-skirts and a sheer red blouse with a matching silky camisole under it. She'd taken a pair of strappy red high heels from her closet and put them on. No jewellery; she didn't need it. She'd surveyed herself in the mirror and smiled with satisfaction. The outfit was a head turner and she knew it.

She had taken a taxi to the bar, telling herself that she shouldn't be driving home after she'd had a few drinks; but she'd known she wouldn't be coming home alone. And she hadn't. She'd singled out Troy Wilson and he hadn't had a chance. He was in town with an oil service crew; a twenty seven year old hottie. She had flattered him and teased him and by midnight he was turning cartwheels, trying to get her to let him take her home; and of course she had surrendered to his charm.

He'd stayed the night and her clean sheets had gotten a good work out. They had grabbed a coffee and toast for breakfast, then spent most of Sunday in bed. He'd been insatiable. He taken her out for a fancy seafood dinner that evening, then brought her home and claimed his payment on her wrinkled sheets.

He kept telling her how sexy she was; exclaiming over and over that he would never have guessed she was thirty nine. He declared that he liked older women. He'd left at around eleven o'clock that evening with her phone number tucked in his wallet, promising that he would call her when he was back in town.

She smiled to herself. There hadn't been any loneliness or boredom. But as she looked back on it, she didn't feel exhilaration either. *Damn Brad! He doesn't know anything about me.* But his words haunted her. *One day you'll wake up and find yourself old and alone.*

She was startled when the phone rang. Christina, her receptionist was on the line. "Colt Thompson on line two."

"Ok, I've got it." She lifted the receiver with a smile on her lips. "Good morning, Colt."

"Hi, Shauna Lee; have you got an hour or so later this afternoon?"

"Colt, I always have time for you," she teased. "At the office or at my place?"

He ignored her words. "I can be at the office at about three thirty, if that's not too late. What time do you close? I could rearrange my schedule, but I've got things I have to take care of this morning and an appointment with Brad Johnson at Windspeer at one o'clock. I'd like to connect with him first, if it works for you."

"Three thirty is fine. See you then."

*I wonder why he's seeing Brad.* Inwardly she winced, hoping their meeting was strictly about business.

She couldn't help it. Anxiety shadowed her all day as she waited for Colt to come. She was surprised when he walked in with his young son in tow. "So, are you giving Frankie a break?"

He tousled the little guy's hair and grinned. "Fran is grocery shopping. She's got Selena with her. I'm showing Sam the ropes early." He sat down and lifted the child onto his lap. "Aren't I, son?" he asked him, pride shining in his eyes.

Shauna Lee's heart curled as thoughts of what might have been threatened to crowd in. *Ben*. She had to force the door closed, but a tear spilled over before she managed to do it. She quickly dashed it away.

Colt was surprised to see the shine of tears in her eyes. He looked at her curiously, wondering why. She smiled. "I'm getting sappy," she said. "It's touching to see you so happy and proud of your family."

"Thanks, Shauna Lee. I can't imagine my life without them now."

Shauna Lee swallowed hard. "I hope you never have to, Colt." She knew she had to get the conversation on a different track. "So what did you want to see me about today?"

"A few things; I know it's not year-end, but I was wondering if I gave you rough figures if you could give me an estimate of where Thompson Land and Cattle will finish up this year. I have our current quota for grain, and I talked to a cattle buyer about the calves this morning, so I can give you an estimate there. Our expenses will be pretty much as other years from here on out. I bought a mobile home this morning. It's a used one in beautiful shape for a good value."

"Why did you buy a mobile home?"

"We have hired a nanny to help Fran with the twins. We're expecting again in May and I want her to have some free time to spend with me before she is tied up with the next little fellow. Ellie Raines, the lady we've found, is wonderful with the twins.

"Just this past week, we all went out to the ranch and she looked after them while Fran went riding with us to round up the cattle. It was like old times having her there. It's really the first break she's had since they were born. She wasn't too keen on getting a nanny, but I persuaded her to give it a try and now she thinks it will work out well. But we both agree that Ellie needs privacy and so do we."

"Congratulations on the new baby. You must be thrilled."

"You can't imagine how much! We both are." Colt shifted on his seat. "The other thing I'd like you to do is calculate what our hydro costs have been for the ranch over the past 10 years. You can pick that up off the computer can't you?"

"It might take a bit to go that far back, but I'll get it for you."

"Do you think you can have it by Friday?"

"Certainly."

"Good. What is your schedule like for Friday right after lunch?"

Shauna Lee consulted her calendar. "Things are pretty slow right now. I haven't got anything booked. Why?"

"I'd like you to come out to the farm with Brad Johnson. I'm giving some thought to putting three or four of his wind powered generators out at the ranch. We've got two water tanks on the grazing lease and it would be handy to have a steady power source out there, so there's always water for the stock in the summer.

"Over the years we've drilled wells at those spots and we have those stationary engines out there, but they are a pain in the ass. If it's hot you have to check every day and start them to pump water and if they decide not to run, you have another problem. I'm pretty sure I can use a float in the tank to trigger a switch that will start and turn off the pump, if we generate power from a turbine."

Sam was pushing at his dad's arm to get his attention. Colt stopped speaking and looked at him.

"Wats asss, dad?" Sam asked.

Colt swallowed his surprise. "Oh, ah…that's just something daddy says to explain things."

"But wats assss?"

Colt looked at Shauna Lee, grinning sheepishly. She was almost bursting with mirth, biting her lip in an effort not to laugh outright. "You know Sam, dad will have to explain that to you later. He's talking to this lady now."

"OK dad."

Colt smirked as he looked over his son's head at Shauna Lee. "Hmmm…little ears catch everything…anyway, the other thing I wanted to talk to you about is finding a manager for the farm.

"It can't just be anyone. I need someone with a track record and good credentials. In other words I'm looking for someone like myself. Don't you have access to some head-hunters that make it their business to find people like that?"

"I'll look into it. I'm sure they are out there. Whoever we find won't come cheap though."

"I'd hope to negotiate for a fair wage. I can't match the big corporations, but I'm thinking about a good wage, with a percentage of the net income of the farm. I know it won't come cheap but this is something I really want to do.

"Fran's concerned about the farm going down-hill. I won't let that happen, but the ranch has always been where my heart is and Fran loves it out there too. I want to raise my kids there."

"What will you do with Ollie?"

"Oh he's there for life; as far as we are concerned he's part of the family."

"That could get to be pretty close quarters for all of you."

Colt grinned. "When I told Fran what I wanted to do, she would have moved into the old house in a heartbeat; after we are satisfied that we have found a good manager for the farm. But I plan to build a new house.

"I took her up to the site on the weekend and she loved it. She demands so little, and I want her to have a modern home with more conveniences for her. I shouldn't say just her, I mean for us; I want a new place for our family."

"That's a lot of changes, Colt. Can you swing it all?"

"Shauna Lee, you know my business inside out. I'm not a poor man. I'm not filthy rich, but I can certainly afford to build a house without it hurting me too much. That's what I want to do for the woman I love."

"She's a lucky woman."

"I'm a lucky man. She has given me something that I never imagined I'd find."

Shauna Lee just looked at him.

Colt looked at his watch and stood up. "I've got to get moving here. I'll phone you with the info that I can give you for the year end so you can give me a rough estimate. And will you have it all when you come out to the farm with Brad on Friday?"

She nodded.

"He'll phone you; but I know he plans to be at the farm by one. He wants to get home early enough to watch the Rough Riders play in Montreal that night. He said something about wanting to be home by four thirty."

He looked at his watch again. "I've got to run. Fran will be waiting for me. Selena with be tired and hungry and she isn't as calm as Sam is. She's feisty and persistent! We'll talk later." He was out the door and gone.

The phone rang as he disappeared. "Call for you on line one, Shauna Lee."

"I've got it," she said wearily. "Hello, Shauna Lee speaking."

"Brad here." She wanted to ask *Brad Who?* just to throw him off his game.

"Colt just left. He told me you'd be calling."

"Sorry, I'm a little on the late side, but I wanted to get this confirmed because I'll be out of town until Thursday night. Did Colt tell you that we are going to be at his place by one o'clock on Friday?"

"He did."

"So I'll pick you up at your office at about twelve fifteen? Will that give us enough time to get there by one? I've never been to the farm."

"That will give us plenty of time. I…I'll be waiting for you."

"OK. I'll see you on Friday then." He hung up. She sat there looking at the phone. *Just what I need; to spend time in confined quarters with a guy who thinks he's my shrink.*

Colt called her the next morning with his projected figures and the price of the mobile he'd just bought, adding in his projected expenses for getting it set up. She had all the paper work he wanted done by Friday morning and she had put out a couple of feelers for a manager.

*Can it be Friday already? The week has gone by too quickly for comfort. I should have told Colt that I couldn't come and sent the information along*

59

*with Brad. I could still plead a headache or something. It will be pretty awkward riding with Brad after our last encounter.*

However, she was waiting in her office when Christina came to tell her that Brad was there. He had followed her and stepped right into Shauna Lee's office. Christina's surprise was obvious. She just looked at Shauna Lee and shrugged, then turned and left them facing each other across the desk.

Brad looked around the room, taking in all the details. It was bright, modern and tidy. "Nice digs you've got here," he said after a moment. "But there's nothing about you here. No pictures of friends, your favourite cat, sailing on the lake. There is nothing that gives anyone any idea about who you are."

She glared at him.

"Why?" he asked. "How do your clients get a feel of who you are?"

"This is a business, not a photo album of my life. It's professional, neat and tidy."

"And there's no sign of personality! It's sterile. Your receptionist has pictures at her desk. I saw a horse, and a picture of her having a beer with friends around a fire pit. There were a couple of others too."

"I don't have a horse or a cat, or pictures of me drinking beer with friends."

"Why?"

She snatched up the file on her desk. "I don't need you acting like my shrink. Either you get back to business and stay there, or I'll phone Colt and tell him I'm not coming."

He chuckled as he watched her fume. "My truck is right outside." He sauntered out with a smirk on his face, winking at the receptionist as he passed. Shauna Lee looked like a thunder cloud when she followed him.

Brad opened the passenger door and waited for her to step up. Then he gave her gentle lift so she could make it onto the seat. He shut the door and walked to the driver's side, whistling as he went. He opened the door and stepped up into the cab. He started the truck, fastened his seatbelt and looked across at her. "All set?" he asked.

60

"Why the hell do they make trucks so high off the ground like this?" She was being snarky. "It is ridiculous."

"Actually those lift-kits are special order."

"Why? What do you get out of it?"

"Well, I get to lift a shortie like you up into the cab once in a while and watch her slide her fancy little tush up onto the seat."

"Screw you," she hissed.

"Hey, you asked. I told you. And as I'm sure you recall, I passed up on that offer last time. I think I'll do the same now."

Shauna Lee flushed scarlet. "That's it! I'm out of here," she stormed, reaching for the door handle.

He put the truck in gear, ready to ease out into the traffic. "You've still got your seat belt on, and it's a long way down to the pavement if you do get it off and try to get out."

She glared at him. He gave her a long look and finally she looked away. She saw Christina watching them from her desk inside. *Oh great!*

"Did you have lunch? I didn't, so I'm going to the drive through at the A&W and order a hamburger and coffee."

She didn't answer him. He grinned. "Cat got your tongue? Oh that's right you don't have a cat, or a horse or…"

She threw the file at him. "SHUT UP. Why are you doing this? We are going to a business meeting. There is nothing personal between us!"

He reached out and grabbed at the file, trying to keep the paper work from falling everywhere. "Hey girl, I'm driving. That's not a smart move." He stopped at a red light and they both scrambled, reaching for the papers that had slid to the floor. She snatched the one he held and organized the file without looking at him.

When he stopped at the drive through at the A&W she was still fuming. "That's it. I'm taking a taxi back to the office. You can take this file to Colt and explain why I'm not with you."

He grinned as she gathered up her purse and reached for the door handle while he ordered. The door wouldn't open. She tried again, then realised that he had hit the child-lock button and she couldn't get out. "You bastard; I'll…I'll…"

He had moved the truck forward to the window to pick up the order. He paid the cashier, took the food and eased the truck forward.

"Oh, you couldn't open the door?" He frowned as if puzzled. "I must have hit the child-lock button. Anyway, I ordered a burger and coffee for you, too. I'm sure you haven't eaten. You need to be on top of things for the business meeting. All that angst your putting out on our personal time has to have taken a lot of energy."

He slid out the cup holder and put a coffee cup in it. "As I remember from the other night you take your coffee black." He laid a foil wrapper with a hamburger in it on the seat and eased it toward her. "I ordered the same for both of us."

He worked his hamburger out of the package as he drove with three fingers of his left hand on the steering wheel. He dropped the wrapper on the seat and transferred the hamburger into his right hand and took a big bite. "Hmmm…that is good. I didn't realise what an appetite I had worked up. You're hard on a guy, Shauna."

He glanced her way, but she was staring stonily out the window. "OK, I'll quit pushing your buttons. I'll shut up. Don't let that hamburger get cold; or the coffee." He pulled back the tab on his coffee lid and savoured the taste. He said nothing more as he drove down the road.

Shauna Lee's mouth was watering. She hadn't eaten breakfast because she had been so nervous about this whole day; the trip out to the farm and back with Brad; being at the farm; she hadn't been there since Colt had married Frankie.

She had released Colt from their engagement without any qualms at the time. But seeing him the way he was now, so relaxed and so in love; she couldn't help but have misgivings. From some little spot in her mind, she sometimes imagined that it was her he had loved, not Frankie. He had changed, maybe she could have too.

A tear slid down her cheek. Brad happened to glance at her as it fell. His heart missed a beat as he looked at her. He could see she was swallowing hard, fighting for control. He pulled over to the side of the road and parked on the shoulder. He reached out to touch her gently. She jerked away.

"Shauna, I'm sorry. I didn't mean to upset you this much." He released his seat belt and reached across her lap to open the small compartment in front of her. He took out a package of Kleenex and extracted a tissue. He handed it to her. She reached for it blindly, refusing to look at him. She dabbed at her cheek and bit her lip, trying to concentrate and take command of the control she always could find, cursing that it seemed to elude her now.

Brad opened her cup of coffee and held it out to her. "Here, have a drink. It'll help." She took three deep breaths and forced herself to relax. Then she reached out and took the cup without looking at him. He opened the hamburger wrapper and searched for a napkin in the brown bag it had come in. Then he handed it toward her.

She hesitated, and then reached for it, still refusing to look at him. He grabbed her hand as he slid the hamburger into it. "Look at me Shauna," he said softly. She still refused. He slid across the seat, still holding the hamburger and her hand. He reached over with his other hand, touching her chin and turning her toward him. He regretted the sheen of tears that he seen in her eyes.

"I'm sorry. I didn't mean for any of this to happen. I intended to pick you up, grab a hamburger and drive out to the farm. And that is what I should have done. But when I walked into your office, I did it on purpose. I wanted to see if it was as...if there was something that showed me more about who you are. But it's just like your house; beautiful, but so impersonal.

"It frustrates the hell out of me. I realize now that I just kept pushing you...a way too far. I wanted to crack that wall of armour that you wear. I wanted to get a glimpse of who you really are. But I never wanted this; I never wanted to make you cry. I can't tell you how sorry I am."

She shook her head and then looked away.

"Eat the hamburger," he urged. "We have to go."

She took a tentative bite, then another."

He turned the key and started the engine. "Can we go now?"

"Yes," she said softly and took another bite.

Brad drove down the highway looking at road signs. When he saw the sign that read, 'Cantaur 12 kms', he turned. He followed the road until he came to Colt's drive way. Then he turned left and started down the long drive.

Shauna Lee finished the last bite of the hamburger. She crumpled the foil wrapper; picked up the one Brad had pushed against her and dropped it in the brown paper bag. "You told me you'd never been here."

"I haven't. I got clear instructions from Colt when I talked to him last night. I didn't say anything to him, but I wasn't sure you would drive out here with me. I thought you might decide to bring your own wheels."

"I thought about it. I should have."

Brad pulled up in front of the house. He would have spoken, but Colt stepped out on the veranda. As Shauna Lee reached for the file, he dropped his hand to cover hers and gave it a gentle squeeze of apology.

Then he released the child-lock so she could get out and shut off the motor. As he got out of the truck, Colt came up to the passenger door to help her out. His touch was impersonal but gentle; definitely different than Brad's lingering hold had been.

"One thing's for sure, Johnson; the lift job you've got on this thing would disappear fast if you ever settled down and had kids. The only thing this is good for is getting a feel of your date's bod' as you lift her up into the cab."

Shauna Lee turned away from Colt. She shot a look at Brad and caught his grin as he shrugged. When he caught her look he sobered up immediately and reached out to shake hands with Colt.

"Nice place you've got here. I think you could use three turbines right here on the farm. They would save you energy and cut your hydro costs."

Colt cuffed him on the shoulder. "I just manage this place. You need to convince the boss about that. She's inside." He turned to lead them into the house. Shauna Lee followed them, wondering at the easy camaraderie that the two men had developed in a short time. She hesitated as she looked at the house.

She'd been here before as a guest of Colt's mom and dad. But now there was a new mistress here. *Suck it up Shauna Lee. Everything is all right; you've got everything under control.* She put a smile on her lips as she walked up the steps onto the veranda.

Frankie came to the door as they stepped inside. Colt slipped an arm around her shoulder; "Honey, this is Brad Johnson. Brad, meet the boss."

She jabbed him in the ribs with an arch look. "You all heard that," she said with a laugh. She extended her hand to Brad. "Hi. I'm Frankie."

"Glad to finally meet you." He motioned to Colt. "This guy's like some newlywed, the way he talks about you. It's nice to see really happy people."

Frankie threw a loving smile at Colt. "Thank you, Brad."

Brad turned to Shauna Lee, and looked at each of them. "Do you two know each other?"

Frankie smiled warmly as she looked at Shauna Lee. "We do." She reached out and placed a hand on Shauna Lee's arm. "Shauna Lee is one of the most generous, understanding people I have ever met," she said softly. She looked at Colt. "And she's a smart business woman too. That's why we wanted her here at this meeting, isn't it hon?"

Colt smiled at Frankie in a way that made Brad feel a tug of loneliness. Shauna Lee pushed all thought into the back of her consciousness.

Colt agreed and suggested that they each grab a chair at the old maple table. "I guess we had better get into this. Brad wants to be home by four thirty so he can watch the football game, so, we've got about two hours to get this finished up." He looked at Frankie. "Do I smell coffee?"

She nodded and he walked to the counter and collected the tray that was all ready set up with 4 mugs and cream and sugar. Frankie brought the coffee carafe and a plate of fresh cookies. Her eyes met Colt's and a knowing look flashed between them. Colt chuckled. "My favourite cookies; she made them the first time I met her at the ranch."

Frankie flushed remembering. She shot Colt a look that said 'don't you *dare*.' Colt bit into one, his eyes sparkling. "That's when…"

Frankie cleared her throat and cut him off. "So where do we start guys?" she asked, adroitly changing the direction she feared Colt's teasing could take. She sat down on the chair at the far side of the table, positioning herself and Colt across from each other and adjacent to both Brad and Shauna Lee.

Brad explained the concept of the wind energy turbines, affirming what Colt had discussed with her. She made sure that Shauna Lee was included in the conversation, and soon it flowed nicely with everyone's input. An hour and a half flew by.

Colt sat back and looked across the table at Frankie. "So, do you think we should go for what we talked about?"

She nodded. "It makes sense. It's a new thing for us, but I agree with you; especially at the water tanks. And you want to put the other two at the ranch near the corrals?"

"I was thinking in a couple of years…"

Frankie's eyes glowed. "Ohhhh…" she breathed softly. "That would be perfect." *My vet clinic,* she thought. *Colt, you are such a darling!*

Colt looked at his watch. He turned to Shauna Lee. "What I'd really like, is for you to go out to the ranch with Brad one day next week. You know the way out there and you know how our business works.

"I'll call Ollie and ask him to take you guys out to both of the water tanks so Brad can get the information he needs. I've shown Ollie where I want the other two turbines put at the ranch. I want to get at this right away before the weather changes."

He looked at Brad. "I'd go with you, but I've got business to take care of here. I've got to get the mobile home set up for our new nanny; a cement pad, hydro and a sewer connection. I want to get it in place as soon as possible so I beat the winter weather."

He looked at Frankie with a slight smile, and Brad caught the knowing look between them. "And we all need our privacy." He looked around the table. "I guess that does it then. We can't make Brad late for his game."

They had all pushed their chairs away from the table, when the patter of little feet could be heard on the top floor, headed for the stairs. The twins came bouncing down them, followed by Ellie. Selena charged into Colt, swinging on his leg as she looked at each person in turn, her brown eyes happy.

Sam came down and took Frankie's hand. He looked at Brad and then at Shauna Lee. He hooked a finger in his mouth, considering her. He watched as they walked to the door and then pointing at Shauna Lee, he said loudly, "Dad, watss asss?"

Shauna Lee looked surprised. Her eyes flew to Colt and she couldn't hide her smile.

"Dad." He was unusually insistent. "Dad, wats asss?" he asked again.

Brad and Frankie looked between Colt and Shauna Lee. "You little monkey..." He looked at Frankie. "Yesterday when I was at the office..." He nodded toward Shauna Lee.

"And you thought he'd forgotten," Frankie said as he jogged her memory. She laughed. "Looks like you've got some explaining to do, dad."

Sam piped up again. "Dad, watsss monky?"

"Possibly not." Colt winked at Frankie. "Dad will tell you later, OK?" Sam nodded, his big blue eyes focused on Shauna Lee.

"Watsss monkey?" he pointed to her. "Ou monky?"

Shauna Lee laughed out right. "You are such a cutie," she said her eyes soft. Brad watched her curiously, thinking how seldom she ever really smiled with a light in her eyes. And he didn't miss the wistful look on her face either.

Colt swept Sam up into his arms. He grinned at him, and pressing his finger to his chest said "Sam is dad's monkey!" He looked at his watch and shook his head. "Brad, right now you will be fifteen minutes late for the game by the time you get home; you'd better get on the road." He turned to Shauna Lee with a smile. "Thanks for coming, ou monky," he teased. "Is that file on the table the information I asked for?" She nodded. "Thanks."

Frankie and Colt stood in the doorway, children in their arms, watching Shauna Lee and Brad go to the truck.

Brad walked to the passenger door and opened it. Shauna Lee looked at him doubtfully. "It's OK," he said reassuringly. He bent over and clasped his hands, palms up. "Put your foot on my hands and your hand on my shoulder, and I'll lift you up." She looked at him sceptically. "It's all right. I promise. I won't harass you anymore today."

She gingerly put her foot onto his hand and leaned her body into his shoulder, steadying herself with her hand as he had instructed her to do. He lifted her up effortlessly and let her lean inside the cab and move her feet onto the floor. He watched until she had turned and lowered herself onto the seat. He smiled at her and shut the door. Turning, he waved to the Thompsons as he walked around the front of the truck to the driver's door.

"I'll talk to you soon Colt, and it was nice to meet you Frankie." He slid in, started the motor and fastened his seatbelt. He looked at Shauna Lee. "Buckled up and ready to fly?"

She nodded and he put the truck in reverse and eased out onto the driveway. They drove in silence until they were half way back to Swift Current. Brad sighed. "I think I envy their happiness; they're still crazy in love and they have three year old twins. You can't miss the looks that pass between them."

He tapped his finger on the steering wheel. "I didn't realize you and Frankie knew each other that well." He looked across the cab at her.

"Actually, we haven't met very often."

"But she said…."

Shauna Lee looked out the window. "That happy family could have been Colt and mine. I was engaged to him when he decided he was in love with her. I didn't hold him to it. That is why she is so generous to me."

"You two were engaged?"

She nodded.

"How can you work together now? I couldn't do it."

"We were friends. Neither one of us were looking for love and romance. We went out together off and on for a few years; no solid commitment, but we went to Mexico and out for dinner and…"

"I get it," he said harshly.

"Any way four years ago he suggested we should get married. At first I thought he was kidding. But he was very persistent, so I agreed. I liked him, but I never had considered marriage with anyone. And I didn't want children and I didn't want to live on the farm.

"He said we would live in town. His mom and dad were living on the farm then. We were engaged for about three and a half months. After about a month, I could sense that something was wrong. And with time he became more unsettled. Before Christmas he came and told me he couldn't marry me because he was in love with Frankie and he wasn't happy without her.

"He was very emotional. He…he broke down and apologised over and over for ever having asked me to marry him. I liked him, but I wasn't in love with him so I told him to go to her. When he found her, she was pregnant with the twins. They are his, there's no doubt of that. They got married immediately."

"Wheww!"

"Now, when I see the way he is with her and the kids, I wish I had held on to him. If he could change so much, maybe I could have too. But it's too late now. They are married and they have the twins. He told me the other day that she is pregnant again. And they are crazy about each other. I missed my chance."

They both were silent until they could see Swift Current in the distance. Brad spoke softly. "Shauna Lee, do you really believe you and Colt could have been as happy as they are?"

She looked away. "Why not?"

"Well, he was engaged to you. He asked for his freedom because he was in love with her."

Shauna Lee sighed. "I've seen how happy he is; how he is with his kids. I've often thought that if I had realized that love could be like that…I'd have been willing to chance it."

He was silent until he stopped at a red light. "Seeing them together…I think they were meant to be. You two weren't meant for each other Shauna, but you could find that kind of happiness with someone else."

"I'll never have that."

"Why are you so certain?"

"Brad, please don't analyze me."

"OK, OK! I'll leave it alone."

Shauna Lee glanced at her watch. "If the game started at four thirty, you're already half an hour late. My house is closer. You could stop and watch it there. I can order pizza in."

"Are you serious?" he asked cautiously.

"Hell no; I get a big kick out of having you turn me down."

"I didn't exactly do that…but…yeah, I do appreciate the offer."

"And know in advance that you are not invited to my bed."

"Yes, let's get that sore point out of the way; I'm not going anywhere near your bed…not yet anyway." He looked at her intently. "I was serious the other night. You interest me, but I don't hunt where others do and I'm not going to be another one of your boy-toys."

"Could you be any blunter?" she asked caustically.

Suddenly he changed lanes. "I have another idea. You have an oven." It was a statement, not a question. "Why don't we make our own pizza?"

She stared at him in astonishment. "Well…yeah, we could. But I have to confess, my cupboard is pretty bare. I need to go for groceries and what about the game? You're already late."

"This won't take long. We'll stop at Safeway and get what we need. It'll be fun." He grinned as he parked the truck. "Are you ready to go?"

She went into the grocery store with him and followed as he whipped through the aisles like a man who knew what he was doing; an onion, garlic, red and green peppers, mushrooms, tomato sauce puree, a bag of shredded Mozzarella cheese a pound of hamburger, a pound of bacon and some limes. He grinned as he picked up a packaged pizza crust. "We'll cheat this time. Next time I'll make the crust from scratch."

"Do you actually do this often?"

"Damn straight. Through the years I ate in so many restaurants I got sick of it. I decided to learn to cook. And I'm pretty good at it, if I do say so myself. Tonight you're in for a treat. We'll make my Hungry Man's Pizza." He looked at her closely. "Have you ever made pizza?

"No. I love pizza, but I always have it delivered."

"Lady, if you're going to hang out with me, you're going to have to learn to cook!"

First thing when they got to her place, she led Brad to the couch and picked up the remote, handing it to him as he sat down. He found the channel with the game on. It was already playing in the second quarter.

She stood watching him. He was immediately into the game, sitting on the edge of the couch, tensing as he watched the players move, cheering when they made a good play, cursing when someone made a bad move.

"Can I get you anything to drink, Brad?"

He looked at the time. "It's only about five minutes until half time." He patted the seat beside him. "Come sit here by me. Do you watch football?"

"To be honest I don't understand the game. I just kind of freak when I see about 2000 man pounds landing on one guy at the bottom of the pile."

He hooked an arm around her shoulder as she sat down, pulling her closer. "I'll help you understand the finer points of the game."

They watched until half time. Then he took over in the kitchen. He didn't let her off the hook though. She sliced peppers and mushrooms while he chopped the onion. He chopped a clove of garlic and added it to the hamburger while she cooked it in the frying pan.

He sorted through her meagre assortment of spices, selecting a handful of this and a pinch of that and tossed them into the tomato paste puree. By the beginning of the third quarter the pizza was in the oven.

"Now, wasn't that fun?" he asked with a happy smile. Then he walked to the fridge and took out two of the Corona beers that they had mutually agreed upon when they had stopped at the liquor store. He hooked a lime with his little finger just before he closed the door, then went to the counter and dropped it on the cutting board. He cut a couple wedges and popped one in each bottle. "I should have asked you; would you have preferred a glass?"

"No. I drink it straight from the bottle."

He grinned as he handed her the bottle of golden ale. "You're a girl after my own heart."

At the beginning of the fourth quarter the aroma of cooking pizza filled the room. "Damn, I'm hungry. That hamburger is long gone. The pizza smells like it is ready," he said, easing himself away from her so he could stand up.

She could see the bulge behind his zipper as he turned toward the stove. Her feminine parts were tight, singing with arousal. Sitting so close to him had sent her hormones into overdrive.

She got up and as he took the pizza out of the oven, she went to the cupboard and took a pizza cutter from a drawer. Then she reached up and took out two plates. "Want another beer?" she asked.

"That's a good plan. Is it all right if we sit over there?" He motioned to the couch.

"I eat there most of the time. I'll pull the coffee table over and you can put the pizza pan on it. I'll bring the plates and some napkins."

He cut a slice and took a bite out of his it. "Mmmm, that is good! We did great a great job with this one."

"You mean you did."

"No, we did. You helped. I'll let you cut the onions next time and you'll remember that you helped," he teased as he carried the pizza past her.

She slid a slice of lime into each bottle of Corona and carried them to the coffee table.

He lifted a slice of pizza off the pan and held it up for her to take a bite. "Now, tell me that delivery beats this, if you dare!"

She took a small bite. "Ohh…that's hot," she gasped, rolling it around in her mouth, trying to cool it.

"Sorry! I didn't think about that. Did it burn your tongue?"

"Yes."

He pushed her bottle of Corona into her hand. "Maybe this will help."

She swallowed a few glugs, and then rubbed her tongue against her teeth.

He groaned, watching her do it. "Here, let me see if I can help." He reached for her, pulling her to him. He kissed her deeply, his tongue working over hers.

"God," he whispered hoarsely. "The pizza isn't the only thing that's hot. I've wanted to do that all afternoon." He pulled her over, laying her across his lap. As she looked up at him she could feel the hardness of his erection against her back. She felt the wetness in her panties and she ached with her arousal.

He kissed her again, then, gave his head a slight shake as if to clear it, and helped her up, so she was sitting on the seat beside him again. His hand trembled as he handed her a plate with the piece of pizza on it. His eyes met hers and held. Then he cleared his throat. "Eat." His voice was husky with emotion.

*What the...* She was trembling as she took the plate. She sat it on the coffee table. Confused she reached for her Corona. She sipped hesitantly.

He turned his attention back to the game, watching quietly. When she had finished eating he reached over and took her hand, lifting it to rest on his thigh. She could feel the tension in his body. They sat in quiet anxiety, side by side, his hand resting on hers, until the game was over.

Brad stood up and gathered up the pizza and the dishes. Shawna Lee picked up the empty bottles and pushed the coffee table back. Then she turned to meet his gaze.

"Shawna. I have to go...*now.*" His voice was strained.

"I...It's still early."

He closed the distance between them and slipped his arm around her waist pulling her against him. She could feel his hardness push into her. "I can't tell you how much I enjoyed this...you and me making the pizza together. Having you watch the game with me. But...I have to

73

go before I…before *we*, do something we can't take back." He kissed her gently, then turned and walked to the door.

She reached out to him. "Brad, please don't go."

He shook his head. "I'm only human, Shauna. If I stay, you know where we'll end up. I don't want to take you to the bedroom tonight. No, that's not true, I damn well *do* want too. But I'm not going to."

He pulled her against him and pushed the hardness behind his zipper against her. "I can't deny what you do to me," he whispered. "I've been so horny for the past three hours, my nuts are aching." He nuzzled the curve of her neck. "But, if I let that happen tonight, sex will take over our relationship. I want to get to know you first. I want to spend time exploring things together; I want to find out what you enjoy…besides sex.

"I think you are going to have to find those things out about your-self too. If I'm wrong, I'm wrong, but I think you've lost touch with who you are. You tell me you've worked and studied, and that's about all. You say you have no family. Do you have any friends, or are your only friends the guys you bring home?"

"Brad, you don't know anything about me."

"But I want to," he whispered. He settled his mouth over hers and kissed her into silence. Then he released her and stepped away. "I *have* to go now. If I don't, I'll be no better than all those other guys." His eyes implored her. "Please…please know you are worth more than that. Stop giving yourself away, Shauna."

He reached out to touch her hand. "I'll call you during the week. If you're not interested when I call, just say so; but if you are willing to see if we can make something lasting…I'd like to explore that with you."

She looked at him with the glisten of tears in her eyes.

He turned quickly and walked out of the house. She moved to the window and watched him stride down the walk way. He got into his truck and sat there for a moment, his head tilted back against the neck support, looking up toward the roof. Finally he sat up and started the motor and drove away.

It was early, but Shauna Lee turned off the lights and went into the bedroom. She took off her clothes, turned back the covers and lay naked on the bed. Her fingers slid down over her breasts to the throbbing ache between her legs. She probed with her fingers, feeling herself swollen and hot. She stroked softly, and then sobbed. She could relieve herself, but that wasn't what she wanted or needed.

She needed what he'd left her without; the warmth of human contact, arms around her, someone to laugh with, someone to share even a few hours with. He'd left her *alone*, like she'd been all her life.

She cried herself to sleep.

# CHAPTER SIX

*T*he next morning she awoke early. Brad was the first person on her mind. He had been cruel when he'd come to pick her up yesterday; asking questions she herself didn't have answers for. Why was he so insistent? Why did he care if her life was *sterile*, as he called it?

The phone rang. She looked at her watch. It was six thirty in the morning. Who would call this early? She reached for the phone.

"Good morning beautiful." The voice was soft, sexy, sleepy sounding.

"Brad?"

"I hope that's who you're thinking about. Are you still in bed?"

"Yes."

"What are you doing?"

"What are *you* doing?" she countered.

"Thinking about you. The cold shower didn't do it last night. I've still got a hard on."

"That's your own fault. I asked you to stay."

"I know that sweetie, but…I'm looking for something I can put my heart into. I'm serious…but for me it's got to be just you and me. I can't share you with other guys. I want to build a relationship with you. I want what I saw yesterday between Colt and Frankie. I want that kind of love for you and me."

She sobbed.

"Shauna? Baby…"

She couldn't control her tears; she sobbed again. Then she hung up.

Fifteen minutes later the doorbell rang. She instinctively knew it was Brad. *Go to hell,* she groaned. She was not getting up to face more torment. But he kept ringing the bell. Then he went around to the back door and pounded on it.

Furious she staggered out of bed and went to open it, not even thinking about the fact that she was still naked. "Jeeze, don't break the place down…" She stopped dead. He stood there in pyjama bottoms, bare feet and no shirt. "Are you absolutely crazy?"

He pushed through the door, forcing her in with him. He closed it and locked it behind him. Then he enveloped her in his arms, pressing her face to his muscular chest. He swept her up and carried her into the bedroom, laid her on the bed and slid in beside her. He cradled her close in his arms and let her cry until she was worn out.

His hands tangled in her hair and he kissed her forehead. "Turn over and let me cuddle you," he whispered. They lay together, spooned. She felt his warmth, the strength of his arms around her. It wasn't sexual. It was peaceful, safe…like finding home after a long exhausting search. They both fell asleep.

Shauna stirred. At first she was confused, enveloped in his warmth. His arm tightened. "Good morning, beautiful," he whispered.

"Uh huh…" she murmured. "What are you doing here?"

"I came by to ask you to go on a date with me. Will you come?"

She moved to turn over. He held her tight. "No. Just stay here in the circle of my arms. Let me hold you."

She was silent for a moment. "What kind of a date?" she whispered.

He whispered back to her. "Breakfast at my house, a lazy day getting to know each other, maybe watch a movie tonight or just sit around and talk. You can stay over if you want…I have a guest room. Breakfast together tomorrow morning; maybe we'll go for a drive. We'll give ourselves a chance to learn to *like* being with each other; learn to be comfortable together; learn to be friends and companions.

"And if it works this weekend, then maybe we'll do something similar again next weekend, and the next one; until we can't imagine life without each other; until we fall in *love*. Lust is no issue; we've got that already; but like and love has to be nurtured and built upon. Are you willing to give it a try?"

She was still for a few seconds. "You are crazy." She thought for a moment. Then she nodded. "But… all right; I'm willing to give it a try."

His arms tightened around her momentarily; then he lightly slapped her naked hip. "Do you want to shower here or at my place?"

"Are you serious?"

"Well sweetie, I don't know if you noticed but I'm not dressed for public places. I just knew you were crying, so I bailed out of bed and tore over here. I thought I might sweep you up and take you home with me right then. But it didn't happen that way. At seven in the morning it didn't seem to matter too much, but at eleven or eleven thirty, it's a little different."

"Can I grab a jogging outfit now and comeback later for necessities?"

"That's great thinking." He rubbed his hand along the cheek of her butt. "Out you get and be quick. I need to get back home so I don't get arrested for indecent exposure!"

Smiling, she slid out of bed, and went to her dresser to take out a pair of panties, a bra and socks. He got out of the bed and made it while she quickly got dressed. She grabbed her cosmetic bag and hair brush and stood waiting for him.

"You're good!" he said with a smile, leaning in for a quick kiss. "Let's go."

Shauna Lee had never given much thought to where Brad lived or what his house would be like. She wasn't prepared for the reality. He lived in one of the new subdivisions on the outskirts of town on a ten acre lot. The house was big and sprawling and the yard was perfectly landscaped.

"Is this your place?"

"I'm pretty certain my name is on the mortgage." He grinned at her. "If you don't like it, I'm…"

"I didn't mean that. I just thought you'd have a condo or something."

"Actually, this is what my Dad calls a 'Bird House.' I bought it with the idea of settling down sometime and starting a family. Now I just have to find a Bird who will share it with me." He looked at her. "You could have first option."

She looked away from him. "Brad. You don't know me. I'm not a prime candidate."

"See, I think you are wrong there. I guess that's something we have to explore. When I first met you, I thought the same thing. I figured you were nothing but trouble; certainly not someone I wanted to have anything to do with. But even that night at the meeting, I saw beyond the...the other stuff."

He smiled as their eyes met. "I knew you were intelligent, and people at that meeting respected you."

"What a revelation that must have been," she said bitterly.

"Shauna, I'm drawn to you in spite of everything else. For whatever reason, it's different for me with you. You frustrate the hell out of me, but you've got me thinking about the future; love and marriage and forever; my gut tells me you are worth the effort."

"We don't want the same things. And I don't want children."

"And yet I saw you with Sam yesterday. I saw you fight tears when you looked at him, and when you reached out to him, you had such a wistful expression. I don't think that had anything to do with him being Colt's son.

"You're smart enough to know Colt's heart is taken, but you know what I think Tweetie Bird? I think part of you wants what you see in Colt, now that he is in love. It's safe for you to imagine that with him because it's unreachable, so you know you will never have to deal with real intimacy."

"I shouldn't have come here."

"You're wrong. You needed to come here. It's not going to be easy Shauna, but I'm in it for the long haul. Little by little, day by day, week by week, month by month, year by year—we are going to peel away the layers and free the woman that you really are. In my heart, I feel that you have been hurt, badly. I want to be the one to show you what real love, *unconditional* love is. I want to share that with you."

He reached out and touched her. "Trust me Shauna. I don't give up easily when I really want something. And I really want to see you happy and in love with me." He opened the truck door. "Ok…session one with the analyst is over."

"Session one? More like session five isn't it?"

"Sorry. I'll drop it for now. It's time for a shower and brunch. How does waffles and strawberries and whipped cream sound?"

He led the way to the house door, unlocked it and swung it open. "Welcome to the nest, Tweetie Bird."

Shauna Lee looked at him. "If I was smart, I'd probably fly away." She walked past him and he stepped in behind her, closing the door. She looked around the large foyer. Ceramic tile covered the floor and flowed into the kitchen and dining room area. Rich dark hardwood could be seen leading down the hall and into other rooms. The kitchen was a modern dream. She stood and looked around in open admiration. "Brad, this is…phenomenal. You have wonderful taste."

"Remember that! I know I do." He smiled into her eyes as he brushed her chin lightly with his fingers. "OK, breakfast first or a shower first?"

"I need a shower. I must look like a nightmare."

"More like a dream." He winked. "I'll show you the spare room. There's an ensuite right off it." He led the way down the hall and stopped at a door at the far end. "Here you are."

She stepped into the room and looked around. It was decorated in a classic contemporary design; understated luxury. "It's beautiful, Brad."

"You'll find towels and shampoo in there. Take as long as you like. I'll grab a quick one in my room. Come to the kitchen when you're ready."

Shauna Lee luxuriated in the warmth and pressure of the shower. She washed her hair, towelled dry and quickly put her clothes back on. She peeked in the drawers, looking for a blow dryer. *None. Well I guess it's a curly mop for me today.*

She wandered down the hallway stopping to look at different groups of pictures on the wall as she went; family, friends, fun events, hunting pictures. This man had pictures everywhere; evidence of his life. *No wonder my place drives him crazy.*

She stepped into the kitchen and watched him beating something with mixer. She walked softly to his side. He removed the bowl from the stand. She could see it was filled with a deep pile of fluffy egg whites and he was shaking a dry mix over them. Then he folded it in gently with a spatula. "From scratch?" she asked.

He grinned as he turned to the hot waffle iron, opened the lip and spooned the mixture onto it. "They are best that way."

She shook her head, knowing she'd never be able to match his cooking prowess. "Can I do anything to help you?"

"You can clean the strawberries and slice them."

"I think I can handle that."

He set out a bowl, a small knife and a cutting board. With an economy of movement, he reached into the fridge and brought out a big carton of strawberries. "There you go," he said with a smile. He turned to check the waffles and lifted a fluffy, golden brown one off the iron. He slipped it onto a plate in a small compartment below the wall oven.

"What's that?" she asked looking toward it.

"Oh, it's a warming drawer. I would hate to be without it."

He spooned more of the mix onto the waffle iron and closed it. Then he reached for a small electrical whipping wand and started making the whipped cream.

"Can I set the table?"

He nodded. "The plates are up there," he said nodding at a cupboard, and the cutlery is over here." He pulled open a drawer to show her.

*He is so organized, he scares me; everything in its place,* she thought as she watched him put the waffle mix bowl directly into the dishwasher and give the counter a wipe down.

He looked at her with a happy smile. "Pull up a chair and dig in," he said as he carried the waffles, whipped cream and strawberries to the table. "I'll put coffee on for after we eat."

She sat down and waited for him to join her. "Help yourself," he said, leaning over to tousle her curls. "I like these," he said softly.

They ate with relish. "Brad this is wonderful. Those waffles sure beat the toaster pop-ups I buy."

"Shauna, Shauna. You don't know what you're missing. And the best part of it is the fun of doing something like this with someone special…like you."

"But I didn't do anything."

He shook his head, pointing to the strawberry stains on her fingers. "Yes you did. And you set the table. And you are great company. You know, it gets lonely being here, no matter how beautiful the place is."

She nodded. "I understand loneliness," she said wistfully.

He took their plates and cutlery and slid them into the dishwasher, then poured them each a cup of coffee. "Do you ride horses? I guess I should ask if you ever have, since it seems like you don't do anything much except work and…"

She put her hand up to stop him. "I rode when I was about eight; that's so long ago I doubt if it counts now."

"Do you want to go for a walk out back? I've got a couple of horses out there.

She looked sceptical but nodded. Brad got up and went to a cupboard and slipped something small into his shirt pocket. He reached out his hand and threaded his fingers through hers. "We can go out the back door."

It was a beautiful day and they wandered down a trail that ran through a large landscaped back yard, into a fenced pasture. In one corner there was a small barn and a corral. Brad whistled sharply and in seconds they could hear the pounding of hooves coming their way.

Brad filled a small bucket with oats and stepped forward to meet the horses, then led them into the corral and shut the gate. "Do you want to come in here with me or watch from out there?"

"I'll stay out here for now."

He talked to each one of the horses, rubbing their ears softly, running his hands down the length of their backs and down over their hips. He took a curry comb and started working their coats, while they stood with all their weight on three legs, resting a hind one, with bottom lip drooping, tail switching lazily, in perfect contentment.

As she watched, a familiarity from long ago rose in Shauna Lee. Her mind went back to a battered old pole corral and bare dirt. She remembered the old grey gelding that she had loved. She had ridden for hours every day; a lonely child in a dysfunctional family. Her horse had been her love, her only companion. Her eyes glistened with unshed tears. She hadn't thought of those days for years; she'd shut them away like she had the rest of the memories of that part of her life.

"Can I come in there?"

"Of course you can! They are so quiet they won't hurt you."

She entered the corral and went to stand by Brad. One of the horses singled her out, nuzzling her top. Brad expected her flinch away and was surprised when she didn't. A confidence from years ago surfaced, and she responded to the horse like an old friend. She rubbed it and petted it, crooning to it softly as she did so.

Brad watched her silently. A soft look came over her face, and she buried her face against the horse's nose. She breathed deeply several times. Brad watched with wonder, then reached in his pocket and took out the small camera. She didn't even notice that he had taken the picture. He slipped it back into his pocket silently. When she looked at Brad, there were tears in her eyes.

Her voice was emotional. "Can we ride?"

"Do you want to?"

She nodded, burying her face against the horse again.

"OK. I've got saddles in the barn. Let's saddle up."

"Can I ride bareback?"

"Shauna, are you sure?"

"Will he be all right with that?"

Brad nodded, watching her in wonder. "The kids back home rode both of them bareback all the time."

She smiled tremulously. "Will you help me up? I'm pretty rusty at this."

Brad made a step for her with his hands and she pulled herself up and slid over the horses back. She leaned forward and wrapped her arms down around its neck. She laid her face against the animal and stayed there, her face turned away from him.

Brad watched in silence, wondering what this meant to her. Then he noticed her shoulders shaking and he heard her sob. He walked around the horse until he could see Shauna Lee's face. She just squeezed her eyes tightly, sobbing uncontrollably; tears coursing down her cheeks, dribbling down the horse's neck. He lay a hand on her thigh and let her cry.

Finally she sat up, sniffling, hiccupping, her face streaked with the tears that had mixed with the unavoidable dust on the horse. She swiped at her eyes and glared at him. "I don't like you," she cried. "You are prodding me into places that I don't want to go."

He reached up and lifted her off the horse like he might have a child. Then he enfolded her against his chest and rocked from side to side with her. "Let's go inside," he whispered. She followed him numbly. When they got in the house he looked at her with compassion. "Shauna, I don't know what happened out there, but that was a big emotional dam you let loose. Do you want to lie down for a while? You have to be exhausted."

She nodded. He took her hand and led her down the hall, but not to the guest room. Instead he took her to the door of his bedroom. He picked her up and carried her to the bed. He slipped her runners off, then went into the bathroom and came out with a damp face cloth. He wiped her face tenderly. "Lay down sweetheart. I'll go take out some steak for supper and I'll be right back."

She was tense and curled up like a child when he came back.

He walked around to the far side of the bed and slid in against her back. He wrapped his arms around her, cradling her close. Gradually she relaxed and eased into his embrace. She fell asleep, snuffling once in awhile. Brad didn't sleep immediately. He was lost in wondering what had happened to this beautiful woman.

When she woke up she squiggled in his arms. She turned around and faced him. "I'm sorry. I...I didn't mean what I said to you out there."

He kissed her forehead. "I want to believe that."

"It's just that you won't let go. I've cried more in the past week than I have in years. Probably since I…"

"Since you what?"

"Brad, I can't talk about this now. I don't know if I'll ever be able too."

"OK sweetheart. We'll take as long as you need."

"You don't know what you're asking of me. Will you just accept me as I am? Please?"

"I will for now. But sweetheart, you're going to have to face the past some time. You're a prisoner to it now."

She turned away and sat up. "Don't push me anymore, Brad." She stood up and walked out of the room.

When he followed she wasn't in the kitchen. He looked in all the rooms, and then went to the back door. She was heading to the corral. He wanted to go after her, but resisted, knowing he had to give her space.

It was dark when she came back in. He had a salad on the counter, potatoes baking in the oven and steak waiting to go on the grill.

She went to the cupboard and took down two plates and put them on the table. Then she went to the drawer and picked out the cutlery, adding a steak knife when she saw the steak on the grill. He put a butter dish, salt and pepper, sour cream, chives and bacon bits on the counter and she transferred them to the table. Brad reached for two wine glasses, and went to the wine cooler, bringing back a bottle of red wine.

They both worked in silence, and even as they sat down to eat it wasn't broken. He looked at her for permission to pour the wine and she nodded. They finished the meal and cleaned up.

Then Brad silently took her hand and led her into the family room. He turned on the electric fire place and motioned for her sit on the couch. He picked up the TV remote and selected a country music station. Then he sat down beside her and snuggled her against him. They sat in the quiet, the music pouring softly around them.

Brad was lost in his thoughts. Shauna Lee was drifting; suddenly the words of a song caught her attention. Brad noticed and listened to the words. "That's Aaron Prichette singing."

She buried her face in his chest. "I didn't know who was singing. I was listening to the words. That is my song Colt; that is me. I don't want to deal with the past. I just want to hide away. I want to find *a warm, safe place.*"

"I'm here for you, Tweetie Bird. I'll be your warm, safe place."

They sat close for a couple of hours. He looked at his watch; it was ten o'clock. "You are staying the night aren't you?"

"Is it OK?"

"Sweetheart, I want you too. This day hasn't exactly gone the way I expected. I don't want to take you home. I want you here with me."

"Be my safe, warm place?" she murmured.

He held her close. "Are you ready to go to bed? We didn't go get your things today. I'll give you one of my shirts to wear to bed."

"Will you sleep with me and hold me?"

"I have every intention of doing that. Let's go."

She waited while he shut off the lights and came to her side. He led her to his bedroom and turned on a bedside light. Then he went to his closet and pulled out a white shirt. "You'll swim in it, but it will do."

He swallowed hard when she came out freshly scrubbed, wearing his shirt. He groaned inwardly. *I must be a masochistic fool.*

When he came out of the bathroom, she was curled up under the covers. He turned off the light and then went to the other side of the bed. She turned and lifted the sheet for him to get in. Then she rolled to her side, back to him, cuddling into his arms as they spooned in the bed. She threaded her fingers through his. "Thank you," she whispered.

He squeezed her and kissed the back of her head. Then they drifted into sleep.

Hours later, Brad awoke with a start, disoriented at first. Arms were flying, fists flailing, legs kicking; a bundle of fury in his bed. *What the hell....*

Shauna Lee cried out. "No..no..please don't. Not Poko..." The words came from her own private hell.

"Shauna. Shauna, it's all right. It's just a dream." Brad tried to hold her, but she struck at him, pushing him away. Suddenly she bolted up right in the bed, sobbing, eyes wide and full of anguish.

Brad reached for her, enfolding her in his arms. "It's just a dream, sweetheart. I'm here to protect you." He let her lie against him and sob. When she finally pushed away from him to wipe her tears and her nose on the shirt that she was wearing, he let her go.

"Oh, Brad," she moaned. "You must be sorry you ever brought me here. I've been such a mess this weekend."

He shook his head and reached out to touch her wordlessly.

"I don't know what's happening. I haven't dreamed like that for years."

"Do you want to talk about it?"

She closed her eyes against the thought. "Brad...I've got so much baggage. I warned you...I don't know if I can ever be what you imagine I can be."

"You all ready are."

"I'm not what you *think* I am; I not what I appear to be. If I let you make me start feeling again...I'll have to rebuild my whole life. I don't know if I have the courage...."

"Do you want to tell me who, or what, you were fighting with before you woke up?"

She sat for a long moment, then got up and walked out of the room. Concerned, Brad followed her. He stopped at the large doorway that led into the main living area of the house. He watched her as she walked around the kitchen counter and opened the door of the cupboard where the glasses were. She took out a tall one and ran it full of water from the tap. Then she went to gaze out the window while she drank it.

Finally she turned to look at him angrily. "I can't believe this is happening to me." Her voice was rough with emotion. "This is you... your fault. You wouldn't just leave me alone."

"Shauna, I'm sorry. I had no way of knowing that bringing you here would be like this."

She shook her head. "You wanted to find out who I am. Well now you're getting your wish."

"I care for you Shauna."

"How can you say that? You don't know who I am."

"Shauna…I don't know how to explain how I feel; it seems crazy. We've hardly known each other long enough to have any real feelings; but of all the women I've met…" His look was pleading.

"Brad, I buried an entire existence years ago. I didn't want to remember it then…I don't want to now. I built a new life and started over. You have no idea who I am; maybe I don't know who I really am."

He ran a hand through his hair. "Just believe me." His voice was harsh with emotion. "No matter what the past has been; you reach a spot in me that no one else has touched. I am willing to do anything to try to make this work; anything but share you with those other guys."

"I hope you don't live to regret it." Shauna Lee came up to him. "Brad, I've never known anyone like you before," she said softly. "I almost don't know how to act; how to be with you."

She took his hand and led the way back to the bedroom. She pushed her pillow up against the head board and sat on the bed against it, with her legs pulled up in front of her, arms wrapped around her knees, chin resting on them. Brad slid in on the other side and lay with his elbow propped up on the bed, his cheek resting on his closed fist.

"I didn't have a childhood like you, Brad. I sure as hell did not come from the same kind of a perfect family."

"We weren't perfect."

"Well you were compared to where I came from. My mom and dad may have been in love once; time changes things. But for as long as I can remember, I don't think they loved each other…I think their marriage was just a trap created by circumstances. Dad had a farm, but nothing seemed to work out for him. We were always broke; but he could afford to drink and he did…all the time." She picked at the sheet aimlessly, lost in her memories.

"When I was almost eleven, mom had another baby. Now that I'm an adult, I can't even imagine how that happened. The baby was a boy. They called him Andre and for once dad had something in his life that he was really proud of. Mom loved Andre; because he was her child, but I also think because for once Dad was truly happy. I loved Andre too. He was part of my heart…"

She was silent for a moment, staring at the wall. "I forgot until this afternoon…how could I have forgotten? But I did. When I stood there and watched you brush your horses, suddenly it came back to me. How I used to ride. It got me away from the house, it gave me freedom. I'd go for hours. I had a grey gelding." Her words were softly spoken, almost as if she was talking to herself. "Poko; I loved him so much. He was an old Percheron-cross that dad had for some reason. He was probably ugly as sin, but he was beautiful to me."

She fell into silence again. Finally Brad reached over and touched her toe. There were tears brimming in her eyes when she looked at him. She grimaced. "Dad drank all the time, but he was happy when Andre was with him. One day, when Andre was almost four, Dad was out on the tractor…"

She bit her lip as the tears spilled over. She dashed them away with her shirt sleeve. "Suddenly Andre was there. Dad couldn't have seen him, or maybe his reactions were just too slow. He…"

She was crying uncontrollably now. "He was backing up. He ran over Andre with the back tire. He just laid there…his little body… Dad watched h..hi.m die." Her fingers curled tight into her palms. She looked at Brad. "Dad was so broken. He had to blame somebody."

A sick feeling flooded Brad's belly. "Not you, Shauna. God, not you…"

"If I hadn't been off riding, I'd have been home helping mom. I'd have kept Andre away from the tractor."

"No, Shauna," he groaned. "That was so unfair."

"Dad never was the same again. None of us were. He blamed me;

but he took it out on Poko too because I was riding him. He…he took his gun and sho.o.ott him."

Brad reached for her, but she pushed him away.

"Dad never was a strong man, but after that he drank constantly. He'd drink until he passed out; probably to erase the memory of what happened to Andre from his mind." She pulled the edge of the sheet up over her knees and wove it through her fingers.

"And mom…" she said sadly. "She just drew farther and farther away from everything. She just wasn't there anymore; I guess it was depression. The spring I was fourteen; actually I was fourteen and a half then; Dad caught a ride into town with a neighbour. That wasn't uncommon; but that time he didn't come home. We never saw him again."

"What happened to you and your mom?"

She smiled bitterly. "Well it hardly mattered to mom. But to me… it really scared me. I was afraid that if mom went to the hospital, I would be put in a foster home."

"Christ, Shauna…"

She kept speaking, ignoring his words. It was as if Pandora's Box had sprung open and everything just came spilling out.

"I did the best I could. Mom was like…a…a zombie. She ate very little. She just sat and stared into space or slept." Shauna Lee balled the edge of the sheet in her hand.

"We had chickens for eggs, but when nobody gathers them properly, the hens set on them. In a few weeks they hatch baby chicks. Over the summer lots of them showed up and they grew. Dad had made me learn how to kill them and butcher them, so I had meat.

"Dad had made me plant a garden in the spring, because mom couldn't. Even though he was gone, it grew and I pulled vegetables out of the weeds. There was a milk cow and I knew how to milk.

The neighbour helped me when I asked for help. He brought me fire wood for winter. I didn't think about it then, but now I think that he might have paid the power bill for us, because we didn't. There was no money."

She sighed. "We held on until mom got pneumonia in January. The neighbour told me she had to go to the hospital and he took her into town. She never came back. She went into a nursing home and she died six months later."

"What did you do Shauna?"

Her eyes filled with tears. Her jaw set. "I can't go there now, Brad. I just can't!"

Brad lifted back the sheet and tried to ease her down beside him.

She shook her head and resisted him. "I can't be here now. I…I'll go to the other room." She pushed herself up and stood. Then she walked away without a word.

Brad jumped out of bed and followed her down the hall, into the spare room. She shook her head as she looked at him. "No," she whispered. He watched her pull back the sheet and crawl into the bed. Then he turned around and walked back to his bed.

He was sick at heart when he lay down. *This is my fault. I should have accepted her as she was or got out. No wonder she hasn't wanted to know who she was.*

Brad woke up at five o'clock, his head dull from the emotion of the night before and the lack of sleep. He became aware of warmth at his back and a slender arm around his waist. A tear seeped out of his eyes, as he swallowed hard to fight back more.

Shauna had come back to his bed. She was curled against him, her cheek resting against his back. She was clinging to him, sound asleep. He wanted to turn over and take her in his arms, but she was sleeping and she needed rest. He didn't want to wake her, so he stayed where he was. His mind relaxed. He held her hand, clasping it and holding it against his breast. He fell into a sound sleep.

It was noon before Shauna stirred. Brad had been awake for a while. When he knew she was awake he turned over. She was still sleepy eyed and flushed. Her eyes were slightly red and swollen. He didn't enfold her as he wanted too. He slid an arm around her waist and gave a gentle squeeze. "You don't know how happy it makes me to wake up and find you here, snuggled up against me."

She looked at him solemnly. Then she moved into his arms. "Hold me, Brad. Please?" She lay in his arms and savoured his warmth, his strength. She felt safe.

After they got up and had breakfast, Brad asked her what she would like to do.

"Can we go for a ride?" The sparkle was gone from her; the night's revelation had taken its toll.

"Are you sure you can do this today?"

"Yes."

They went to the corral and Brad whistled for the horses. Shauna Lee smiled wanly, but she did smile as she watched them come up the trail.

"I would like to ride bareback."

"OK, we'll give it try and see how it goes. Do you want to ride very far?"

"How far can we ride from here?"

"If we go out the back of the field, we can follow a trail for a mile or so and then we can ride through fields that a friend of mine own all afternoon, if you want."

"I'm going to saddle up though. I'll be a cripple if I don't. Are you sure you want to go bareback? I have a saddle you can use."

"I've never ridden with a saddle, Brad."

"Oh." *Shit, why didn't I realise that?* "It's been a long time since you rode sweetie...or am I wrong?"

"No, you are right. I never rode again."

"You're not thirteen years old anymore. You might find the saddle is easier on your body. Either that or maybe we should just ride around here in my place and give you a chance to get used to it again. We could go for a longer ride next weekend."

She thought for a moment. "You are probably right. Let's just make it a short ride today."

After an hour of riding, she was shifting on the horses back, trying to find a comfortable spot. "I think I need to get off him. I'm going to be sore."

A glance at Brad's watch told him it was later than he'd thought.

"What do you say we go out for supper?"

"Well, I have to go home anyway. We could…"

"You don't have to go home you know. We can stop by and pick up your things and I'll take you to work when I go in the morning?"

"Brad, I can't stay here with you indefinitely. I have to go home and live *with* myself. I can't avoid my past anymore. I have to face it and… and deal with my feelings as best I can."

"I'll help you. I'm a good sounding board."

"You're a master shit disturber," she said ruefully.

"Shauna…I'm sorry I helped to upset your world. But honestly, don't you think you would have remembered eventually? Being here when it happened; well, at least you were with someone who cared. I was here to offer whatever support I could. It might have been worse if you had been all alone when it happened."

"Recently, something else did happen. Suddenly I was thinking of something so…so horrific from my past…it made me physically ill. I had to deal with it that time, but it was awful." Tears shimmered in her eyes.

Brad stepped to her side. "There have been enough tears for now. No more, sweetheart. Not today." He wrapped her in his arms and kissed her gently. Then he brushed away the one or two that slipped down her cheeks.

They went to her place first so she could drop off her things and change. Then they went out for Chinese dinner. Afterward he took her back to her place.

"Don't hesitate to call me if you need me," he said seriously after he kissed her soundly. "I'll be here as fast as possible, no matter what time it is."

She looked at him in a dazed way, slowly shaking her head. "Brad, are you for real? Can you really be this wonderful and caring? Is it possible that I can really deserve someone like you? This," she motioned with her finger between him and her. "It almost scares me…it's like… like it's too good to be true."

He took both her hands in his and looked intently into her eyes.

"I've told you how I feel and I've told you that I'll do almost anything to make a relationship work for us. Just trust me Shauna." He turned to the door, opened it, and then hesitated. "It doesn't feel right, leaving you here."

She swallowed hard. "Just go. If I need you, I promise to call.

# CHAPTER SEVEN

*S*hauna Lee fell into the sleep of exhaustion. The phone woke her at seven fifteen the next morning. She smiled when she answered and heard his voice. "Good morning, beautiful. Were you thinking about me?"

"Not really. You woke me up."

"I thought I'd call and talk dirty with you for a minute or two."

She laughed and it sounded good to him. "You fool; I wouldn't know how to talk dirty with you. You've never..." She blushed and quit speaking.

"I've never...? What were you going to say?"

She took a deep breath. "You've never played "dirty" with me... other than the fact that it is dirty of you to get me all...you know...hot and bothered, and then walk out and leave me."

"Well, I have company over here that is bigger than life right now; I'm going to need a cold shower again. I have half a mind to come over there right now and take you to bed, like I did on Saturday morning. But this time I'd insist that you put your pyjamas on before we crawled in; there are limits to my restraint."

"Brad...go and have your cold shower. I have no sympathy for you."

"Hear that big guy? She told us to go have a cold shower. What do you think?"

Shauna Lee grinned to herself. *That impossible man!*

"Are you there Shauna Lee? My friend here...he says to tell you he doesn't like cold showers. He says he'd prefer to be somewhere hot and moist."

"Tell him he missed his chance."

"Shauna Lee? I think we just talked "dirty" and you know exactly how to do it with me."

"You are nuts. But I *do* miss you Brad; even just lying in your arms instead of…"playing dirty." Actually it's kind of nice to just be there… not *having* to…you know…. Thank you for caring about me and looking after me," she said soberly.

"I miss you too, sweetheart. I love to hold you in my arms. I'll talk to you later. Now I have to go have a cold shower and make my friend respectable so I can go to work."

Brad didn't phone, and she had to admit she felt disappointed. She took a lunch break and walked down town to do some shopping. When she got back to the office she asked Christina if anyone had called.

Christina said no, with a happy twinkle in her eye. Shauna Lee's disappointment overshadowed her impulse to ask what had made her day.

Shauna Lee went into her office and took a couple of steps toward her desk; then she stopped dead. On the corner of her desk sat a dozen red roses in a crystal vase. Her spirits lifted magically and her face lit up with a smile. She reached for the small envelope that rested in the flowers.

As she started to open it, she noticed two framed pictures sitting next to her computer monitor. She laid the envelope down and leaned over to look at them. She picked up the closest one and gazed at it. *When did he take this?*

It was an excellent picture of her with her face resting against the horse's nose. Then she picked up the other one. He had caught her riding bareback, hair flying, galloping up the trail toward him. She pressed the picture to her lips. "You wonderful man, you," she said softly.

"Ahh…you finally realize that!" She jumped and found herself in his arms. Then he was kissing her, hot and passionately. "It's been about sixteen hours since I did that. I'm a starving man."

"You could have had lunch with me."

"I meant touching you, kissing you, holding you starving. I'm not hungry; I grabbed a hamburger at the A&W while I took care of some important things." He swept his hand toward the desk.

"The flowers are beautiful."

He looked puzzled. "The flowers? They aren't from me." He looked at them. "There's a card. Did you look at it?"

"Well no; I saw the pictures and stopped to look at them. I love them, Brad. You really sneaked them on me." She looked up at him, puzzled. "Are you serious about the flowers not being from you?"

"Damn serious. What does the card say?"

She opened the envelope hesitantly, and then pulled out the card. No one ever sent her flowers. If they weren't from Brad who were they from?

She looked at the card and began to smile. It read, "I hate cold showers. I'd rather be where it's hot and moist." The card was signed, "Brad's friend."

She turned into Brad, and reached down and caressed the hardness behind his zipper. "Thanks big guy, they are beautiful. Talk to Brad about where you'd rather be."

Brad moaned. "Woman," he whispered. "I'm waiting; I still haven't heard the words I want to hear from you."

She looked at him, puzzled.

"When you are ready, they will come. Until then, my friend and I will take cold showers and dream of hot, moist places." He kissed her again. "I have to go do some work now. Can I take you home with me after work and we'll make supper together?"

They had supper together every night that week. Some nights she slept in his arms, others he took her back home. If he took her home he always called her the next morning. He had worked his way into her life and made her want to be with him.

Saturday morning the ringing of Brad's phone woke them. He uncurled himself from holding her and reached for it.

"This had better be good," he growled. "I'm still in bed. In case you hadn't noticed, it's Saturday morning."

Shauna heard Colt laugh. "You know people die in bed!"

"Maybe I just did. I thought I was in heaven, until you called."

"Well it's time you got your ass out of bed! It's nearly ten o'clock. What you need is a good woman and a pair of twins and a nanny in the house with you. Believe me you'd be up by now!"

"I've been giving it some thought; the good woman part, I mean. I'm not sure about the twins or a nanny. But a good woman…" He curled his arm and pulled Shauna Lee closer. "Yeah, I'm waiting to get a green light and I'm in for that."

"I've got news for you man; if you wait for a green light, you'll probably never get one. You've got to be proactive and turn on the light yourself."

He laughed and looked at Shauna Lee, knowing she could hear the whole conversation through the hand set. "Women aside, what's on your mind this morning, Colt?"

"I intended to call you all week about going out to the ranch to get the specs for the turbines. I've just been too damn busy getting a pad poured for the trailer and getting everything else set up for it. I know it is Saturday, but I wondered if you could make it today?

I've tried to get a hold of Shauna Lee a couple of evenings this week, but she never answers. I worry about that woman. I hope she doesn't get herself in a heap of trouble, doing some of the stuff that she does."

"Yeah," Brad drawled as he gave her a squeeze. "She could get herself into a heap of trouble, all right. I seen her last night and she looked pretty damn hot."

"Was she with some guy?"

"Yeah, she was."

"Damn it. You know, after that night at the restaurant I told Fran what had gone down. She suggested maybe I should try to talk to her, but I don't want to get involved in that. I just worry that she'll find herself in a situation she can't handle one of these times."

"She easily could find herself in a situation she doesn't know how to handle. But the guy she was with last night was different than the others. I think she may be getting it right this time."

"She's a good person, Brad. Like Fran said, there has to be someone out there for her. I'd like to see her as happy as I am. I'd like to see her with someone who deserves her."

"She's pretty smart. I'm sure she will figure it out. Now, about going to the ranch today…" He looked at his watch. "Colt, it is almost ten o'clock all ready. It's getting kind of late. We could do it tomorrow and leave early, if that works for you. We are more likely to get everything done if we do that."

"You are right. If we wait until tomorrow, we can bring Ellie's things here and get her moved into the trailer today. She's a prize, but I miss being able to run around the house in the buff if I want or being able to grab a morning quickie with my wife."

"OK man, I get the picture! Do your thing and we'll go out to the ranch tomorrow. What time do you want to leave; around seven o'clock?"

"That will work for us. I'm going to bring Fran along."

"Oh great; we'll spend another day watching you love birds! Just seeing you two together makes me horny. You are so…aww, forget it; I'm just envious. Bring her along. I'll work on Shauna Lee. She's so hot, she could light a fire."

"Just be careful you don't get third degree burns!"

Brad laughed as she squirmed. "We'll see you tomorrow. I'll stop in at the office today and get everything I need. I'll get Shauna Lee lined up too. We'll be at the farm by seven."

He hung up the phone and grinned at Shauna Lee. She gave him an elbow in the ribs. "You are so *bad!*"

"Well, I didn't think you'd want me to tell him that you were here in my bed, and that I was the guy you were with last night!"

"I'd have died of embarrassment. They say women are gossips…. jeeze."

"I basically told him the truth. I just left out the juicy stuff. Speaking of juicy…" He ran his hand over her hip and pulled her back against the hardness of his erection. He groaned, and pushed her searching hand away gently. "Shauna, this is killing me, but I don't want to just fuck you. I need to know that it means the same to you as it does to me."

"Brad…I don't know what you want. I've been ready since that night when you left me all alone. I cried myself to sleep that night."

He eased himself away. "Tweetie Bird. You've been ready for sex. I want more; and I believe that eventually you will too. When I know the time is right, I'll make love to you like no one ever has. Until then," he put his hand around his swollen shaft. "More cold showers and lovers nuts, buddy." He stood up and headed into the ensuite.

Shauna Lee glared after him. "Fuck you!"

He stopped and looked at her. "I'm counting on you doing that! But not before we make love, sweetheart."

"Bull! I'm beginning to wonder if you aren't gay."

He stopped short and stared at her. Then he laughed harshly and with one swift move pushed his pyjama bottoms over his hips and let them drop to the floor. He walked back to the bed. A flash of fire burned in his eyes as he pulled her up onto her feet.

He jerked her against him, then grabbed her hand and pushed it onto his erection, forcing her fingers around it. "If I'm gay, why do I pack this bone around every time I think of you? And that seems to be damn near all the time lately."

She pulled her hand away. "You're a pervert," she fumed as she flounced out of the room.

She went into the spare room and sat on the bed. She ached for release. "He's a sadist," she mumbled, fighting tears of frustration. "Why do I put up with this? What the hell does he want from me?" She stood up. "That's it! I'm not sleeping with him anymore."

She showered, dried off and blew her hair dry. Then she pulled on a pair of jeans, and a red long sleeved top. She was still sulking when she went to the kitchen. He was whistling to himself as he made breakfast and she had an urge to hit him. *How can he be so damn happy?*

She walked around him and went to the cupboard. It was a familiar ritual now. Two plates, two coffee cups, two sets of knives and forks. *Like a couple,* she thought. *That doesn't have sex. Cripes!*

Bacon was sizzling on the grill, and she saw him look in the oven and check on the hash browns. She set the table and got the Ketchup from the fridge for his hash browns. Then she moved to the toaster and popped in three slices of toast; two for him, one for her. She took the butter down from the shelf and got a knife to spread it with. The moves were automatic now. It was part of their routine.

He came up behind her and slid his arms around her. She stiffened. He turned her into his arms, even though she resisted him. "Not talking to me?" he asked softly. He ran a hand up her back, along the length of her neck and through her hair. She felt herself melting.

"This looks great, but I really do prefer your curls when we're here by ourselves on the weekends." Then he kissed her gently, and held her closer against him. "My Tweetie Bird," he whispered on a sigh.

He stepped away, going back to the grill to turn the bacon. She watched him crack three eggs onto the grill. He cooked his sunny side up and hers easy over and firmer the way she liked them. *He so maddening about some things, but then he is so wonderful too.*

"Breakfast is ready," Brad said cheerfully as he put everything on a plate and took the hash browns out of the oven. Shauna Lee picked up the coffee carafe and carried it to the table. They ate in silence that wasn't broken until she looked at him and said, "That was yummy. Thank you."

"I love doing it for you, sweetheart. I love having you here with me."

Her expression turned to frustration. "I'm so mad at you."

"I sense that."

"You are a tease. You are tormenting me and I've decided that I'm not going to sleep with you anymore."

"I'm not teasing, Shauna. I'm betting the rest of our lives on this. I'll miss you in my arms. I'll miss your warmth, the cuddles. I'll miss listening to you breathe. But if you don't want to sleep with me for a while, then I'll have to accept that."

She stood up. "Damn you," she cried. She turned and flounced to the back door.

Her runners were there. *As if I live here*, she thought as she put them on.

She was feeling miserable and frustrated as she went outside and followed the trail to the pasture. She got a bucket of grain from the barn and called the horses. She smiled as she heard them running through the trees.

When they reached her, she let them take turns eating out of the bucket. When the grain was almost gone, she poured the remaining kernels on the ground and then she petted them both. Finally, she put a bridle on *her* horse (that was how she thought of it now) and swung up onto its back.

Brad watched her from the back door as she rode bareback down the trail and out of sight. He sat down on one of the chairs and gazed into the field where she had disappeared. *Am I expecting too much?* He rested his elbows on his knees and buried his face in his hands. *She's been hurt so much. God only knows what she hasn't been able to tell me. But I don't want to settle for less than love.*

He sighed deeply, and then stood up and went inside the house to his office. He turned on the computer and pulled up a file, considering what he needed to take with him the next day.

He was still at the computer when Shauna Lee came back into the house two hours later. He heard her come in, but decided that he would let her seek him out when she was ready. He listened to her footsteps through the house as she looked for him, stopping in each room as she went.

He didn't look up when he heard his half closed office door push open. She hesitated uncertainly before she stepped into the room.

He looked up at her. "Enjoy your ride?"

She nodded and stepped to his side. He swivelled the chair so he could reach out and slip his arm around her waist. He pushed back from the desk and pulled her down onto his lap. She sat there; her eyes held his in a long look. Then she broke the connection and laid her cheek against his shoulder. He nuzzled her hair, noticing the smell of the crisp freshness lingering in it.

"Brad?" she said softly.

"Uh-hum?"

She sat up and threaded her arms around his neck. "I'm sorry. Sometimes I act more like a petulant teenager, than a grown woman. I was childish this morning. You are so wonderful to me and I thanked you by acting like a spoiled brat." She looked past his shoulder, avoiding eye contact. Her voice grew hoarse with emotion.

"You…you confuse me. I've never met a man who wouldn't have sex with me. And with you…it…it *hurts* so much to know that you won't. I don't know how to do what you want me to do; I don't understand what you want from me."

He sighed. "Sweetheart, I…"

She cradled his face with her hands. "Brad, you know I've had meaningless sex with lots of guys."

He grimaced. "Don't…"

"No! I need you to understand. I didn't realize it then, but now I know that I was lonely. I wanted companionship; but you've changed all that." She looked deep into his eyes. "Brad, with you it wouldn't be meaningless. You've given me so much."

She bit her lip. "I…I *want* to be with you that way. I want to give myself to you. I need to feel you inside me. Don't you see? Being together with you that way…it's the closest that I can get to you. It hurts that what I have to give you isn't enough. That you are looking for something more."

Now he was fighting emotion. "Tweetie Bird, it's not that; not that what you have to give me isn't enough." He closed his eyes and swallowed hard. "I…I'm not rejecting you. I never, ever wanted to *hurt* you. You mean too much to me to do that."

He sighed. "This hasn't been easy for me. I love to hold you close, but I'm a man. A night hasn't gone by that I haven't ached with wanting you."

He shook his head, his eyes reflecting his anguish. "I…I don't want to fight this anymore. Maybe I've been unrealistic." He helped her stand up, and then took her hand as he stood. "Come with me."

He led her to his bed.

He wrapped his arms around her and held her close. As he kissed her, he slid his hand up the back of her shirt and caressed her. It moved around to cup her breast. He played with the nipple through her bra. He shifted his mouth to trail down her neck, nipping her, kissing her, licking her lightly as he went.

She whimpered.

Desire flooded through him like a tsunami. He was as hard as a rock; so hard he ached. *Maybe I've been a fool,* he thought; *she wants this. God knows, I want this.*

He pulled her against him as his fingers fumbled to undo her jeans. He pulled down the zipper, and eased them over her hips, letting them slide to the floor. Feverishly, he slid his hands into her panties and inched his fingers slowly downward. He slipped them into the small patch of fluff at the entrance he sought and he gently invaded her.

He groaned. She was hot and moist.

She gasped and bucked against him. He reached for the hem of her shirt with frantic hands and pulled it up over her head. He unhooked her bra, slid it down her arms and let it fall.

Fire raced through him, burning away all his former reasoning. *The rest doesn't matter right now; I just have to trust her feelings,* he thought as he undid his jeans. He let them slide to the floor and he jerked off his shirt. He ripped his socks off and threw them to the side, then picked her up in his arms and laid her on the bed.

He tugged off each of her socks, leaning over to lick the toes on each foot as he exposed them. She jerked her foot away. She squirmed as he kissed his way up her legs, moving along the inside of her thighs until her found her juicy moistness. His tongue danced and probed, as she twisted and sobbed.

He continued his way up, worshipping her body with his mouth; tracing his tongue along her belly, thrusting and twirling it deeply into her navel. Every inch of her was sacred to him and he kissed her everywhere. When he reached her breasts he suckled them and slathered his tongue around each hardened nipple.

Her fingers threaded through his hair and she tried to reach his mouth with hers. Finally he laid his length over hers, giving her what she sought. He took her mouth in a hot, probing kiss. She was twisting, grasping beneath him.

Their eyes met. "Brad, are you sure?"

He groaned. "There's no going back now, Tweetie Bird." His voice rasped. He cried out as he pushed into her. He tried to go slow, but he was beyond control; this moment had been put off for far too long. He was taking her hard and deep. She made a muffled sound against his neck and he felt her convulse inside, squeezing around him. Their cries mingled.

"God, oh God, oh my god," he whispered as he collapsed and rolled off of her.

She was crying softly, running her fingers through his hair as she kissed his mouth: his eyes: his neck. She buried her face into his chest and he felt the wetness of her tears. He gathered her close and held her.

They lay there, bathed in perspiration, satiated, until their breathing steadied.

"Brad...this is OK isn't it? I know you didn't want too...you're not disappointed are you?"

He groaned. "Sweetie, how could I be disappointed? We...I...you left me breathless." He kissed her forehead. "I love you, Tweetie Bird. I just wanted to know that you loved me before we went this far. I don't want to get my heart broken."

She looked at him sadly. "I hope I never...I *won't* ever break your heart, Brad. I want to be with you; *only you.* Even when I was so mad at you this morning, I realized how much a part of my life you've become in such a short time; how much like a couple we've become. It's been so many years since I've let anyone into my heart; given anything from deep inside me to anyone. *You* have that."

Brad reached for her hand, his love shining in his eyes.

She let him take it, but her eyes filled with tears again. "But I can't let myself love you. I can't even think about that." She dashed the tears away impatiently. "Everyone I've ever loved has either hurt me or left me or died. I can't ever do that again and I can't lose you."

"Sweetheart, I'm not like the others. I'm here for the long haul."

"Brad, when someone dies they don't have a choice. That is the long haul for them."

They lay entwined together, silent for a long time. When Brad stirred, he realized that he'd dozed off. He looked at his watch. It was after six in the evening and he was hungry. And they had things to do.

"Tweetie Bird," he whispered. "I'm hungry! That took a lot of energy, and we still have to go into town and get what we need for tomorrow."

Shauna Lee stretched. She reached up and traced his lips with her finger tip. "I don't want to move in case this is a dream and I have to wake up and it will fade away."

"This is a dream, sweetheart; a dream come true. It's not going to fade away. But we have to get going. I have to go to the office and pick up supplies and you probably have to do the same. Then I think we should go out and celebrate in the best restaurant in town."

"That's right here in your kitchen, isn't it?"

"It's the cook's night off. Do you like seafood?"

"Brad, anything is all right; even a hamburger at A&W."

She moved tight against him and buried her face into his chest. "I want you to know, being with you wasn't…I couldn't be a virgin for you; but it's never been that way for me before," she whispered. She shivered involuntarily. "It wasn't just sex…it was so far beyond that …."

She leaned her head back and looked at him. "I just want to wrap my arms around you and pull you inside me and *feel* like that forever."

He chuckled. "I don't think we can stay like that forever. We'll need to eat, and go to work occasionally. But Tweetie Bird, I told you that first day when I brought you here; you have the first option on my heart, everything I am."

"How can you be so sure? We haven't really known each other very long. There's still a lot that you don't know about me, Brad."

"It's a knowing; like recognition in my heart. All that other stuff is

106

nothing to do with you and me. It's what happens from this day forward that counts."

He rolled onto his back and eased away from her. "Right now, we have to get moving. We'll come back here later, I promise."

He chuckled. "You've exhausted the insatiable beast. See?" He flicked his "friend" with his finger. It remained unresponsive and limp. He looked over at her and grinned. "Look at that. After all those cold showers, the shock just wiped him out."

He gently slapped her naked hip. "You're as bad as he is! Up and at it, girl; we've got to get moving. And breakfast was one hell of a long time ago."

She groaned in protest as she rolled to the edge of the king sized bed and sat up. "Party pooper."

"I'm just going out for re-enforcements! You can have the bathroom," he said as he pulled on his shirt and jeans. "I'll go down the hall to the spare room."

Even though Brad was hungry, they went to their respective offices first and collected what they needed for the next day. After asking if she needed to stop at her house, he drove to one of the nicer restaurants in town. They ate their meal as they drank wine and looked into each other's eyes and savoured their happiness.

As they were leaving they met Josh Kendall in the lobby. He sneered when he saw Shauna Lee. "Got another sucker on the line, eh bitch?"

Before Shauna Lee could even flinch, Brad leaped forward, catching Josh by surprise and shoving him against the wall. "You're the only sucker here. And now, I'm telling you what you told me the first time I met you, you weaselling little prick; *she's mine for tonight, so you're out of luck this time buddy.*"

Brad pushed him against the wall a little harder. "In case you didn't get the message, I'm telling you again. She is mine tonight and every night here after! Got it?"

He glared into Josh's shocked face. He released him from against the wall and gave him a firm shove away. "You're the looser. Take my advice and stay away from her or you'll answer to me. One more thing; don't *ever* call the woman that I love a bitch again."

Then he slid his arm around her protectively and guided her out to the truck. Josh stared after them, sputtering idle threats and straightening his shirt.

# CHAPTER EIGHT

$\mathcal{C}$olt Thompson glanced at his watch as he stepped out on the veranda. It was almost seven o'clock and darkness still hung over the land. He stretched and inhaled the crisp fresh air. The sky was cloudless, the partial moon riding high in the sky. The smell of coffee brewing in the kitchen wafted on the air, and he could hear Fran and Ellie in muffled conversation from behind the half closed door behind him.

"Brad should be here soon," he thought. "Hopefully he has tracked down Shauna Lee. I'm glad we could get on this today. I want to get those turbines in place before it gets too cold to pour the cement for the bases."

He watched as lights came into view on the main road, and grinned when the signal light flashed and the vehicle made the turn onto the laneway. "Right on time; the more I have to do with Brad, the better I like him."

The truck pulled up in front of the house and Colt walked down to greet its passengers. As Brad partially opened his door, the inside light came on, revealing that Shauna Lee was with him. They were laughing about something and he saw Shawna Lee reach across the seat and slap Brad playfully with the file folder that she held in her hand.

Colt opened the passenger door as Brad got out on his side. Shauna Lee was relaxed and happy when she smiled at him. "Good morning, Colt. You owe me big time for this! He rousted me out of bed at a quarter to six this morning. It's Sunday!"

Brad laughed. "And she's been nattering at me all the way out here. Even the fact that I stopped at the drive through at Allan & Wright's and bought her a coffee and a breakfast sandwich didn't stop her."

Colt reached up to help Shauna Lee slide out of Brad's 'monster truck' as he laughingly called it. "Johnson, you need to put a pull down step on this thing, so short people can get in and out."

"You are missing the point, Colt. It gives me a chance to get up close and personal when I help a shortie get in. Besides, I don't travel with many short people; just her." He nodded at Shauna Lee with a grin.

"Come in. Fran's got coffee on. We can grab a quick cup and head out."

Frankie greeted them with a happy smile and motioned to the coffee pot and the cups set out beside it. "You've been here before guys, so you don't qualify as 'guests' any more, and company has to help themselves this morning. I'm going to run up and say goodbye to the twins. Ellie is upstairs with them."

Colt looked at them. "Help yourself guys. I think I'll run up and get a hug too. We'll be right back to join you."

Shauna Lee poured two cups of coffee and handed one to Brad. They shared a quick kiss, followed by a look of conspiracy. "We'll keep it our secret for a while?" she asked in a whisper. He nodded in agreement and they sat down at the table. Moments later Colt and Fran came downstairs hand in hand, laughing happily.

Frankie poured a cup for each of them and carried it to the table. She looked at Shauna Lee and reached out to touch her hand. "I like the curls, Shauna Lee. You look so relaxed and happy."

Shauna Lee smiled warmly. "I didn't have time to use the curling iron. This getting up with the birds...."

Brad grinned. "Tweetie..."

Shauna Lee blushed softly. Frankie caught the rise in colour and the quick little look that passed between the two of them. *Hmm. Am I imaging things or is there something going on there?*

Colt missed it all. He guzzled his coffee and stood up. "Shall we hit the trail guys?"

"Colt," Frankie protested. "Give us a chance to finish our coffee."

"Oh...sorry; I'm just anxious to get going."

Brad stood up. "You're right, Colt. We need to hit the road. We have a lot to do today and it's what; a two and half to three hour drive to the ranch?"

He looked at Shauna Lee, a smile dancing in his eyes. "Hustle it up girls."

Frankie smiled as she gathered up the cups and put them by the sink. *Something is going on between those two,* she thought.

"We can take my truck." Brad offered. "Everything we need for today is in it."

Colt nodded as he put on his coat. When they got out to the truck Shauna Lee turned to Colt. "You can sit up front with Brad. I'll get in the back."

"Are you kidding? Have you any idea how seldom I get to sit in the backseat and make out with my wife? We never got to do those things before we got married," he said, giving Frankie a hug. "I know that was due to my own stupidity, but now I'm grabbing every chance I can get. Before too long the baby will be taking up cuddle room." He rubbed his hand over her slight baby bulge and grinned. "But I'll happily move over."

He looked at Brad. "You'd better get with it. You have no idea how wonderful this baby thing is."

"Give me time man." He lifted Shauna Lee up so she could get up onto her seat. He made an exaggerated show of running his hand down her leg. She slapped at him, flushing scarlet.

"I've decided I'm going to work on Shauna Lee today and see if I can make any headway."

"Johnson, I've got witnesses. That's harassment. It can get you into trouble. Maybe more than you want to deal with."

He laughed as he shut her door. When he got in he looked across at her. "I might be willing to take my chances."

"Brad!" she protested.

He chuckled and looked into the back at Colt and Frankie. Colt had his arm around Frankie and held her tucked close. "OK you two. No indecent behaviour back there. I'm a sex starved old man, and I don't want any distractions while I'm driving."

111

"Keep your eyes on the road. You'll be OK. This seat is too small for any more than a little necking."

"You guys," Frankie protested. "Get down to business."

"I'm trying too, but I keep getting interrupted," Colt responded.

Frankie jabbed him in the ribs with her elbow.

Shauna Lee looked out the window, a soft flush in her cheeks and a small smile on her lips.

They arrived at the ranch at eleven thirty. Ollie met them at the door. He looked at the four of them, then past them to the truck. "Didn't you bring the twins?"

Colt answered. "Not this time. It would have been too crowded."

Fran smiled as she watched some of Ollie's excitement deflate. "You know Ollie, you can stop by any time for a visit."

"Yeah, I know. I just…"

"You don't have an excuse not to now that you have Patch here. Speaking of Patch, where is he?"

"He went out to check the cows. He's really conscientious. One of them wasn't acting right at feeding time this morning; she was kicking at her belly. She might have eaten something that gave her a belly ache. Anyway, he went out to check on her again."

Frankie looked up, expectantly. "Should I go and check it out?"

"That might be a good idea; take the quad. It'll be at the shop. Patch walks everywhere."

Frankie turned and headed out the door. Colt went to the cupboard to get cups and Ollie brought the coffee pot to the table. "Does anyone use cream and sugar? Oh, Patch uses both so I'll put it on."

"Who is Patch?" Shauna Lee asked Colt.

"Oh, he's the new ranch hand. He's been here for about 6 weeks; I just haven't gotten the paperwork from Ollie. You'll meet him when they come in from checking the cattle."

He glanced toward the door, as if expecting them. "Ollie is really impressed with him. He's kind of quiet and reserved, but a good cowhand."

Ollie poured the coffee and they each took a cup. Colt took a few sips and then turned back to Shauna Lee. "Have you found anything new in your search for a manager for the farm?"

"I've got a couple of possibilities. Just names on my desk right now, but I've got feelers around, checking them out."

Brad joined the conversation. "Are you looking for a manager for the farm, Colt?"

"Yes, I told Shauna Lee I wanted her to start looking for one."

"What exactly are you looking for?"

"I want someone to take over the operation and the management of the farm. He has to have the right credentials and experience. I've been thinking about offering a percentage of the net income of the farm, as well as a competitive wage. By competitive I mean comparative to this situation, not to a big corporation."

"What are you going to do? Move out here?"

"This is where I had always intended to be, until Dad had his heart attack. Then it was necessary for me to take over on the farm. But I love it out here and Fran does too."

He smiled and shook his head. "She was working here when we got together. I refused to accept that I was in love with her and I almost lost her because of my stupidity. I did my best to push her away and she left."

He moved a finger between Ollie and Shauna Lee. "I have to thank these two for urging me to go find her."

Ollie snorted. "Well, he was moping around like a sick calf. He just needed a good kick in the ass. Those two were a perfect fit right from the beginning, but they were both to stubborn to admit it.

"I knew she was head over heels in love with him when she left. When I confronted her and asked her if she was pregnant with Colt's baby she finally admitted it. But she was just as stubborn as he was; she made me promise not to tell him."

Colt was sober. "He didn't tell me either. He just tore a strip off me and told me to suck it up and act like a man. He did tell me where I could find her though."

Ollie chuckled. "The best phone call I've ever gotten, was that New Years Eve, when they woke me up at two o'clock in the morning and told me they were getting married right away and they were having twins! I danced a jig. And then I couldn't go back to sleep."

Colt looked at Brad. "Yeah…well now you know all our dirty laundry!

Brad shrugged his shoulders. "A lot of people have dirty laundry, Colt. Thankfully our past doesn't have to control our future."

"You are right, Brad. And now we are moving on; I plan to build a house up on the bench and move my family out here. It will be a wonderful place to let the kids grow up."

Brad looked thoughtful. "I'm thinking; I have a friend who might fit the bill for you as a farm manager. He's from the Peace River country. He's got degrees in agriculture; I'm not sure what all, but he's a damn smart business man and he ran the family business for twenty years and made it pay.

"They had thousands of acres of grain farm and all the modern machinery; you know, the GPS stuff and 'white shirt cabs' with stereos and air conditioning, 70 foot plus wide air seeders, fancy sprayers. Name it, they had it.

"Then his dad died. His mom had died a few years earlier, so there was no one to check the inheritance free-for-all. There are six kids in that family and the fight was on. Everyone wanted their share of the pie in cash and they all thought they were going to be multi millionaires. In the end, between everyone's greed and the lawyers, the family business had to be sold. A major corporation bought it."

"Did they offer him the management position?"

Brad sighed. "They did. But while the inheritance fight was on, his wife went for the jugular. She divorced him. Last I heard he was just looking for a new start anywhere away from there. If you want to check him out, I'll give you his phone number and address when we

114

get home. His reputation has been solid. He might be your answer."

Colt nodded. "I have confidence in your judgement, Brad." He nodded to Shauna Lee. "You can call Shauna Lee and give her the info. I'm going to be flat out with everything else going on. She knows what I'm looking for and she has good instincts about that sort of thing."

Shauna Lee smiled. "Thanks Colt."

"Well, it's true…" He stopped as he heard the door open. "They're back." He stood up and walked down the hall.

"Hi there, Patch." Patch nodded to Colt as he hung up his coat. Colt looked at Frankie. "So how is the cow?"

"I think she is all right. She's eating. Her eyes are clear and her nose is moist. I couldn't get close enough to examine her, so I told Patch to just keep an eye on her."

She smiled happily. "It felt so good to be out there again. We have to find a manager and get busy on the house so we can move out here next year!"

"Speaking of managers; Brad knows someone who might fill the bill. He's going to give Shauna Lee the guys phone number and his address. She'll check him out."

He slipped his arm around her shoulders. "We'll take time for you to grab a coffee and then we'd better get moving."

As they came into the kitchen, Shauna Lee handed Frankie a hot cup of coffee and was pouring another for the new hand. Ollie introduced Patch to Brad.

When Patch spoke in acknowledgement, a shiver went up her spine. She trembled as she sat down the coffee pot and slowly turned to look at the new comer.

Colt motioned to her. "Patch, this is Shauna Lee Holt. She's been our accountant…"

The color drained out of Shauna Lee's face. She reached for the counter top to steady herself. Brad was instantly on his feet. He strode to her side and slid his arm around her waist. "Shauna…are you OK?" Her hand grabbed his shirt and clenched it. "Sweetheart…?"

She didn't seem to hear him.

Everybody's eyes flashed to Patch. Shock registered on his face. "Leanne?" he whispered.

Colt shook his head. "No, this is Shauna Lee."

Patch stared at her. "No," he said hoarsely as he reached out to her. "Leanne?"

She leaned into Brad. He could feel her trembling. "No," she whispered.

"I know my own daughter. Those eyes! No one could miss them; and that golden curly hair. No matter who you call yourself, you are Leanne Bergeron."

The floor slid away from her and Shauna Lee collapsed against Brad. He held her against him and then lifted her in his arms. "Shauna. Sweetheart…talk to me."

He looked at Patch in confusion. "What the hell is going on here?"

Shauna was conscious in a moment. She looked into Brad's eyes as tears filled hers. "Take me home," she whispered. "Get me away from here, away from him…please, just take me home."

He glared at Patch. "If you really are her dad, you were a heartless bastard. Do you have any idea how much damage you did to her?"

He looked at Colt. "We're headed home. I'll come back during the week and do the job."

Shauna Lee put her arms around his neck and pulled up to look into his eyes. She shook her head. "No. No, that's not fair. I'm sorry. This was just such a shock…just get me out of here…we can go out and do the work. Put me down please, Brad."

"Are you sure?"

She closed her eyes and nodded. He slid her feet to the floor and let her stand beside him.

She stepped toward Patch and looked him right in the eye. Her voice trembled but she held strong. "Leanne Bergeron does not exist anymore, so you are not my father. You never were a father to me. You didn't care about me. You walked out and left without a backward glance. Mom was so sick…"

"Leanne…what I did was cowardly; inexcusable. But there are

things you don't know about the life we lived; your mother and I. I read about Marie's death. I read about you and what happe…."

She slapped him. "Shut up! SHUT UP! Don't you dare! Don't you dare go there!" She flew at him, beating him backwards. "I buried Leanne Bergeron with everything else that I buried back there. I'm Shauna Lee Holt. I have made a new life. I have become a new person."

She started to cry. "And guess what; nobody noticed. Nobody cared. Nobody even gave Leanne Bergeron another thought." She pushed past him and ran outside.

Brad was right behind her. He caught her before she got to the end of the cement sidewalk, grabbing her from behind, holding her close. "It's OK now…I'm here with you." He turned her into his chest, enfolding her in his arms, pushing his hands gently through her hair.

Frankie followed them out, carrying the shoes that both of them had left inside. She came up beside them and stretched her arms around them to hold them both. Shauna Lee cried until she was wrung out. Then Brad picked her up and carried her to the truck.

He motioned for Frankie to open the back door and he slid her in. He reached for the shoes that Frankie handed him and put them on her feet. Then he pushed himself up onto the seat beside her and slid his arms around her shoulders.

She leaned into him and rested her face against his chest. "I'm sorry I'm such a screw up."

Frankie watched as he kissed Shauna Lee's forehead. *Thank goodness she has Brad.* She went around to the passenger side and pulled herself up onto the front seat, staring out the window as she waited for Colt to come.

Colt didn't appear for ten minutes or more. He slid behind the steering wheel, turned to look at Brad who gave him a nod. He started the truck, fastened his seatbelt and headed for home. The entire drive was made in silence.

When they arrived at the farm, Brad lifted Shauna Lee out of the back seat and stood her on the ground. He led her around to where Frankie waited by the passenger door. As he bent to lift her up, Frankie rested her hand on his sleeve, her eyes imploring. He nodded and she stepped in front of him and wrapped her arms around Shauna Lee.

She felt Shauna Lee stiffen momentarily, then relax into her embrace. "I'm glad you've got Brad," she whispered. "I want you to know that Colt and I are here for you, Shauna Lee."

Shauna Lee hesitated, then lifted her arms and hugged her in return. "Thank you," she whispered. Frankie stepped away and let Brad put Shauna Lee into the truck. He closed the door and walked around to the front of it to meet Colt.

"Don't leave her alone tonight, Brad," Frankie said softly. "She needs somebody. If it can't be you, I'll come. This obviously was a terrible shock to her."

"You don't know the half of it. Anyway, I'm not leaving her alone. She's coming back to my place tonight. We'll see how things are tomorrow. I may phone her office and just tell them she's not coming in and I won't go in either."

Colt looked at him with concern. "Are you guys…"

"Together? Yes. It hasn't been easy, but we are. I know it must seem sudden, but it's like I've been waiting for her; like I've always loved her."

Colt sighed and reached to shake Brad's hand. "Hang in there buddy. She is basically a good person. I think she's worth the effort if you love her."

"I know that. I'll talk to you in a couple of days and work something out to get this job up and going."

# CHAPTER NINE

*B*rad looked across at Shauna Lee as they entered the Swift Current city limits. "How are you doing, sweetie?"

"I'm OK," she answered dully.

"I'm going to swing into the drive through at A&W and pick up a coffee. Do you want to grab something quick to eat too? I'll make pizza when we get home."

She shook her head. "Just drop me off at my place."

He was silent while he ordered coffee and a hamburger for both of them. He pulled forward and picked up the order, then pulled into a parking space and shut off the motor.

She looked at him questioningly. "What are you doing?"

"Well, first we are going to eat something. I'm hungry. That bacon and egg sandwich we had for breakfast is long gone." He opened a hamburger wrapper and handed it to her. "Eat," he said softly as he handed it to her.

She shook her head. "Just take me to my place."

"Shauna, please. It's been hours since you ate. You need something now. Then, we'll talk about going to your place. You've had a tough day."

She took the hamburger and looked at him, tears shimmering in her eyes. "I'm such a screw up, why don't you just give up on me? Take me to my place and just forget about me."

He opened her coffee, pulled out her cup holder and sat the cup into it. Then he looked at her. "Is that why you want to go to your place? Because if it is, you should know it is not going to happen. If I take you to your place, I'm staying there with you. I'm not leaving you there alone. I'm not giving up on you. I'm not forgetting about you."

He took her hand. "And in my opinion, *you* are not a screw up. Now your old man…he's another thing."

119

She started to sob.

"Sweetheart…I'm sorry. I can see this isn't going to work. We'll just go home." He started the truck and headed for his place. She didn't protest.

He parked the truck, then got out and went around to the passenger door. He opened it and reached for her. She leaned into his arms and let him lift her down to stand on the ground; then she slipped her arms around his waist and clung to him. He wrapped his arms around her and held her. They stood like that for what seemed to be countless moments. Then she pulled back and looked up at him. "Thank you," she whispered.

"Let's go inside," he said softly.

Once inside, Brad looked at her closely. "What do you want to do, sweetie? Are you hungry? Do you want me to make some coffee? Do you want to lie down?"

"I must sound like such a baby, but I honestly don't know what I want to do. I'm exhausted. I'm numb. I…I don't know."

"Look, I'm damn hungry. I'll go out and grab those hamburgers… No! On second thought, let's get you tucked into bed for a rest first. Then I'll grab something quick and start making pizza for supper. OK?"

She nodded and turned toward the hall. He slid his arm around her shoulder and led her to his bedroom. He pulled back the cover and stepped aside as she lay down. Then he pulled the cover back over her, and leaned over to drop a kiss on her cheek.

"Have a nap, sweetie. I'm sure you'll feel better then. And remember this; I'm here for the long haul, so don't ever think that I'll abandon you."

She reached up and touched his face gently, then closed her eyes.

Brad went out to the truck and collected the hamburgers and coffee. He took a bite and grimaced. He stuffed it all in the brown paper A&W bag that it had come in and dropped everything in the garbage can as he went into the house.

He went to the fridge and took out a beer, then made the pizza crust and set it aside to rise. He went to the bedroom to check on

Shauna Lee; she was lost in the oblivion of sleep. As he looked at her, he replayed her confrontation with Patch in his mind.

"What happened to you, Tweetie Bird?" he wondered. "What was so terrible that you wanted to completely forget your life; even go so far as to change your identity? Surely more than having your dead beat father leave you and your mom."

Troubled, he went back to the kitchen. He leaned against the counter and finished his beer as he gazed unseeingly out the window. *There are things you don't know about the life we lived.* Patch's words rang in his mind.

"Shit! Secrets and lies destroy lives time after time." He shook his head. "People never realize how much they can hurt others without physically touching them. Bruises and broken bones heal. Scars in the mind stay there forever."

He went to the fridge and got another beer. Then he started preparing the topping for the pizza. When he finished browning the hamburger and chopping onions, peppers, celery and mushrooms, he punched down the crust and rolled it out to fit the pizza pan. He arranged the toppings, then put the pizza in the oven and set the timer. He checked his watch; almost five o'clock.

He slipped into the bedroom and checked on Shauna again. She was still sleeping peacefully. He touched her hair gently and went back to sit down in front of the TV. He flipped through the channels and found a football game. The Rough Riders were playing in Edmonton. He turned the volume down low and sat there, not really watching, lost in his concern for Shauna Lee.

He didn't realise that she was there, until she touched his arm. He looked up startled. "I just checked on you and you were sleeping."

She smiled wanly. "I woke up as you were leaving. I felt you touch me."

He took her hand and tugged her over to sit by him on the couch. He slid his arm around her. "Feeling any better?"

She nodded. "I needed that." She took his hand and lifted it to her lips, pushing against it with a soft kiss. "Are you watching the game?"

"Not really. It's just on. I couldn't concentrate; I was just sitting here, thinking about today."

She sighed. "I was totally blindsided. I haven't seen him since I was fourteen and a half. After all these years, I couldn't have imagined seeing him there. When I heard his voice…"

"That bastard."

She shook her head. "I think he was just as shocked as I was. He's hidden himself so well for all these years…I'm sure he never imagined he'd run into me there."

"It's interesting that you'd mention that. He didn't try to distance himself from you. He claimed you. He could have just slipped away and left the place. It'll be interesting to see if he quits his job, that's if Colt doesn't put the run on him."

She shook her head. "Colt shouldn't fire him if he is working out well at the ranch. It doesn't matter to me if he works there. As far as I'm concerned he is not my father. The girl who was his daughter has been buried for twenty years.

"I have no reason to see him again. I do the accounting for Thompson Land and Cattle Company. Aaron Bergeron is just a name…no he doesn't call himself Aaron any more. Who is he now? Patch? Whatever…it means nothing to me."

"Shauna, you know it's not that simple. You and I need to talk about all this eventually; your dad, you; all that stuff. But let's just sit and relax for now. The pizza will be ready in a few minutes. I think we should eat first. We can talk as much as you are comfortable with later this evening."

She nodded, biting her lip.

"We can't brush all this away and pretend it never happened." He kissed her cheek as he squeezed her gently. "I love you, Tweetie Bird. I've told you before, I'm not cutting out. But you can't keep living a lie.

"I know you had to have been hurt beyond comprehension to have taken such drastic actions. That kind of thing doesn't heal in a hundred years if you bottle it up and try to lose it inside yourself. It's still there; still hurting you."

She sighed and laid her head against his shoulder, closing her eyes. They sat like that until the timer went off. She shifted and sat up so he could move. He stood up and took her hand, helping her to her feet.

They walked to the kitchen hand in hand. He turned off the timer and took the pizza out of the oven. She went to the cupboard; *2 plates, 2 knives, 2 forks, napkins. He loves me. He must. I have to tell him. Can I open up to all that pain again?*

He put the pizza pan on the table. He went back to grab two bottles of Corona and a lime from the fridge, and snagged the pizza cutter on his way back to the table. They sat down together and she waited as he made the first cuts.

"Mmmm. That smells yummy Brad. I just realized that I am hungry." She looked at him. "Did you eat something earlier?"

He nodded at the beer. "I got a head start on you. I had a couple while I made the pizza. I checked out the hamburgers but they were cold and not very appetizing, so I ditched them in the garbage."

"I'm sorry. I just couldn't eat then."

"And I should have realized that. You see, I don't always know what the best thing to do is, even when I think I do. It's a man thing, I guess." He reached out and brushed her cheek. "You proved that when you forced my hand yesterday."

She blushed.

"And I can tell you, it felt so damn good to give in and admit you were right. I felt like I'd died and gone to heaven; and it made such a change in you. You relaxed…"

"It wasn't just the sex, Brad. That was incredible; but it was having you accept me…"

He smiled. "I've accepted you for quite a while, sweetie. One day soon, I hope you will be able to accept that I love you unconditionally and that you are worth my love."

Her eyes misted.

"No more tears now. Eat!" He cut the lime and stuffed it into her bottle, then slid it to her. They ate in silence, then gathered up the dishes and loaded the dish washer. Then they stood looking at each other in an awkward silence.

Shauna Lee reached her hand out and took his. "I guess…we have to talk," she said haltingly.

"We do, Tweetie Bird." He pulled her close and kissed her gently.

"Where shall we sit? Where are you most comfortable?"

"On the bed?"

"Are you trying to distract me? It might work for tonight, but we still need to talk about this; if not tonight, then tomorrow."

"Kiss me again?"

He cupped her face in his hands. "I think I could." And he dropped his lips to hers. The kiss lit the fires that always sprung to life when their lips met, only now he wouldn't deny them. He picked her up and carried her to the bed room.

They made love slowly, sensually; it was a deeply satisfying, healing experience for both of them. They lay on the bed quietly, afterwards.

Shauna Lee lay against Brad, as soft and pliant as melting chocolate. Brad's heart was full. He watched her lashes drift down to rest on her cheeks. *I love you so much girl; we'll talk tomorrow. I can't bear to make you face all that ugliness tonight.* He kissed her cheek softly and drifted off to sleep.

Brad stirred; something wasn't right. He stretched his arm out, feeling for Shauna. She wasn't there. He got up and wandered through the house, but didn't find her. His heart was pounding. *Where can she be?*

He turned on the light in the kitchen and looked at his watch. It was midnight. "Shauna, where are you?" he wondered out loud. His truck was in the driveway, so she hadn't taken it and gone home.

He ran a hand through his hair. "Ok, settle down Johnson," he said to himself. "Where would she go? It's dark. Would she have gone out to the horses? She's happy with them."

He stepped out the back door. The sky was full of stars, the moon shining brightly. Suddenly he saw movement, a dark image running up the path toward him.

"Brad," he heard her call. "I'm here." She flew into him, arms outstretched. "I woke up and couldn't go back to sleep. Suddenly I felt I had to come out here." She hugged him close. "I'm sorry if I worried you. I didn't think you'd wake up; then I saw the light go on in the kitchen. I knew you were looking for me. I'm so sorry."

"You gave me a scare. I went through the whole upstairs; I didn't check the downstairs. I never thought of that. I saw that the truck was still there, so the next thing for me to do was to look out here."

"I wouldn't take your truck without asking," she said stepping back to look at him. She reached down and took his hand. "Let's go in. It's chilly out here and I'm wide awake now."

Brad shivered. He had just pulled on a pair of pyjama bottoms before he'd gone out. He looked her over. She had put her clothes on and grabbed one of his jackets from the coat hooks by the back door. "At least you got dressed! Did you find what you were looking for out there?"

"I think so. I know I have to talk to you about what happened to-day. Can we do that now? Before I chicken out?"

"Any time you want. Do you want me to make a coffee and sit in here, or on the couch? Or do you want to go back to bed? What will work best for you?"

"Coffee would be good. Can we sit here? This isn't easy for me. I don't want to spill any more blood in the bedroom. I want to have happy memories in there; like earlier tonight."

Brad hugged her. "Coffee is coming up."

She drummed her fingers on the table while she waited. When Brad sat two cups on it, she sighed as she reached for hers. She played with the handle and then looked at him. "Where do I start?"

"Well, is there anything more that you need to tell me about your dad? Did he abuse you?"

Her eyes widened. "You mean sexually? Heavens no! He wouldn't even give me a hug. He sure as hell didn't do that."

"I'm glad, Shauna. I would kill him if you told me he had."

"Brad, please! He has caused me enough pain; please don't let him take you from me too. If you went after him that is what would happen."

"I just would like to even the score for what he did to you!"

"It's the past."

"But it isn't in the past Shauna. It is still part of you. It has coloured your whole life."

She shook her head. "I told you everything about dad. He ran out and left us, flat broke. Mom died and I was alone."

"Yes, and you were afraid Social Services would take you. When I asked you what happened to you after that you said you couldn't talk about it then. Sweetheart, none of this justifies you taking an assumed name, starting life over. That's big."

" I…it's so hard Brad. I…"

"Shauna. Please don't play with me."

She looked stricken.

"Sweetheart, I love you; the choices that you made away back then will not change how I feel about you. But I need you to be honest with me. I need to be able to understand you."

"Brad…I was 15 years old. I had no home, no money, nobody to care. I moved in with a guy in the neighbourhood; Dave Trutcher. He was in his twenties. A rough and tumble farmer. I…I got pregnant immediately."

She looked down at her hands as she twisted them together. "The baby was a boy. I called him Ben." She swallowed hard. "He was born with a bi-lateral cleft lip. To me, he was beautiful and so perfect, even though his mouth was deformed.

"He was part of me and I just loved him even more because of the problems he had. He needed me. I knew that he'd need special care and eventually he would need a lot of surgery to repair his lip. But he was mine and I loved him with all my heart.

"But Dave was revolted by the way he looked. He always referred to Ben as 'the freak,' and he wouldn't touch him. He insisted that my genes were responsible for the defect, because no child with his lineage would have been born looking like that."

Brad exploded. "What an asshole! Where the hell does this pain end, Shauna?" He held her in his arms and rocked her.

"It..t..'s not the end yet. There's more."

"Ben would have started to have corrective surgery when he was about eighteen months old." She began to cry. "But he...he didn't l..i..v.e.. l.ong.g en..ough for that."

Tears filled Brad's eyes and trickled down his cheek. Shauna Lee wiped them away.

"I changed my name after that. I...I decided to bury Leanne Bergeron with her baby and start life over with a clean slate. I become Shauna Lee Holt. That was my grandma's name—my mother's mom." She mused for a moment. "She was the only person who ever truly showed me that she loved me."

Brad grabbed her hands and held them to his lips. "You've got me now."

She sighed wearily. "I know that...I'm so tired, Brad."

"I know. I'm sorry I prodded you to talk about all this. I wanted to help you, to understand you, not to hurt you more."

"Brad this isn't your fault. Seeing Dad today was a shock...but he obviously knows about Ben; the baby. He started to bring it up this afternoon at the house. I couldn't listen to him; I couldn't let him do that to me."

She sobbed. "I guess I blame him for what happened. If he had been a father to me; if he hadn't been such a drunken coward; if he'd stayed and made a place for us to live, I wouldn't have been in such a mess. But I had nowhere to go."

Brad's heart ached for her. "He is the poorest excuse of a father that I've ever heard of." He leaned forward and brushed her lips with his. "And tonight, you've done enough of this; I've heard more than enough. Let's go to bed. We need to get some sleep and I want to hold you and make you feel safe."

She nodded and stood up, reaching for his hand. They walked together to the bedroom. He helped her slip out of her clothes and slide her naked body onto the sheets. Then he gently covered her, dropping a kiss on her forehead as he tucked the blanket over her.

He undressed quickly, turned off the light on his side of the bed and eased himself in behind her. The feel of their bodies touching, skin to skin, was warm and comforting. She relaxed against him, settling into his arms. Sleep soon claimed her.

Brad lay for a long time, listening to her even breathing. He couldn't forget her words; *he didn't l..i..v.e l.ongg en..ough for that.* He cursed her father and Dave Trutcher. No wonder she had closed herself off. Everyone who had been a part of her life had hurt her; let her down.

He finally slept fitfully for a couple of hours. When he awoke, he checked the clock on the bedside table. It was six-thirty in the morning. Shauna was still asleep and he was emotionally and physically exhausted. He considered for a moment and then shifted so he could reach his cell phone on the night table.

He dialed his office and left a message saying he would be in on Tuesday. Then he dialed Shauna Lee's office and left a message for Christine, telling her that Shauna wouldn't be in until the next day. He shut off the phone and put it back. Shauna stirred lightly, reaching for his hand in her sleep. Brad smiled and kissed her shoulder, then fell asleep.

It was noon when he woke up. Shauna was gone from the bed. He listened for sounds of movement in the house and then smiled as the aroma of coffee wafted on the air. He was just starting to sit up when she tiptoed to the door. She smiled when she saw that he was awake and walked to his side of the bed, bending down to slip her arms around his shoulders. She sat down beside him and held him close and kissed him.

She leaned back and looked at him. "I just talked to Christina. She said you phoned in earlier and said that I wouldn't be in. Thank you; but when did you do that?"

"I didn't sleep very well. I woke up early and knew that I wasn't in any shape to go in to work today. I thought you needed some time to recoup too, so I made an arbitrary decision, without checking with you first. I hope that's OK."

"It's fine. I appreciate you thinking about my needs and taking care of things. I'm not used to that."

"Get used to it Tweetie Bird," he said with a soft smile as he reached to tangle his fingers in her curls. *She's slipped right back into happy mode,* he thought. *How does she do that after everything that happened yesterday? It must be a defence mechanism. I guess that's how she has survived all these years.*

"I made coffee. And," she smiled shyly, "I made breakfast…or at least I tried to."

Brad grinned. "What? Did you buy a package of frozen waffles?"

She punched him lightly in the shoulder. "No. I made pancakes from scratch." She wrinkled her nose. "I think they are all right."

He pulled her close and rubbed his face in her hair. "I'm impressed! I'm hungry too, so let's go eat."

When they went into the kitchen he was surprised to see that the table was set and everything ready. "Sit down," she said with a proud smile. She went to the warmer and took out a plate of golden brown pancakes, as well as a plate with crisply cooked bacon. Then she brought the coffee carafe and poured two cups full.

Brad took two pancakes and commented on how light and fluffy they were. He slathered them with butter and drowned them with pancake syrup. Then he took a couple of bites. "These are really good! You've been holding out on me, Tweetie Bird."

"No. I just paid attention to what you do and I'm a fast learner! So are they really good?"

"No kidding. Try them yourself!"

She smiled after she took her first couple of bites. "They are good; hey, I did all right."

Later in the afternoon, Brad went into his office to look over his schedule. Shauna sat watching TV for a few minutes, just relaxing. "Shauna," she heard him call.

"Yes"

"Will you come here for a moment?"

As she wandered into his office, he swivelled his chair and slid his arm around her waist and pulled her close. "I'm looking at my schedule for the next few weeks. I have to go up north for a maintenance check on a couple of places where I've installed turbines. I could do it on the November eleventh long weekend. Would you come with me?"

She smiled as she ran her fingers through his hair. "How far north?"

"Well, I've got one set up at a dugout near Glaslyn, and we put two up at a house on Chiteck Lake a couple of months ago. They aren't big jobs, just maintenance checks before winter sets in. It's quite a bit of driving, but the roads are good. It will be an easy weekend away from home, and we'll get to spend it together."

She looked into his eyes and smiled brightly. "I think it could be fun. Besides, what would I do for three days without you? I'd miss you like crazy."

He squeezed her gently. "Now those are words I'm happy to hear." His look turned sober. "I've got another trip I have to make too. I'll be gone for a week, but it's something I have to do. Around the end of November I have to fly to China. Several months ago I had an inquiry from a company over there that is interested in finding out more about the turbines.

"I've contacted The Canadian Consulate in Beijing and worked out some preliminary things. Doing business in China is a lot different than here. This trip will basically just be a fact finding mission; testing the water. I'm going to be meeting with someone who will translate for me, and show me the ropes over there; what to do and what not to do. If this contact materialises it would be a real boost for the business, but nothing is for sure and it's not going to happen overnight."

"Brad! That is so exciting."

"Yeah, but I won't be able to take you with me this time."

"I'll be all right. It's just a week."

"I know. But I may not even be able to call you. I'm not sure what things will be like over there."

"But you'll be safe?"

"I wouldn't go if I wasn't certain of that. I plan to spend many, many years with you!"

"Then I'll sleep in your shirt every night and be waiting here when you get back."

# CHAPTER TEN

"Want another coffee?" Frankie asked, holding up the coffee pot.

Colt nodded. They were catching precious minutes alone, before Ellie came over to the house and the twins woke up.

"Well, I wonder how Brad and Shauna Lee made out last night. She seemed pretty shell shocked."

Colt was thoughtful. "It's hard to imagine that I've known her so many years and have no idea what her life has been all about."

"Yesterday was a shocking glimpse into it. What happens to somebody that is so terrible that they totally deny their life; change their name completely? It had to be really painful."

"Even when we were seeing a lot of each other, she never talked about family. In fact she always said she didn't have any."

"Well, she certainly was shocked to see Patch there." Frankie thought for a moment. "He was surprised too. But did you notice, he acknowledged her; even claimed her. But she would have made him vanish if she could have."

"Well its plain there's some painful history there and Brad knows about some of it. He was pretty defensive of Shauna Lee and he certainly expressed his anger towards Patch."

"I'm glad he's there for her."

Colt grinned. "Yeah, the sly dog; she was probably there with him when I talked to him Saturday morning. It's pretty sudden; especially to say he's in love already."

Frankie gave him a little nudge with her toe. "Not everyone is such a hard sell as you were!"

Colt grabbed her hand and kissed it. "I was pretty thick headed. But when I got it right, I fell hook, line and sinker."

She smiled. "And you don't even fish! When we're at the ranch we're going to have to teach you how to relax and fish. Every kid should learn how to drop a hook. I did that with my dad."

Colt grinned. "Riding horses is just as relaxing."

Frankie smiled. "I agree, but it's good to learn something new too. Anyway, back to Patch. He seems like such a nice guy. I guess people can change."

"He offered to quit yesterday, after that happened with Shauna Lee and him."

"What did you say?"

"I told him I didn't want him to. What happened years ago with Shauna Lee and him isn't anything to do with his working out there on the ranch. He may have been a lousy father but he and Ollie work well together. His recommendations are second to none. He stayed at the Gang Ranch for over fifteen years, through different changes in ownership. I didn't vet Ollie when he came. Who knows what his past history is, but he's a good man and we'd be lost without him."

"I'm glad. At this point he seems like a good fit. You can just make sure that he and Shauna Lee don't have to be in contact."

Colt nodded. "Which reminds me; I should check in with Brad's office and see if he is working. I want to get moving on the turbines out at the ranch."

Frankie handed him the phone. "Here you go. Make the call."

Colt dialed and waited for a pickup. "Mmmm. I just got the answering machine. He's not going to be in until tomorrow. Things must have been tough for Shauna Lee last night. I'll check in at his place this evening and see if we can go out to the ranch tomorrow."

"So what are we doing today?"

"Do you want to go into the office and look at house plans? We need to get started on that too."

"Let's go. The kids aren't up yet and Ellie will be here any minute."

Frankie gathered up the cups and put them in the dish washer. Colt took the coffee pot back and slid it onto the coffee maker. They reached for each other's hand and walked to the office.

132

"So where do we start?" Frankie asked.

"I picked up a few books of house plans. That will give us a place to start from."

"Have you looked through them?"

"Yeah; I found a few that might work, but I want you to go through these on your own and look at them. Then we'll see if there are any that we both pick out."

"Ah; no outside influence, eh?"

He smiled and nodded. He handed her the books of house plans and motioned to the chair behind the desk. "Take your time. I'll go check in on the twins and then I'll make a few phone calls from the kitchen; we'll compare notes later."

The twins came into the office to say good morning and then Colt took them back into the kitchen where he and Ellie supervised their breakfast routine. Frankie could hear squeals of laughter and general banter between the four of them. Afterwards the house fell silent when Colt took the twins out for a walk.

She heard Ellie go upstairs to tidy their room and then come down and go to the laundry room. "We are so lucky to have found her. She is so much more than a nanny! I hope she stays until all the kids are grown up. And then we could keep her on as member of the family."

By lunch time Frankie had carefully looked through all the plans and picked out three designs that she liked best. Colt was back with the twins and she could hear them all in the kitchen.

When she joined them, Colt was at the stove. Ellie had Sam settled in his chair at the table, and was putting a recalcitrant Selena into hers. *Her patience amazes me*, she thought as she considered whether she should reprimand the child or not. She looked at Colt, who shook his head as he watched. *Ellie can handle her. No point in interfering and undermining her authority,* she thought.

"What's for lunch?" she asked.

Colt motioned to two empty boxes of Kraft Dinner lying on the counter. "Ellie got out voted this time. But we had to agree to eat some carrot sticks, cucumber slices and red pepper strips along with the Mac 'n Cheese. It's ready now."

Frankie picked up the plate of vegetables and Colt took the pot of Mac 'n Cheese to the table. He dished a portion onto each of the twin's plates and Frankie held out the vegetable plate and let them help themselves. Sam took an acceptable amount without fussing, but Selena protested.

Frankie looked at her seriously. "Did you tell Ellie you would eat the vegetables if she agreed to have Mac 'n Cheese for lunch?"

A sulky look settled over Selena's face. She nodded.

"And so do you think it is all right for you to break your word to her?"

Selena looked down at her plate, avoiding Frankie's eyes.

"Selena?"

Selena shook her head.

"So what if Ellie did what you are doing. Should she take away the Mac 'n Cheese and give you something else?"

Selena shook her head again.

"So what are you going to do, Selena?"

Selena had played this game before and knew she couldn't win. One time Ellie had actually taken away her favourite dish. Begrudgingly she reached out and took some carrot sticks."

"What about the other vegetables?"

Selena looked at her mom and then gave in. She reached out and took three more pieces of each.

Frankie smiled. "I'm proud of you Selena; you kept your word." She looked at Colt, who smiled as he met her eyes and winked.

While everyone ate, Selena and Sam excitedly told Frankie about what they had seen on their walk. After lunch Ellie took them upstairs to their room and Colt and Frankie cleaned up the lunch dishes.

"So, did you find anything that you liked?" Colt asked.

"Actually I found three plans. They all have good points. It's hard to pick out one, but we can make adjustments can't we?"

"For sure; these plans just give us a good reference to start from. I know an architect in Swift Current. She's good and she's flexible. She'll have ideas of her own to suggest, but she'll make sure we both get what we want. Let's go compare notes."

They went into the office and Frankie showed Colt the plans she had chosen. He looked at her with a twinkle in his eye. "We've picked two of the same ones."

"Show me the other ones that you liked," Frankie said. He showed her three more plans, and she could see good ideas in each of them. "So now what?" she asked.

"Well, I think I'll phone Mona Blake and see if she has time to work with us now. I want to get on this right away. The sooner we get our design finished and blueprints ordered, the sooner we can talk to a contractor."

"This is exciting Colt. I love this old house, but to be out at the ranch! I can hardly wait. But we've got to find a manager first."

"We can do both. Brad and Shauna Lee will collaborate on finding a manager. We'll work out the plans for the house and we'll have everything on the go as soon as they can start building in the spring."

Frankie gave him a warm hug, excitement lending a flush to her cheeks and a sparkle to her eyes. Then she handed him the phone.

Colt's call was answered on the second ring. He talked extensively with Mona. When the conversation was finished he looked at Frankie with a smile. "She's just finished up a big job. She says she'll let her assistant tie up a couple of other loose ends and she wants to see us any day this week."

"I'm going to phone Brad in an hour or so. I just don't want to press him too soon, but if we could, I'd like to go out to the ranch with him tomorrow and get this turbine business underway."

"In the meantime, we could pick apart these plans and decide what we want to incorporate in our house. If we have an idea of what we want before we go to Mona, we'll have a head start."

Colt reached into a bottom drawer in the desk and pulled out a pad of graph paper. Then he took a yellow note pad out of the top drawer. Frankie pulled up a chair and sat beside him and they started dissecting the various plans, making notes about what they liked, what they would tweak and what they each wanted to add.

Time slipped by quickly. When the phone rang, Colt glanced at his watch as he answered it. It was four o'clock already. He pointed to the time as he answered. Frankie looked surprised. She slipped out of the room to put on the roast that she'd taken out the night before and put five potatoes in the oven with it for supper.

When she came back to the office, Colt wore a satisfied smile. Frankie gave him a questioning look.

He stood up. "That was Brad. We're a go for tomorrow. But even better news is that he tracked down his buddy from the Peace River country and talked to him. Shauna Lee talked to him too. She thinks he's a good candidate for manager. He's interested, so he's going to fax his résumé to her tomorrow, and I'll get it from her on Wednesday."

He hugged her. "Things are going our way, hon."

"Speaking of Shauna Lee; did Brad say how she was?"

"No, and I didn't ask. He may not want to say anything; it may be something that stays between the two of them. I talked to her though and she sounded good."

"That's pretty amazing. After what happened yesterday...how could she just put on a happy face and be OK today?"

"Possibly because she has always done that; if you think about the things that were said between her and Patch yesterday, I'd say there's probably more to the situation than we have any idea about. She's obviously lived with something painful for a long time. He mentioned that he heard about when her mom died and then he started to say something else and she just flew at him."

Frankie was thoughtful, remembering. "She did. And she was yelling at him to shut up, and warned him not to go where ever she knew that conversation was going." She sighed. "What happened to her Colt? She said she'd buried the person she had been and nobody had even noticed. No one had cared." Tears shimmered in her eyes. "Colt: what a terrible realization to have to live with."

136

Brad arrived at the farm at seven the next morning. Colt asked him in for coffee and Frankie joined them.

"Brad, is Shauna Lee OK?" Frankie asked.

Brad sighed. "It's amazing how she bounces back. I can't talk about all this with you guys. She's trusted me enough to confide in me. But I...her life has been..." He rubbed his hand across his face. "Sometimes you have to wonder how much one person can take."

"Brad. Just let her know that we support her."

"She could use your friendship; if she'll let you in. She has closed herself off from everybody for years...I shouldn't be telling you this..."

Frankie frowned. "Shauna Lee has really invested herself in her work. When I was working at the clinic, everything centered on my work too. Relationships got to be pretty impersonal; everyone I met was just an acquaintance.

"Some of us are not social butterflies, Brad. Truthfully, I...I haven't made many close friends either. I have one girl friend that I've been close to forever, but she lives in Calgary. But other than that, I lived in a 'man's' world until we got married. Now I have Colt and the twins; they are the center of my world. Well throw Ollie and Ellie in there too. But I'm busy; I don't have time to make friends. I never feel like I need friends."

"But you have family...you have *someone* in your life..." He shook his head. "I shouldn't be talking about this. But it's hard to love someone and see so much pain!"

"But she has you now, Brad."

He smiled. "Yes, she has me." He turned to Colt. "I guess we'd better get on the road."

"I'm ready. Let's get rolling." Colt leaned over and gave Frankie a kiss. "If you have time, you could look at those house plans some more. Anything you think of, just write it down. We are going to meet with Mona later tomorrow afternoon."

Frankie nodded. "At three thirty. I'll spend some time looking at the plans again. I'm so excited I can hardly think about anything else!"

She walked to the door with Colt and Brad, waiting as they

shrugged into their jackets. She kissed Colt again. "Travel safely, love. See you later."

She stepped through the door to where Brad stood on the veranda. "Brad."

He turned to look at her. "Hang in there. I'm glad you are there for Shauna Lee. She needs you."

He smiled softly, touched by her compassion. "Thanks, Frankie. I know she needs me. I'm waiting for her to realize that she loves me. Right now, she can't even consider the idea of that...love, I mean. But I love her and want her, and I'm in this for the long haul."

She squeezed his arm, then turned back to smile at Colt. He dropped a quick kiss on her lips. "I love you *and* I want you too," he whispered before he followed Brad down the steps. She stood and watched, waving as they drove away.

Brad and Colt talked about everything, except Patch and Shauna Lee, as they drove to the ranch. When they got close Colt said, "We probably should go right out to the water tanks on the grazing lease."

"That makes sense. Just tell me where to go."

"Take the road through to Loch Levan. There will be sign coming up pretty soon. When we get there, we'll go through the park, across the Gap road and then I'll give you directions to the first tank at the corrals."

"This really is different country compared to the Swift Current area," Brad commented as he drove.

"It is. It's totally unexpected in this part of the world. I love it out here; the hills and the different trees; the different animal species out here. It's like a small piece of the foothills set here in the middle of the flat prairies. My heart is here. So is Frankie's. That's why I'm going to move heaven and earth to get us out to the ranch by next fall."

Brad nodded. "That's where you should be, if you feel that way."

"Speaking of that; thanks for getting in touch with your friend in the Peace River country. Shauna Lee seemed to think he is a really promising prospect for the manager's position."

"I think he could be. But you'll have to decide that for yourself, Colt."

The time went quickly as they traveled to the two water tanks. Brad took measurements and explained how the bases would have to be made so the turbine towers could be anchored and set up solidly.

Both realized that they were working against time as the probability of winter cold loomed on the horizon.

"We can put a conditioner in the cement to deal with a degree of cold, but I'm a lot more comfortable with getting it poured before it starts freezing. I think you get a better strength in the cement."

"These are the critical ones for now. The others at the ranch can be put in next year. Right now they will just be a fill in on the power grid, but their end purpose will be to power a vet clinic for Fran to work out of. That's a couple of years down the road; after this next baby arrives and we get settled in at the ranch."

"Frankie's a vet?" Brad asked with surprise.

"A good one and I want to give her a chance to use her training. She spent years in vet school; she should get to make use of it. I think the locals will use her services once word gets out."

"I never even thought of her being a vet. People are full of surprises."

"Aren't they?" Colt said. "Anyway, I think we can head back to the ranch now. I'll show you where I plan to set up the other two turbines; we might as well cover it all while we are out here."

Brad pulled onto the driveway that lead up to the ranch site, and Colt noticed that Ollie and Patch were across the field, working on the fence. He pointed them out to Brad.

Brad's countenance visibly shifted. "I'd rather not have to see that asshole right now, Colt."

"Patch?" Colt looked across the field. "You probably won't have to. If Ollie comes in, he'll probably leave Patch to work on the fence."

"If I ran into him today, I'd want to strangle the bastard."

"I understand Brad. I know it's got to be awkward for you, but he's a good worker and his resume is sound. Ollie likes him…"

"Colt, when it comes to that man, my give-a-shitter is broken. He was an inexcusably rotten father to Shauna. No damn wonder she wants to forget she ever knew him. The way he treated her; the way he walked out and left her and her mom; those things have scarred her for life."

"I get it Brad. But I'm not going to fire him for what happened years ago between him and Shauna Lee. He works well with Ollie. Shauna Lee is my accountant. She doesn't usually come out here. She never has to see him again."

"That's the amazing part; Shauna said exactly the same thing, but I'm telling you man, I'd kick his ass all the way to Timbuktu. Then, he'd never get a chance to screw with her head again."

Colt looked across the field at Ollie and Patch. He didn't answer, but instead directed Brad to take a turn onto a trail that lead toward the corrals. He showed Brad where he wanted to put the remaining turbines. They discussed the site and agreed it would be a better plan to install them in the spring.

When they were finished, they got back into the truck and Brad made some notes on his ipad. When he was finished he closed the screen down and shut it off. As he started the truck, he noticed Ollie coming across the field on the quad. He noted with relief that Patch had stayed at the fence line. He looked across at Colt. "I guess we'll wait for Ollie to get here."

Colt nodded with a grin. "He'll be here in a moment."

Ollie pulled up next to Colt's window on the passenger side. "Howdy do, Boss." He nodded to Brad too. "Guess you're checking out the turbine sites, eh?"

Colt explained their morning activities. "I see you're fixing fence."

"Yeah, it needs to be done. And Patch has been pretty bummed out since Sunday, so I've been trying to keep him busy and work with him so he doesn't have so much time to think."

Brad clenched his jaw, but kept quiet. Colt just nodded to Ollie. "It's smart to tie up the loose ends like the fences; one more thing to cross off the to-do list.

"I'm going to take Brad up to the bench and show him where we're going to build the house, so I guess we'd better get moving here. I'll give you a call this evening."

As Ollie drove away, Brad put the truck in reverse. His anger was simmering, barely below the surface and Colt knew it. He sought to divert Brad's explosive response to the mention of Patch's feelings, by changing the focus of his thoughts.

"Just drive back to the drive way, and turn right. You won't go far and you'll see a trail to the left. That will take us up onto the bench where we plan to build.

"I haven't gotten too far into thinking about this, but I've been toying with the idea of putting two or three turbines up on the ridge behind the house. I like the idea of the house being energy independent of the power grid, and I'm sure we'll get enough wind up there to make it work."

Brad drove up to the bench in silence, but when they arrived there he looked at the panoramic view and smiled. "You've got it all here, Colt. This is great. What kind of house design are you looking at?"

"We're looking at plans now. We're both pretty much set on a rancher style. It will fit in well up here."

Brad nodded. "I can see it. How big is it going to be?"

"Well, what we are looking at right now, the main floor will be about thirty five hundred square feet. The twins are young, and we're thinking about maybe having another one after this bambino arrives. And then we need an apartment for Ellie. So we'll be able to use that much room and more."

Brad looked up at the ridge above the house. "Are you thinking of putting turbines up there?"

"Yes. What do you think? Will two do the job? Or should I put up three to be safe?"

"I guess that depends on how much you plan to have going on. Three would make a total of seven turbines in all. I'd have to sharpen my pencil a bit, but I'm sure we could work a package deal, and save you quite a bit.

"Not only that, but you probably would be eligible for provincial or federal government green energy grants; in fact you might be able to get both of them. Besides that, you can feed the extra energy into the power grid and it will cover a substantial part of the ranches hydro expenses."

"Well, let's put our heads together over the next couple of weeks and see what we can come up with," Colt agreed. "I'll have Shauna Lee look into what's available for grants too."

Brad nodded in agreement. "We need to get started with putting up the forms and pouring cement out at the water tanks. This weather isn't going to hold forever. It'll be too late to get everything lined up today by the time we get back, but could you go out there with me on Thursday? We could probably do both the sites."

Colt thought for a moment. "I'll make that work. Fran and I have an appointment with the architect tomorrow and I need to get on that too."

They talked amiably as Brad drove toward home. Once they reached the main highway he reached for his cell phone and hit a speed dial. Colt could hear it ringing: then Brad smiled as he spoke into the phone.

"Hi there Tweetie Bird," he said softly. "How are things going today? Are you all right?"

Colt could faintly hear Shauna Lee's laughter, but her words were indistinguishable to him. Brad chuckled. "I'll see you in about two hours. Love you." He closed his phone and sighed. *She's amazing*, he mused to himself.

Colt marvelled to himself at how invested Brad had become in Shauna Lee in such a short time. *Love*, he thought. *There is no accounting for it sometimes*. He smiled as he recalled how hard he and Fran had resisted it. Brad was the exact opposite. He had plunged right in, heart first. *I wonder where Shauna Lee stands on this*.

Frankie and Colt went over the house plans again that evening, comparing notes and looking for anything they had missed. "I'm certain that Mona will have suggestions. She'll look at this with a fresh eye."

Frankie smiled. "Yes, and she's has so much more experience, she

may think of things that never crossed our minds." She hugged him. "I am so excited Colt. Everything is falling into place so neatly." She touched her small baby bulge and Colt rested his hand over hers. "A new baby, a new house, us moving to the ranch. I am so lucky!"

"We are so lucky!" Colt murmured as he kissed her.

# CHAPTER ELEVEN

*S*hauna Lee looked at her watch. It was eleven o'clock. It was Wednesday and the office was slow. She picked up the picture of her and "her" horse, that Brad had put on her desk the first time he'd introduced a 'personal touch' into her office.

She ran her thumb softly over the glass as she looked at it. "Brad," she thought, remembering how defensive and supportive he had been for her when she had met her dad at the ranch. "There's never been anyone like him in my life before."

She set down the picture and reached for the one he had brought in most recently. She smiled softly as she examined it. She had known when he had taken this one. He had put his camera on the tripod and set the timer. Then he had stepped behind her and aligned his face with hers. He had pulled her slightly into him and the camera had caught them in a joyful, laughing moment.

*He makes me smile,* she thought as she stood looking at it. She looked at the other pictures sitting in different spots around the room. "He's determined to build a life for me," she said with a sigh. "He cares so much, it scares me. I'm afraid something will go wrong; that I'll lose him."

The ring of the phone startled her. She reached for the hand set. "Hello."

"Morning, Tweetie Bird. What have you been doing since I saw you two and a half hours ago?"

"You goof," she said softly. "It's been pretty slow so far. But I did some checking on Timothy Bates. Everything he put on his resume checks out; but then of course you knew that. I'm going to suggest that Colt have him come for a personal interview."

"That's a good idea. I'll look forward to seeing him too. Anyway, I wanted to ask you something."

"Oh, what is that?"

"Well, Colt and Frankie have an appointment with an architect later this afternoon. Remember I told you he's going out to the ranch with me tomorrow? I need to discuss a few things with him. Would it be OK with you if I invited them over for supper?"

There was dead silence. Shauna Lee's chest tightened.

"Shauna?"

"It's your house, Brad. You can invite who you want."

"Shauna, it's pretty much been our house these past few weeks. I wanted to ask you how you felt about having them. If it makes you uncomfortable we will go to a restaurant."

Shauna took a deep breath. *Damn.* The silence seemed to hang forever. She knew she should say something. She should tell him it was all right to have them come to the house, but...

"You know sweetie," he said gently. "It has been a long day and I have to leave early tomorrow morning. It's probably best if we just go to a restaurant."

"OK," Shauna Lee said so softly the word was almost a whisper. She was almost overwhelmed with relief. Having people for dinner was too...it was like opening the door, letting people get in too close.

After they said goodbye, she got up and took a couple of files out of the filing cabinet. She stared at the words and figures but nothing registered in her mind. *I'm not being fair to Brad. He would have enjoyed making dinner for Colt and Frankie.*

She reached for the phone and speed dialed Brad's number. It ran three times: four times: five times. He didn't answer. She hung up, guilt forming a knot in her breast. She put down the phone and rested her head in her hands.

"Damn! He does everything for me without hesitation and I...I..."

The phone rang. She reached for it quickly. "Hello?"

"Hi Tweetie Bird; you called."

*Tweetie Bird!* Her eyes misted at the sound of him saying his crazy little pet name for her. "Yes. I've been thinking. Is it too late to invite Colt and Fran for dinner?"

There was a silence. "Why?"

"I'm sorry I acted the way I did. I..I'm...this sort of stuff is hard for me...it's like..."

"I sort of figured that out, sweetheart. It makes you feel too vulnerable?"

"Sort of..." Her eyes glistened with tears. *He understands*, she thought.

"We'll just take little steps." She heard the reassurance in his voice. "I've already talked to Colt and we are going to meet at the Steakhouse at around five o'clock. They want to get home before eight so they can tuck the kids in, so going to the restaurant works better all the way around tonight."

She let out a sigh of relief. "I can leave here any time after four thirty."

"I still have to go to the lumber yard. It'll save time tomorrow if I have all the pieces cut to length."

"OK, I'll be ready when you get here." She hesitated. "Brad...I...I hope you know how...how much I appreciate you."

"I think I do, sweetie." There was a smile in his voice. "I'll see you as soon as I get things finished up here. And Shauna; you know that I love you." Then the phone went dead.

She swallowed hard. She couldn't tell him she loved him; it was just too frightening.

Supper with Colt and Frankie was easier than she had imagined it would be. They were bubbling with excitement about their plans for the new house. Colt and Brad talked about what they needed to do when they went out to the ranch the next day. Shauna Lee filled Colt in on the information she had about Timothy Bates and he told her to set up an interview as soon as possible for them to meet at the farm. These were all impersonal things that she felt totally comfortable with.

She was less at ease with Frankie; she could feel her reaching out to her. She went out of her way to be friendly, even suggesting that they get together for a girls day. *A girl's day? I wouldn't know how to act. And with Frankie? It would be awkward wouldn't it?*

She found herself watching Colt and Frankie interact. *They are so happy* she thought. *Brad was right. They are meant for each other.* She looked at Brad. His eyes met hers and warmth flooded through her. *Could we be like them? Could I be that happy? But what if something goes wrong?* She reached out and touched his arm. He took her hand in his and pulled it under the table, resting it on his thigh, her fingers entwined with his. He squeezed her hand gently.

As they were saying goodbye, Frankie hugged her. Shauna Lee stiffened momentarily. Other than her grandmother years before, she couldn't remember when a woman had shown her affection; had hugged her. *Except for when Frankie hugged me that Saturday.* Her thoughts were conflicting. *It feels good,* she finally admitted, fighting tears. She hugged Frankie back tentatively.

Frankie's lips brushed her cheek as she released her. She smiled as her eyes met Shauna Lee's and she trailed her hand down her arm to her hand. She squeezed it gently and said softly, "Take care."

Then she nodded at Brad and turned to take Colt's arm. "We'd better get going daddy," she said with a smile. "We don't want to take advantage of Ellie. Heaven help us if she went on strike."

Brad was smiling as he put his hand against the small of Shauna Lee's back and guided her to the truck. She was silent and thoughtful as he helped her up into it.

"They are so pumped about life right now," Brad said with a smile. "Everything is coming together for them; the new baby, moving to the ranch, planning the new house. There is some pretty exciting stuff going on there."

Shauna Lee nodded her head. "When I think of where Colt was five years ago; bitter and angry, defensive and determined to never fall in love again...it's good for the soul to see him like he is now. It makes me wonder if..."

"If...?" Brad prompted.

"You know... could I ever be that happy? Could *we* ever..." She stopped, color suffusing her face.

"Could we ever be like them?" he prompted.

She looked away. "I don't know if I could… "

Brad heart lurched. *It hurts to hear you doubt us like that, Shauna.* He sighed. *I'm so certain about us and I'm not giving up, but I can't do this all by myself. Somewhere along the way, you have to begin to trust in us; open up to accept my love and return it.*

They rode in silence the rest of the way home. parked the truck and then went around to help Shauna Lee get out. He lifted her down to stand on the ground, then turned and hooked his thumbs in his back pockets and looked up at the stars in the clear sky.

He tried to shake off his disappointment. *Why is this bothering me so much? I've never doubted us before. I can't now. I love her…but will she ever love me?* He sighed deeply and then turned to find her looking at him. He smiled at her and reached for her hand and they walked to the house.

Shauna Lee saw the pain in his eyes. *I've hurt him,* she thought. *But how can I say yes, when I just don't know if I can give him what he wants? What he needs?* She swallowed hard.

Brad went to the fridge and got himself a beer. It was a reflexive act to his cover his disappointment; to avoid facing her, giving himself time to collect his feelings and open up again to the love he felt; the *unconditional* love he knew he had for her.

He had almost closed the fridge door when he caught himself. He looked at her. "Sorry, do you want one?"

Shauna Lee looked at him, apology in her eyes. She hesitated. The ache in her heart numbed her. She nodded. As he reached into the fridge again, she reflected that sitting and drinking a beer with him might give them time to overcome this painful awkwardness.

Brad cut a lime and pushed half into each bottle. He took one and handed her the other. Then he took her hand and led her to the couch. After they sat down he reached for the remote and turned on the TV.

He flicked through the channels, not really focusing. Finally he found a program about China and settled on it. He looked at Shauna Lee, then sighed heavily as he slid his arm around her shoulder and pulled her against him. He leaned his head against hers, nuzzling her hair.

She snuggled into his shoulder, savouring the warmth of his body against hers, troubled by the tension that still hung between them. She took a couple of sips from the bottle, but she struggled with the pain of knowing that she had hurt him; the fear that lurked in the background that he would give up on her damaged heart and leave her. She tried to force her fears aside, but a tear slipped down her cheek. She tried to stifle them, but more came.

Brad felt a drop fall on the hand that cupped her shoulder. He looked at her. Her eyes were downcast, refusing to meet his. He lifted his hand and brushed it along her cheek. It was wet with tears.

"Sweetheart?"

She shook her head, but a sob slipped out.

"Shauna?" He put down his beer and wrapped her in his arms. "Why are you crying? Was it that hard for you to be with Colt and Frankie tonight? You...you don't still have feelings for Colt, do you?"

She shook her head. "NO!" She sobbed again, rubbing her tears away. "No, definitely not. It's not that."

"Then what...?"

She looked at him, her expression pained. "I'm so sorry; I know I hurt you...and I didn't want too. I...I just..."

Brad suddenly understood. He pulled her against his chest. "Oh sweetie...I'm not going to deny that it hurt to hear you say you didn't know if you could love me like that. It did. I've...It seems like I've waited so long." He tightened his arms momentarily. "But... I realize that I was pushing you again. You were being honest. You didn't just tell me what I wanted to hear, when it's not how you felt. In the end, that would hurt more."

"In the end?" Fear threaded through her. "You mean when you get tired of waiting and give up on me?"

"Sweetheart, no; I promise you, I am in this relationship for the long term. I won't be leaving unless you tell me irrevocably that you don't want me to stay. And then I'd have a hard time letting you go. I love you, Shauna."

He unbuttoned his shirt and took it off. He bunched the back of it in his hand and used it to gently wipe her tears away. Then he tossed it aside and leaned into her, kissing each eye lid. He settled his lips on hers and kissed her gently. It was a kiss of promise, a kiss of under-standing, a kiss of comfort. Sexual arousal was not there.

She gave herself entirely to it, savouring its healing message. She threaded her arms around his neck and relaxed against him. They both absorbed the essence of their closeness. Finally Brad pulled away gen-tly, looking deep into her eyes. "Let's go to bed," he whispered. He stood up and helped her to her feet. They held hands as they walked to the bedroom.

They both undressed and Shauna Lee pulled back the sheet on her side of the bed. She lay down and reached to cover herself, but Brad was there, reaching to tuck it around her. His hand smoothed her hair gently.

Then he went around to his side of the bed and got in and inched across until his body found hers. He slid his arm around her waist, nestling her back against his chest, spooning her. She relaxed against him, savouring the feel of their nakedness touching. She lifted his hand from her waist and kissed it, then put it back, tugging it so he was holding her tight against him. He dropped a kiss on her shoulder. Then they lay quietly as they drifted off to sleep, both thinking that this was how love felt.

The next morning they were up early so Brad could meet Colt at the farm by seven o'clock. They realized that Shauna's car was still at her place, so Brad had to drop her off there on his way out of town. He had walked her to the door and went in with her. She chuckled as he made a tour through the place, making sure everything was all right before he would leave.

When he was satisfied, he kissed her goodbye and made her prom-ise she'd be at his place when he got back, knowing that he would be late. He and Colt would work until dark before they started home. He left after telling her that he would call her at the house when he was on his way into town.

Shauna Lee put on a pot of coffee and looked around. It felt strange to be here. She had spent the last month at Brad's place, only stopping in here to make quick checks periodically, or to grab a few clothes from her closet. She realized that "home" was there with him now, not here in this lonely place.

As she drove to work later she caught herself missing Brad's company, wondering where he was right then. She checked her watch and calculated where he'd be. *Somewhere near Maple Creek if they got away from the farm right away.* She smiled. Brad had planned to slip into the drive through at A&W for a coffee and breakfast sandwich on his way out of town. *He's been doing that a lot lately,* she thought. *He should own shares in the place.*

The office was busy that day and time went by quickly. She contacted Timothy Bates and set up a date for him to meet with Colt at the farm. They had consulted their calendars, and decided to set a date in mid November, after the long weekend. She told him she would double check with Colt and confirm the time.

Her phone rang at about two o'clock. To her surprise it was Frankie. "Hi there, Shauna Lee. I have to run into town to take the architect some more information. I know the guys will be ravenous when they get in. I'm putting on a pot roast for supper and I was thinking...I'll be in town anyway; could I pick you up and bring you out here? The four of us can have dinner together. We'll get to catch up on their day and you can ride back with Brad and keep him company on the way home. I'm pretty certain he'd like that."

Shauna Lee's first instinct was to say "no" and close the door on the invitation. She quickly said, "Oh, I have my car here today."

"Couldn't you drop it off at your place? I could follow you there from your office and pick you up."

Shauna Lee grimaced. *Damn.* But a little voice whispered in the back of her mind. *This would make Brad happy. It won't hurt you. Open up just a little bit, Shauna Lee.* She swallowed hard and heard herself say, "That would work, Frankie. And Brad would be thrilled."

"Good! I'm looking forward to having you come. What time can I pick you up?"

"I've got things pretty much under control here now. I have a meeting with a client at three fifteen. He's just bringing me some paperwork, so it won't be a long one. Any time around four o'clock should be all right. Christina will close up the office at five, if I ask her too."

"That will work out perfect. I'll see you then."

Shauna Lee hung up the phone, misgivings stirring in her mind. She tried to squash them but old habits die hard. "What am I doing?" she wondered. The tentacles of old fears tugged at her. She wanted to phone back with some excuse and cancel. She reached for the phone, but the thought of Brad made her stop. *If I'm going to make things work with Brad, I have to get past this*, she thought. "And I want to make this work," she whispered.

She sat back in her chair thinking about the night before. She remembered the pain in his question. *You…you don't still have feelings for Colt, do you?* That had shocked her.

She hadn't thought of Colt in that way since the day Brad had confronted her, pointing out that it was obvious that Colt and Frankie were meant for each other. She had tried to push that truth away, but deep down she had recognised it.

Slowly Brad's persistence, his unflagging understanding, his declarations of love, had worked a fine crack into the bastion of the lifetime of defences she had built. The fortress hadn't crumbled yet, but she knew he had given her a glimpse of something that she didn't want to lose. She closed her eyes.

Her heart twisted with fear. *He wants love; and he is worthy of love. But am I? Can I truly let all this pain go and freely give him what he needs? It should be easy; he offers me so much. But this fear of losing again…it just keeps coming back. It haunts me.*

She turned back to her desk. "I can do this," she said determinedly. "Going to Colt and Frankie's tonight is a start. I won't let myself be held captive anymore."

When Frankie came to the office, Shauna Lee was ready to leave. She greeted her with a smile, then went to her car and started it. As Frankie followed her to her place, a lump burned in her chest, but she resolved to push it out.

When she got into Frankie's van, she felt like a frightened child; she wasn't in control now, she couldn't just walk away if she wanted to. She'd given up that thread of comfort and security when she'd left her car at her place. But she vowed to take control of her emotions, of her heart, of her mind. This was another step toward a new, happier life. She would make it work.

Frankie saw the uncertainty behind Shauna Lee's smile. *She's uncomfortable.* Frankie smiled warmly, hoping to ease her mind. She concentrated on driving, giving Shauna Lee time to relax. She commented on what a nice day it was and maintained a neutral conversation. Gradually she felt Shauna Lee relax. By the time she turned onto the long, tree lined lane that led onto the farm, the conversation was much easier. Shauna Lee had even laughed a couple of times.

When they went into the house the twins ran to greet Frankie, hanging on her legs and talking excitedly over each other, each one vying to get her attention first. She bent down and encircled them both in her arms, holding them against her breasts in a warm, loving embrace. "Ok kids, we have company here. Remember Shauna Lee? Be nice now and say Hi."

Selena went to Shauna Lee and reached out her hand. Shauna Lee took the child's hand, looking into her smiling, beautiful face. Her dark eyes were dancing with mischief.

Selena tugged on her hand. Her little body twisted with exuberance as she braced herself to pull. "Come on," she commanded with a giggle. Frankie had picked up her son and nodded when their eyes met. Shauna Lee gave herself up to the child's persistence and followed her into the kitchen.

Selena guided her to a chair at the table and patted the seat, indicating that Shauna Lee should sit down. "Would you like some coffee?" she asked in a matter of fact way.

Shauna Lee chuckled and gave Frankie a quick look. Frankie nodded. Shauna Lee looked into those sparkling happy eyes again. "That would be very nice, Selena."

Selena whirled to her mother. "Coffee, mom." She pointed to Shauna Lee. "She wants coffee."

Frankie bent to put Sam on the floor. "It's coming right up, Selena. I'm proud of you for being such a good hostess. Do you want to help me make it?"

Selena ran to pull a chair away from the table and slide it up to the cabinet, next to the coffee maker. "Can I put the coffee in mommy? I know how. Four scoops. Isn't that right?"

Shauna Lee watched with interest. *This is how it should be*, she thought remembering her 'children should be seen and not heard' childhood. Suddenly she felt fingers tug on her pant leg. She looked down to see Sam looking up at her, his big blue eyes calm but interested. "U monkey?"

Her mind flashed to her last visit and her heart did a somersault. *He remembers!* She reached down and picked him up, setting him on her lap. He twisted so that he could look into her eyes. He touched her face thoughtfully and smiled. "I 'ike oou."

For Shauna Lee time seemed to stand still. She took his hand in hers and lifted it to her lips. She held him close and whispered. "I like you too."

Selena was still bubbling over and talking to her, but Frankie had turned in time to see the interaction between Shauna Lee and her son. For that fleeting moment, Shauna Lee had let her guard down. Frankie saw the pain and longing in Shauna Lee's face as she hugged the child and whispered to him.

*There's so much more to her than we know,* Frankie mused thoughtfully as she took two coffee cups down from the cupboard. She poured the coffee when it was ready and carried the cups to the table. "You take it black, don't you?"

Shauna Lee nodded and let Sam go. He looked into her eyes and smiled, then slid off her lap. He walked over to his mom and looked at her solemnly. "She 'ikes me mommy."

Frankie smiled at her son. "You are a very special little boy, so I can see why she likes you, Sam." He leaned on his mother's knees and stuck his thumb in his mouth. He looked at Shauna Lee for a long moment. Then he smiled and it was like sunshine in Shauna Lee's heart. He pointed at her. "Oou monkey! I 'ike oou."

Shauna Lee smiled as she lifted the cup Frankie had sat in front of her. The eyes she lifted to meet Frankie's had the shimmer of unshed tears. "You have such sweet kids. And you are such a good mother. Not all children are so fortunate."

"Thank you Shauna Lee. These children," she touched her tummy, including the new one, "they are such a gift. Colt and I are so lucky."

The twins ate early and Ellie ate with them. Afterwards Frankie took them upstairs and bathed them. After they were in their pyjamas they came back down stairs to play until Colt got home to say good-night and tuck them in.

Sam came over and took Shauna Lee by the hand. "Come," he said tugging on her hand. Shauna Lee smiled at him and stood up. He pulled on her hand, leading her to a box of toys in the family room. He sat down on the floor and patted the spot beside him as he looked up at her. "Oou sit."

She smiled and sank down on the floor beside him. He took a toy tractor out of the box and showed it to her. Shauna Lee smiled. Then he took the toy and pushed it around on the floor. "vrrrrm." he said looking at her as he moved it. "Daddy goes like this."

Frankie watched Shauna Lee play with her son. *Colt said she swore she never wanted to have children, but look at her. She's good with them.* She watched as Selena introduced Shauna Lee to her stable of toy horses. Shauna Lee picked up a grey horse and looked it over. "What is this horse's name, Selena?"

"His name is Starlight."

"Do you ride your daddy's horses?"

"No; not yet. Mommy says they are too big for us to ride yet. Isn't that right, mommy?"

Frankie looked up at her and smiled. "Yes, they are, Selena. This summer we will check out the ones at the ranch. There may be one there for you guys to ride."

Frankie turned to Shauna Lee. "Do you ride Shauna Lee?"

"From the time I was eight, until I was almost fourteen, I rode all the time. Brad has a couple of horses and I've gone for a short ride a couple of times on one of them."

Sam sidled up against her, tapping her on the arm. "Whatss oou 'orses name?"

"My horses name was Poko. He was my best friend and I loved him."

Selena took some plastic panels for toy corrals out of the toy box. "Will you help us build a corral?"

Shauna Lee slid down and rolled over on her stomach. She began to fit the pieces together, helping Selena make them into a corral. Sam brought a toy barn to her and set it in front of her. She smiled at him as he plunked down beside her.

When Colt and Brad came in the door, the first thing they saw was the three of them playing on the floor. Brads eyes flew to meet Frankie's. She read his surprise and nodded as she smiled at him.

As soon as the twins heard Colt's voice they jumped up and ran to greet him. Sam was carrying the grey horse by its back leg. "Dad, Dad." He held the horse up to show him. "Is Poko." He pointed to Shauna Lee. " Poko iss 'er 'orse."

Shauna Lee had stood up. Her eyes met Brads. She smiled softly as he winked at her." *She told them her horse's name was Poko,* he marvelled. *Oh, Tweetie Bird. You are making progress.*

He walked over and put his arms around her, dropping a light kiss on her lips. "This is nice …finding you here. Now I don't have to drive home alone. Frankie told Colt you'd come out with her."

She nodded. "It's been…fun."

He squeezed her shoulders. His grey eyes were bright. "I'm proud of you," he whispered.

Frankie had the table set in no time. Ellie had gone to her trailer earlier, so Colt took the twins upstairs and tucked them into bed. The four of them lingered over dinner, discussing the events of the day.

Finally, Colt yawned and looked at his watch. "Well I don't know about the rest of you, but this has been a long day and I'm ready to hit the sack. It's nine thirty already, and it'll be another early morning tomorrow. We have to go back to the ranch and finish the job."

He looked at Brad. "Are you sure you don't want to spend the night?"

Brad shook his head. "It's not that far. Shauna Lee has to go back to town anyway."

Colt nodded. "It's your call, man. We are ready to pour the cement now. We shouldn't need all day to do those two forms. Maybe we can make it a little later. How about getting here at eight instead of seven?"

"Let's see how morning feels. I'll give you a call when I'm leaving Swift Current. I'd sooner get to work earlier and make sure we get the job done. We can always come home early, but I'd rather not have to go back on the weekend."

When they got to Swift Current, Brad and Shauna Lee stopped at her place to pick up her car. She looked at him and smiled softly. "You're tired. We could spend the night here you know. There are no groceries so you'd have to stop at A&W in the morning again, but we are right here and we could be in bed in 10 minutes."

Brad yawned. "You are right. It'll simplify everything in the morning too. And you won't have to drive your car home alone now." He parked the truck on the street and they went inside.

"Brad, do you want me to throw your clothes in the wash? I'll put them in the dryer first thing in the morning, before I make the coffee. They'll be dry in half an hour or a bit more."

He looked at his jeans and his shirt. "That might be a good idea. They are a little worse for wear."

When Shauna Lee came back from the laundry room, Brad had turned back the sheets and was already in bed. He had fallen asleep while he waited for her. She smiled as she turned off the light and slid in beside him. He stirred in his sleep and mumbled something as his arm slid around her.

The next morning Shauna Lee was awake by five o'clock. *I can't believe I am awake this early!* She swung herself out of bed and darted into the laundry room to put Brad's clothes into the dryer. Then she wandered out to the kitchen and made coffee.

Humming she looked through her cupboards. "Pretty bare," she murmured to herself. "And there isn't any milk or eggs. Ahhh, what's this?" She pulled a plastic package off the top shelf. "Buttermilk pancake mix. All it needs is water." She smiled. "I know it's almost sacrilege, but we could have breakfast together."

She opened the sealed package and measured out the ingredients. She added an extra teaspoon of baking powder and water and stirred it with a whip. As the electric griddle heated, she rifled through the freezer and found some bacon. She popped it into the microwave to thaw, while she poured four portions of pancake mix on the hot griddle.

She was intent on her cooking and did not hear Brad slip up behind her. She jumped with a squeal as he slid his arms around her waist, pulling her back against his chest. "Are you sick?" he asked, reaching up to feel her forehead. "Singing in the kitchen, while you're cooking… at five thirty in the morning?" He stuck his finger in the pancake mix. "And you told me you didn't have any groceries….what is this?"

"Oh, it's just some of my magic."

"Hmmm…I never thought of your magic showing up at the stove at five thirty in the morning." He turned her toward him. "This is where I've always found your magic." He pulled her close and settled his mouth on hers. The kiss was deep and passionate. His response was immediate. So was hers.

"Breakfast or dessert?" she whispered.

"Both?" he whispered, sweeping her into his arms.

"Turn off the grill," she said with a giggle.

He pulled the electrical cord from the plug in the wall and carried her to the bed. He slipped off her housecoat and let it fall to the floor. He laid her on the bed and they made love, fast and furious and passionately. In ten minutes it was over except for the deep breathing, the little shivers of ecstasy and the marvellous afterglow.

"You are going to be late."

"I'm sort of the boss. Colt won't mind if I'm late; he even suggested it. And since you went to all that effort to make breakfast, I'm going to eat it."

"It's just a mix," she confessed.

"No; not just any mix. It's a mix that the woman I love made with a song on her lips, after she dried my clothes...I hope."

She smiled. "I didn't forget! I'll do almost anything for the most important man in my life. Even get up at five o'clock in the morning to dry his clothes and find a way to make breakfast so that I can share it with him."

He pulled her close and kissed her again. "If I don't get out of here, I might have to stay at the ranch to finish the job up tomorrow. That wouldn't be good for us...because I plan to do this properly tonight; slow and simmering, not like this morning's firestorm." He sat up and swung his legs off the bed. "And if I have to stay at the ranch...they'll have to tie me up to keep me from pounding your old man to pulp."

"Brad, he's not worth it."

She went into the kitchen and plugged in the grill. Then she opened the package of bacon and put some on to cook. Brad was dressed when he came out and found her going through the fridge looking for pancake syrup. She found a bottle with half an inch in the bottom. She waved it triumphantly, grinning as she opened it and put it on the table.

Brad went to the cupboard and took out two plates and two mugs. She smiled at him as she went to the cutlery drawer. She smiled even broader as she picked out two knives, two forks and two spoons.

"What are you thinking?"

She looked sheepish and shrugged her shoulder.

"Fez up!" he said, wrapping his arms around her.

"Just silliness."

He looked into her smiling eyes. "You are going to make me really late, Tweetie Bird."

"Two plates, two mugs, two knives, two forks, two spoons, the two of us, here or there. Just silliness."

"That's not silliness; it makes perfect sense to me!"

She took the pancakes out of the oven and put the bacon on a plate, then took it to the table. She bent down and whispered in his ear, "Eat. You've got five minutes until you have to hit the road. I want you home tonight."

They ate breakfast and finished their coffee and then Shauna Lee stood up and led him to the door. He kissed her deeply before he put his shoes on.

She groaned and then pulled away. She reached down and stroked the hardness behind his zipper. "Hey buddy, take your friend and get him out of here. He has to finish the job at the ranch, so he can get home and keep his promise to us tonight."

He grinned as he rubbed himself. "Sorry friend, she's throwing us out." He turned away to put his shoes on, grumbling good-naturedly about having lovers nuts all day.

She laughed as he put his hand on the doorknob. "Let's see if you fall asleep tonight as soon as you hit the pillow like you did last night."

His hand snaked out and grabbed her wrist, pulling her close. "I love it when you're happy like this," he said dropping his lips on hers for one more kiss. Then he went out the door.

She called after him. "Be sure to phone Colt right away. Tell him to meet you running when you pull in at the farm. And hurry home. Tell your friend I'll even leave the office early if you're back!"

His walk turned into a run. He blew her a kiss as he jumped into the truck. It roared to life and he spun his wheels, snaking down the street until he was out of site.

Shauna Lee was chuckling as she went inside. She looked around the room. "Yesterday this place seemed so empty, so uninviting. But this morning it feels like home. He makes any place feel like that when I'm with him."

Shauna Lee was in a good mood all day. She hoped Brad would make it home early but he didn't call until three thirty that afternoon. "We are at Maple Creek, sweetie. I'm thinking about kicking Colt out at the highway and making him hoof it to the farm so I can hurry on home."

She chuckled. "You can't do that. It'll just take half an hour to go in and drop him off and get back to the highway."

She could hear Colts voice in the back ground, then Brad came back. "He says I'd better rethink that. He hasn't paid me yet."

"Shall I meet you at your place or mine?"

"Sweetie, no offence, but I really prefer the king sized bed."

"I'll meet you there and I'll order in a pizza for supper," she teased.

"That will be fine; I'm more interested in desert anyway."

"See you later," she said softly.

Shauna Lee left work early, with Christina's promise to close up the office for the weekend. She stopped at Safeway and bought a pork tenderloin roast, as well as some broccoli and a head of Romaine lettuce. She selected two smooth, new potatoes for roasting and made her way through the till. Then she headed home to Brad's place.

When Brad got home the house was filled with the savoury smells. The table was set and candles flickered in the dim room. He sniffed appreciatively. "I can see we need to create a morning firestorm more often." He pulled her into his arms and nuzzled her hair. "What a welcome home, he whispered. "I've been thinking about you and me and this, all the way home." He rubbed himself against her so she could feel his arousal.

"Dessert first?" she asked.

"I want to so badly. But you've gone to all this trouble." He shook his head. "And I am hungry too…for food, that is. I don't want to rush anything tonight. Not this," he said rubbing against her again. "And I don't want to rush supper either. Let's relax and enjoy it while we eat here in the candlelight."

Shauna Lee laid her head against his chest. "We have the whole evening." She stepped back, running her finger along his bottom lip. "I still have to steam the broccoli. Can I get you a beer or a glass of wine to help you relax while it cooks?"

"I'll have a beer."

Shauna Lee went to the fridge and took out a bottle of Corona. She grabbed a lime and cut it, then slipped a piece into the bottle and handed it to him. Then she poured herself a glass of wine. She turned on the steamer, and took his hand.

"Let's sit on the couch. We can nurse our drinks while you tell me how your day went."

He sat down and pulled her beside him, tugging her to his side. He bent to kiss her, but she shook her head. "Enjoy your drink, and tell me about your day. Consider it a bit of foreplay before we eat, OK?"

He groaned. "I've been in foreplay mode ever since I left this morning."

She giggled. "You're the one who was worried that I would let sex take over our relationship."

He shook his head. "No…I said it would take over our relationship; I didn't say that you would be the only one to let that happen. I knew how much I wanted you, too."

"I want to hear about your day."

He put a hand on her thigh and held her next to him. "What do you want to know? We went to the water tanks and poured cement at both sites for the turbine bases." He tugged at the crotch of his jeans as he looked at her. "And I had lover's nuts that ached all day. I also had trouble concentrating all day, just like I am right now."

He put his Corona on the end table at his elbow; then he took her glass of wine away from her and sat it next to it. "Damn it woman," he groaned. "You are torturing me." He pulled her on top of him as he slid down on the couch and drew her into a passionate kiss. She reciprocated. Then she let her hand slip down to his bulging crotch, moving further down to massage his scrotum through his jeans. He broke the kiss with a gasp.

A beep from the steamer signalled that the broccoli was cooked.

"To hell with the broccoli," he rasped. He tugged at the jogging pants she had changed into when she came home, taking her panties with them. She wiggled to help him get them off and toss them aside.

She was fumbling with the button at the waist of his jeans. He pushed her hands aside and dispensed of the jeans and his shorts. He took her there on the couch in a firestorm of passion. In moments they had both spent their lust and lay half on, half off the couch, savouring their release.

He rolled onto the floor, pulling her down on top of him. He sighed as he ran his hand through her hair. "Oh, Tweetie Bird," he whispered. They lay entangled, catching their breath, waiting for the pounding of their hearts to subside. Lethargy slipped over them, the release of the height of their sexual tension leaving them both exhausted.

Fifteen minutes later Brad kissed her forehead. "We'd better get up; the broccoli will be mush."

She giggled, rubbing her head against his chest. "To hell with the broccoli," she said softly.

"I'm hungry now."

They slowly got up and got dressed. Brad shook his head as he looked at her. "What have I gotten myself into? I'm thinking I'm in a way over my head."

She slapped his butt. "Which one; the big one or the little one?" she teased. He made a grab for her but she eluded him and went into the kitchen.

She took the meat out of the warmer and set it on the counter. Then she reached for the carving knife and laid it next to it, smiling as she looked at him and motioned to them. He sauntered around the counter and took out a plate, gently slapping her hip as he passed her. Grinning, he picked up the knife and started to carve the meat.

Shauna Lee took baked potatoes from the warmer and put them on a plate. She put the broccoli in a bowl and brought the salad from the fridge. Then she retrieved Brad's beer and her glass of wine from the end table. "Do you want a glass of wine?" she asked.

He looked at the table and smiled. "Anything that sumptuous deserves wine. I'll finish the beer later." He walked to the cupboard and got another wine glass, then carried the meat to the table and sat down across from her. "You've out done yourself, Tweetie Bird. This looks great."

They relaxed and took their time, enjoying the meal; settling into normal couple talk. The sexual tension had been relieved; Brad was able to think clearly now and willingly elaborated on the work that he and Colt had finished out at the ranch. They were sitting back, enjoying a cup of coffee when Brad looked at her and chuckled. "The twins were outside with Frankie when I dropped Colt off. They have put it together that you are with me now. Sam asked about you."

Shauna Lee looked surprised. "What did he say?"

"Oou monkey? Wheres oou monkey?"

She laughed. "He is so cute. You just have to love him."

"He's no dummy. At first I wondered if he was a little slow," Brad commented. "But Selena is so advanced for her age that I think she makes him seem that way."

"She is so hyper. He is so calm and laid back; they are two totally different personalities."

"Well, he sure likes you." Brad smiled softly. "And from what I saw last night, the feeling is mutual."

She looked at her cup for a moment. "I like both of them, but all I have to do is look into his calm blue eyes and…he touches me here." She placed her hand over her heart. Her look was wistful, but there were no tears.

"That's good, sweetheart," he said softly, reaching out to touch her hand. "I could tell you were enjoying them last night when we came home. It made my heart stop for a moment; seeing you down there playing on the floor with them. Sam was sitting so close to you, leaning on you, watching you and Selena playing with the horses. He was holding the grey one; when he called it Poko, I knew you had told him about your horse."

She turned her hand over and entwined her fingers with his. "It's odd, but it was easy to tell Selena and Sam about him and how much I had loved him. Of course I didn't…"

He shook his head as he squeezed her hand gently. "Of course not."

# CHAPTER TWELVE

$\mathscr{S}$aturday morning Brad and Shauna Lee awoke to a beautiful fall day. The morning sun streamed in through the bedroom window. They shifted onto their backs and looked at each other. Shauna Lee reached for his hand and threaded her fingers through his. "Good morning," she said softly. He smiled and raised her hand to his lips. He kissed the back of it gently, then turned it over and slowly licked the palm, with a glint in his eyes as he measured her reaction.

Heat flared in her instantly and she tried to pull away, but he held her hand firmly, licking, then twirling his tongue into its softness. She turned into him, squirming against his assault on her senses.

"Brad." It was a plea.

"What?" he teased.

"You know what."

"Tell me."

"You're driving me crazy."

He pulled her on top of him, smiling as he heard her intake of breath when she landed on his erection. He adjusted his body until her legs straddled over him. He arched his back pushing up against her until he found her soft moistness. He probed until he gained entrance. Then he pushed her up until she was sitting over him, enveloping him, taking him into her. She moaned, clenching around him. Then he turned, holding her tight, rolling on top of her.

He kissed her as he withdrew, trailing his lips along her neck, across her breasts, down over her stomach; no place was sacred. She answered him with equal passion. They kissed, touched, probed, and sucked until they were both crying with need, wound tight in anticipation. Brad kept bringing them to the brink of ecstasy, then pulling back, letting them coast down to start over again.

Shauna Lee was whimpering. She wiggled and turned until she had him beneath her. Then she pushed herself over him, moving deeply, quickly until she found the release she sought. He cried out as he found it too. She collapsed on him as he enfolded her in his arms.

"You horny animal," she whispered. "Jeeze, I'm going to get a chastity belt. It's not safe to be around you."

He chuckled. "I dare you! In two minutes, you'll be searching for the key so you can get it off."

She nipped his shoulder with her teeth.

"Oh, Tweetie Bird, who would have imagined we would be so well matched."

"Yeah, especially since you refused to have sex with me for so long that I was beginning to wonder if you were gay."

"That was a low blow. But I think we've cleared up that misconception now," he said lazily.

They drifted languidly in the morning sun that shone on the bed. Finally Shauna Lee stirred. She lifted her head and looked at him. "People die in bed, you know."

"I am certain I've died once or twice already. I've seen a golden haired angel. I'm sure I have."

She tickled him. "You're mistaken. This angel has just turned into a devil…a hungry devil." She hit him with a pillow and then jumped out of bed. "I'm going to take a shower. Haul your ass out of there or I'll go to A&W by myself."

Brad laughed as he got up and headed for the shower. He was sitting in the kitchen when Shauna Lee came down the hall. He smiled at her as he stood up and held out his hand to her. "Come on, you little devil."

He drove downtown and past the A&W. He grinned when she threw him a questioning look. "I need a real breakfast."

Brad stopped in front of Smitty's Pancake House. "It's time to eat." He glanced at his watch. "It's ten minutes after twelve. I guess this is lunch!"

They shared light hearted banter as they ate. When they were finished Brad reached across the table and touched her hand. He was smiling. "I love it when you are like this."

She wrinkled her nose at him, but her heart was light and happiness bubbled out of her. "Like this?"

"All bubbly and happy."

She squeezed his hand. "I have you to thank for that, Brad."

"I'm just playing the supporting role, sweetie; you are doing the hard work." He stroked her fingers with his thumb. "I'm so proud of you, Shauna."

She looked down at their joined hands. "Thank you. I am trying. I want to…" She looked up at him. "I want to make this work. I want to trust. I want to be able to give you what you want; what you give me so freely. I want to be able to love you, Brad."

He leaned forward and kissed her hand. "You already do sweetheart. You already give me what I want; what I need. Shall we go?"

He helped her into the truck, shut the door and got in on his side. He looked at her as he reached to turn the key. Her eyes were swimming in tears. He slid over and pulled her close. "What's wrong, Shauna?" he asked softly.

She smiled tremulously. "Nothing, Brad. These are happy tears."

"Oh…" He kissed her gently. "So, uh…" *Happy tears… Tweetie Bird, you just threw me off track,* he thought as he looked into her tear washed eyes. "Well…It's a beautiful day. We aren't likely to get many more like this before winter sets in. What would you like to do? "

"Can we go home and go for a ride on the horses?"

He tousled her hair. "I like that idea."

They took the horses out through the gate at the back of the horse pasture and followed the trail to the gently rolling fields. They rode in companionable silence, enjoying the crisp fresh air and the serenity of being away from everything else.

Shauna Lee sat astride her horse and threw her arms wide open, embracing the world. "I love this; total solitude: no sounds of traffic: no telephones: no computers!" She turned to smile at him, happiness overflowing.

"I know what you mean. I get that same feeling when I go hunting in the mountains. Dad and I ride away back off the beaten track. You feel like no else has ever been there. The mountains are so majestic, the air so clean and the scenery so spectacular.

"It's like being transported into a totally different world. For two weeks we become different people; I always think we become the people we really are meant to be. Life is simple, with no outside pressures. It recharges my batteries. One day I'd like to take you with me."

Shauna shook her head. "I couldn't go hunting."

Brad looked out over the fields. "Shauna, man has been a hunter for centuries. Dad and I always use the meat we take. How can I explain it to you? For us, it's almost a spiritual thing; being so close to nature; to the creator."

"So why can't you just go out into the mountains?"

"I could. But I'd miss pitting myself against the animals. They are cunning and they have instincts that man can never equal. Spotting a goat or a herd of caribou on a mountain ridge across a valley is only the beginning of an arduous journey.

"You can ride your horse so far, but after that you are on your own. You are the one on foreign terrain. They are right at home and they know the trails. They are sure footed and travel a lot faster than you ever can.

"Its damn hard work, often outright dangerous, when you are climbing high up in the mountains but it's such a thrill when you stalk them and beat them at their own game. In truth there have been many times when I've dragged my ass back into camp, so exhausted that I've almost been afraid that I would collapse on the trail before I got there and I've never even gotten close to them. But I'm driven by the challenge, and I'll go out again the next day."

She looked at him thoughtfully. "I could be interested in going for the trip, without a gun."

He shook his head. "That would be foolish sweetie; certain animals see everything as prey, including humans. You need a gun for your own protection." He looked thoughtful. "But we could take a camera along if you wanted to go into the mountains with me, and make picture taking the main reason for being out there. I'd love to share that experience with you."

"Did you go this year?"

Brad shook his head. "No, I was too busy, but who knows; maybe *we'll* go to the mountains next year and hunt with a camera, but we'll take a gun along for a back-up in case we need it." He glanced at his watch. "We'd better start for home. It's four o'clock already. It'll be getting dark soon."

"I hate for this day to end." Her face was relaxed and beaming. "I've enjoyed this ride so much. I have always ridden alone before; it was wonderful to be able to share it with you."

They took their time on the way home and it was dusk when they got back to the corral. Brad unsaddled his horse and took the saddle to the tack room in the barn. Shauna Lee slid off her horse and petted it, telling it how much she loved it.

Brad handed her a curry comb, then poured a measure of grain in the trough for each animal. While the horses ate, Brad and Shauna Lee curried them, lifting their coats to allow fresh air to move through the hair and release the moisture and salt from their sweat, cooling the animal naturally. The horses' postures changed, reflecting their appreciation.

Darkness had settled in by the time Brad and Shauna Lee put away the grain pail and the curry combs. They joined hands as they walked the along the path to the house. When they reached the backdoor, Brad slid his arm around her shoulder. "This has been a great day, all the way around hasn't it?"

Shauna Lee tilted her head against his shoulder. "It has been incredible. Thank you, Brad."

He squeezed her shoulder gently, then opened the door and let them inside.

That night they ate leftovers from the night before. Afterwards they each took a bottle of beer and settled on the couch to watch TV. Brad surfed through the channels without finding anything that caught his eye. He handed the remote to Shauna Lee. She clicked on CSI and snuggled against him to watch.

In minutes she noticed a change in his breathing. He had fallen asleep.

Hours later Brad stirred and looked at his watch. It was one o'clock in the morning. Shauna Lee was snuggled against him, sound asleep. His shirt was damp where she had drooled on it as she slept. He eased himself away from her letting her slide to the seat. He stood up and worked the kinks out of his limbs, before he lifted her in his arms and carried her into the bedroom.

He hesitated deciding what he should do. He laid her on top of the bed, unbuttoned the waist of her jeans and eased the zipper down to make her more comfortable. He reached for a comforter that lay on the chair in the corner and placed it over her. He took off his jeans and socks, then eased himself under the comforter and moved over to lie against her. She automatically rolled onto her side and eased her back against his chest.

He slipped his arm around her waist, a soft smile curving his lips. *It's habit all ready…like coming home.* Sleep claimed him in moments.

Sunday morning they awakened to another clear and beautiful day. Shauna Lee stretched and then realized that she must have fallen asleep watching CSI. She turned in Brad's arms and traced her finger along his lips. His eyes remained closed, but he smiled. "Are you awake?"

"Well," he said lazily. "I am now."

"What time did you bring us to bed?"

"One o'clock"

"Are you serious?"

"Would I lie?" he asked sleepily, his eyes still closed.

"Yeah, you might; but I believe you. I must have just died!"

"Well, you were out like a light, but you were still breathing so I took that as a good sign."

She pinched his nose gently. His eyes opened slightly as he grabbed her hand. "You are asking for trouble, Tweetie Bird."

She tickled his ribs. "What kind of trouble?"

He moved to grab her. "Damn," he groaned.

"What?"

"I'm sore in places I forgot existed. I haven't been on a horse for a while."

She chuckled. "Poor baby; I suggest you soak in a hot bath to loosen up. I'll run the tub for you and then I'll make breakfast."

She went into the ensuite and started to run the tub full of warm water. She looked through the storage cupboards and found a small bag of Epson salts pushed into the back. *That man is full of surprises! Imagine him having Epson Salts,* she thought. She opened the bag and poured about half of it into the tub. She reached in with her hand and stirred the water to be sure it fully dissolved.

She stepped back to look in the bedroom. Brad was standing up, bending and stretching his muscles. "The tub is waiting."

He looked at her. "I'm stretching the stiffness out. I'll be OK."

"You dumb ass! Get in here. I've run the tub and wasted half a bag of Epson Salts in it. I'm going to be really ticked off if you don't use it."

He grinned and walked toward her. "You're cute when you get mad."

She walked to his side and delivered a light kick to his backside. "I'm serious. Get in there and soak for at least fifteen minutes. It'll do wonders for you."

She heard him chuckle as she left the room. She went to the kitchen and made a pot of coffee. She poured a cup for herself and considered what she could make for breakfast. "I'm not feeling creative this morning. In fact, I don't feel like doing this now, but I guess I'd better suck it up."

When Brad came into kitchen, she was browning hamburger in a pan. She had tossed in chopped onion, diced red and green peppers, a minced clove of garlic and added a generous helping of Taco spice and salt and pepper. She had another pan on the grill heating.

"What have we got here?" he asked, looking over her shoulder.

"A surprise. How do you feel now?"

"You were right. Soaking in the tub helped a lot." He lifted her chin and dropped a quick kiss on her lips. "Thanks for looking after me." He got a spoon and dipped it into the hamburger mixture. "Uhmm. Taco…mexican flavour. That's good."

He watched her whip two eggs with a fork, add salt and then pour it into the second pan. She pulled the mixture into the middle until it was starting to set.

"What kind of an omelette is this? I assume the hamburger mix is the filling?"

"It's a Mexican omelette. You put salsa and sour cream on it. I ordered it in a restaurant once and I liked it. I've kind of guessed at the recipe. I hope it turned out all right."

He reached out and took her hand. "It'll be wonderful. The hamburger tasted good, so let's try it. I'm hungry."

They took their first few bites. Brad lay down his fork and looked at her. "This is really good, Shauna. You'll have to make this again. I really like it."

"Are you serious?"

"Deadly. You never fail to amaze me. My mother would like this recipe."

Shauna Lee smiled as warmth from his praise flooded through her.

He picked up his fork and started to eat again. When he finished, he pushed back his plate and picked up his coffee. He smiled at her as he spoke. "Speaking of my mom; I've been thinking about Christmas, Shauna. How would you feel about going to my folks for Christmas this year? I'd like you to meet my family."

Shauna Lee tensed.

Brad shook his head. "Don't stress about it now, sweetheart," he said softly. "We've got a while to think about it before we have to decide. And if it makes you too uncomfortable to go for Christmas, we'll go another time. We can stay here or go somewhere warm."

"That isn't fair to you," she protested. "You should go to see your family at Christmas time."

"No. I'm going to be with you; where ever that is. You are my priority now. What do you usually do for Christmas?"

"Not much. Christmas has never meant anything to me. Sometimes I've just stayed at home; a few times I have caught a last minute trip to Mexico or somewhere warm."

"Well Tweetie Bird, Christmas is a big deal to me; I'm going to have so much fun sharing it with you!"

She smiled. "I've never had anyone to share the holidays with for years, but you have a way of opening new doors for me. I'm sure it will be fun!"

"Count on it!" He looked out the window. "You know...it looks like today is going to be another great day. What shall we do?"

She gave him a wicked grin. "We could go riding again."

He grimaced. "I was thinking of something less painful." He frowned. "You rode bareback all afternoon; I cannot understand why you are not in major pain. I had a saddle for support and I was damn sore this morning."

She stood up and reached over to tweak his ear. "You've done some pretty serious riding out of the saddle the past couple of days. Maybe that's what has caught up with you."

Brad slapped her butt lightly and grinned. "Careful..." he said softly.

She looked deep into his eyes. "You're too sore to back that up," she teased. "So what were you about to suggest we do today...since you don't want to ride?"

He stood up and pulled her to him. "Well, soaking in the tub took away most of the pain; I think I've changed my mind. I could be interested in a ride."

"Well let's go then," she said turning toward the back door.

He pulled her back against him. "No, no. I don't want to spend all day in a saddle. But..." He rubbed against her.

Her eye's twinkled. "Oh! I put my chastity belt on this morning. It won't unlock until nine o'clock tonight." She feigned regret. "So we'll have to go to plan C, I guess. What else did you have in mind?"

"I'll bet I can get it off without much trouble."

Shauna Lee shook her head. "You pervert! Now who is letting sex take over the relationship? It would be a shame to squander this beautiful day. What else were you thinking about?"

He kissed her softly. "You intend to make me cry uncle don't you?"

"Until tonight; consider it a day of foreplay! So where are we going?"

He tugged at the crotch of his jeans. "Hey, big guy" he ran his fingers up and down the bulge behind the zipper of his jeans. "I think she's serious. We're going to have to tough this out; I'm sorry about the lover's nuts, again."

She laughed at him, and gathered up the dishes on the table. As she put them in the dish washer, Brad put away the sour cream, salsa and ketchup.

"So, what are we doing?" she asked as she wiped the table.

"I've never been out to the 'Big Muddy Badlands'. Have you?"

She shook her head. "Where are they?"

"About two hours south east of town. It would be a nice drive and we'd get to see some new country. There's lots of history in the area. There's a natural formation called Castle Butte; it apparently stands out there all by its self; sort of a mini mountain in the middle of a desert like area.

"There are some caves out there too. American outlaws used to come across the U.S. border into Canada and hide out in them. I checked the area out on the internet a while ago. There was mention of Butch Cassidy and the Sundance Kid, and some other guy."

He snapped his fingers, trying to remember. "What's his name... Sam Kelly! It said he enlarged a wolf den for his living quarters and the cave is suppose to still be there, pretty much as he left it. He was into a lot of shit across in the U.S., but he and his gang specialized in stealing horses and cattle. They would hide them in caves close by for a while and then they would take them back and sell them."

Shauna Lee's eyes sparkled. "Good grief; the original wild west!"

"Part of it anyway; so, are you up to it?"

"Absolutely. Should we pack a lunch and some coffee?"

"No, we'll go to a little place called Coronach for lunch. There are a couple of restaurants there. We'll find out where to go from there."

"Let's go then. I'll grab my purse and a jacket and put my runners on."

When they went to the truck, Brad took her hand and led her to the driver side. "I want you in here, right beside me; nice and close."

She smiled as he helped her up into the cab. His hand lingered on her waist and slid down over her hip as she got in. She eased under the steering wheel and past the gearshift. He got in and started the engine. Then he dropped his hand on the inside of her thigh and pulled her over against him. He grinned as he reached for the gearshift and eased it down until his hand was resting between her legs.

His eyes twinkled with mischief. "I'm going to start working on that day of foreplay right away. I'm thinking we can melt that chastity belt before too long. We haven't stopped on a back road and made love yet."

"You're a sex maniac."

"That's your fault. You've made me aware of what I've been missing all these years. I…we've got a lot of catching up to do."

He eased out of the driveway and headed down town. He stopped to fill the truck with diesel and brought two cups of coffee back with him after he had paid for it inside. He handed them to her and she put them in the cup holders.

He got in beside her and turned the key. Before he put the truck in gear he leaned over and dropped a light kiss on her lips, teasing them with his tongue. Then he shifted the gears and pulled back out onto the highway. When he had shifted the last gear, he let his hand rest on the seat against her crotch.

She tried to ignore its warmth, the familiar tightness that gathered at that spot. She shifted her hips slightly hoping to defuse the small flames that began to lick inside her. Then she took his hand in hers and held it on her leg. She saw him smirk, but he didn't comment.

They chatted, observing the landscape as they traveled the road to where it intersected with highway. When Brad slowed down so he could stop at the intersection, Shauna Lee released his hand so he could shift again. When he was finished his hand fell back between her legs again, but this time he stroked her gently.

"Are you planning to torment me all day?" She took his hand in hers again and held it.

His eyes twinkled as he smiled at her. "I'm working on that chastity belt."

It was shortly after noon when they stopped for lunch. The locals were friendly and happy to tell them how to get to Castle Butte. When Brad inquired about the caves, the owner of the restaurant said that they were only accessible through private property and the people who owned the ranch were away.

Brad paid for the meal and they went outside. As they got into the truck one of the locals followed them. Brad lowered his window and talked to him. The man told him that it was the end of the season for the guided tours.

Nobody lived in the old house on the Giles Ranch, any more, but he knew the owner. He told Brad he would have to park the truck at the road, but if they crawled through the barbed wire fence and followed the trail they would find the caves. He gave him directions to the old ranch and Brad thanked him.

He was grinning when he started the truck. He put his hand on the inside of her thigh. "Are you game for the adventure?"

"It sounds like fun."

Brad pulled up to the ranch gate and stopped. He read the sign; "Giles Ranch: Trespassers will be given a fair trial then hung." He smiled crookedly as he turned to her. "Hang man's noose and all! Do you think we should risk it?"

"Well it sort of makes us outlaws; I guess that's fitting with the history of the area."

He chuckled as he hooked his arm around her shoulders and pulled her against him. "Are you ready?"

Shauna Lee nodded and they got out. He grabbed the camera, and then reached under the seat. He pulled out a small package and put it in the inside pocket of his jacket. Then he pressed the automatic lock button and shut the door. They walked to the fence and he put a boot on the bottom wire and took the middle one in his hand, pulling them

176

apart so she could go between them. When she had slipped through the fence, she did the same for him.

He whistled a soft tune as they walked hand in hand down the trail. They went a fair distance before they saw what appeared to be a cave at the bottom in the coulees.

"That could be what we are looking for!" she said, excitement sparkling in her eyes.

They stopped and looked out over the terrain. "Can you image this country over a hundred years ago, with outlaws and Indians roaming these hills? If I remember correctly, Sitting Bull even hid out here a time or two," Brad mused.

Shauna Lee's face glowed as she turned to him. "I never knew about any of this, and I've lived in Swift Current for thirteen years!" She threaded her arms around his waist. "Brad, you are the best thing that has ever happened in my life. You just keep showing me more about life."

He pulled her tight against him and lifted her face to meet his. "That is a two way street, you know. I love having you to share things with." He looked deep into her eyes. "For the first time in my life, I've finally found what I've been waiting for. You are the missing piece of the puzzle." His arms tightened around her. "You make my life complete."

She reached up and cupped his face, bringing his lips down to touch hers. He needed no encouragement. Brad kissed her deeply. His tongue slipped between lips that opened to accept it. It mated with hers in a sensuous dance. Heat and moisture flooded her. She felt his answer to it grow ridged against her belly.

"Oh Brad," she whispered. He nuzzled his face in her hair, savouring the feel of her against him. Her hands kneaded his back. He closed his eyes against the desire that rolled through him.

"Let's go." His voice was rough with emotion.

He took her hand and led her down the trail to the caves. They saw a sign that read 'Sam Kelly's Outlaw Caves'. He smiled as he pointed at the sign. "We've hit pay dirt! Will you stand over there by the sign and let me take your picture?"

GLORIA ANTYPOWICH

She took his picture too, and then he found a dead branch with a crotch in it. He pushed it into the light soil and put his camera in the join. After he assured himself that he had everything lined up, he set the timer and ran to join her. They stood one on each side of the sign when the camera flashed. He grinned. "That's another picture for your office!"

They looked in the cave that was largest. "This is probably the one they used for the animals" Brad said looking around. "It's huge."

He hooked his arm around her shoulder and walked with her to the other one. It had been reinforced. "I think he actually lived in this one for awhile after he gave up rustling and came back here to settle down." They stepped through the opening and looked around. The ceiling was low and Brad had to stoop to avoid bumping his head on it. "He must have been short."

Shauna Lee smiled as she looked at him. "Not tall, dark and handsome like you." Shauna Lee looked around, taking in the dirt walls and floor. "Can you imagine living in a wolf den? He had to have enlarged it a lot."

"I guess he did what he had to do." He turned to her, his eyes burning with lust. "How many times do you think he made love in here?"

She looked at him, wide eyed, reading his need. "Brad…The truck would be more…more civiliz.."

He stopped her words with a burning kiss. "I'm not feeling very civilized right now; I feel more like a cave man." he groaned. His fingers found her crotch, probing gently, seeking her sensitive spot through the fabric of her jeans. He took her hand and pushed it into him. He cupped her buttocks and forced her against him. "Let's make love now, Tweetie Bird." His voice was hoarse. "Here in this cave." He nibbled at her lips. "We can spread our coats out and lay on them."

She sucked in her breath. *It's a dirt floor.* The thought flitted through her mind, but her aching need overruled reason. She eased back and slipped out off her jacket. His eyes held hers. She swallowed hard and looked at the floor. He pulled her against him and kissed her desperately again. Then his hands were working at the button at her waist. She was tugging at his. He returned his lips to hers, as he reached

178

inside his coat. He drew out a small package. His arms went around her, his hands busy behind her as he worked to open it, while he ravaged her mouth with his.

She was unbuttoning his shirt, pushing it away from his chest. Brad growled; it was a rough sound of need that sprang from deep inside. She was vaguely aware that he had flipped something and was shaking it behind her.

Then he pulled off his coat and shirt. He tossed it behind her and lifted her in his arms. As he knelt to the floor, he rested her legs over his lap, cradling her with one hand, as he worked with the other one to spread out the jackets before he lay her down. He straddled her body and stripped off her jeans and panties along with her socks and shoes. He pulled his own clothes off and then, supporting his weight with his arms, he lowered himself over her. He held his breath, savouring the touch.

His desire was fierce. He fought the temptation to force himself into her and take what he needed; give her what she needed, quickly. But he wanted more than that now. He took several deep breaths to regain control; then they made love, tenderly but passionately, slowly but hungrily.

Shauna Lee sobbed as she climaxed. Brad's exclamation echoed throughout the cave. They collapsed, entwined together. Eventually Shauna Lee moved her fingers, feeling for their clothing. Her fingers found something slippery. She grasped it her with her fingers, and turned her head to see what she held. It was light weight and silvery.

Brad lifted his head. He smiled as his eyes met hers. "It's an emergency space blanket for camping. I put it in my coat." He kissed her shoulder. "I couldn't take you on the dirt floor."

It was four o'clock when they got back to the truck. Brad looked at her as he unlocked the door. "Should we go any farther today or should we come back another day?"

"I don't think I can take in anything more today; it's hard to top the ultimate." Shauna Lee smiled lazily. "I'm content to go back. It's going to be dark by the time we get home any way."

Brad put his arms around her. "You don't mind do you? That I'm so…that I'm like a..a randy teenager?" He moved his hands to cup either side of her face and looked deep into her eyes. "Sometimes I almost feel embarrassed that I'm like this…that I want you so much…I mean that I'm so horny."

"Mind? Jeeze Brad! How can you ask me that after what we just shared?"

His face was serious as he touched his finger to her chest, over her heart. "I hope you know deep inside that I'm not like the others; I'm not just an opportunist, using you for…"

She put her hand over his mouth, silencing him. "Don't," she whispered. "I've never thought that! Brad, you don't take from me; you share with me; you give to me."

They sat shoulder to shoulder and thigh against thigh on the drive home, chatting easily, relaxed now that the sexual tension was released. The November long weekend was coming up and they discussed the trip they were going to make to the northern region of the province. They decided to leave on Thursday, so they could be home by Sunday night.

# CHAPTER THIRTEEN

Thursday, Brad and Shauna Lee were on the road to Glaslyn by eight o'clock in the morning.

"How far is it?" Shauna Lee asked. "Will we get there early enough for you to do the maintenance check at that site this afternoon?"

"It's roughly a six hour drive; maybe six and a half with stops for fuel and food." He gave her a teasing look. "Mind you, if we park somewhere on a back road for a quickie, it will take longer."

"Brad! We're making this trip so that you can do a maintenance check on the turbine. Let's just focus on that for now. No side trips."

"I love it when I get you all tied up in a knot! Sweetie, I promise you I'll do my 'work job' first and save the other one for the motel room...or maybe on the way to it. We haven't initiated this buggy yet."

"Jeeze; a monster has been created here. You've gone from being a man who refused to have sex with me to being one who is insatiable."

"It's your fault."

She stuck her tongue out at him.

He ran his tongue around his mouth. "Maybe we'd better stop here for a moment. I can't resist that tongue."

She shook her head as her hand flew to cover her mouth. She hurriedly undid her seat belt and slid across the seat to sit against the passenger door. She grabbed that belt and clicked it into place.

He grinned at her. "You just hurt my feelings, Tweetie Bird."

"Bull! You've been tormenting me. I'm staying here until we get to the turbine and you check it out. After that..."

He gave an exaggerated sigh. "OK, you win."

They drove to North Battleford and stopped for lunch and fuelled up the truck. Brad had stopped teasing her and the trip had relaxed into a pleasant drive. After lunch, when they went back to the truck

Brad took her hand and led her to the driver's side. She hesitated, looking up at him suspiciously before she allowed him to help her into the cab.

"I promise I'll behave." He leaned over and kissed her gently. Once he got in, he pulled her close beside him before he started the truck. When he shifted gears, his hand landed between her legs, but he moved it to rest on her thigh.

She smiled as she placed her hand on his. She squeezed it gently and then turned to place a kiss against his shoulder.

Brad lifted her hand to his lips and kissed it, then returned it to where it had rested over his on her thigh. "It's roughly an hour drive from here to Glaslyn. The turbine is set up in a pasture about fifteen kilometres out of town. I should phone Bob Matzlan now and let him know where we are. He's going to meet us at the site."

Shauna Lee listened to him as he made the call. She realised that she hadn't seen him interact with clients. She'd seen him with Colt, but they had a friendly relationship as well as a professional one. It bordered more on casual, but now as she listened to him talk to Bob Matzlan, she glimpsed the truly professional aspect of the man.

He shut off the phone and put it back into its holder. "He'll meet us there and he'll be on time, which is good." He looked at his watch. "It's almost two o'clock now. If everything is all right, it'll take about an hour to check out the turbine; an hour and a half max. I should be done by four thirty.

"Spiritwood is about thirty five kilometres from Glaslyn. That may be the best place to go for a motel. When I went on line and checked out the town, I saw that there is a fairly new one on a service road adjacent to the highway. The rooms looked decent and there are a few restaurants down town where we can catch something to eat there."

"That sounds good. What is Bob Matzlan like?"

"He's a nice guy. I'd guess that he's in his late fifty's or early sixties. I think his father-in-law lives there with him. The boys call him grandpa, but as I remember Bill didn't introduce him as his dad. Come to think of it, I've never met his wife, but there are 3 boys. The oldest is about thirty two, and I'd guess the youngest is about twenty five."

"Are the boys interested in farming?"

"Bill is the oldest one. He has taken over the family farm, but Bob is still working with him."

Shauna Lee shook her head. "I can't imagine anyone wanting to farm."

Brad looked at her curiously. "Why? It's a time honoured way of life that has been the backbone of this country."

"And a lot of the time it's been a damn skinny old cow, with every vertebrae of that backbone almost poking through the hide."

Brad frowned. "Shauna, you must have quite a few accounts for farmers and ranchers. A lot of them are very successful. Colt seems to have done well."

Shauna Lee looked out the window. "Yes, Colt and his dad have done well. But Brad, I lived on a farm when I was a kid. Believe me; our life was nothing like theirs is."

He squeezed her hand. "Probably not; but that was thirty five years ago or more. Times have changed a lot since then. Farmers like your dad was, scarcely exist now. A quarter-section is not enough to even survive on, unless the owner really specializes in something unique. I know a couple who raise fancy little dogs and they do really well, but they cater to their buyers and they understand marketing."

"I know you're right about that. But I can't shake the memory of the smell of cow shit, dirt and dust and poverty."

"Well, there still is the odd one like that. They've gotten stuck doing what their father did, what their grandfather did. But the majority of those people have never gotten an education beyond the basic reading and writing and arithmetic. And honestly, most of them have no vision; they can't even begin to imagine creating a better life."

Shauna Lee sighed. "That is true. They look at people who succeed and make all kinds of excuses for themselves. They wallow in self pity; everything is someone else's fault."

"In my opinion, a lot of those guys don't have the initiative to make the effort to do things differently or they have other social problems. Alcohol is a big one, but some of them get into drugs too; how the hell they can afford it is beyond me. Both habits are expensive."

Shauna Lee snorted. "But they always do. Dad could always squeeze out enough money to buy his whiskey. It didn't matter what else didn't get taken care of."

Brad slowed down and signalled, turning right at the intersection. "We don't go right into Glaslyn. We turn here and go east for about five kilometres. Then we turn off on a gravel road and go in about ten kilometres, to the turbine.

"Bob Matzlan is a pretty sharp guy. He is one of the thoroughly modern farmers. He and his son farm several thousand acres. I don't know how much education Bill has, but he is no dummy. He was the one who got interested in wind turbines and researched them on the internet. He and Bob came to Swift Current to meet me."

Brad slowed down and signalled to turn left onto a gravel road. He smiled when he saw a white crew cab parked on the side. As he pulled up behind it, all four doors opened and four men got out and walked back to them. Brad got out and shook hands with all of them in turn.

When he came back to the truck, they followed the other vehicle down the road. They turned into a field and a few hundred yards further, as they rounded a curve in the road that passed a clump of poplar trees, Shauna Lee caught her first glimpse of a wind generated turbine mounted on a tower.

Brad's smile was one of pride. "There it is! And they are happy with the set up." He opened the truck door and slid out. "Do you want to get out? The air is a bit nippy, but it's refreshing. I'd appreciate it if you'd take a few pictures for me; some of the four of them and me looking at the tower and working around it. I have to check the storage batteries and I want to climb up and look at the turbine too."

"Where is the camera?"

He opened the back door, reached inside and took a small leather pouch out of a storage box he had set on the seat. "Just click away. I'll keep the ones I can use and discard the rest."

Shauna Lee took it from him. He gave her a quick hug and joined the others. Shauna Lee played with the camera, adjusting the lens focus from close up to wide angle. When she was satisfied she followed the men and took pictures.

To her surprise, Bob Matzlan came over and stood beside her. "I don't think we've been introduced. I'm Bob Matzlan."

Shauna Lee looked at him and smiled. "I'm Shauna Lee Holt." She looked at him closely, attracted by his startling blue eyes.

"I'm pleased to meet you, Shauna Lee. It's strange, but there is something very familiar about you; like I've known you from somewhere before."

Shauna Lee's heart skipped. She tried to sound casual but all the red flags were up. "I don't think so."

"Funny. It's just a feeling. I'm trying to think. You said your name is Holt. Are you married?"

Surprise registered on her face.

"Pardon me. That was rude of me. I was just wondering if that was your family name."

She swallowed. "It is a family name." She looked at him. "There is nothing familiar about you for me."

"I guess it is just my imagination. You are a very striking young woman; one that would stick in a person's mind."

She smiled at him. "I guess I should take that as a compliment. Thank you."

She moved away from him and kept taking pictures. She could feel his eyes on her and it unnerved her. *I have never known anyone from Glaslyn.*

Bob approached her again as she was taking a picture of Brad climbing up the tower. "Do you live in Swift Current?"

She nodded and then took another picture.

"Do you know if any of your family ever lived in this area?"

*Jeeze! He's like a dog with a bone.* "No. In fact I'm sure they didn't."

"Life is funny. When I was a young man, my first love was a pretty young woman. Her name was Marie Holt. You remind me of her. I don't know why, because you don't really look alike…"

Shauna Lee almost choked, but he didn't notice. He was lost in his remembering.

"We lived at Medstead at the time. Then my family moved to Glaslyn and we lost touch. I never forgot her. In fact, I happened to run across her a few years later at a house party in Junor. She hadn't forgotten me either, but she had married a Frenchman. He got so drunk that he passed out that night and she was really mad at him. We had been drinking and dancing and one thing led to another. We went outside and ended up in the barn. It wasn't the right thing to do, but we made love in the hay that night. I have never forgotten her. I've often wondered…"

*Shit, shit, SHIT! This is way too much information.* She felt sick. *How can this be happening? All these freaking years later!*

She was relieved to see Brad walking toward her. She smiled as she stepped forward to meet him and handed him the camera. "Do you want to check the pictures and make sure some of them are what you want?" He studied her face as he took it. *Something has upset you, Tweetie Bird.* He glanced through the pictures quickly and assured her that she had done well.

Then he glanced at his watch and turned to Bob. "Everything is working fine. Like I mentioned when we installed the turbine, they very simple in design and require no regular maintenance. But if it's reasonably close, I make it a policy to check out every installation before the first winter as a precaution. It helps me keep on top of any possible problems too."

He shook Bob's hand again and said he had to be getting on the road. Shauna Lee smiled and said goodbye, then led the way to the truck.

Brad didn't say anything until they reached the highway and headed east again.

"What happened back there?" he asked.

"Wh..aa.t do you mean?"

He took her hand. "This is me, sweetheart. My radar picked up on something back there. What was it?"

186

"You are like a damned lie detector machine."

"So what was it?"

She sighed and rested her head back against the seat, looking up at the roof in the truck. "Damn it Brad; I can change my name and run, but it seems that I can't hide."

"What are you talking about?"

"Bob Matzlan. He kept asking me questions and telling me that I reminded him of someone." Tears shimmered in her eyes as they met his. "It turns out he...he had a thing about my mom when they were young. Shit, Brad; he had sex with her after she was married to dad." She wiped away the tear that spilled over on her cheek. "He told me all that. He just started talking and blurted it out; jeeze, as if I needed or wanted to know all of that."

Brad was thoughtful. "Did you tell him who you were?"

"Are you kidding? I just kicked myself over and over for using grandma's married name when I decided to be Shauna Lee Holt. I should have chosen VanWinkle or something like that, instead of Holt. But mom was gone, grandma was gone and grandpa was dead before I was born. I never imagined anyone would connect the dots."

"Well Bob's curiosity will probably not go any further. You gave him a happy glance into the past. I'm pretty sure he won't give it another serious thought."

"I hope so. I don't want any more ghosts from my past to raise their heads. I thought I had put all of that behind me years ago, when I changed my name."

"Where did your parents live, Shauna? You said you lived on a farm, but where was the farm at?"

"A few miles from a little place called Junor. In the early homestead days it was a thriving little community; the railway line ran by there. But when we lived in that area, there wasn't anything much left of the town."

"Is that near here?"

"I couldn't honestly say. I never went very far from the farm when I was growing up and I left there when I was fourteen and a half. I've never been back."

Brad took her hand. "Would you like me to help you find it?"

"NO, No, no! I don't want to go anywhere near the place."

"OK sweetie, we won't do it. I just thought...well sometimes it helps to face our demons. It can take away the power that they have to hurt us; lay them to rest."

She shook her head. "I don't want too; I can't!"

Brad pulled her against him and held her there, as he drove the last few kilometres to Spiritwood. He turned off the highway and drove along the service road until he came to the motel that he was looking for. "Here we are," he said as he pulled up in front of the office.

Shauna Lee waited in the truck while he went in to make arrangements for the room.

He came back to the truck and got in. "Are you all right?"

She nodded. "Where is our room?"

"Down at the far end. I'll park down there in front of the door." He started the truck and moved it, and then they both got out and went inside.

Brad looked around the room. It was large and comfortable with a table and two comfortable chairs and good lighting.

Shauna Lee gave him a nudge in the ribs. "A King sized bed? How on earth..."

"It's the only one they have, and it normally costs twice as much as the others; but what the hell?" He could hardly control his delight. He walked over to an open door. "Come and look at this."

Her look was quizzical, as she joined him and stepped inside the room. "Brad!" Her gasp turned into a giggle. "A Jacuzzi tub."

"Big enough for two," he whispered.

"You are unbelievable." She was laughing. "Where is the toilet?"

"Over there," he nodded to the closed door behind them. "Toilet, sink and shower."

"And a 50 inch flat screen TV, behind here," he said with a chuckle as he folded out the doors.

"How long are we staying?" Shauna Lee was laughing. "It's so over the top, for a small town like this; it's crazy!"

"I booked it for two nights. It's the end of the season, so she gave me a good deal."

"Two nights?"

"It's about a forty five minute drive to Chitek Lake from here. I'll finish up early there and then we'll come back here. We can soak up the luxury and sleep in. We'll still get home in plenty of time Sunday night."

"Decadent; I like the way your mind works!"

"Now, I'm hungry. The receptionist said there's a restaurant on Main Street that she would recommend. I don't think it's nearly as luxurious as our room, but she said the food is great. Shall we go check it out?"

They drove around down town and then parked in front of an older, rundown looking building. When they went inside the decor was just as dismal.

Brad raised an eyebrow. "I haven't noticed any cockroaches!"

"Yukkk!"

"Well, the girl at the motel said the food was good, so we'll see."

The waitress who came to their table was neat and tidy; her clothes were clean and her shoes were shiny. She left them menus and went to get them each a coffee.

Shauna Lee smiled. "Well that is encouraging! At least the waitress is clean. Maybe that means that the kitchen is too," she whispered.

They looked at the menu and both decided to order Salisbury steak."

Brad picked up his coffee cup and looked it over. "No lipstick stains; no old coffee runs down the side." He took a sip and smiled. "Ahh... that is a great cup of coffee."

The waitress brought them both a cup of beef vegetable soup and a fresh dinner roll. Brad dipped a spoon into it and took a sip. "Hey, this is good!"

Shauna Lee tasted hers. "I guess you should never judge a book by its cover!"

When their Salisbury steaks arrived, they looked across the table and gave each other a thumbs up. The food was excellent. When they were finished the meal, the waitress brought two pieces of carrot cake for dessert.

Shauna Lee groaned. "I can't eat this now." The waitress amiably suggested that she could put it in a takeout box, so they both decided to take desert back to the motel. While Brad was paying for their meal, he checked to see if the restaurant was open for breakfast. The man at the till assured him that they were open in the morning. Brad and Shauna went back to the motel satisfied and happy.

Once they were inside, Brad swept her up in his arms and sat her in the middle of the bed. He picked up the remote and turned on the TV, then sank down bedside her. They both scooted up to sit against the headboard. He pulled her against him, while they listened to the last few moments of the evening news. After the news Brad flipped through the channels and finally selected a channel that played soft music.

"I didn't get my job done today," he said softly as he turned to pull Shauna into his arms and kissed her.

"You did."

"Not this one. I didn't get into the fo…"

"Foreplay," she finished his sentence as she touched her lips to his again. "I think you made a really good start," she whispered against his mouth. "With this king sized bed and the Jacuzzi tub."

He silenced her words with his tongue as he thrust it into her mouth, to dart with hers, stroking it and twirling in the warm, moistness.

As they moved and twisted with their passion, they slid down onto the mattress. Their hungry hands caressed and groped each other. One by one each piece of clothing came off until they were naked. Brad slid off the bed then scooped her up and carried her to the tub. He stood her inside it and then got into it with her. He turned on the water and sat down with her.

"Isn't this a little backwards?"

"I don't think so; it lets me admire your beautiful body as the water fills up. I see that as good thinking."

They played in the tub for three quarters of an hour. Finally Brad let the water drain and helped her out. She rubbed him down with the towel and he dried her off. They held hands as they walked to the bed. He tossed the extra pillows on the floor, then pulled back the sheet and let her slide into the bed. He rolled into it beside her and they hungrily reached for each other. They made love slowly, savouring the pleasure. When they were satiated, they lay hand in hand, side by side.

Shauna Lee became very silent.

"What are you thinking," Brad asked softly.

"Nothing."

"Sweetheart, you can't lie to me. What's going on in that pretty head of yours?"

"I was thinking about what Bob said today."

"And?"

"Brad...you'll hate this..."

He pushed himself up on his elbow. "Spill it, Tweetie Bird. What are you thinking?"

"Brad, you know my past...about all those guys."

"Sweetheart, don't do this to yourself; you were lonely; you were needy; you were looking for affection."

"But what if that isn't the reason. From what Bob said, mom had sex with him while dad was passed out at a house party. Brad, that's bad. That's acting like a slut. What if I am like her?"

"You're not a slut!"

"I acted like one; so did she."

"Sweetie, you can't assume that about your mother. Maybe she was empty and lonely, just like you were."

"But she was married."

"The marriage could have been empty and lonely; it could have felt like a trap if she hadn't married the man she loved."

"But why would she do that? Why would she marry dad if she didn't love him?"

"Bob told you his family had moved and he'd lost touch with her. Maybe she loved him; maybe she thought she'd never see him again so she just got married. In those days women didn't have the choices that they do today."

He reached for her and pulled her against him. "You are a beautiful, wonderful person who has never known love before. Even your mom couldn't give that to you. Maybe she just didn't have it left to give."

"I hope I deserve you," she whispered.

"I have no doubt about that." He turned off the music and the light. She rolled onto her side and he pulled her against his chest. He held her close and waited for sleep to come.

The next morning they went back to the restaurant for breakfast. They were on the road to Chitek Lake by nine thirty. Brad had phoned to let his client know that they were on their way.

Brad pulled up in front of a modern, two story house situated at the edge of Chitek Lake. The lawn was beautifully maintained and she could see the two turbines spinning on the breeze.

Brad opened the door and helped her out of the truck. "You will like these folks. They are down to earth people. When they got to the door, Brad knocked. They could hear footsteps scurrying through the house.

The door opened and a petite grey haired woman smiled as she looked at Brad. "Come in. I just put the coffee on and I made fresh cinnamon rolls this morning." Her eyes slid to Shauna Lee. She hesitated, shock whitening her face. "Oh my! LeeAnn, is it really you? She reached out and pulled her close. She kept repeating her words. "Oh my, oh my: LeeAnn." She looked over her shoulder and yelled. "John, John…hurry up and come here. You will never believe who is here."

Brad watched in stunned disbelief. *Oh Tweetie Bird. The past is determined to find you on this trip.*

John Potter came bounding to the door. "Who is here?" He slid to a stop. "LeeAnn? LeeAnn Bergeron? It's been so long since we've seen you."

Shauna Lee faltered. Brad reached out and steadied her. "It's all right sweetheart. I had no idea that you knew the Potters."

"Come in, come in," John Potter insisted. He reached to pull

Shauna Lee into his embrace. "How have you been LeeAnn? We tried to find you several times throughout the years, but we always hit a dead end. It was as if you had just vanished. I guess I couldn't have blamed you if you had, after everything that happened."

Brad put his arm around her protectively. "John, Shauna didn't know we were coming here. I had no way of knowing she knew you. Can she sit down and have a chance to collect herself?"

"Oh, yes. Come in and sit at the table. Bring her a cup of coffee, Marion."

Shauna Lee sank onto the chair. Her face was pale and she looked devastated.

Brad looked at their hosts. "John and Marion; she is with me now. Once she is settled and comfortable, I'll go out and check the turbines. I…I think it might be good if the three of you had a chance to catch up. Obviously there has been a connection between you. I…I'm going to be honest about this; there are still things I obviously don't know about the past. I just know that it was painful." He hesitated. "Please be kind to her."

He turned to go outside, aware of the puzzled looks on the faces of the Potters. He was almost at the door when Shauna Lee called to him.

"Brad…please stay." Shauna Lee looked at him with tears in her eyes. "You have to hear about this sometime. I tried to tell you that night, but you said…"

He nodded. "I know. I said we both had dealt with enough that day. Are you sure you want me to stay?"

"Yes," she said softly. "I want to get this all out in the open now. You know most of it; but this part is the most painful, the ugliest." The sadness in her eyes hit him like a kick in the gut. Brads heart faltered. *How much more could there be?* John was looking at her with compassion. Marion's eyes swam with tears. He pulled over a chair and sat next to Shauna Lee, reaching for her hand. She smiled at him wanly.

"I don't remember much about the months after Ben's death, Brad. They are a blur; a nightmare of pain that just steam-rolled over me. My arms ached with emptiness. My heart was broken. I would have gladly

193

died; I wished I could, but I didn't. John and Marion saved me; saved my sanity."

She looked at John and Marion. "I need to tell you something right away. I changed my name after you took me to Saskatoon. That's why you couldn't find me. I'm Shauna Lee Holt now. I buried LeeAnn Bergeron with Ben and the rest of my life when I left here."

Surprise flickered over John and Marion's faces.

Shauna Lees look was apologetic. "Please forgive me. I knew I should have told you. You had been so kind to me." She looked down at the hand that Brad held in his. "So much had happened. You know how big the trial was in the news."

Brad stiffened. *Trial? What the hell?*

Shauna Lee continued. "LeeAnn Bergeron was a household word. Everyone knew that name, even if they didn't know me. I couldn't face all the questions, people's pity, never knowing when the media would be in my face, asking me stupid questions or just keeping tabs on what I was doing.

"I wanted anonymity; to simply disappear and start a completely new life. I didn't want *anyone* to be able to find me." She looked at them, imploring them to understand. "If one person knew, it could slip out and others would find out. The next thing I knew, people I didn't want to know could find out. So I didn't tell anyone.

"My dad had walked out; mom had died. Grandma was the only person who had ever made me truly feel loved. She died when I was six. I decided to take her name. Why I kept the Lee part, I'm not sure now. Maybe deep down I did want to keep a little piece of myself. Whatever; I became Shauna Lee Holt and that is who I have been for the past twenty one years."

She looked at John and Marion. "I have told Brad about Ben being born with a cleft lip, and I've told him how his..father..felt about him. I told him that Ben didn't live long enough to have the surgery he needed. I haven't told him what happened though. This is so painful..." Tears slipped down her cheeks as she looked at Brad.

"Ben was a fussy baby. He had trouble swallowing and he'd get infections. I was so tired that night; I fell asleep with him cradled in my arms. He had one of the ear infections that he often suffered from and he had cried and cried for hours. He started to cry again and it took me a few moments to fully wake up.

"Before I realised what was happening, Dave jerked Ben out of my arms. He was shaking him furiously and Ben was screaming. I jumped out of bed, and started fighting with him, trying to take Ben away from him. I was hysterical, begging him to stop.

"He...he swung Ben into me like he was a baseball bat. I fell down. He dropped Ben onto me." She was sobbing. "Ben wasn't crying anymore. He was just dangling silently over my arm."

Brad closed his eyes. Pain knifed through him. *Oh Shauna, no.* Tears were running down everyone's cheeks now, including his.

"I was terrified. I...screamed at him, telling that he had to take us to the hospital, but he just turned away and grabbed a bottle of rum off the table. He...he just kept saying that the little freak had finally shut up and he went out the door."

"The fucking son of a bitch," Brad growled. He looked up, shocked at what he'd said out loud. "I'm sorry guys, but..."

John waved his hand, dismissing Brad's apology. "We've all said and thought that about him; and much worse! I could have strangled him with my bare hands. I often wished that he would have gotten shot for resisting arrest, rather than put LeeAnn through the ordeal of the trial."

Even though Brad was holding her, Shauna Lee hugged herself, pushing away the coldness that ran through her, struggling to swallow the bile that rose in her throat. Her stomach rolled as she remembered holding her son's precious little body close to her breast. "I ran across the field to John and Marion's."

John read her pain. He reached across the table and touched her hand. His voice was full of compassion. "Let me tell the rest, Lee... Shauna Lee."

She nodded, sobbing. Brad held her close, smoothing her hair. *Damn. I feel so helpless.*

"We knew right away that the baby was dead when she came to the door. She was clutching his body against her chest, but he was blue and still. She was crazy with fear; babbling incoherently and crying hysterically; begging us to take them to the hospital right away.

"Of course we took her. It was clear that there was nothing to be done for the baby, but LeeAnn was close to a breakdown. She needed help. Dave had never hidden how he felt about the baby. He had nothing but contempt for Ben and LeeAnn.

"Today we would have reported his behaviour to social services and had her taken out of that situation; but twenty years ago you minded your own business. I did go into the back room and phone the police before we left. I reported what had happened. They came out and took Dave into custody."

Marion's expression was full of compassion. "Lee…I mean Shauna Lee; you were so young; just a girl yourself. I don't know how you dealt with his cruelty."

Shauna Lee sobbed. "I…I had nowhere else to go. I had a roof over my head and food to put on the table; a place to sleep. I didn't grow up in a very loving home and until the baby was born, life with Dave wasn't that bad. But after Ben was born…" She buried her face in her hands. "He despised me, and poor little Ben. Dave would have h.h.. it him over the head like he did the ru.n.t p..igs and thro..w.n him on the manu..r.e pile with them. H..ee told me he wou..l.d. But Ben was m..my ba.by. I lov..ed him."

John Potter spoke, breaking the sickening mental image. "LeeAnn came back here after she got out of the hospital and she lived with us until after the trial. It took several months for the case to get to trial. Lee..sorry…it's going to take a while to think of you as Shauna Lee. Shauna Lee testified against Dave. He should have gotten life without parole, but they gave him twenty five years.

Brad sat upright. "Twenty five years," he exploded. "It won't be long before he is released. In fact he could be out on parole now if he behaved himself in jail."

"That was one reason I changed my name; leaving no trail. He hates me. I was afraid he would come after me."

John nodded. "He hated a lot of people. We'll all be looking over our shoulders when he is released." He looked at Shauna Lee. "Do you live in Swift Current now?"

She nodded. "I've been there for thirteen years."

Brad's voice reflected his pride in her. "She's worked hard and she's done very well for herself."

"So what did you do after you left here," John asked.

She sighed. "I rented a single room in a private home. I did house work and cooked meals for my board and room. They both worked. They liked me and eventually they recommended me for babysitting and house-sitting jobs on the weekends. I stayed with them until I finished high school.

"I...I was driven and determined to leave fear and poverty behind me. I vowed to make a good life for myself; to never be dependent on anyone else for my survival again. I vowed I would never be vulnerable to my emotions again. I would be the master of my own ship. Nothing was going to stand in my way. And on the surface I've done that."

"What do you do," Marion asked.

"I became a Chartered Accountant. Then I worked for an old accountant in Swift Current and when he retired I bought the business. It was a good investment for me."

John and Marion both nodded with approval. "Good for you," Marion said.

John drummed his fingers on the table. "Did you change your name legally?"

Shauna Lee shook her head.

"But how did you get into school?"

"Well when I enrolled in high school I simply registered as Shauna Lee Holt, but I realized that I had to get a birth certificate that I could use." She grimaced. "I did what I had to do. It took me a while, but once I had that, I got my social insurance number too. Then I could get a real job."

John eyes were sad as he looked at Shauna Lee. "I wish you had come to me."

"You had already done so much for me, John. My top priority was to disappear and leave my old life behind. If I turned to anyone for help, I would lose my anonymity. I was totally focused on building a new life. I did what I had to do."

Her expression was pained as she looked at Brad. "I even resorted to…to prostitution a few times. It paid a lot more and I needed money to…to get a birth certificate." She hid her face with her hands. "I'm sorry Brad, but it's true. I hope you can forgive me."

Brad closed his eyes and squeezed her hand. *Oh, Shauna.* "The past is the past, sweetie. I've told you that before and I still mean it. What happens from here on out is what matters." He dropped a kiss on her hand.

John looked at Brad with admiration. "You are a fine man, Brad. I am so glad to see that Shauna Lee has someone like you in her life."

"Thank you, John. From what I've heard here today, you were probably more like a father to her than her own dad was."

"She needed someone."

John looked at Marion. "Can we have some hot coffee, mom; and some of those cinnamon buns?"

She nodded and went to make a fresh pot of coffee.

Shauna Lee looked at John. "I didn't think that anyone would recognize me. I've changed a lot since those days; or at least I thought I had."

John looked at her thoughtfully. "You have changed a bit. You're older and you've filled out, but those eyes are unmistakeable; and there is still vulnerability about you. One first glance I may have missed the resemblance because I wasn't expecting to see you; but on a second look, it would be hard not to see it."

Marion had brought small plates and the cinnamon buns to the table. "I knew you right away, Shauna Lee."

Shauna Lee sighed. "Obviously I'm not as invisible as I'd thought I was"

Brad held her close. "You've spent too many years hiding from your life Shauna. You can't do that anymore. We'll face this together."

After they drank coffee and enjoyed Marion's fresh cinnamon buns, Brad and John went out to inspect the towers. Shauna Lee and Marion chatted, catching up on the past twenty years. John and Marion had sold the farm five years previously and bought the house on Chitek Lake. Life was comfortable for them now. They traveled quite a bit and they both liked to fish on the Lake. After all the years of struggling they were enjoying retirement.

When Brad and Shauna Lee left for Spiritwood, the Potters assured them that Shauna Lee's secret was safe with them.

Brad was sick at heart as he watched Shauna Lee huddle against the passenger door. She had refused to sit next to him when he had asked her to. She had become strangely calm; as if she had removed herself from the situation. *That has to be how she has survived all these years.*

At eighteen, Shauna Lee had been stripped naked. Emotionally she had been numb. She'd had no possessions, no education, no family, no life. But she had drawn on a strength deep inside her; one that had always been there and that was how she had survived. Now she was doing that again. Would she lock herself in that world, or would she reach out to him?

When he drove up to the motel door, Shauna Lee sat up and opened her door. Brad was relieved when he saw that she sat on the edge of the seat, waiting for him to help her down to the ground.

Before he opened the motel door he glanced at his watch. It was four fifteen. He swung the door open and let Shauna Lee step inside. He went in behind her and locked the door behind him. He watched her as she stood at the end of the bed, looking at him uncertainly.

He stepped in front of her and unzipped her jacket. She let him take it off her and then she turned and sat down in one of the chairs. *She's keeping her distance,* he thought sadly. He took off his jacket and laid it on the bed beside hers. He hesitated and then sat down in the other chair. He was silent for a moment; then he cleared his throat. "Do you feel like talking?" His voice was soft.

"What is there to talk about?"

"You could tell me how you feel. This has been a tough day. I'm here for you and I'm a good listener." He smiled gently. "I'm even better at if I can hold you in my arms and listen."

She smiled wearily. "I'm sort of numb. I don't know what to say."

"Can I hold you?"

She shook her head. "I just need some time, Brad."

"Do you want me to just leave you alone for now?"

"Please?"

"Maybe you should lie down and relax. I can sit here and watch TV."

She hesitated, then nodded. He stood up and extended his hand. She placed hers in it and let him help her to her feet. He led her to the bed and let her sit on the side of it. He bent down and removed her shoes, then swung her legs up. He squeezed her hand, then walked back to the chair and pulled it over so he could watch TV.

He flipped through the channels, but found nothing that interested him. Finally he selected a soft music channel and sat slouched down in the chair, letting the music wash over him. He let his head fall against the back of the chair and stared at the ceiling. He was deep in thought, going over the horrific story he had heard that morning. *Someone should have killed that bastard*, he thought. *A man that would kill his own child; Jesus! Poor Shauna, no wonder she just shut down and locked up!*

"Brad." He jerked up in his seat. She was sitting up, looking at him.

"What, sweetheart?"

"You don't look very comfortable there. Why don't you come and lay down?" She patted the far side of the bed.

"I don't want to crowd you."

"If you just lay there you'll be more comfortable and you won't be crowding me."

"Are you sure? I'm OK, you know."

She smiled wanly. "I'd like to know that you are close to me; close enough that I can reach out and touch you if I want to."

His heart lightened. He kicked off his boots and lay down. He fought his desire to hold her close, to protect her; instead he forced

200

himself to breathe deeply and relax. He vowed to give her the room she needed.

Slowly he drifted off to sleep. Somewhere during that time she had rolled over beside him and placed her hand on his arm. He surfaced briefly, smiling as he turned toward her. She mumbled in her sleep as she rolled over and snuggled her back into his chest. He slipped his arm around her waist and they fell sound asleep.

When Brad woke up the TV was still playing music. He looked at his watch. It was two o'clock in the morning. They had slept for at least eight hours. He was wide awake...and hungry. The coffee and cinnamon buns were long gone. He shifted carefully, trying not to awaken Shauna Lee, but with his slightest movement she stirred. She stretched, then turned over and looked at him.

"What time is it?" she whispered.

"Two in the morning," he whispered. Then he grinned. "Why are we whispering?" he asked softly.

"Because it's two in the morning," she replied just as softly. "Jeeze, we've already had a full night's sleep. And I'm hungry!"

"So am I. We didn't eat that carrot cake last night, did we. There is a coffee maker in here. We can make coffee and eat the cake."

"Right now that's better than nothing." She rolled off the bed and went to set the coffee maker up to brew. Then she opened the small fridge and took out the two pieces of cake. She came back and sat down beside him and handed him a piece.

They gulped it down, then looked at each other and laughed. "I'm wide awake," she said.

"So am I." He got up to pour them each a cup of coffee and brought her one. He looked at her as he sipped. "Well, what are we going to do now?"

She looked at him. "We could head for home and sleep the rest of the day after we get there."

He looked at his watch again. "It's twenty to three. If we leave right away we'll be home around nine o'clock. That will give us time for breakfast along the way too."

She leaned forward and kissed him softly. "Let's go."

They quickly packed up their bags and were on their way. When they reached North Battleford it was still dark, but they decided to have breakfast at a twenty four hour truck stop. An hour later they were back on the highway.

The stereo was blasting and Shauna Lee was by his side. *Life is good*, Brad thought as he shifted gears. He let his hand rest on the seat between her legs.

She smiled at him. "What are you up to?"

"About six inches."

"You wicked man."

He moved his hand and let his fingers caress her jeans. He felt her contract. "Like that?" he whispered.

"We are still a long ways from home."

"Ahh…it's called foreplay," he said softly stroking her again.

She wiggled. "It's called torture," she whispered and leaned over to lick his ear.

He stroked her through her jeans again. "Maybe it's called a quickie?"

She shivered. "Maybe it's called initiation?" She reached over and stroked him. "Ahhh..a good six inches."

He slowed down.

"What are you doing?"

"There has to be a back road here." He turned onto an approach. The lights shone on an abandoned farmstead. Tumble down buildings with rows of trees that formed a windbreak around the perimeter out lined it. He expelled his breath softly. "This is even better." He pulled in between a row of granaries, and a row of leafless trees. He shut off the motor and the lights extinguished. He pushed her over onto the passenger side and flipped the level that laid the seat back.

Brad looked at his watch later when he parked in front of the house. "We are home," he said with a smile. "It's nine thirty."

"You are half an hour later than you estimated," Shauna Lee teased.

He laughed and pulled her against him for a kiss. "I didn't allow for the initiation!"

Shauna Lee flushed.

"Sweetheart, are you blushing?" He looked at her more closely. "You are!"

# CHAPTER FOURTEEN

$\mathcal{F}$rankie and Colt sat at the kitchen table, enjoying their morning coffee. Colt looked out the window and shook his head. "I can't get over the way this great weather is holding. November tenth, and it is plus six degrees. I can't remember when I've seen this before."

"It must be Global Warming," Frankie said with a smile.

Colt chuckled. "Whatever it is, it's a god send. If these temperatures hold for another week, Brad and I should get the towers and turbines up at the water tanks before winter sets in for real. That will be a big load off my mind. It will make things so much easier next summer."

"Modern innovation is amazing isn't it?"

Colt nodded. He glanced at the clock on the wall. It was seven thirty. "We have half an hour before the twins get up. Could I talk you into snuggling on the wicker lounge on the veranda with me and have another coffee?"

"It's warm for this time of the year, but it's still chilly."

"That's the reason for cuddling. It will be refreshing and the morning sky still beautiful."

Frankie laughed. "Well, it's either a very romantic idea or an insane one. I'll get a warm jacket."

"You are a real trooper. I'll refill our cups and put my coat on."

They settled on the wicker lounge, cups in hand. Colt hooked his arm around Frankie and pulled her into the curve of his shoulder. "Look at that sunrise," he said softly. The sky was flushed fuchsia and pink with touches of yellow.

"It's beautiful."

Colt looked toward Ellie's trailer. "It looks like Ollie is there; at least both vehicles are there."

"Don't be nosey," she chided.

"I'm not being nosey. I'm being proactive. She's our nanny. He's our ranch foreman. I don't want anyone screwing up the system."

"Colt! That sounds awful!"

"Well, what did you think when Ollie showed up here yesterday?" He laughed. "He was as nervous as a teenager going out on his first date! He shocked the hell out of me when he asked if Ellie could have the afternoon off."

Frankie shook her head. "Not me! I saw that coming when we were out at the ranch for the round up. Ollie got a light in his eye and a spring his step the moment he set eyes on her." Frankie chuckled. "I remember thinking that there might be snow on the roof, but Ollie still had a fire in the stove! I'm surprised he took this long to make a move."

"You're kidding! I missed all that. I guess I didn't expect it of him."

"Why? Because he's older; even old guys get lonely…and horny!"

"Horny?" Colt laughed. "The old dog, he stayed the night there. Do you think..?"

"Colt! Now you really are being nosey. If they did that's up to them. They are old enough to make their own choices, with no observations from you."

He looked at her with a twinkle in his eye. "So, are you willing to make a bet?"

"Do you think he's going to come out here and tell you everything, you pervert?"

"If he's wearing a shit-eating grin and walking bowlegged, we'll know."

She gave him dig in the ribs. "He already walks bowlegged and he could be grinning from ear to ear because he's happy."

"Because he got to grease his pole."

"That is so crude! You are disgusting." They heard the trailer door close. "Shhh…here they come."

They watched Ellie and Ollie come toward them. When they saw Colt and Frankie sitting on the lounge, they spoke quietly to each other. Then, they both laughed.

"See that shit-eating grin?" Colt murmered.

Ollie let Ellie precede him up the steps onto the veranda. Frankie stood up and smiled. "Good morning, you two. We came out to drink our coffee and admire that fabulous sunrise." Her eyes met Ellie's. "Did you have breakfast or are you going to join us?"

She led the way indoors and Ellie followed her.

Ollie looked at Colt with a twinkle in his eye.

Colt couldn't control his grin. "So you old dog; did you have a good visit?"

"Sure did. She's one hell of a woman. We were awake half the night." He stepped toward the door, and then looked back at Colt. "Get your mind out of the gutter, you young pup. We weren't having sex: we were talking. Not that it's any of your business, but I can hear the wheels turning and I don't want you to disrespect such a wonderful lady."

Colt had the grace to look embarrassed.

Ollie laughed. "Gotcha! We took a bet on it when we saw the two of you sitting there. She didn't believe you'd think that, but us guys... well, we all think pretty much alike. I could read your mind as soon as I saw you sitting there."

"For god's sake, don't tell her. She's our nanny! I couldn't face her..."

Ollie was still chuckling when he went through the door. Colt followed him a few moments later, hoping his discomfort didn't show.

Ellie and Frankie had gone upstairs to get the twins dressed. Colt offered Ollie a cup of coffee and asked him how everything was at the ranch. Ollie's eyes still twinkled, but he took up the conversation and Colt's embarrassment eased. When Ellie and Frankie came down with the twins, pandemonium broke out. They ran to meet Colt and then they crawled all over Ollie.

Ollie's affection for them was undeniable. He beamed with pride like the grandfather he never would be, might have done.

Colt offered to help make breakfast, but Ellie and Frankie shooed him out of their way. He suggested Ollie join him and they went into his office.

"I'm going to give Brad a call and see if we can finish putting up the turbines this week. I'm anxious to get that out off the way before we get cold and blowing snow."

The phone rang several times and finally went to the answering machine. Colt leaned back in his chair. "He isn't answering. He said something about going north to check out some of his turbines. He was taking Shauna Lee with him. He said they hoped to be back today."

Ollie checked the time. "Well, it's only nine thirty. They probably aren't back yet."

Colt nodded, tapping his pen against the desk. "You are right. And who knows what they'll end up doing." He grinned. "He and Shauna Lee seem to have a good thing going."

"Shauna Lee." Ollie looked thoughtful. "I wish she would sit down and talk with Patch. There are things that she needs to be told. He has talked to me some; I'm not excusing his actions, but there seems to be more to the story than she knows."

"It's hard to imagine that happening. Brad is really defensive of her. He has no respect for Patch whatever. He sees red whenever he is mentioned."

Ollie shook his head. "Everyone has a story, Colt; but sometimes they aren't read correctly."

Colt opened his mouth to speak when the telephone rang. He looked at the call display and smiled. "Good morning, Brad."

They exchanged the ordinary conversation and then Colt got to the point. "Could we finish installing those turbines this week while this weather is still holding?"

"I've been planning to do that. I have a few things to finish up before I head off to China on the twenty third of this month. I can work with you tomorrow and the next day if that works for you. We should be able to finish up by Tuesday night."

"We could stay at the ranch tomorrow night. It would speed things up."

"You can. I'm coming home. I want to spend as much time with Shauna as I can before I leave. I'm going to be gone for a whole week."

Colt laughed. "You've got it bad, man!"

"Keep your opinions to yourself, man. How often do you go away for a week without Frankie? Besides, Patch is still at the ranch isn't he? The more I learn about Shauna's past, the more I want to strangle that bastard."

"Brad, there may be another side to ..."

"Screw that noise. I'm not interested."

After breakfast, Ollie and Ellie took the children for a walk. When they came back Frankie volunteered to give them a snack and put them down for their nap, giving Ellie the afternoon off.

Ollie and Ellie walked back to the trailer.

Frankie and Colt went out and sat on the wicker lounge again. She looked at Colt and grinned. "So, you pervert. Are you mind-peeking into Ellie's bedroom again?"

He grinned sheepishly and shook his head. "That sneaky old dog; I asked him if he'd had a good visit. He gushed about what a wonderful woman she was and about how they'd been awake half the night. I didn't say a word, but then he told me to get my mind out of the gutter. He informed me that they hadn't had sex; they had just talked."

"That is priceless!"

"That is not the best part. Or is it the worst part?" He grinned. "That old bugger guessed what I'd be thinking and he'd made a bet about it with her."

"Colt! That is awful!" She covered her face with her hands and groaned. "What did Ellie think?"

"Let's hope we never find out."

Ollie left at five o'clock that afternoon. Colt grinned and shook his head as he watched him drive down the road. "He's going to get home late. I guess age is irrelevant when you've got the hots."

"Do you realize that teenagers and twenty year olds probably think we are too old for sex? What do you think your parent's love life is like?"

"I've never actually given it much thought. After dad had his heart attack..." He grinned. "But he is my dad. I guess he probably is still interested. I'm sure I will be at ninety five. And you; I'll probably have to run to keep up with you."

# CHAPTER FIFTEEN

*B*rad and Shauna Lee watched the evening news and sipped a beer. When the news was over Brad looked at her. "I'm curious. How did you get your new birth certificate?"

"Brad...do we have to go through this?"

"I'm just curious."

She shook her head. "I'm not."

"You were a kid. How the hell did you do it?"

"You just have to get in touch with the right people."

"But how did you do that."

"Damn you..."

"I'm not judging you. I'm just...it boggles my mind."

She sighed heavily, knowing he wouldn't give up until she told him, "I...well, I told you that I...I slept with guys for money."

"You said that before."

"Well...one of the guys I got to know was a salesman. He traveled all over the country and he knew lots of people."

"How did you meet him?"

"I met him at the bar." She brushed away Brad's angry expression. "I know, I know...I was too young to be in bars, but when I dressed up sexy, and put my hair up and wore lots of makeup, I seldom got checked for ID; that only happened a couple of times."

She sighed. "Jeeze Brad, I don't want to tell you all this stuff. I really didn't...sleep with many guys; and after I met him I didn't go with anyone else. He only came through town once in a while. He was older; probably thirty five or so. Actually he was a really nice guy. He realized how young I was after the first time, and we never had sex again.

"He wanted to know why I was doing what I was doing; he didn't like it. I explained what had happened; that I just wanted to be

209

anonymous and start over again and I was trying to save money so I could find a way to get a new birth certificate. I needed to have one so I could get a social insurance number and get a real job.

"After that, when he came into town, he would take me out for dinner and we would just talk about all kinds of things. He always paid me a lot and he was nice to me.

"When he came through town one time, he told me he had talked to someone who knew someone, who could take care of everything for me. I was thrilled. I told him I wanted to keep the name I was using and my birth date because I was already using that information.

"Three months later when he came back, he had everything I needed.

"I had a complete identity as Shauna Lee Holt and a complete history to back it up. I was born in Nanavut. My parents were Gregor and Helena Holt. They worked independently as geologists, doing mineral exploration around Ennadai Lake. I was born in a small cabin by the lake, out in the wilderness. My father delivered me and the place of birth was recorded in latitude and longitude.

"My parents were friendly with the Ihalmiut Inuits. Sometimes I stayed with them, while mom and dad flew out to camps further away. When I was five years old my parents were both killed in a plane crash. An Inuit family took me in and I lived with them until I was seventeen. Then I came to Saskatoon and started going to high school there. They even included some back ground information about what it would have been like to live with my imaginary Inuit family."

She shook her head. "Brad, my new life was complete to the last detail. I could have been that girl; I became that girl."

"How much did it cost you?"

"He refused to take any money and he never told me how he got the paper work. But I've built my whole life around that information. For the first few years I was scared to death; you know, always looking over my shoulder, afraid that someone would show up and expose me as the fraud that I was. But once I got through university I relaxed and accepted my life."

"So what did this guy want in return?"

"Nothing; he made two stipulations. First, I had to use my new identity to get a real job; which was what I wanted it for anyway. The other was that I would never make money...selling my body...selling sex...again, but when he came to town he wanted to see me. And honestly Brad, he never slept with me again. He only came back a couple more times and then I never seen him again. I often wondered what happened to him."

"This is damn freaky, Shauna. Think about it; if he could get you a new identity...you damn well weren't the guinea pig. Whoever did it was pretty sophisticated about what they were doing; they had to have had access to government records or I don't know how it could have worked."

Shauna Lee sighed and buried her face in her hands. Then she looked at him. "I know. It used to drive me crazy. For awhile, I would go on line and search to see if Gregor and Helena Holt really existed or if they were just made up. It took me several searches, but I did find them for real, Brad. They did live in Nanuvit and they were geologists and they did die in a plane crash up there."

"Christ. That's identity theft. Well not exactly but it's certainly manipulating a dead person's identity to create another."

She sat staring at the TV. "I didn't mean any harm. I was just trying to protect myself." She wrapped her arms around herself. "But I really am just a fraud, Brad. My whole life is a lie." Tears shimmered in her eyes. "I'm so sorry I got you involved. I know you love me, but you need to just walk away. Sometimes, no matter how much you care, the price is too high."

A look of shock crossed Brad's face. "Shauna that is *not* what I was getting at. No one could blame you for wanting to escape your past. After what I learned this weekend, I don't know how you held yourself together. I am proud of you.

"I'm even...I'm grateful that this man helped you; no matter what other shit he may have been involved in, he was sort of a...a guardian angel for you. It's the old double edged sword; good and evil. Life is seldom black and white; there are always shades of grey. It depends on the point of view you look at it from. From your…from *our*… point of view, he did a good thing for you. He gave you a chance to escape a horrific past that was the result of a seriously dysfunctional family; he gave you a chance to build a new life."

He pulled her hands into his and held them tight. "But think about it; people are actually out there doing this kind of thing. I know, you read about it in books and you see it in movies. And I have heard that people do use false ID's, but I never dreamed that they did such a thorough job. It's unnerving. Can you trust anybody or anything?"

"I've been me, like this for over twenty years. I trust in me."

"Shit, I just keep pushing my foot farther down my own throat here; when will I ever learn to leave good enough alone?" He pulled her into his arms. "Sweetheart, none of this really matters now. I wasn't judging you. And please don't keep thinking that I'm going to leave you. It isn't going to happen; I'm stuck to you like crazy glue."

Shauna was strangely calm; withdrawn and solemn. When he pulled her to her feet she didn't respond with her usual smile. He put his arm around her waist and guided her to the bedroom but her movements were automatic. *I've hurt her.* He reached to help her unbutton her shirt, but she shook her head and brushed his hand away.

"Shauna…"

"Not now, Brad."

He turned away and went into the bathroom. His heart was heavy. When he came back to the bed she was lying on her back, staring at the ceiling. He slid into the bed from the other side and reached for her, but she didn't turn into his arms, and she didn't turn so he could hold her and spoon her from the back. She just lay there. The message was clear. She didn't want to be close tonight.

He reached for the hand that lay at her side next to him. He enveloped it in his, needing to touch her, to reconnect. She didn't pull it away, but let it lie limp in his clasp. Eventually Shauna Lee fell into a sleep of exhaustion. Brad lay beside her, cursing himself for pushing her once again. Tears of anguish squeezed out of the corner of his eye; spilling his grief for the pain she had suffered.

The next morning Shauna Lee responded to his touch. She kissed him, and she gave him a hug, but he still felt the emotional barrier she had erected. The sparkle wasn't there, the spontaneity. He felt like they'd lost their special connection and his heart ached.

Colt noticed his preoccupation when he picked him up. They had driven for several miles when he looked across at Brad. "OK man, something is going on here. Do you want to talk about it?"

Brad shook his head. "Sorry Colt. I didn't realize I was such an open book. I can't really talk about this."

"Is it Shauna Lee?"

Brad nodded. "Her past just keeps coming back to hurt her. I want to help somehow, but sometimes I think I do more harm than good."

"Well, you are right; this isn't something we should talk about. All I can suggest is that you have patience, man. I'm sure that you have gotten closer to her than anyone else. If you love her don't give up."

"I'm not giving up. I just don't want her to shut down on me."

Shauna Lee was making dinner when Brad got home that night. She turned to smile at him. "I wasn't sure what time you'd get home. You are a little earlier than I expected."

"We have one tower and turbine up and ready to go. We'll do the other one tomorrow. I didn't want to be late tonight." He walked over to stand in front of her and put a hand on each of her shoulders. "It bothered me all day; you know, the way things went between us last night.

"And I know you were trying this morning, but you weren't there yet. I just wanted to get back here, so I could hold you like this." He wrapped his arms around her. "And I wanted to kiss you like this." He bent his head and claimed her lips. He felt the resistance in her yield and soften against him. "I love you, Tweetie Bird."

"I know that, Brad." She cradled his face between her hands. "It's just that sometimes I feel like I'm such a liability."

Brad worked his hands over her back, across her shoulders and up her neck where he threaded his fingers in her hair. "Tweetie Bird, you have never been a liability. You are not a liability. You never will be a liability." He looked into her eyes. "Quit questioning my judgement and good taste. You'll give me an inferiority complex."

She pressed her cheek against his chest. "I hope you always feel that way."

"There you go, questioning my judgement again." He kissed her forehead and then looked toward the stove. "I'm hungry, and something smells wonderful. What are you making?"

She lifted the skillet lid. "I cheated tonight. I picked up a package of hamburger helper and some fresh hamburger. I sautéed some chopped onions, peppers, celery and garlic and added it to the hamburger and left the meat to brown. After I added the hamburger helper package, I threw in a fancy mix of frozen vegetables and left everything to simmer."

"It smells yummy. How soon can we eat?"

"After the table is set and I finish making the dressing for the salad." She opened the fridge and took out a salad bowl and set it on the counter. "Do you want a beer?" she asked as she reached for a salad mix container.

Brad nodded as he went to the cupboard and took down two plates. Shauna Lee grabbed a lime and two bottles of Corona out of the fridge and put them on the counter. She grinned as Brad took out the cutlery.

He bumped her hip as he walked past her, murmuring softly in a sing song voice. "Two plates, two cups, two knives, two forks, two spoons, always the same…"

She giggled. The sparkle was back in her eyes and her face was soft again.

They relaxed as they ate and shared the events of the day. Shauna Lee leaned forward and touched Brad's hand. "I got a call from Timothy Bates today. He'll be in Swift Current on Wednesday. He's going to meet Colt on Friday."

"That's great news." He looked thoughtful. "Would you…?"

"Would I be comfortable if you invited him to stay here on Wednesday night?"

He nodded.

"I thought about that earlier. It is instinct for me to close up; you know that. But the answer is yes: invite him. I know you would enjoy having him stay for the night."

"And will you enjoy having him here?"

"He's your friend, so I probably will. It's not like he's going to be here forever and it'll give me a chance to get to know him a bit. I may have to take him out to the farm on Thursday. Colt wants him to go out there so he can show him around. At least he isn't anyone that can spring any more shocking news from my past on us!" She smiled apologetically. "I hope not anyway."

"Can you take Friday off?"

"Why?"

"Well, I leave for China on Sunday night."

"Already? I forgot it was so soon."

"Well it is and I want to spend as much time as possible with you before I go. If you can play hooky, I will too."

She gathered the dishes off the table and put them in the dishwasher. "I'll have to give Christina a week off for filling in for me so often, but I think I can persuade her let me off the hook for Friday."

"Tell her I'll bring her something special from China."

Timothy Bates arrived at eleven-thirty, Wednesday morning. He had called Brad when he came into town and got directions to the Windspeer office. He chuckled when his old friend came pushing through the door as his pickup rolled to a stop. Brad was opening his truck door before Timothy undid his seat belt.

"Hey there guy. Is it ever good to see you. How was your trip?"

"It was pretty good, except for your crappy Saskatchewan roads. Don't you guys pay your taxes? I came across from Edmonton to Lloydminster; the roads were perfect. I spent the night in Lloyd' and then headed down here this morning. Man, talk about narrow and rough roads from there to here; the pavement is falling apart in some places."

"They are working on them; things are getting better. Now that you've had your bitch session, how is everything else?"

"Well, your folks say hello. And I really appreciate you putting in a word for me here. I hope this job works out. I want to get away from the Peace River Country. There is still a lot of crap going on there with the family. And Marsha is still twisting the knife, wanting to bleed some more out of me.

"Christ man; you were smart to never get married. I'm counting on you to hit me on the head if I ever get stupid enough to consider it again. Put me out of my misery before it gets started!"

"Ouch! You are a tad bitter. They're not all like Marsha, Tim."

"Show me one who isn't. In a hundred years I might be interested." He closed the truck door and turned to Brad. "So what is Colt Thompson like?"

"I've done business with him and we've formed a friendship. As far as I'm concerned he's an all-around straight-up guy. He's got a good operation at the farm and I think you'll find him fair to work with. He's looking for a manager because he wants to move back to the ranch that he owns in the Cypress Hills. He's got a great wife, twins and another one on the way. They are a happy family."

"And Shauna Lee Holt? I talked to her first. Is she his accountant?"

"She is. We're meeting her for lunch in about ten minutes. I think she is going to take you out to the farm tomorrow."

"Does everybody know everyone else around here; or did I just land into the middle of a nest? It seems you guys all know each other."

"It just turns out that way in this case. I certainly don't know everyone in town. Anyway, we should get over to Shauna's office."

Brad considered their recent conversation. He hadn't seen Tim for two or three years and he was surprised by his attitude. *He's damn bitter. I hope I didn't stick my neck out to get it chopped off by giving him a good reference to Colt.*

He pulled up in front of Swift Current Accounting and

Bookkeeping Services. "This is it guy. Shauna owns this place and she does Thompson Land and Cattle's accounting. So if you and Colt work out an agreement, you will get to know this place well. Let's go in."

Christina's smile lit up her face when Brad walked in. "So what will you bring back for me from China?"

"Give me some ideas! I'll do my best to find something worthwhile; maybe a statue of Buddha."

She laughed. "Yeah; I'll put it in my shrine to you!" She gave him the 'Trudeau salute', with a laugh. "Just go on in. I think you know the way," she said with a wink at Tim. "She's expecting you any time, now."

Tim found himself wondering what was going on between Brad and the receptionist as he followed him to a half closed office door. Brad pushed the door open and stepped inside. A petite, blue eyed, blonde turned from an open filing cabinet to greet them.

Her smile was radiant when she saw Brad. "You're here!" Her look shifted to Tim. "And you have to be Timothy Bates," she said extending her hand.

He took her hand and smiled. "Call me Tim."

"Ok, Tim. Did you have a good trip?"

Brad laughed. "He's really impressed with our Saskatchewan roads!"

Shauna Lee chuckled as she grabbed her coat and purse. "Shall we go?" Her eye's met Brad's and held. As she walked up to him, he slid his arm around her waist and dropped a quick kiss on her hair. "I take it you're playing hooky on Friday."

"Did Christina tell you that?"

"Not exactly; she just asked me what I was going to bring her from China."

She gave him a quick smile. "I gave her next week off too. She's filled in a lot for me lately and if I keep really busy while you are gone, time will go faster for me." She reached up and touched his cheek.

Brad looked at Tim. "Sorry guy. I should have introduced you. This is Shauna Lee Holt. She is Colt Thompson's accountant, but she's my Tweetie Bird. You'll get to know her better when you stay over at our place tonight."

217

Tim's surprise was obvious. *Tweetie Bird,* he thought. *Whoa fellow! I'm a way behind the times here. Brad with a woman; and she is living at his place! I hope he knows what the hell he is getting into.*

Tim nodded his acknowledgement to Shauna Lee, then followed Colt and her out of the room. Shauna Lee stopped at her receptionist's desk.

"Tim, this is my receptionist and my right hand around here: Christina Holmes.

"Christina, this is Timothy Bates. He is a friend of Brad's from B.C., but he is here for an interview for the manager's position at Thompson Land and Cattle Company. You remember earlier this fall, we were searching through the different head-hunter sites for someone suitable to manage the farm? Well Timothy is the man Colt decided to go with."

Christina stood up and reached out to shake hands with Timothy. As she shook his hand she could sense his closed attitude. The energy he gave off was flat, the look in his eye was guarded and cool. Christina's bubbly nature immediately sensed his remoteness and she drew back. *Yuk! What a bloody cold fish,* she thought.

Shauna Lee smile's included both of them. "If things work out the way we hope they will, you two will get to know each other well."

*Don't hold your breath,* Christina thought.

The next morning it was decided that Shauna Lee should drive her car out to the farm and Tim would follow her. She would come back to Swift Current to meet with Brad and Tim could decide if he was coming back to Brad's place for the night, or if he would stay overnight at the farm.

Brad had shown him where the spare key was if he came back and they weren't home. He had made it plain that he was taking the day to spend time with Shauna Lee because he was going to be away.

Brad and Shauna Lee spent a lazy day at home, relaxing and enjoying each other. He insisted on taking her out to a Steak and Seafood restaurant for supper. They enjoyed the meal, drank wine and relaxed. When they came home, Tim hadn't returned, so they spent the evening cuddling, kissing and stoking the sexual fire that smouldered between them. When it had fanned into a hot flame they retired to the bedroom and exhausted it. They fell asleep in each other's arms.

Sunday morning came too quickly for both of them. Brad held her against him as they lay in bed. "I don't want to go, Tweetie Bird," he whispered. "I'm going to miss you."

Her fingers traced his lips. "I'm going to miss you too. Just be sure you come home to me."

He laid his head against her hair. "I promise you; I will come back."

"I'll be here waiting for you. We'll make up for the lost time when you get back." She kissed him, darting her tongue between his lips. "Remember this," she flicked her tongue again. "Take the thought with you and bring it back to me."

Brad smiled and pushed back the sheets. "Let's go make breakfast. I want to remember you sitting across the table from me, with those big blue eyes sparkling and that mass of soft blonde curls bouncing." He pulled on his pyjama bottoms and went out to the kitchen.

She put on a cotton wrap and followed him. By the time she wandered into the kitchen, he had the coffee brewing.

He nodded to a brown paper bag on the counter. "You can empty that bag. I'll make scrambled eggs and bacon."

She looked at the bag. It was a large heavy brown paper one. As she reached for it Brad glanced over his shoulder. "It's delicate. Be careful how you open it."

"What are you up to now?"

He just smiled as he turned back to making breakfast.

Shauna Lee opened the bag carefully and peered inside. She looked in quickly, pulled back, then looked again and frowned. "What on earth?" she said softly. She reached in again and touched a mound of black hair. Suddenly it moved, squirming, wiggling. Two dark eyes looked up at her. She gasped and jerked her hand back.

Brad laughed out loud. "It's not going to hurt you. Take it out and hold it. You'll love it."

"What is it?" She reached her hand into the bag again and a

tiny tongue licked her fingers. She let her fingers close around the squirming, twisting little ball and she pulled it out. Brad watched her, savouring her incredulous expression.

"Oh, you little darling." Her eyes filled with happy tears as she buried her face in the tiny ball of fluff. "Brad, this is so…so special. What a tiny little puppy!"

She walked around the counter and leaned in to kiss him. "How old is he; or is it a she?"

"She is fourteen weeks old."

"She is so little. What is she?"

"She is a toy Havanese. She will always be a tiny little bundle of energy. She doesn't shed and apparently she is anti allergenic. I wanted you to have something to keep you company; something for you to love and cuddle with while I am gone. And when I get home we'll both love and cuddle her, but she is yours. Her name is Karma."

"Karma." She nuzzled the puppy. "I like that."

"There is just one thing I want to make clear. She does not sleep in our bed with us. I refuse to share you there."

She snuggled the puppy in the crook of her arm and slipped the other one around Brad's neck. She pulled his ear down to his lips. She hesitated, then grinned as she shot the tip of her tongue into his ear and twirled it around. "She wouldn't be any competition for you; no one would."

Brad chuckled. "I hope not! I think we'd better eat now. We have to leave for Regina by ten o'clock."

Shauna looked at him. "What am I going to do with her?"

"There is a small carrier in the back entry for her. I thought you'd want to take her with you; at least until she gets used to us and the place."

Shauna gently placed the squiggly little package in his arms, and ran to get the carrier. It was full of goodies; tiny doggy bones, some little toys, a dainty little collar and leash, water and food bowls, a soft pad in the bottom for her to lie on.

Shauna's eyes sparkled. "Brad! You thought of everything! You'll be a perfect daddy; to Karma I mean!" She blushed.

Brad's eyes met hers and held them. "I intend to be a perfect father when the time comes. And you'll be a perfect mother."

Shauna Lee looked away. She picked up the puppy and deposited her in the carrier. She petted and talked baby talk to the dog as she reluctantly closed the door and secured it.

"Brad Johnson. You are the most wonderful, thoughtful man I have ever met." She wrapped her arms around his neck and rested her cheek against his. "I don't know how I'd live if I ever lost you."

He grabbed her by the arms and looked into her eyes. "You don't think that way anymore. Remember? You are not going to lose me."

"I'm sorry. I've been afraid for so long, the thought just comes without me thinking about it."

"Start practicing then. '*Brad will be right here with me forever*'. Say it over and over and every time you start to doubt, say it again."

She buried her face into the curve of his neck.

Tears trickled down Shauna Lee's cheek as she watched the Air Canada fight taxi down the tarmac, lift into the air and disappear in the distance. A tight knot twisted in her stomach as she walked outside and went to her car in the parking lot. She unlocked the door, reached in the back seat and took out Karma's carrier and put it in front on the seat beside her.

She opened the door, took the little black ball of fluff out and tucked it against the curve of her neck. She sat, stroking it absently, her mind winging through the sky with Brad. Loneliness overwhelmed her. She broke down and cried.

Ten minutes later she placed Karma back in the carrier and started the car. She glanced at her watch. Brad was one third of the way to Calgary already. At four thirty, Alberta time, he would board his connecting flight and he would be in Vancouver at four fifty nine, B.C. time. It would be six fifty nine at Swift Current when he landed in

Vancouver. She sighed. "The provincial time changes really mess up your head when you look at your watch."

She grabbed her purse, took out her cell phone and turned it on. He would probably call her when he landed in Calgary and she didn't want to miss him. She needed to hear his voice.

Brad called before she was half way home. His voice was full of love and concern. They didn't talk for long because he had to hurry to make his connection to Vancouver.

Shauna Lee arrived at the house at six thirty. She brought Karma's carrier into the house and took her out of it. She put her on the floor and let her try her legs on the ceramic tile. The puppy stretched, enjoying her freedom. Shauna Lee put out a small dish of soft food and some water and watched her eat daintily. Her cell phone was on the floor beside her and when the phone rang she answered it before it could ring once more.

"Brad?"

"Hi, Tweetie Bird. Are you home yet?"

"We got home about half an hour ago. I'm sitting beside Karma on the floor and she is eating out of the new bowl you bought her...daddy. Where are you?"

"I'm waiting for my luggage to arrive on the carousel, Mommy. One day we'll discuss this mommy and daddy stuff, but now isn't the time for that."

"Brad...I don't think I could ever do that again."

"We'll take everything in little baby steps, just like we have up until now. I miss you sweetie. I can almost feel you right here beside me. I can't tell you how many times I've already reached for your hand. It's almost a shock to realise that you're not there."

"I know. I'm going to sleep in your shirt and take Karma to bed with me."

"That's all right when I'm not there. Just don't let her get the idea that she belongs there. Remember...I won't share you; even with her."

"Brad, where did you get Karma?"

He chuckled. "I owe Christina big time. She helped me."

"Have I told you how much you mean to me?" she asked softly.

"I'm listening. Tell me more."

"I miss you."

"I miss you too. My luggage just went around for the fourth time. I guess I'll have to go love; I'll talk to you in the morning before I leave. I have to get to bed early. I have to be up at three in the morning to get to the airport in time. I fly out with Continental at six o'clock. I'll call you at five, B.C. time. That'll be seven o'clock your time."

"OK." She kissed into the phone and said goodnight.

Loneliness washed over her as the line went dead. She scooped up Karma and went to sit on the couch. She cuddled her and caressed her. Karma luxuriated in her affection. Shauna Lee bent down and dropped a kiss on her head. Memories flooded through her. For a moment she was holding Ben again. Her heart filled with love as she looked into his beautiful little face.

Karma jumped up and tried to lick her face. Shauna Lee startled, coming back to reality with a jolt. Her eyes brimmed with tears as she lifted the puppy to her face and kissed it. *My baby.*

She turned the TV on in an effort to dispel her loneliness. She surfed through the channels, finding nothing that held her attention. Finally she went to bed, taking Karma with her. She slept fitfully, missing Brad's warmth, his arms around her. Karma was a comfort, but she couldn't compete with Brad.

When the phone rang at six o'clock, she snatched it from the night table. Before she could say hello she heard Brad's voice saying, "Good morning beautiful. I hope you slept better than I did." His voice spilled over her, rich and sexy.

"Didn't you sleep?"

"Not much. I missed you."

"I missed you too. You don't need to worry about Karma. Sweet as she is, she is no competition for you."

"That's a big relief! I was worried."

"You adorable goof. Where are you?"

"I'm waiting in line at the airport. I'm calling a little early, but I just wanted to hear your voice."

"Oh Brad. Do you have to be gone a whole week? Couldn't you do all this over the internet and come back home?"

"I've already done as much of that as I can do. I'll be home earlier if I can, but my schedule is pretty tight as it is. I'll call you when I get to Beijing. I have to go now Tweetie Bird, I'm next in line. I love you."

"I hope you know how much you mean to me, Brad."

"I do Sweetheart. Maybe you even love me a bit."

Tears filled her eyes. "Maybe," she whispered. "Hurry home to me!"

"I will. Bye love; I'll talk to you soon." The line went dead.

She held the phone to her lips and kissed it. *Maybe you even love me a bit.* "Why can't I say it to him?" she whispered. "I love you. Three little words; but they just won't come. I know he loves me and I know he won't leave me. Cripes, he knows all about me now and he's still here. What's wrong with me?"

Shauna Lee had a busy week. She had made sure of that when she had given Christina the week off. She took Karma to work with her every day. The junior associates made over her, but for the most part she stayed in the carrier under the reception desk, by Shauna Lee's feet.

Colt and Tim stopped in on Tuesday. From all appearances everything was working out, and Tim would probably take over management of the farm. Colt was taking him around town and introducing him to the merchants that he dealt with regularly.

They were still negotiating some of the finer points of the agreement but everything sounded positive. Shauna Lee smiled as they left her office. It felt good to know that her intuition had not let her down. She was sure that Brad would be happy to have his old friend in town too.

Brad called three times that week. Each call was a hurried message of loneliness and love. Business in China was not nine to five. His contact was guiding him through the maze of culturally proper considerations, but Brad was finding that missing her, compounded by constantly having to be careful not to slip into the North American casualness that could be interpreted as disrespectful by his hosts, was wearing on him. He knew he couldn't hurry the trip, but he was chafing to be on his way home.

When Shauna Lee opened the office Friday morning, loneliness was heavy on her heart. She was early and she sat behind the reception desk with Karma on her lap. Shauna Lee stroked her and talked to her softly, thankful that Brad had anticipated her loneliness and given her something cuddly and living to focus on. "One more sleep and daddy will be home," she whispered.

Christina stopped in for coffee at three o'clock. She brought each of them coffee from Tim Horton's and half a dozen donuts. Christina took over her chair at the desk and picked up Karma. She looked at Shauna Lee with a smile. "Isn't she a sweetie?" She ran her fingers over the puppy's head with a smile. "Shauna, I hope you realize how lucky you are. Brad is so crazy about you. I might even settle down if I met a guy who loved me like he loves you."

"I do know how lucky I am. He is wonderful and I have missed him like crazy. I'm counting down; one more sleep until he's home. Karma is a sweetie, but she is definitely not him."

Christina laughed. "He is good for you. You probably have no idea how much you have changed since he's come on the scene."

"I know one thing. I never imagined anyone could work their way into my heart like he has. I don't know what I would do without him now."

"I'd say you don't have to worry about that." She held out the box of donuts. "Eat! You look like you have lost five pounds this past week. You'll blow away if you keep it up."

Shauna Lee drained her cup of coffee and tossed it in the garbage. "Will you stay at the desk while I go to the washroom?"

"Go!"

When Shauna Lee came back down the hall, she heard Christina talking. She stepped into the reception area and stopped dead. Her face went white and momentarily, she couldn't find her voice.

Christina looked at her with surprise. "Shauna? What is wrong?" She turned to look at the man in front of her, puzzled.

"I'm her dad. She doesn't want to see me, but I have to talk to her."

Shauna Lee gasped. "How dare you come here? You know I don't want anything to do with you."

Patch Bergeron held his ground. "I'm not leaving until we talk."

"Screw you!" Shauna Lee yelled. "You didn't want anything to do with me thirty five years ago. I haven't seen you for over twenty years. Why the sudden urge to see me now?"

Shock registered on Christina's face. *What the hell is going on here,* she wondered.

Patch nodded, his hazel eyes holding Shauna's blue ones. "I was wrong. In twenty years I've come to realize that. I am ashamed of what I did, but I need to explain; to tell you the truth."

Shauna Lee stormed into her office and slammed the door. Christina stared after her, and then looked at Patch.

"I'm not leaving until I talk to her."

"I…I'll go in and see what I can do." Christina slowly opened the door. Shauna Lee was standing at the window, staring outside. "Shauna Lee," she said softly.

Shauna Lee's cheeks were wet with tears when she turned to face her.

"He says he's not going to leave until he talks to you."

"Jeeze, I wish Brad was here. He'd throw him out into the street. What does he think he has to say that's so important now; after all these years?"

"Look Shauna. I don't know your history with him, but he is determined. I'll come in and sit with you if you want."

Shauna shook her head and dashed the tears from her cheeks. "Send the useless bastard in here. There's nothing he can do or say that will make any difference now."

Christina went out and brought Patch to the door. Shauna Lee glared at him as he closed it behind him. She crossed her arms over her chest, symbolically closing him out. "All right. Have your say and then get out."

"LeeAnn, will you sit down…can we sit down?"

"LeeAnn does not exist anymore."

"No matter what you call yourself, you are still LeeAnn Bergeron."

She sneered. "I guess you would know, wouldn't you. How did you decide on Patch?"

He looked at her steadily. "My first name is Patrick. It always has been. Aaron is my middle name. My family called me that because my dad's name was Patrick too. Patch is the nickname the ranch hands gave me. After all these years it's become my name.

"And after all these years I am Shauna Lee Holt." She walked to her chair behind the desk and sat down. She motioned to him. "Sit down and let's get this over with; tell me your story and get out."

"It's not a story; it's the truth."

"As if I would believe anything you said."

Patch ignored the jibe. "Lee...Shauna Lee. Your mom and I..."

Shauna Lee bristled. He didn't miss that fact.

"Just listen, please. When I married your mom, I was crazy in love with her. She was beautiful. You remind me of her...except for your coloring and those...those big blue eyes.

"She was sexy and full of fun. But after three years of marriage, I discovered that I...I...that she didn't really love me. I was just a fill in."

"How can you say that?"

"Because, one time when she was mad at me she told me so and I knew that she meant it." He twisted his hands together. "I was hurt. No I wasn't just hurt; I was devastated. I should have set her free, but part of me still loved her and part of me wanted to hurt her the way she'd hurt me.

"Besides that; where would she have gone? What would she have done?" He looked at her. "In those days, it wasn't like today. We didn't have any money. We would have both been struggling on our own. And I had my damn pride; what would people think?"

He shrugged. "I started drinking. It helped me forget; it helped me make her angry; it helped me get even with her for what she had done to me. The bottle became my lover."

He looked out the window and swallowed hard. "Then she got pregnant. I felt ashamed. I'd never touched her with love since she had told me there was someone else." He shook his head. "We had sex, but

I never made love to her. She submitted to me, but I made sure she knew that I...that I hadn't forgiven her."

He stood up and walked to the window. "When you were born, I couldn't help but be proud. You were so beautiful. But as you got older...you didn't look like either one of us. You had blonde curls and those big beautiful blue eyes. No one in my family had blue yes. And your mom's eyes were so dark, they were almost black. Your grandma Holt's eyes were as dark as your moms."

He turned to look at her. "Your eyes were so striking. They haunted me. And I kept thinking about them. Then one day I remembered where I had seen them before."

Shauna Lee sucked her breath in. *Oh, no, no, no!*

"It was like a kick in the gut when it came back to me. One night, before you were born, we were at a house party. There was a guy there that night. I suspected that Marie had known him before. She danced with him all night. She flirted with him; they were all over each other. I was jealous and I drank until I passed out.

"When I put it all together in my mind, I confronted her with my suspicions. She denied that anything had happened. But I couldn't let it go. I kept after her about it day in and day out. One day I pushed her far enough; she defiantly admitted that she had gone to the barn with him.

"I couldn't stand looking at you after that; seeing your curly blonde hair and those blue eyes was like a knife in my heart. I couldn't deny what stared me in the face every day. You were not my child. I knew you were his."

Shauna Lee covered her face and sobbed.

Patch walked over to her. He put his arms around her for the first time in thirty five years. She stiffened and then collapsed. "I am so sorry, LeeAnn. I couldn't think clearly for years; not until I left and got away. But your mom and I; we were both selfish and filled with anger and misery. Without thinking about what we were doing, we hurt you the most and you were the only innocent one." He kissed her forehead.

"I've had twenty years to think about what we did to each other, and to you. I was so stubborn and proud that I wouldn't forgive her.

She knew she had hurt me, but eventually I just wore her down and she became lost in the defeat of my endless rejection. We continued to live in that same vicious cycle year after year, destroying each other and everything around us."

Shauna Lee cried until she was exhausted and he held her until she pulled away.

"When I got older, I realized that you didn't love each other," she said. "I have wondered how Andre was ever conceived."

"I forced her one night when I was drunk; I'm ashamed to admit that I did that quite often in those days. But she never got pregnant. I thought I was sterile. When she got pregnant I thought she must have been with someone else. But she was so wrung out, so despondent; I couldn't imagine her having sex with anyone else.

"When Andre was born, he looked like me right from the start. I couldn't deny it. And I loved him like I loved no one else; except your mom when I first married her."

"Things were better between you and mom for a while weren't they?"

"Yes. It's amazing what our guilt and our love for Andre did for a while. And then..." Patch walked back to the window. His shoulders were shaking and she heard him smother a sob.

Shauna Lee did the unimaginable. She walked over to him and put her arms around him. "And then Andre died," she whispered sadly.

He shook his head. "No! Then I *killed* him. I was drunk and I ran over my own son with the tractor."

"It was an accident."

Patch was crying, his body wracked with sobs. "I'll never forget that...seeing him lying there. I felt like my own body had been torn in a thousand pieces. I wished I could trade places with him; you can't know much how I wanted to.

"I couldn't face what I had done; I needed to blame someone else, so I blamed you. And I shot your horse. I was so...I was so cruel to you... and to your mom."

He tried to collect himself and control his emotions. "After that I totally lost myself in the bottle, and your mom lost herself in the black hole I'd forced her into. Then, like a coward, I ran away and left you to fend for yourself."

He pulled away from her. "I've been a coward all my life, Lee… Shauna Lee. I didn't have the guts to try to make things work with your mom; I made her life hell. I was a shameful bastard to you.

"I don't expect forgiveness. I don't deserve it. I can't forgive myself. I've thought about ending it all, but in some way I know that living with all this is my punishment. I live in my own hell every day."

They clung to each other; two strangers crying together; a father and a daughter as they had never been.

Patch cradled Shauna Lee's head. "It's too late to change the past, but I had to tell you the truth. I couldn't live with you believing that your own flesh and blood could have treated you the way that I did. Real fathers don't do that. I realize that I was the only dad you ever knew, but I never truly was a dad to you."

There was a gentle tap at the door. Shauna Lee looked at her watch, knowing it was Christina. "Just lock up and go home, Christina."

"Are…are you sure? Are you OK?"

"We'll be done here pretty soon. And Christina; thanks for filling in for me."

Shauna Lee walked back to her chair and sat down. Patch looked at her uneasily. She motioned for him to sit down as she reached for the box of Kleenex. She pulled out a couple of tissues and handed them to him, then took some for herself. After they had both wiped away the tears and blew their noses, they sat and looked at each other.

"I'll leave now, if you want me to."

She shook her head. "I'm not sure what we do now." She sighed. "I wish Brad were here. He'd know what to do."

Patch smiled ruefully. "If he was here, we would never have had this conversation. That's why I came today. Ollie mentioned he was gone so I decided I needed to do this while he was away."

Shauna Lee was shocked. "You came here today because he was away?"

"Well, he's very protective of you; like a bloody guard dog. He has no use for me; he's made that clear." He smile was drawn. "I'm glad that you have someone like him in your life. It's plain that he loves you and he makes it his business to take care of you. He's a good man Shauna Lee."

"He is. He is the first person who has loved me unconditionally in my whole life. I never intended to let anyone into my heart, but he was so persistent, before I realised it he was there. I don't know how I would live without him now."

Patch looked at his watch. "I don't know how you feel, but this has been exhausting for me. And I'm hungry. Would you let me take you out for dinner?"

She pleated the sleeve of her shirt with her fingers. "We can't go back and change the past; and I closed the door on my life as LeeAnn Bergeron over twenty years ago. I tried to bury everything; forget it ever happened. But Brad says it has coloured my whole life and it is still is part of who I am. He has helped me deal with a lot of memories. Meeting you at the ranch that day was such a shock."

She looked at him. "Good, bad or indifferent, you are the only dad I've ever known. To be honest, until Andre was born I didn't realize that you didn't love me. I guess even then, I didn't get it. Sometimes I wished you would play with me the way you did with him. I knew you and mom fought. I was devastated when Andre died; but when you shot Poko…then I despised you. And I have ever since."

Patch shifted in his seat uncomfortably. He swallowed hard and looked away.

She sighed "Instinctively, I want to slam this door closed right now." She shuddered. "But I guess that would just continue the cycle of pain and the lack of forgiveness that made such a mess of all our lives from the very start. Neither of us can start to heal until we face this."

He looked at her then, his eyes brimming with tears.

"I have to tell you, I'm glad you insisted on this meeting," Shauna Lee continued. "What you've told me has made some of the things I couldn't understand make sense. I understand how hard it had to be for you to look at me every day and know what had happened." She shuddered as she covered her eyes with her hands.

Patch swallowed hard. "It doesn't excuse how I acted; you were innocent; the product of our selfishness."

Shauna Lee shrugged and reached for her purse. "I can't tell you that I'll ever love you. And after what you have told me; forgiveness is not an issue. I guess we have twenty years to work through. I'll go for dinner with you."

She stood up and reached for her jacket. Patch stood and went to the door ahead of her. He opened it and waited as she shut off the lights and stepped past him. His hand reached out to touch her arm.

"Thank you," he said softly.

She nodded and went to the reception desk. Christina had closed Karma's carrier and left it on top of the desk. Shauna Lee looked at Patch. "I want to let her out and let her run around a bit. She is trained to use a little box in the back and I should give her a little bit to eat. Is it all right if we wait about fifteen minutes?"

He nodded. "She is a cute little thing."

"Brad gave her to me the day he left for China. He wanted me to have her so she would keep me company."

Patch smiled. "He is a good man."

Shauna smiled. "He is wonderful." She thought for a moment and then reached for her cell phone. "I'm surprised I haven't heard from him." She checked her messages.

"Damn," she said softly. "He called four times. How did I miss him?" She checked her phone. "Oh, the ringer shut off. He has probably left Beijing already. With the time difference…he'll be in the air by now. And he'll be worried about me."

The evening went quickly and Patch and Shauna Lee made a tenuous start to healing their relationship. He filled her in on his years at the Gang Ranch. She shared with him how she had gone to University and got her CA, and ended buying Swift Current Accounting and Bookkeeping Services. He did not bring up anything about the baby and if he had, she would have refused to discuss the subject.

They parted easily. She knew she could have offered to have him spend the night at the house, but she didn't. She needed time to absorb everything and time to think. It had been a day full of unexpected revelations and she wished Brad were here. She missed him.

# CHAPTER SIXTEEN

*B*rad arrived in Vancouver at nine thirty Saturday morning. It was ten fifteen by the time he reached the luggage carousel. He had not been able to connect with Shauna before he'd left Beijing; worry and anxiety gnawed at his gut. He flipped open his phone and dialed her cell again. It rang three times before she answered.

"Brad?" she cried. "Is that you?"

Relief flooded through him. "Tweetie Bird. You had me worried. I couldn't get you before I flew out yesterday. Where were you?"

"When I realized that I'd missed you it was too late. I accidently shut the ring tone off. Yesterday was a crazy day. Normally I would have been checking it constantly but yesterday I was fighting to keep my equilibrium."

"What happened?"

"I'll fill you in when you get here. Just hurry home. I'm missing you like crazy. I needed to feel your arms around me so badly last night."

"Where are you now?"

"Karma and I just left home. We are on our way to Regina to meet you." She smiled. "Do you want me to book the honeymoon suite at the Coast Inn, or do you want to drive home and sleep in our own bed?"

"Do you mind if we drive home? I want to be in the comfort of our own bed with you tonight."

"That sounds good to me. We can sleep in tomorrow."

"I can hardly wait to feel your body against mine. I love you, Tweetie Bird."

"Uh huh, maybe, too. I've missed you like crazy too!"

"Did I hear you say you loved me?"

She smiled. "Maybe."

"Be careful, Sweetie. One of these times you are going to slip up and say it. I'll see you at about four thirty."

She smiled as the line went dead.

Shauna Lee was at the airport two hours early. She was walking Karma through the parking lot, letting both of them stretch and get some exercise. Excitement bubbled in her mind, anxiety knotted in her gut and sexual anticipation tightened in her groin.

She alternated between checking the time and peering longingly into the sky. Her logic told her that Brad's plane was barely half way to Calgary yet, but her emotions told her that time was passing at an agonizingly slow pace.

She stooped to pick up Karma and snuggled her in the curve of her neck. "I love you sweetie." she whispered. *Both of you,* she thought. She closed her eyes and swallowed hard. *I don't know if I should dare to think that, but I do love you Brad.* A flicker of uncertainty rippled through her, followed by a shimmer of fear. "No," she whispered, pushing it away. "Brad would never hurt me."

At four o'clock she put Karma back in her carrier and put it on the back seat, out of the sun. She opened the back windows a small crack and locked the car. While she walked into the airport terminal, she looked into the sky, searching for Brad's plane.

When she stepped through the door she realized that her heart was pounding and she felt nervous. She stood looking out the airside viewing area, watching for it to land. She heard the arrival announcement and then it was taxiing up the runway.

She moved to stand near the escalator. She was shocked to realise that she was trembling. She wrapped her arms around herself, attempting to control her involuntary reaction. Her eyes were glued to the landing at the top.

She was so intent that she almost missed seeing Brad come bounding down the stairs next to it. His eyes were focused on her and the smile on his face was dazzling. When their eyes met she gasped and moved toward him. Tears of joy were spilling down her cheeks as he enfolded her in his arms.

They were kissing hungrily, their hands groping and pulling each other close.

"Shauna," he whispered. "It feels so good to hold you. I never knew a week could be so long." He pulled back and looked into her eyes, smiling as he brushed her tears away. "Tweetie Bird, I missed you so much." He hugged her against him again. "God, I love you."

"I love you too, Brad."

She felt him tense and then he looked into her eyes. "What did you say? Did I hear you right?"

She smiled through her tears. "Maybe."

"We'd better get out of here before I embarrass us." He grabbed her hand and led her outside. "Where are you parked?"

"What about your luggage?"

"Oh shit, I got so excited I forgot about that." He turned her toward him, a hand on each arm. "You did say you loved me, didn't you?"

She smiled. "Maybe."

"I guess I'm going to have to make love to you slowly, until you are begging me for mercy and then you'll say it again. After this past week, I definitely up for the challenge." He grasped her hand and pushed it against the hardness in his jeans. "Don't you agree?"

She kissed him quickly. "Quit talking and go get your luggage. I'll bring the car around to meet you."

He watched her dart across the parking lot, then turned and went inside. When he came back out she was waiting at the curb for him.

He was grinning from ear to ear. "It is so good to be home and have you close. I can't wait to get even closer."

"Hang on big guy. It's a little small in this car. And I don't know of any caves around here. So we'd better get on the road. We've got a two and a half hour drive ahead of us."

He groaned as he reached across the consol and slid his hand along the inside of her thigh. She shivered and grabbed it in hers, holding it still.

"I've changed my mind. I can't wait that long. I've dreamed about the feel of your skin against mine all week; and my poor friend here…"

236

He stroked the hardness behind his zipper. "He's so tired of cold showers. He deserves a hot moist place before he suffers from hypothermia."

He leaned over and slid his tongue into her ear. "Find a motel, or a hotel room…whatever, just make sure it's sound proof and has a king sized bed. I don't want everyone else to hear you begging…just me."

She pulled away as his tongue twirled around in her ear. She shivered. "Behave yourself and help me decide where to go."

"It can't be that hard to find. There's a Days Inn near the airport. I remember looking at it online and it had king sized beds."

"Karma is here too."

"I'll put her in my garment bag."

"You are bad."

"But I am good!"

When they walked into the King Suite at the Days Inn, Shauna Lee whistled softly. "Brad. How much did this cost?"

"Insane, but I intend to get my money's worth." He grabbed the *Do Not Disturb* sign and put it on the door. Then he reached for her. His kiss left her weak in the knees, clinging to him. He groaned as her rubbed himself against her. He reached to the hem of her shirt and started to lift it.

"Brad," she drew back. "Karma; we have to take her out of your garment bag." She smiled softly as she traced his lips with her finger. "And I think we are going to be busy for a while…we'd better give her something to eat and some water before we get too involved."

He groaned. "You're right." They laid some bath towels in the tub and put Karma onto them. Shauna Lee gave her some soft food on a saucer that she took off the counter by the coffee pot. She put water in the ice bucket and set it by the drain. "I feel mean, putting her in the tub."

"It gives her more freedom than she'd have in her carrier, and she's fed. And I'm hungry," he said as he reached for the hem of her shirt again, "for you."

She sighed as he guided her out of the bathroom and back to the bed. His lips trailed down her neck as he reached behind her to unhook her bra. He groaned as it slipped down over her breasts. His hands became frantic as he slid it down her arms and let it fall on the floor. His hands caressed her breasts.

She gasped as he licked her nipples. Her hands tore at his shirt and slow and sensuous morphed into fast and frantic as they tore each others clothes off. He lifted her onto the bed and she pulled him with her.

Everything happened quickly. Blatant lust fuelled their urgency. There would be time later to savour their lovemaking but for now the overwhelming need won out. They took each other eagerly, their passion hot and demanding.

Brad felt himself explode after the first few strokes. "Damn, I lost it," he groaned. As he collapsed onto her, he slid his fingers into her heat, stroking her gently until he felt her convulse beneath him. Her hands threaded into his hair and balled it as she moaned. He rolled over and pulled her with him.

"So much for making you beg," he whispered. "I have missed you; I've missed us...so much. I don't know what I'm going to do. I don't want to leave you behind the next time I have to go." He looked into her eyes. "I kept reaching for your hand; on the train, in a car, in the bed. It felt like part of me was...missing."

"I missed you too."

His arms tightened around her briefly. "I love you so much, Tweetie Bird."

She buried her face against his chest. "I..." She shut her eyes. "I love you too, Brad." She raised her head and looked into his eyes. "There. I...I said it." Tears filled her eyes. "I love you," she whispered.

He expelled a deep breath. "I wasn't sure that I would ever hear you say that." He cupped her face. "I've waited so long to hear you say those words. Sweetheart, you can't imagine what it means to me."

"I'm afraid, Brad. I can't lose you. Anything I've ever loved...."

He touched his finger to her lips. "Shhhh... remember, you aren't supposed to think that way anymore. That is not going to happen."

"What if I am a jinx?"

He held her close. "You're not a jinx! Shauna, everything and everybody that you have lost; that all happened before you were eighteen years old, and none of it was your fault." He nuzzled his face into her hair.

"And look at what you have done since then. You are strong and resilient and what you have achieved is beyond most people's imagination. You started over with nothing and you fought tooth and nail to build a life for yourself. And you have done it."

She rolled onto her back and stared at the ceiling. "When it comes down to it, I am the reason that everything went wrong in the first place."

"Shauna..."

"I had a visit from my dad...I mean Patch, yesterday."

Brad shot up on the bed. "That bastard..."

"He came to the office and he wouldn't leave until he had talked to me."

"You mean he came to shift more blame onto you; what an asshole."

"He didn't do that. He apologized for being such a bad father."

"I guess he should have," Brad responded heatedly.

"Nothing is simple Brad. He explained things that made more sense about what I remember happening between him and mom."

"Why would you believe anything he said?"

"I probably wouldn't have if I hadn't gone to Glaslyn with you."

"What has that got to do with anything?"

"Do you remember what Bob Matzlan said to me about him and mom meeting at a party?"

Brad thought for a moment and then he nodded.

"Well dad pretty much confirmed what he said."

"No...."

"Dad didn't know who Bob was, but he knew mom had been with him."

"Damn it, Shauna..."

"He told me he was crazy about mom when they got married. A couple years later they had a fight and she told him she had always loved someone else. He was hurt, and angry and he couldn't get past it. He started drinking.

"One night they were at a house party and some guy showed up. He said mom and the guy danced and flirted all night. He said they were 'all over each other'; Dad felt angry and jealous and he drank until he passed out.

"Later when mom was pregnant, he was excited because he thought it was his child; even when I was born he still thought so. But I was blonde and I had these blue eyes. It bothered him because there were no blue eyes in his family. Mom's eyes were so dark they were almost black and so were grandmas. Eventually he remembered the guy at that party; his blonde hair and blue eyes, and he knew. I guess eventually mom admitted that she'd gone to the barn with him."

She turned and looked at him. "I was a constant reminder of her betrayal, and he...he couldn't stand to be around me."

"That would be hard." Brad admitted. "But why didn't he divorce her instead of making your life hell."

"He said he should have, but part of him still loved her and part of him wanted to punish her for what she had done. He never forgave her. They just lived year after year in their own hell. And I was the reason."

"That is not true. I could pound that man into the ground. How dare he dump that on you?"

"No, Brad. That's not what he did. He wanted me to know that my own flesh and blood had not treated me the way he had."

"Damn! I leave you for a week and this happens. Are you OK?"

"I am fine. I really wished you were here last night; but I can't count on you to rescue me all the time." She looked at him seriously. "Brad... he couldn't have told me this if you'd been here. You would have run him off."

"Damn right, I would have! The nerve of him coming to your office."

"But I'm glad he did. Finally, I understand what happened. When I was young it was hard to accept that he wouldn't play with me; especially when I saw him with Andre. I couldn't comprehend why he wasn't the same with me. He wouldn't even touch me."

He pulled her close. "Sweetheart, that doesn't make you a jinx. That was their problem. You were a victim."

"It seems like my whole life has been like that."

Brad shook his head. "No sweetheart...that first part of your life was, but everything that happened; even you ending up with that Dave jerk. All of that happened because you didn't have a real family."

"Brad, do I know how to be different?"

"Shauna..." His voice was filled with anguish. He shook his head. "I wish my love could heal you. But...you have been through so much." He looked into eyes. "Sweetheart, maybe we need to get professional help."

She stiffened. "What are you saying?"

"Maybe we need to go for therapy."

"You mean a psychiatrist?" She pulled away. "No! I'm not going there!"

"Shauna, you have been hurt so badly. And you have never really dealt with any of it. You just pushed your pain down and buried it." He reached for her chin and tried to turn her face toward him.

"Brad, you say you love me. Why can't you ever just accept me the way I am?" She pushed his hand away and rolled over, turning her back to him.

"Sweetheart it's not that I don't accept you. I don't want you to live in fear or always feel that you are not worthy of happiness."

"Well it feels like you're telling me I'm not good enough the way I am!"

Brad's heart fell. He sighed. "Shauna...that is not what I meant. I would be with you every step of the way. I need to understand all this too."

He slid his arm around her waist and tried to snuggle against her, but she pushed his arm away.

"Well you can forget it. I am not subjecting myself to that; I've bared my soul to you and now that isn't enough."

"Sweetheart?"

She lay tense and didn't answer.

*Shit. I stuck my foot in my mouth again.* He groaned.

They both tossed and turned but sleep wouldn't come. At nine o'clock Brad got up and walked to the window. Shauna Lee got up and went into the bathroom. She came out with Karma in her arms.

Brad turned to face her. He could see the hurt in her eyes. He crossed the room and pulled her into his arms. Karma wiggled between them. Shauna Lee did not relax against him.

He sighed. "Shall we go home? This hasn't turned out the way I planned." He walked away to pick up his garment bag. "I think it's got to be these King sized beds. The last time we rented one we didn't sleep either." There was no humour in his voice; only anxiety.

Shauna Lee picked up the dog carrier and put Karma into it. She collected Karma's things from the bath tub. She gathered up the towels and threw them on the bathroom floor. Wordlessly she put Karma's toys in her overnight bag and picked up her jacket.

Brad tucked Karma into the garment bag and looked around. "I guess that's everything. Are you ready to go?"

Shauna nodded and opened the door. She stepped out into the hall and Brad followed. They took the elevator down to the lobby. The clerk looked puzzled when Brad dropped off the key and told him that they were checking out.

Shauna Lee handed him the car keys and the two and a half hour drive home was made in uncomfortable silence. When they drove into Swift Current, Brad pulled into the A&W drive through. "I'm starved. I haven't eaten since breakfast. How about you?"

Shauna Lee swallowed hard. She started to shake her head and then changed her mind. "Yes. I am hungry."

"Do you want a hamburger?"

"Yes, please."

Brad ordered two cups of coffee and three hamburgers.

"I guess you are hungry," Shauna Lee said with a faint chuckle.

"I am. I was so excited about coming home that I didn't think to grab lunch. And then I couldn't wait to make love to you…"

"And I spoiled that," she said sadly.

He reached for her hand and she let him take it. "You didn't spoil it, Tweetie Bird. I should have thought before I spoke. I didn't mean to upset you. You have to know I would never hurt you; that I was only thinking of what would help you.

"I know, but I don't want to talk to a stranger about my life."

"We'll drop the subject. It was just a suggestion."

They stopped in the parking lot and ate. "That felt good. I was hungry. And that was my first hamburger since I touched down on Canadian soil again."

"I needed to eat, too. It's going to feel good to get home and fall into our bed now," she said with a faint smile.

Brad reached out and squeezed her hand. "I've missed cuddling with you."

Tears glistened in her eyes. "I have missed it too. Karma is adorable, and she did sleep with me, but she is no substitute for you."

They went straight to bed. Their sexual desire had been subdued. They both needed the healing comfort of feeling skin against skin; Brad's chest against Shauna Lee's back with his arm around her waist holding her against him, their legs tucked together.

Shauna Lee lifted his hand to her lips and kissed it softly. "I do love you, Brad Johnson," she whispered.

"And I love you, Tweetie bird."

The skies were grey when they woke up the next morning. Shauna Lee turned in Brad's arms to face him. She ran her hands along his jaw, up over his cheeks and into his hair.

Brad shifted onto his back and eased her into the curve of his shoulder. "It is so good to be here, holding you like this. This may not be good timing and it's not how I planned to do this, but I thought about it all the time I was gone.

He pushed up on his elbow and looked into her sleep flushed face.

"Tweetie Bird, I hope you'll think about it. Don't answer me right now because your first reaction will be "no". But I want to marry you and spend the rest of my life with you."

Her blue eyes widened. She looked frightened as she shook her head.

He kissed her. "I did say I wanted you to think about it for a while." He lightly brushed the tip of her nose. "You always say 'no' at first. And I haven't asked you yet. But I'm going to do it now; will you marry me, Shauna Lee Holt?"

Tears filled her eyes.

He smiled. "I know what your answer would be right now. Just think about it for a few days or hours and then give it to me."

She shook her head. He placed a finger across her lips. "Not now," he said with a teasing smile. "Get used to the idea. And remember, when I really want something…"

"…you don't take no for an answer." She finished his sentence. "Brad you know this scares me to death."

He nodded. "That's why I told you to think about it. The question is open ended, with no pressure! Well not much. I'll wait an hour or two for your answer." His hand slipped down to tickle her ribs.

She writhed and he laughed. "I thought about that when I was in China, too. I didn't know if you were ticklish. I had to find out before I married you."

She smacked him playfully. "No pressure, eh?"

"Of course not; just say 'Yes' and I'll go shopping for a ring tomorrow, like I'd planned to do before I lost my head and jumped the gun."

# CHAPTER SEVENTEEN

*S*unday morning, Colt sat behind the desk in his office. He smiled across it at Tim Bates. "So are you satisfied with everything?"

Tim reached across the desk and Colt clasped his hand. "I think the arrangement works well for both of us. I'm happy if you are."

"So now we just need to find a place for you to live."

"I'll check around town. Brad should be back this weekend. He may have some ideas."

Colt stood up and stretched. "We'll come up with something between the two of us. Let's go have a coffee."

They went into the kitchen. Frankie was sitting at the table poring over house decorating magazines. She rubbed her lower back as she looked up them. "Ideas, ideas, ideas! This is so exciting, but how do you decide which way to go?"

"Talk to Mona. It's her job to help you decide." He walked over to the coffee pot and set it up to brew. "Tim and I have made a deal. Now we just have to do up the paper work and he will officially be the new manager of the farm. Next, we have to find a place for him to live until we move out to the ranch."

Frankie stood up. She grimaced. "That's great news Tim." She leaned forward and rested her hands on the table.

Colt moved to stand beside her and placed his hand on her back. "Is your back still aching?"

"Yes, it is. In fact it seems to be getting worse. I think I'll go lay down for a while."

"Can I do anything to help?"

"Would you heat the gel pack for me? Not too warm, though."

"Is it still in the hall closet?"

She nodded. Colt frowned as he watched her go up the stairs. "She never complains about anything. She has to be really bothered, for her to let it show." He went to the closet and got the gel pack and put it in the microwave.

Concern showed in Tim's face. "How far along is the pregnancy?"

"About nineteen weeks. She's due in April."

When the beep signalled that the gel pack was warm, Colt took it out of the microwave and bounded up the stairs with it. He offered to massage her back but Frankie insisted that he go back down stairs and have coffee with Tim. He helped Frankie position it under her lower back and looked at her with concern. "Should I take you to the doctor, hon?"

She shook her head. "I'm sure everything will be OK. My body is probably just stretching, making room for the baby."

"Did this happen when you were carrying the twins?"

"No, but every pregnancy is different. Just let me lay down for a bit." Frankie laid down and closed her eyes. The warmth didn't seem to help. Her discomfort drove her from the bed into the bathroom. She pulled down her jeans and sat on the toilet. "This never happened with the twins. It must be gas." She found no relief, so she stood up and started to pull up her panties. She started in shock as she noticed a red stain on the crotch. Fear struck at her heart. *Blood; there shouldn't be blood.*

She pulled up her jeans and went back to the bedroom. She sat on the edge of the bed. "Ok…I just have to get a hold of myself. I remember reading somewhere that spotting is not unusual. It's not heavy. I'll just rest here and see if it gets any worse."

She lay down and tried to relax. In half an hour she was up again. She went into the bathroom to check her panties. There was more blood but it was still light in colour and not heavy. When she stood up she noticed that the ache in her lower back seemed to reach around into her stomach and pelvic region. *Maybe I should call the doctor. There shouldn't be a problem, but this didn't happen the last time. Still, I don't want to be an alarmist. I'll just lie down again.*

Colt came into their room and sat on the side of the bed. "How are you doing? Any better?"

"Not really. There's a bit of blood on my panties, but not very much. But the ache has moved around into my tummy and the pelvic area. I'm not sure what to do. This didn't happen when I was carrying the twins."

"Fran, why don't I take you to the hospital? We don't want to take any chances with your health or this precious little bundle." He rested his hand on her tummy, looking concerned.

"I guess you are right. I just didn't want to be silly about it. I've read that spotting is normal sometimes."

Colt took her hand and helped her sit up. He put his arm around her and guided her down the stairs. Worry was etched on his face as he looked at Tim.

"I'm going to take Fran into emergency just to make sure everything is all right. The twins are sleeping. Would you go over to the trailer and tell Ellie what is happening? I know Sunday is normally her day off, but she'll need to fill in here while we are gone. I'll call home when I know something more."

"Don't worry. Between the two of us, everything will be looked after here." He gave Frankie a serious look. "It's good that you are going in now and don't worry about the twins."

She smiled uneasily and followed Colt out to the truck. After he helped her get settled, he got in on his side and started the truck. He reached for her hand as he let the motor warm up. "I've been pretty preoccupied this past week, with Tim and getting this farm manager thing set up. I guess I haven't asked how you've been. Have you had any problems before now?"

"Not really. I've been more tired than usual I think; not sleepy, just no energy. And my stomach has been a bit queasy the past few days, but I think that's just part of being pregnant. I remember feeling that way earlier on with the twins."

"You didn't say anything."

"Colt, I can't run to you with every little bump in the road. You were busy. Getting things settled with Tim is huge in the big picture."

"Honey, you and my family are the big picture for me."

"I'm sure everything is all right. But you are right, it is best to check it out and know for sure."

They checked into Emergency. The doctor who attended her was woman. She asked her who her OB/GYN was, along with a few general questions; then she placed the stethoscope at various places on her tummy. She gnawed on her bottom lip as she listened.

Concern filled Colt. "Is everything all right?"

She smiled. "I'm sure it is, but this little one isn't co-operating. I'm not finding a heartbeat, but that is probably because of how the baby is laying."

She consulted Frankie's chart. "You are nineteen weeks now. Are you feeling movement yet?"

Frankie frowned. "Not yet. But that's not unusual is it?"

"It's your second pregnancy, so it is possible that you could, but it's not unusual that you don't. I'm going to send you for an ultrasound though. We want to cover all our bases."

Colt's stomach tightened, even as he smiled reassuringly at Frankie. *Everything has to be all right,* he thought, reassuring himself. Frankie got dressed and sat on the bed. Colt was holding her hand when Dr. Wilfred pulled back the curtain and stepped in by the gurney bed.

"Hello there, Frankie." He looked at Colt and reached to shake his hand. He looked down at the chart he was holding, and then touched Frankie's shoulder kindly. "So tell me exactly what has been happening with you, my girl."

Frankie explained what had happened that morning and mentioned her tiredness and the couple of days of nausea. He smiled reassuringly and reaffirmed that they would do an ultra sound as soon as the technician was available.

The technician appeared with a wheel chair almost immediately. Frankie protested that she could walk, but the doctor assured her that this free ride was one of the few that people got in the medical system and she should enjoy it.

Colt went into the room with Frankie and stood out of the way as the technician prepped her; then he moved up and stood on the far side of the bed, where he could watch the sonogram screen too.

Dr. Wilfred watched intently as the technician dabbed jelly on Frankie's tummy and started to move the head around on it. Tension grew heavy in the small room as she searched for the pulsing of the heart. There was no telltale rhythm. Frankie's face crinkled up as tears filled her eyes. "Where is the heartbeat?" she pleaded anxiously.

Doctor Wilfred and the technician looked at each other, and then quickly broke contact. The technician cleaned up and pushed the machine back. Doctor Wilfred looked at Colt sadly, then reached for Frankie's hand.

"There is no heart beat Frankie. I'm afraid your baby has died. What you are experiencing now is the body releasing the uterine lining and expelling it, because it senses that the embryo is no longer viable."

Frankie began to tremble. "But,why? Why would my baby die in.. si.de me? What did I do wrong?" Tears spilled and she looked at Colt, her eyes imploring him. "I'm so sorry. I'm so sorry I didn't take better care."

She collapsed into inconsolable tears as Colt bent over her. He pulled her close. "Fran don't...honey, this is not your fault. You didn't do anything wrong."

"But I didn't keep it safe. I...I let it die."

Doctor Wilfred stepped up and laid a hand on each of them. "About ten to twenty percent of known pregnancies end in early miscarriage. It is the body's way of saying that the fetus is abnormal and not growing correctly so the uterus expels the embryo. We don't know why this happens, but it does.

"As a rule the baby has already died before the miscarriage starts. That is what has happened here. But even if you had come in before the heart had actually quit beating, once the process starts it is almost impossible to halt. Something didn't fit together genetically with this embryo. Nature takes over in these cases and neither one of you could have done anything about it."

Colt brushed away the tears that slipped down his cheeks. "So what happens now?"

"We'll go back to emergency. I need to examine Frankie and see how far she is dilated. She's not bleeding heavily yet, which indicates to me that this process is just starting. We will do a D and C (that's a dilation and curettage) in the next day or so and scrape the womb to remove all the embryonic tissue and make sure that there is no chance of infection.

"I know this isn't any real comfort right now, but this does not mean that you will not have another child. You have successfully carried twins already."

Frankie started to sob again. Colt helped her sit up and supported her as she moved into the wheel chair.

When they arrived back at emergency, Doctor Wilfred looked at Colt. "If there is a room available, it would be wise to keep Frankie here over night. I believe she needs some sedation so she gets a good rest."

Colt nodded. "I agree. But I'm going to stay here with her."

Dr. Wilfred secured a private room and had Frankie moved into it. He requested a cot for Colt too. While the doctor examined Frankie, Colt went to the parking lot and phoned the farm.

Ellie answered. She shed emotional tears when Colt told her what had happened and encouraged him to take as much time as necessary to get Frankie back on her feet. She assured him that she would look after the twins and everything at home would be fine.

He thanked her, and then wandered over to the truck. He opened the door and slid inside. He leaned his head back against the head rest. His chest was tight, aching with unreleased emotion. *All our hopes and dreams for this baby; poof and they are gone.*

He squeezed his eyes tight, fighting the disappointment and loss. Tears trickled down his cheeks, and finally he gave in to the pain. His sobs were deep and ragged. He gave them free reign and let the intensity of his emotion exhaust itself. Then he wiped away the tears and collected himself. *I have to stay strong for Fran. This is going to devastate her.*

He locked up the truck and went to join her in her hospital room. In the few minutes he had been out, the doctor had examined Frankie and the nurses had gotten her settled and administered a sedative. She hovered in the hazy twilight zone between the medically induced fog and the blessed nothingness of sleep. When he came into the room she reached out and pulled him close. She had been waiting for him. "I'm so sorry," she whispered as she succumbed to the drug.

Colts eyes swam with tears. *She can't keep blaming herself. She didn't do anything wrong.* Colt was exhausted too. He drifted off to sleep, his forehead resting on the bed, her hand clasped in his. He woke up an hour later when a nurse checked in to see how Frankie was doing. After she left the room, he went outside and phoned Frankie's parents.

Cameron and Rayelle Lamonte were shocked by the news. Their immediate concern was for Frankie and how she would handle the loss. They decided they would leave early the next morning and be in Swift Current before nightfall. They would stay with Frankie and Colt as long as was necessary.

Then Colt phoned his parents. Selena and Bob were out, so Colt left a message for them telling them he would call in the morning.

When Colt went back to Frankie's room she was sleeping soundly. *I don't want to be gone when she wakes up, but I'm going nuts just sitting here thinking.* He walked down the hall, looking for the nurse who had stopped in Frankie's room.

"Mr Thompson. You should go out for a while. Your wife will sleep for a good eight hours and when she wakes up the doctor has left orders for her to be sedated again. She needs the rest and so do you. You have a lot to deal with too."

She put an arm around him. "Go kick a tire, shake your fist at the sun, swear at the moon, cry a few tears or talk to a friend; whatever it takes to release your pain. Your wife is going to need your support and you'll need hers too. Doctor Wilfred has requested a cot for you so you can stay the night. Come back later and we'll have one in the room for you."

Colt walked out into the dreary, cloud filled day. Somehow he was glad the sun was not shining. The clouds were more appropriate. He unlocked the truck and got in. *What am I going to do now? I'm hungry but I think I'll gag if I try to eat. And where would I go.*

He linked his hands together and rested them at the top of the steering wheels. He gazed off into space. "Brad and Shauna Lee; I'll call Brad," he said out loud to himself. He took out his cell phone and dialed Brad's number. He sighed with relief when Brad answered.

"Hello, Colt. How are you?"

"I need someone to talk too. Can I come over?"

"Sure, but what's up man? You sound serious."

"I… it is serious. I'll fill you in when I get there. See you in fifteen minutes or so."

Brad's mind went around and around as he tried to figure out what was going on with Colt. When he told Shauna Lee what Colt had said, they both were puzzled.

When Colt came to the door one look at him told them that something was very wrong. His face was drawn; his eyes were strained and red.

Shauna Lee gasped. "Colt!" She pulled him into her embrace. "What has…where is Frankie? What has happened?"

"She…the baby." His eyes filled with tears. "We lost it today. Fran's in the hospital."

Brad stepped forward. "Colt, is she all right?"

"Physically she will be. But she is blaming herself for what happened and it's nobody's fault."

"What happened?"

"The doctor says it happens fairly often. For some reason, the baby's heart stopped. It died in the womb. Today Fran woke up with a backache and then she started spotting. We came to the hospital and they did an ultra sound." He shook his head. "There was no heartbeat. The baby is dead."

Shauna Lee paled. "No! Oh no."

"We have been able to share everything about this pregnancy. I've regretted that I missed so much with the twins. Fran carried the full load that time. This time it was going to be so different and we were looking forward to the baby's birth, but now…"

Brad put his arm around Colt's shoulder and gave him a gentle hug. "Words are pretty hollow right now, Colt. I don't know what to say, except that we are here for you. If there is anything that we can help with, just let us know."

Colt looked at Brad and Shauna Lee. "It helps just to be able to let some of this go; talk about it. I can't fall apart in front of Fran. I have to be strong for her. We haven't had a chance to talk very much because they sedated her right away, but the little that she has said makes it plain that she is blaming herself and feeling that she let me down." He shook his head. "Of course that isn't true. But how do I make her see that?"

Brad looked at Shauna Lee. Her eyes shimmered with tears when she spoke.

"Colt it's hard to lose a child. She has carried the baby for all this time; no matter how much you love it, it's different for her. That child is literally part of her." A tear spilled over. "Just be there for her and have lots of patience. I don't think Frankie is the kind who will be able to just let this go and move on right away."

Brad looked uncomfortable, not quite knowing what to say or what to do. "Colt, can I make a coffee or get you a beer or something?"

"I shouldn't drink. I have to drive back into town. They are putting a cot in Fran's room, so I can stay in there with her." He sighed. "Make it a coffee, please. And could I have a sandwich or something? I haven't eaten since breakfast."

Brad went to cupboard and took out a mug. He looked at Shauna Lee. "Do you want coffee, sweetheart?"

She shook her head as she opened the oven. "Colt, we just ate. There's some hot chilli. Would you like some?"

Colt nodded. "I just need something to eat." Brad set a cup of coffee in front of him while Shauna Lee filled a bowl with chilli. She grabbed a spoon on her way to the table and put both of them in front of Colt. "What else? Some bread?" She went to the fridge and got two dinner buns and some butter.

Brad sat down on a chair and pulled Shauna Lee down onto his lap. He held her hand, his thumb rhythmically caressing hers. *I feel so helpless,* he thought. *What do I say to make things better? Is there anything I can do?*

He held Shauna Lee closer and her eyes met his. *Life can be so uncertain…we take so much for granted.*

Colt ate in silence. Shauna Lee and Brad sat in silence with him, not knowing what to say; feeling that they should be able to do more, but not knowing what they could do. When Colt was finished he pushed the bowl aside and sipped at his coffee. He sat staring out the window. Then he shifted and looked at his hosts.

"Thanks you guys. You have helped me more than you can imagine. I needed to get this off my chest; you know, just to breathe, just to talk about how I felt about losing the baby and my concern about Fran. I'd better go to back to the hospital now. If she wakes up I want to be there."

Shauna Lee stood up. "Colt, have you called Frankie's mom and dad?"

Colt nodded. "Yes, they will be here tomorrow. I called my mom and dad too, but I had to leave a message. They'll get back to me."

Brad cleared his throat. "And your nanny is with the twins?"

"Tim is out there too. We came to an agreement this morning. Now we need to find a place for him to live in until we get the house built at the ranch." He looked at Shauna Lee. "Could you work on that for me?"

She nodded. "I'll do that." She swallowed hard. "And Colt, say hello to Frankie. Tell her we are thinking of her…of both of you."

Frankie was still sleeping when Colt slipped into her room. He tossed his jacket on the cot, and then went to sit down beside her. He took her hand in his and lifted it to his lips. "I love you hon," he whispered. "We will have another baby in time, but right now we have to come to terms with this."

An hour later, Frankie began to stir. Colt was still holding her hand when her eyes fluttered open.

"Hi there love," Colt whispered. She smiled softly, then her eyes flew open.

"Colt? Where am I?...Oh...the baby..."

Colt kissed her hand. "We lost the baby, honey. It was one of those things that no one could have prevented. We...we loved it while we could. Now we...we have to let it go."

Tears filled her eyes. "I...we...wanted it so much. How could this happen?"

"Dr Wilfred says it happens quite often and doctors don't understand what causes it." He laid his head on the bed beside her. "I'm sorry this happened to us. You have nourished this little one and looked after it so carefully this long. You are such a wonderful mother." He kissed her cheek. "I called your mom and dad. They will be here tomorrow night."

"Thanks. I'm glad you did. When can I go home?"

"They still have to do a D&C. Maybe they'll do that tomorrow. I'm not sure if they will keep you in for a day or so after that. Dr. Wilfred will tell us later."

Frankie's tears spilled over. "I want to go as soon as possible. I want to see the twins."

"Yes. We are so lucky to have them to go home to."

She turned her face away and her tears ran freely. "I know that. But I wanted to share this pregnancy with you right through to the birth. And now that will never happen."

"Not this time love, but maybe in the future."

"I'm so tired." she whimpered.

"Go back to sleep. Dr. Wilfred wants you to get plenty of rest. He gave you a sedative." Colt squeezed her hand gently. "I'm staying here with you; they've put a cot in here for me."

She nodded and closed her eyes. "Is this real? Or is it just a bad dream?" she whispered.

He swallowed hard. "No Fran, this is no bad dream. It's real life." Tears swam in his eyes, but he blinked them back. *I have to be strong for you, my love.*

Dr. Wilfred made his rounds by eight the next morning. He came in and told Frankie that she was scheduled for a D&C at eleven o'clock. He explained what the procedure would entail and told her that she would certainly go home the next day; possibly even that evening if he felt it was prudent.

Colt followed him out of the room. "Dr. Wilfred, if she could get a good sleep here in the hospital tonight, it might be best. Her mom and dad are coming late this afternoon. No matter how much she wants to go home, there is going to be so much activity and emotional stress. If everyone sort of gets settled in first, I'd feel better about taking her home."

"Let's weigh everything when I see her later on. Some of it will depend on how pressed we are for beds too."

At four fifteen, Frankie stirred and slowly woke up. She smiled wanly when she opened her eyes to see Colt beside her. "Have you been here all day?"

"I slipped down to the cafeteria for coffee and an egg salad sandwich. But other than that I've been right here where I want to be; right next to you." He leaned over and kissed her softly on the lips. "I had a call from your mom and dad. They left at four o'clock this morning. They'll be arriving at the farm anytime now."

She smiled wanly. "They can help Ellie with the twins."

"I talked to Ellie just after lunch. I asked her to change the sheets in the spare room for your mom and dad. Tim is going to stay at Brad's place until he finds a place to live. I asked Shauna Lee to help with that."

"Did you see her?"

He nodded. "I...I went out to Brad's yesterday, after they sedated you. I...I needed to talk to someone. I'm comfortable with Brad and I've known Shauna Lee for so long; they listened to me and they gave me coffee and some chilli. It helped."

He lifted her hand to his lips and kissed it. "They were both concerned and Shauna Lee said to be sure that you knew they were thinking about you. She was really upset."

"She likes children, Colt. You can see it when she is with the twins; especially Sam."

"And yet she always swore she didn't want any."

"Well, we don't know what has happened in the past. There may be a reason why she feels that way."

"I hope you don't mind Fran, but I asked your mom and dad to wait until we come home to see you."

"Why..." she started to protest.

"If you really want me to I'll call them. But they have had a long day and I thought it would give them a chance to settle in and they can visit with the twins. And you have had a full day. I'm hoping they will give you a sedative tonight so you get a good rest. How are you feeling now?

"I'm cramping a bit."

"Dr Wilfred said he'd stop by later."

"That's good. I would like to talk to him."

Just then a nurse came into the room. "How are you feeling Mrs. Thompson?" Then she took her temperature, blood pressure, pulse and listened to her chest. She looked at Colt. "I'm going to ask you to leave, while I check out what is happening with your wife."

Colt chuckled. "I think I'm old enough; besides that, I've seen it all before."

"Don't be cheeky! It's the rules. Out you go."

Colt dropped a kiss on Frankie's lips and went out into the hallway. While he was waiting there, his cell phone rang. He glanced at the call display and smiled. *Mom* and *Dad!* "Hello you guys. Where are you?"

Colt was shaking his head when the nurse stepped outside and told him he could go back inside to see his wife.

"I just got a call from Mom and Dad. They made a last minute decision to take a bus tour to Florida with some friends. They offered to come back home but I told them there wasn't any need to do that.

Everything is covered at this end and they never travel like that, so they'll see us when they get home."

"I'm glad you did that. Things will be better by the time they get back."

Colt took her hand and rubbed his finger over the back of it in an unconscious gesture. "So what did the nurse have to say?"

"Not a lot. The cramping is pretty normal and I am bleeding, but not abnormally. It will just take time. She said Dr. Wilfred had a busy afternoon and he will be in early tomorrow morning." She smiled. "I will be able to go home then. I want to see the twins."

"And your mom and dad are there."

Frankie nodded. "I'm happy to see them too; but honestly, as much as I love them," her eyes filled with tears, "I just want to be home with you and the twins. I have to get used to the fact that we won't have this little one."

She touched her tummy automatically." Tears spilled over to slip down her cheeks. "It is still hard to get my head around this; to accept that its little heart just stopped beating. I don't even know if it was a girl or a boy," she sobbed.

Colt sat on the bed and folded her in his arms. "We'll get through this together hon." He swallowed hard, fighting his own emotions. "I'm sure Dr. Wilfred will tell us what our baby was; boy or girl." He felt her collapse against him. "And then we will help each other heal emotionally, and we will enjoy the two children that we have. In time we'll have another one."

"But not this one," she replied sadly.

"No, not this one," he agreed.

The next morning everyone came out onto the veranda to meet them when they arrived at the farm. Cameron and Rayelle Lamonte couldn't hide their sadness for their daughter's loss and Ellie's face was full of concern. But Selena and Sam were bubbling with excitement as they bounded down the steps to meet them. Frankie's face broke into a radiant smile, for the moment her grief shoved aside by her love for her children.

Colt knelt down, so his eyes were level with theirs. He took their hands in each one of his. "Mommy is really happy to see you, but you guys have to be really careful. Mommy has a sore tummy. She can't pick you up for a while because she can't lift anything heavy...and you are both getting to be big kids. So when we go inside, you have to wait until she sits down and then you can sit by her and hug her and kiss her, but you have to be careful not to jump on her tummy. Do you understand?"

They both looked at him with big eyes, and then turned to Frankie. "Can we hold her hand?" Sam asked.

Frankie nodded and smiled as she reached out to them. "Please take my hands. I can hardly wait to hold you close."

She leaned over to give her mother a kiss as she passed her, but her hands held her children's tightly. She smiled at her dad and buzzed his cheek also. Ellie smiled as their eyes met and ran her hand down Frankie's back as she passed her.

The twins propelled her to the couch and waited for her to sit down. Then they crawled up beside her and wiggled over to sit close to her. She put her arms around them and cuddled them close. Her eyes filled with tears. She bent to rub her head against each of them. "Mommy is so happy that she has you two," she whispered.

They lay their heads against her breasts, each being careful not to touch her tummy. Sam looked up at her. "We missted oou, mommy."

Selena flew off the couch and ran to Colt. "We missed you too, Daddy. And Grandpa and Grandma came to visit while you were gone." She danced with excitement.

Frankie hugged Sam again. "I want to say hello to grandma and grandpa now," she said softly as she helped him get down off the couch. He slipped his thumb into his mouth and stood beside her, hugging her leg.

Ellie made coffee and everyone sat around the table and talked. Frankie tried to minimize her parents concern for her, insisting that while the loss was a disappointment, she would be all right.

Rayelle Lamonte frowned. *My dear daughter, all of this is much more difficult than you are pretending it is. I know, I have been where you are now. No matter how brave a face you are putting on, this is going to hurt for a while.* Her heart ached for Frankie.

Frankie's parents stayed for a week, and she felt relief as she watched them drive down the lane when they left. Colt slid his arm around her waist as they waved. Ellie took the twins inside when the car was out of site. Frankie laid her head against his chest and heaved a big sigh.

"Are you all right, hon?"

"I am such an ungrateful daughter; I know mom and dad are concerned and they wanted to do everything to help here, but honestly I just couldn't wait for them to leave. I just want to be here alone with you and the twins."

"And Ellie; you need Ellie's help."

"Of course; she is part of our family now." She turned to him. "Colt, can we go for a walk? Just you and I?"

"Are you sure it won't be too much for you?"

"We don't have very go far. I just need some quiet and fresh air; and some time to look into the morning sky and say goodbye to our little girl with you." Her eyes glistened with unshed tears.

Colt held her tight. "Shall we walk down the lane?"

She nodded. They held hands as they started to walk. "What shall we name her?"

Colt was startled. *I should have thought of this myself.* Guilt flooded through him. "We hadn't discussed a name before. What have you thought of?"

"I've been thinking about 'Cherish'. I will always cherish our dreams for this little girl. She will always be a part of me; even though she never got to be here with us."

Colt swallowed hard as he turned Frankie toward him. He tried to push away the tears, to be strong for her, but he lost the fight as he looked into her eyes. A tear slipped down his cheeks. "Cherish is a perfect name for her."

Frankie reached up and brushed the tear from his cheek. He grabbed her hand and kissed the palm of it. "We'll plant a tree in memory of her; maybe a weeping willow or a flowering plum? What do you think?"

"I'd like something happy; the flowering plum would be a beautiful reminder of her every spring. And the blossoms are pink; for a little girl."

"We'll plant a flowering plum. Should we plant it here or at the ranch? Or maybe we should plant one at each place?"

"Can we do that? She would have been born while we are here, and we would have taken her to the ranch with us."

Life at the farm fell into a steady rhythm. Frankie spent most of her time with the children, reaffirming how lucky she was to have them. She pushed away the sadness that constantly threatened to creep in.

When she couldn't control the emptiness she went to the bedroom to take a nap and let the tears flow. Other times she made an excuse to go to the bathroom, where she would flush away the tears with water from the tap. Colt heard her sobs when she thought he was asleep. Anxiety knotted in his breast. He tried to talk to her about her feelings but she brushed his concerns away.

Ellie saw the stress in her eyes. *I've never had a miscarriage*, she thought. *But she is not the happy person she is trying to appear to be.*

Ten days after she came home, Colt took her into town for her check up with Dr. Wilfred. Doctor Wilfred confirmed that she was healing nicely, but he advised them to put off having intercourse for another two weeks. He suggested they make an appointment before the New Year for another check up.

# CHAPTER EIGHTEEN

*B*rad and Shauna Lee had both gone to their respective offices on Tuesday morning, but when Tim showed up at Brad's place, he had phoned Shauna Lee and asked her if she could leave early and go home with them. They were anxious to hear news about Colt and Frankie, but Tim could tell them little, except that Frankie's mom and dad had arrived. Shauna Lee felt relief, knowing that.

She picked up Karma and cuddled her in the curve of her neck. She was surprised how much it had hurt her when she had learned about Frankie's miscarriage. Feelings of her own loss had flooded through her.

True, the circumstances were different, but it was still was the loss of a mothers hopes and dreams and her heart ached for Frankie. She thought about how devastated Colt had been and realised that in normal circumstances it was a crushing loss for both parents.

She looked at Brad. *He will be a loving father*, she thought. She stopped petting Karma, and swallowed hard. *Will be? What am I thinking?*

She walked out of the room and went and sat on the bed where he had asked her to marry him. He hadn't pressured her for an answer. He was giving her time. She got up and walked into the bathroom and stood in front of the mirror. She looked into her own wide blue eyes.

"Why am I waiting?" she asked herself. And suddenly she knew. "I'm being a fool. I shouldn't wait," she whispered. "I won't! He loves me and I...I love him. I don't need to be afraid."

Brad came around the bedroom door as she turned. "Here you are! You just disappeared. Are you all right?"

She nodded, her eyes shining with unshed tears. She leaned over and put Karma on the floor. Then she reached up and threaded her arms around his neck. "I know this isn't the right time to tell you this, but the answer is YES!"

"Yes?" Then she saw understanding flare in his eyes. "Tweetie Bird; there is never a wrong time to tell me that!" He laughed, then spanned her waist with his hands and lifted her off the floor, twirling her around. "Shall I send Tim away?"

"No" she whispered. "But is it all right if we just keep it our secret for now? I just admitted it to myself; I want to be your wife. And when you came in here now, I just had to tell you, so I didn't get cold feet and change my mind."

"Tweetie Bird, you have just made me the happiest man in the world!" He took her hand and led her back into the kitchen.

Tim looked at them with amusement. *Fools in love; they've got it bad,* he thought. *I only hope it lasts longer than mine did before the knife goes to the jugular.* He looked at Shauna Lee. "Brad says you may have a place for me to rent until the Thompsons move out to the ranch."

Shauna Lee gave Brad a puzzled look, and then understanding crept into her eyes. "Yes…yes I could have." She gave Brad a happy smile. "I do. I have a house in town and I never stay there. In fact, I won't be living there anymore now that we are getting married." Her hand flew to cover her mouth and she blushed scarlet.

Brad hugged her with a happy grin. He looked at Tim. "I asked her to marry me when I got home from China. Shauna doesn't make hasty decisions about things like that and she kept me waiting until just a few minutes ago. She wanted to keep it a secret for a little while, but now you heard it from her. We are getting married!"

"Congratulations, you guys. It must be something in this Saskatchewan air. You two are like the Thompsons." Tim's expression darkened as he looked out the window. "I hope you are always so happy." Brad caught the bitterness in his voice.

"We are going to make sure we stay this way. We are not young kids and we know relationships need to be worked at." He smiled at Shauna Lee. "In fact, we've had to work hard to get this far."

Shauna Lee laid her head against Brad's chest. "This man never takes *no* for an answer. He just wouldn't give up on me. And now," she reached up and caressed his cheek. "I can't imagine life without him."

Brad winked at Tim. "I offered to kick you out for a while this morning after she told me the answer was 'yes', but she said not too."

"Brad! You are so bad." She struggled to hide her embarrassment. "Just ignore him, Tim… and getting back to the house; it's fully furnished, and it's comfortable enough. You can take a look at it and see if you like it."

"I'm not fussy. It's just a roof over my head and a place to sleep."

Brad chuckled. "Until you get caught up in this Saskatchewan air. Look at what happened to me."

"Been there and done that once already and believe me, I have no intention of getting burned again." He stood up. "Tell me how to find your place and I'll get out of your hair right now."

"No Tim," Shauna Lee protested. "We'll go with you. If the place works for you, I need to take my personal things out of there. There isn't much left, but I'd like to tidy up a bit."

Brad released her and stepped away. "Are you ready to go now?"

Shauna Lee nodded. "I'll get a jacket and my purse." She went into the bedroom and picked up her purse. She scooped Karma up off the floor and carried her into the kitchen. "Can we take her, or would it be better to leave her here?"

"We are going to be busy at the house. Maybe we should put her in the carrier and leave her here for now. We shouldn't be more than a couple of hours."

Tim liked the house. He walked through it, looking into each room. "This works for me. In fact, it's more than I'd ever expected to find. And the furnishings work for me too. Does the TV stay?"

Shauna Lee laughed. "I don't need it. This is where it belongs, so I guess it stays."

"All right, let's draw up an agreement, and I'll move in tonight." He grinned. "I've never liked being the odd man out. I'll leave you two alone to celebrate your engagement."

"You don't have to run away!" Shauna Lee protested.

Brad grinned. "But you can move in tonight if you want. We can do the paperwork tomorrow."

Shauna Lee blushed. "Brad. That is rude!"

Tim laughed; the first real laugh Brad had heard out of him since he had arrived in Swift Current. "Think nothing of it Shauna Lee. As you said, this guy doesn't take 'no' for an answer. And I doubt if a quick kiss when you told him 'yes' is what he has in mind to celebrate your acceptance of his marriage proposal."

Brad grabbed Shauna Lee and pulled her close. "Spoken like a man who understands a man!" He gave her a squeeze. "Go gather up all your lacy bras and panties, and whatever other sexy stuff you have left around here."

"Brad," she protested, blushing again.

"I'll help you. I saw a laundry hamper by the washer." He went to get it.

Shauna Lee looked at Tim. "I'm sorry..."

"Don't be sorry. It's good to see him so happy. In all the years I've known him, he's never been like this. He's like a teenager again. I could envy him, but I've been there already and I hope this works out better for you guys than it did for me."

"Don't let bitterness rob you Tim. I...I was like you. Brad should have run like hell from the person I was back then, but he wouldn't let me hide behind my pain. Like I said, he is a persistent man when he decides what he wants. I believe in love now. He has shown it to me in so many ways. You may find it too."

"I'm cured of that illusion."

"Colt Thompson thought that once too. Look at him now."

"Good for him, but it's not in the cards for me."

"Don't be too sure, pal." Brad leaned against the bedroom door, a smile on his face. "Maybe we should toss a sexy nightie into his bed. You don't wear them anymore!"

Shauna Lee gasped. "Brad! Will you stop that?" She took the hamper from him and started going through the drawers, gathering up the few remaining personal items.

Brad went into the bathroom and collected the remnants of makeup and medication, including an empty birth control package. "Are you still on these?"

"Are you kidding? I'd have been pregnant within the first week after we had sex if I wasn't."

"Hmmm…well a guy can hope." He dropped the things he'd collected in the laundry hamper. "Is that it now?"

"I'm pretty sure." They walked into the kitchen to find Tim looking through the cupboards.

Brad chuckled. "You won't find much in there man. I'm sure this woman never cooked when she lived here, but she's pretty good at it now."

Tim grinned. "I was checking to see what I could pack up for you, but you're right, there isn't much in here."

Shauna Lee shook her head. "Tim, I'm not taking anything. The pots and pans are yours. Brad is a great cook and he already had everything when I started staying there; my meagre collection of cooking utensils looked like it belonged to a hopeless bachelor. If there is anything you can salvage in the cupboards, feel free to use it. Otherwise throw it out."

"I'm getting a sweet deal here. And it already feels good to know that I'll have a place of my own; a fresh start without painful memories around every corner. Thanks guys."

Brad looked at Shauna Lee. "It's seven o'clock and I'm hungry. I think we should take your new tenant out for supper; what do you think?"

Tim protested but Shauna Lee agreed. Brad opened the door. "Hurry up man. The invitation was only for supper. Then you can come back here and I'll take this woman home and thank her properly for agreeing to be my wife."

The next morning Shauna Lee was sitting in her office, doodling on a yellow notepad when her cell phone rang. She smiled as she reached for it. "Hi Brad," she answered softly.

"Hi, Tweetie Bird; what are you doing?"

"Not much. I've been acting like a lovesick teenager, day dreaming and practicing my new signature. I've been trying to decide whether it should be 'Shauna Lee Johnson,' or maybe just 'Shauna Johnson,' since you call me Shauna. Or I could make it 'Tweetie Bird Johnson'." She giggled. "Or, I could be 'Lady Bird Johnson', too. What do you think?"

"I like 'Tweetie Bird Johnson'. It has a great *ring*...no pun on words."

"The ring. Ohhh...did you find one?"

"Sweetheart, I want you to go with me."

"Brad...I'd like you to pick out the ring. I'll love it just because you chose it."

"You know me, I never take 'no' for an answer. Anyway, can we go for lunch together?"

"Hummm, let me check my calendar. I've almost filled this page, practicing my new name. I think I can manage it. What time do you want to go?"

"What is your schedule like today? Do you have any appointments?"

"No, today is a paperwork day."

"Could you take the afternoon off? It's a beautiful sunny day. We could go to Regina."

"I left early yesterday and now again today? You are a bad influence on me." She laid down her pen and pushed the yellow pad away.

"I'm sure Christina will take care of the office and everyone else is working hard. I'm the only one off in lala land, so I might as well get out of here. When are you coming?"

"Give me forty five minutes, and I'll be there."

Shauna Lee stood up and stretched. Then she walked out to Christina's desk. "If I cut out again this afternoon will you cover for me?"

Christina grinned. "Well, if Brad brings me something as gorgeous as that silk kimono that he brought me from China, I'll cover for you any time. Where are you off to today?"

"Brad just called me on my cell. It's a nice day, so he would like to go to Regina. I feel guilty about taking off but…"

Christina brushed her words away with the sweep of her hand. "Don't! It's one of the perks of owning the business." She grinned as she looked at Shauna's happy face. "That man has made such a difference in you. You are so alive now and we all notice it. It is good to see you happy, like you are these days."

"Thanks Christina. You know, I always vowed I would ever let myself fall in love with anyone." Shauna Lee's eyes sparkled. "But Brad just wouldn't give up. He wore down all my defences and now I love him so much it scares me."

"Anyone can see how much he loves you. You have nothing to be afraid of except your own fear, Shauna Lee."

"I actually do know that, but I…I have a ton of emotional baggage from…from before, and sometimes the past creeps up and bites me."

Christina smiled at her. "Do you know something? We have worked together for ten years and I have learned more about you in the last few months than I ever even got a glimpse of in all those years."

"Have I really been that unapproachable?"

"You have been all business; and nothing else. I guess that worked for you; but the rest of us have become a family. We know each other's spouses, their children, and their interests. We get together and do things socially.

"But we really know nothing about you as a person. You are a fair and consistent boss, but until Brad came along your personal life didn't seem to exist. I felt sorry for you. I couldn't imagine living such a lonely life."

"I didn't have a personal life. I was lonely, but I was afraid to let anyone get close to me." Shauna Lee smiled sadly. "That really bothered Brad. Remember that day when he followed you into my office?"

Christina smiled and nodded.

"He did that on purpose, so he could see if my office was a 'sterile' as my house; that's how he put it. It drove him crazy that I didn't have any pictures. He was unrelenting about it, wanting to know how anybody who dealt with me got any idea of who I was." She sighed. "I honestly didn't think it mattered. I wanted to keep my life private. I was so mad at him."

"I know that. He gave me a big wink when he walked out and you followed him, looking like a thunder cloud." Christina chuckled. "And when he helped you get into the truck, I had to laugh. You looked like you were ready to kill him. And he was enjoying the whole thing!"

Shauna Lee found herself laughing. "He's got that lift kit on that truck and those big tires. I am too short; I just can't get into it without help."

Christina was laughing too. She glanced up as the door opened. "Speak of the devil! Here he is."

Brad grinned. "Was she telling you our secret?" He looked at Shauna Lee. "You couldn't wait?"

Shauna Lee shook her head frantically. "No Brad…"

Christina looked from one to the other. She reached out and grabbed Shauna Lee's hand to check her ring finger. "Are you getting engaged?" She let out a squeal of happiness. "Is that why you are going to Regina; to look for a ring?"

Shauna Lee flushed and Brad reached over to hug her. He placed her hand against his coat pocket and she felt the tiny box in it. Her eyes widened. "You got it?" She reached into his jacket and pulled it out of his pocket. "Show me!"

"Hey; I wanted to do this right."

"To hell with doing it right," Christina blurted. "Hurry up and show her. I want to see it too."

Shauna Lee was fumbling with the box. Brad took it from her. "Are you sure?"

"Yes! I don't want to wait."

Brad opened the box and watched Shauna Lee's expression. Her eyes filled with tears. "Oh Brad…I love it; the setting is gorgeous. It's so unique."

He took the ring out of the box and slipped it onto her extended finger. Then he shoved the box back into his pocket and took her in his arms, oblivious of the fact that Christina had rushed through the office and collected all of Shauna Lee's employees. All six of them applauded as he kissed her.

"All right, you two," Christina said with a laugh. "Go get a room! But let's see that ring first."

Brad turned Shauna Lee in his arms, so her back was against his chest and she was facing her staff. She held out her hand and let them admire the ring. They all exclaimed about the diamond set in the unique combination of white and yellow gold.

Christina winked at him. "I knew you were a keeper the first time you came in here with Shauna Lee."

"Thank you. It didn't take me long to know that she was a keeper too. And believe me, she hasn't come easily!"

"I'm glad you hung in there Brad. She has become a different person since you came into her life." She shifted back and rested a hip against her desk. "So when is the wedding?"

Shauna Lee blushed again. "Jeez—we just got engaged! Give me time to catch my breath."

Brad laughed. "I like the idea of a winter wedding. Or better yet, we could elope this weekend."

"Don't you dare," Christina exploded. "We want to celebrate a wedding." She turned to the others. "Hey guys. We want to put on a bridal shower and all that stuff, right?" There was a shout of cheers. Christina shook a finger at Brad and Shauna Lee. "No cheating! You cannot elope!"

Brad leaned forward and looked into Shauna Lee's face. She shrugged and they both laughed. "I guess she just laid down the law."

"I just had to make sure you've got that straight. Now you two get out of here and do whatever newly engaged people do." Christina turned to the others. "Back to work everyone; the real boss is leaving and I get to crack the whip for the whole afternoon." She twirled around, making the motion of cracking a whip. Everyone laughed and went back to their desks.

Christina threw her arms around Shauna Lee. "I am so happy for you!"

She grabbed Brad's hand. "Congratulations!"

When they got into the truck Brad pulled Shauna Lee close against him. "Well, once again, I'm going to have to take you home and thank you properly. How is it that nothing goes quite the way I plan for it too?"

Shauna Lee touched his cheek. "It turned out perfectly." She stretched out her hand to look at her ring. "I love, love, *love* my ring. You have beautiful taste."

He kissed her. Shauna Lee shot a quick look at the office window. Christina was standing there, pretending to be watching them through binoculars. She laughed out loud. "Let's get out of here. They are probably all watching us, just like she is!"

Brad started the truck and pulled out onto the street.

"Where are we going?"

"I had planned to take you to the park and give you the ring there. That's where we first spent time together at the car show. It's sunny and nice out. Do you feel like going there?"

"You are so romantic. Let's do it. And then let's go home and make pizza like we did the second time and have a beer."

He chuckled. "But I'm warning you right now, I *am* going to bed with you tonight."

They walked through the park and sat on a bench for a while. Shauna Lee told him about her conversation with Christina, explaining to him how her staff viewed her. "I realize now that you were trying to tell me that, but I couldn't see it."

"Sweetheart, that's because you have hidden yourself all your life. You struggled to be anonymous. And you did the same thing with your staff." He hugged her. "You tried to do it with me."

"Why didn't you just move on?"

He chuckled. "I must have been drawn to your pheromones! I *wanted* to know you. Why? I guess it was meant to be, because I would have run a mile from anyone else like you. But with you, I never considered giving up."

When they got back to the house Tim had left a message on Brad's cell, wondering about the rental agreement. He had gone to Shauna Lee's office and Christina and he had obviously clashed. In his message he had referred to her as the "officious bitch".

Shauna Lee laughed. "Christina thinks he is a cold fish."

Brad chuckled. "Wouldn't it be funny if they got together?"

Shauna Lee was thoughtful. "I'm ashamed to admit that I really don't know anything about Christina, except that she's not married. She's worked for me for ten years and I don't think she ever has been."

"I'll phone Tim and tell him not to worry about the agreement today. We'll get at it tomorrow."

Shauna Lee sighed. "I'll phone Christina and ask her to pull the forms and fill in all the information that she can. I'll see her in the morning and get everything finished up. Then I'll give him a call and he can come down and we'll both sign them."

They worked together and made pizza like they had that first evening. As they worked they discussed Christmas.

"We can go to your family's place for Christmas," she offered.

"I wanted to at first, but after you told me how you've always celebrated Christmas, I made up my mind to celebrate it with you, right here in our home. We'll buy decorations and lights for the house and the tree.

"And we are going to have company. We'll have Tim and Colt and Frankie and the twins for dinner; a day with coffee and donuts at the shop for my clients; one for your clients at your office; a Christmas party for your staff right here at the house so they get to know us. December is going to be full and overflowing."

Shauna Lee groaned. "Brad! Why don't we just have a Christmas wedding? We could do everything at once."

"You just want to take the easy way out." He grinned and shook his head. "There isn't enough time. You need to meet my family. And I want us to have a real wedding. It is the first one for both of us and I want to look back on the memories and the pictures and admire my wife in her beautiful dress."

"Who will we invite?"

"My family, the Potters, Colt and Frankie, Tim and your staff; it will be big enough for a celebration, but not over the top enough to make you nervous."

She sighed. "You know me; I hate being the center of attention."

"Yes, I know you, but everything will be all right. Trust me. And you know, if we didn't have a wedding Christina would never forgive us."

"I know...it's just uncomfortable for me. Who will I have for a bridesmaid? I don't have any friends."

"Tweetie Bird. That's not true. Frankie is a friend. And I'll bet Christina would love it if you asked her to be your bridesmaid. And Selena could be your flower girl and Sam could be the ring bearer."

"Who would be your best man?"

"I'd like to ask Colt."

"Not Tim?"

Brad thought for a moment. "Well, Tim will be living here and he is an old friend, but right now he is so bitter about love and marriage."

"So I've noticed." She looked at her ring again.

"When do you think we should get married?" he asked.

"We're into tax time at the office after the New Year, but I don't want to wait until June! I want to be your wife sooner than later."

"I love hearing you say that." He kissed her gently. "December is going to be busy and if it's all right with you, I'd like to fly us to Dawson Creek for New Years. We'd only be away from home for four days, if we left Regina on the twenty ninth and came back on January first.

"We can sleep on the flight back because we will be tired. My family will howl because I haven't been home for a while, but I'm thinking of work...and you. Families can be overwhelming if you aren't used to them."

"I love you for realizing that," she said softly. "And going to your family for New Years is fine by me." She chewed her lip. "I have no idea how long it takes to put a wedding together. I could ask Frankie. I know they were married within a couple of weeks. But her mom helped her with the details. And I'm not sure how Frankie will be feeling now. She is probably struggling emotionally."

"Maybe it would be a good diversion for her." He took her hand. "Let's go into the office and check out a calendar." They looked at different dates, and then decided that she could ask for Frankie's help in a couple of weeks. In the mean time Shauna Lee would phone Christina and ask her if she'd ever helped plan a wedding.

Christina was delighted that Shauna Lee had called her. She said she had helped her sister four years earlier and she would call her and pick her brain. She was dancing with excitement when she hung up, telling Shauna Lee she would talk to her at the office in the morning.

"You were right Brad. Christina is wild with excitement because I called her."

"Tweetie Bird, once you open up to people you will be amazed at how helpful and friendly they are."

"I feel like I don't deserve it. I didn't intend to be distant and unapproachable but I guess I have been. They must think I am a terrible snob."

"Just be the person I've come to know, Sweetie. If they ever thought that, they will soon forget it."

She threaded her arms around his neck. "I'm so glad you are so persistent. I love you, Brad Johnson."

Brad phoned his parents and told them he was engaged and that he was planning to bring his bride-to-be home for New Years. He also shocked them when he told his mom that they were planning to have the wedding in late January or early February. He could hear the unspoken questions. He chuckled as he assured her that he wasn't going to make her a grandmother for a year or so.

Shauna Lee blushed as she listened to him. He was grinning when he hung up. "Everyone will be buzzing now!"

Next he phoned and made reservations for their flight to Dawson Creek. Shauna Lee cringed when she heard him affirm the cost, but Brad just smiled. "Sweetheart, I have waited forty two years for you.

I'm not a bottomless pit, but I've never been a playboy, and I've invested wisely. The cost means nothing to me."

He slid his hands around her waist, and lifted her up, twirling her around. "I am as happy as a kid! It seems like I have known you forever."

"I know. Sometimes it scares me when I realise how short a time it's really been. Are we rushing things?"

"Do you have any doubts?"

"No...I don't. But I could see why people might think we are crazy."

"I know in my heart that this is right. If you don't have any doubts, I don't care what anyone else thinks." He sniffed the air. "And I smell pizza. Let's go eat!"

They ate pizza, drank beer and jotted down ideas for the Christmas holidays. By the time they went to bed, Shauna Lee felt good about what they had come up with. With Brads input, planning for the holidays would not be so daunting. It had been a wonderful day.

The next morning, Christina was dancing with excitement when she arrived at the office. She looked at Shauna Lee. "Did you sleep last night?"

Shauna Lee smiled. "Yes, why would you ask me that?"

"Because I didn't; I'm so excited that you asked me for some help with your wedding. I talked to Julie last night! She gave me a few suggestions and ideas. Have you set the date?"

"As soon as possible! Well not in December; it's too busy all ready. Brad wants a real wedding...fancy dress, cake, invitations etc."

"Shauna Lee! You want it too."

"Yes, once I got past the intimidation of the whole idea, I admit I do." Her smile sparkled. "I am excited. So, how quickly can we put a wedding together? The office really gets busy by the end of January with tax time and I have to be on the ball then; I can't be distracted by planning a wedding. But I don't want to wait until spring. Soooo..."

"So, we'd better get the ball rolling! I know December is busy, but we can order invitations, book a caterer, book a church, book a photographer, and make up the guest list. You need to get your invitations out as soon as possible since the wedding is going to be coming up fast."

"I'll call Brad and see if we can meet for lunch. If he is free, could you have lunch with us today so we could discuss some of these things?"

"I'd love to."

"I'll give him a call right away. I'll call his cell and then I'll be sure to get him."

Brad chuckled when he answered the phone. "Let me guess; you're up to your neck in wedding plans!"

"Are you psychic too?"

"No, but I can imagine you and Christina at it."

"You're right. What are you doing for lunch?"

"I have an appointment at one, but I'm pretty flexible until then. What's on your mind?"

"Well, we need to make some decisions. Could you come over before lunch?"

"I could come right now if you want."

"Umm…all right, we can get together in my office. We need to set a date and we need to think about where we are going to get married so we can order invitations. Things like that."

"I'll be right over. Shall I stop at Tim Horton's and pick up some donuts?"

"That's a great idea. Bring enough for the whole staff. And Brad, please bring a large coffee each for the three of us."

Shauna Lee phoned Christina. "Brad has an appointment at one, but he's free right now so he is on his way over. And he's bringing Tim Horton's coffee for the three of us and donuts for everyone; I mean the staff as well."

Christina chuckled. "I wish I had met him first! I like that man."

Brad arrived twenty minutes later, bringing coffee and a varied selection of donuts. Christina brought a paper plate into Shauna Lee's office and let everyone pick two goodies each. Then she took the box into the coffee room. She turned on the intercom at her desk so they could hear if any one came in. Then they sat around Shauna Lee's desk with a calendar.

They tossed around different dates and then settled on the first weekend in February. Shauna Lee was surprised to learn that Brad's family were devout Baptists. *I wonder what other little things we don't know about each other,* she mused.

He grinned as if he had read her mind. "When we go there at New Years, we won't be allowed to sleep together."

Christina howled with laughter.

Frankie looked shocked. "Are you serious? We live together!"

He chuckled. "Not as far as my parents are concerned! And sleeping together in their house is a definite "no, no" until we are married. That's another reason why I only plan to spend two nights there!"

She shook her head. "I guess Tim will have to sleep at the house on the weekend of the wedding, so I can move back into my place."

"Or you can 'live' at my place for a few days," Christina volunteered.

"Would you do that for me?" Shauna Lee asked, her eyes glinting with a sudden flood of unshed tears.

"Of course I would. It's one way to make sure I get invited to the wedding," she said with a laugh. "Besides that, it's bad luck for the groom to see the bride before the wedding, so you couldn't stay at the house the night before the wedding anyway. I want you two to be 'Happy Ever After' so I'm going to be the watch dog." Christina shook a warning finger at Brad.

He reached over and grabbed the finger, "We will be 'happy-ever-after' regardless."

They all laughed and then Shauna Lee reached over and touched Christina's arm. "Brad and I talked about this last night. Would you be one of my bridesmaids?"

Christina looked stunned. Then she jumped up and hugged Shauna Lee. Her eyes brimmed with tears. "As long as the bridesmaid dress isn't a chartreuse colour and it doesn't make me look fat!"

"I'm going to ask Frankie Thompson to be my maid of honour. I hope she is up to it by then."

"Why wouldn't she be?"

"Oh...Christina I thought you knew. She had a miscarriage last Sunday."

"Oh, no! I am so sorry to hear that." She blinked hard. "That is such a painful thing to go through, and it takes a long time to get over it. One day you are so happy and full of anticipation. The next, your dreams are all gone."

Brad and Shauna Lee looked at each other, wondering at her words. They let her pull herself back into the present and Brad changed the subject.

"So I guess we need to count up the guests. For my family there could be nine adults and if the kids all come that would add another seven. So that is a total of sixteen. And Tim makes seventeen. And you will want to invite the Potters won't you?"

She nodded. "And Frankie and Colt and the twins make twenty three, and I want to invite all the staff from here."

Christina counted on her fingers; that is another fifteen if the children are included. That makes thirty eight...and *me*. That makes thirty nine, plus you two; that totals forty one."

"Is there anyone else you would like to invite Shauna Lee?"

"No..."

"What about your dad sweetheart? He's an asshole as far as I'm concerned, but he was, or I should say *is* the only dad you ever had. It's up to you."

Shauna Lee looked at the floor and chewed her bottom lip. Brad and Christina waited for her answer. She sighed. "He is the only remnant of family that I have. Would you hate it if I asked him?"

"Tweetie Bird. I hate what he did to you; he hurt you so much in ways he never knew. But if you want to invite him to the wedding, I'm fine with that."

"It's still hard for me to accept him, but after what he told me." She shrugged. "We were all hurting, Brad. Am I any better than him...or mom...if I shut him out? We need to heal." She shook her head. "I know it would mean a lot to him. He is a troubled man too."

Brad took her hand and gave it a gentle squeeze. "Maybe we should invite Ollie too, so he will feel more comfortable."

"And we can't forget Frankie & Colt's nanny; Ellie."

"How many is that now? Forty four?"

"We were going to have a small wedding!"

"Don't worry; you will love it."

Christina grinned. "So I guess the first thing to do is make sure we can get the Baptist Church for February the fourth. We can't decide about invitations until we have that nailed down. And where are you going to have the reception?"

"Could we use the church basement?" Brad asked.

Christina spoke up. "Or possibly one of the hotel banquet rooms; they will cater too."

Shauna Lee smiled. "That is a good thought, and would probably simplify things."

"All right; Brad can you check out the church before lunch to see if it is available and if we can get married there? I'll go on the internet and check for banquet rooms and catering businesses around town and make some calls."

Christina stood up. "Someone just came in the office." She went out into the reception area.

"Is Shauna Lee in?"

"Damn," Shauna Lee said softly. "That's Tim. We were supposed to have the rental agreement ready this morning. I forgot."

Brad stood up and gave her a quick kiss. "I'll ask him to go to the church with me." He chuckled. "He'll be as thrilled about that as he is about weddings!"

Shauna Lee chuckled. "It will buy some time for me to get that agreement finished."

When they stepped out of Shauna Lee's office, Christina and Tim were bristling with antagonism as they dealt with each other. Christina was opening a folder that contained the rental agreement.

Brad stepped forward. "Hey man, I need some back up here. Will you come with me for half an hour or so. I'll bring you back and we'll take these two girls for lunch. They'll have the rental agreement ready by then."

"Do I have to go to lunch with that cold fish?" Christina grumbled as the two men went out the door.

"Get used to him, girl. He'll probably be your escort at the wedding. He is an old friend of Brad's and he's going to ask him to be his best man. He's going to ask Colt too, but I'm sure he'll be with Frankie."

"Shit…when I said no Chartreuse dress, did I forget to say no Tim? I'm sure that man hates women. He is such a prickly, arrogant jerk."

"He just went through a very nasty divorce so he probably does not like women right now. You are right though, you can literally feel his scorn for love and marriage." Shauna Lee gave Christina a wicked smile. "You could take him on as a challenge."

"Not likely. He'd freeze me to death."

"We'd better get this paperwork done or we could find out how hot he can get. He can't be impressed; he expected it yesterday."

Christina and Shauna Lee accomplished a great deal by the end of the first week in December; the church was reserved, the reception and catering arrangements in place, a photographer booked and the invitations were at the printers. Colt met them after work on Friday and the three of them went for supper at the local steak house.

Brad looked around the room after they sat down. He took a second look and then grinned at Christina. "Tim is sitting over there all by himself. I think we should invite him to join us."

"Don't put yourself out on my behalf," Christina grumbled.

Brad chuckled. "You know, Christina, the poor guy doesn't really know anybody in town. It's got to be kind of tough."

"I'm not running an escort service either. If he'd get off his high horse he might meet other people, but he is such a bitter, arrogant jerk that he doesn't exactly attract anyone to him."

"We've been friends for a long time, but I have to admit he is pretty jaded right now."

Shauna Lee and Christina were toasting their success with the wedding plans when Tim walked up to their table.

"Hello Brad."

"Tim, it's good to see you. Grab a chair and join us." He motioned to the empty chair beside Christina.

Christina glared at Brad as she moved her purse. She barely acknowledged Tim when he sat down.

Shauna Lee sent him a warm smile. "So are you getting settled, Tim?"

"Yes. I am very comfortable. It is a perfect place for one person."

"I always liked it, until I met Brad." She looked at Brad and smiled. "But the last time I stayed there by myself it felt empty. It just wasn't home for me anymore."

"Well, I'd buy it from you if I wasn't going to be moving out to the farm next fall. It's perfect for my situation and I have no plans to change that."

"How are things at the farm?" Brad asked.

"I go out there every day. I'm getting familiar with the books and the equipment. From what I see, I am really impressed with Colt's management style. I'm excited about taking the place over. He's flexible and open to new ideas which I appreciate. I think we'll work together well."

"How is Frankie doing?" Shauna Lee asked.

"She's putting on a good front, but loosing the baby has been hard on her. It's been hard on both of them. Colt struggles with it, but he tries to be strong for Frankie. And Frankie tries, but the sparkle that was there when I first met her is missing now."

"Well, it hasn't been very long. It is a death of their child and all their dreams for it," Shauna Lee said soberly.

"That feeling of loss doesn't go away over night either," Christina said.

Brad and Shauna Lee looked at each other, wondering. This was the second time Christina had spoken about miscarriage as if she had firsthand knowledge. Tim glanced at her quickly, and then looked away.

When Brad and Shauna Lee got home they talked about Colt and Frankie. "Brad could we invite them for supper on Sunday night? We need to talk to them about the wedding. I don't feel comfortable that we haven't told them yet."

"I did mention that we were engaged when I phoned Colt the other day."

"I am glad you did. I wanted to phone Frankie. She reached out to me before, but it almost feels wrong for us to be so happy when they are hurting so much right now."

Brad pulled his cell phone out of his pocket. "I'll give them a call now and invite them over Sunday afternoon. We could get a tree tomorrow and some decorations. We could put it up on Sunday. The twins might have fun helping us decorate. I'll run the idea past Colt."

Brad was smiling when he clicked off his phone. "Colt asked Frankie how she felt about coming over on Sunday and she was open to it. And not only that, they always get their tree from a farm where they pick their own and cut it. They went there last summer and tagged one. We may not find one we like, but it could be fun to go with them. What do you think?"

Shauna Lee hesitated.

Brad chuckled. "I know what you are thinking. Look, just think about it overnight. I'll let him know in the morning."

*Am I so predictable? That is silly. I have to change and the time to start is now.* "No, you can phone him now, Brad. We should give them as much time to plan as possible."

Brad pulled her to her feet and kissed her. "That's my girl! I'll call right now."

Brad and Shauna Lee met the Thompsons at highway junction, early on Saturday morning. The weather had changed and the morning was cold and frosty. Everyone was dressed in warm jackets, gloves and winter boots. It was a two hour drive to the Christmas tree farm, but everyone was caught in the spirit of the season and no one seemed to mind.

The tree farm offered rides on a wagon pulled by two grey work horses. The wagon was stacked with hay bales and the driver took them down the trails though the rows of trees, stopping periodically so they could look at them.

There was six inches of snow and Shauna Lee made snowballs with the twins and showed them how to make snow angels.

Brad's heart filled with love as he watched her. He smiled as he looked at Colt and Frankie. "Look at her; she's the woman who doesn't want kids. She is great with them."

Colt nodded. "Sometimes it's hard to believe she is the same person I knew for all those years. She has changed a lot since you have come into her life, Brad."

"Christina says that she has changed too. I can't take credit for that, though. I have supported her...and pushed her sometimes too; but she has done the hard work." His face turned serious. "Some of it has been damn hard for her."

Colt and Frankie found the Scotch Pine that they had marked earlier and cut it down. The twins struggled to help Colt and Brad carry it to the wagon. Brad and Shauna Lee selected a Balsam Fir that grew three rows over. Brad cut it with a saw that the farm provided, and they carried it to the wagon together.

It was snowing by the time they got back to the old barn where the tree farm office was located. Everyone had hot chocolate and warmed up around the wood stove. Snow was falling heavily as they headed home. Winter had come and they would have a white Christmas.

Brad pulled into A&W when they got to the city. "I'm damn hungry. That cup of chocolate was just a teaser. Can we make this supper? It's quick and easy."

Shauna Lee nodded. "I'm starved too."

Brad peered out at the snow as they waited for their order. "I want to put lights up around the outside of house. What do you think about stopping at Costco after we are finished eating? We can get decorations for the tree and lights for the house. They have all kinds of stuff there."

"We need a tree stand too."

"I didn't think of that. Is there anything else?"

"I think we need to shop for groceries. What are we going to make for supper tomorrow?"

Two hours later they were laughing like kids when they came out of Costco with two shopping carts filled to the brim. Their excitement carried into the evening while they ate popcorn and examined their purchases.

Brad leaned back, watching Shauna Lee as she sat on the floor in the living room, boxes scattered around her as she examined the brightly coloured ornaments they had bought. Her eyes were sparkling, excitement bubbled from her. *She's like a child,* he mused lovingly.

He pushed boxes away so he could crouch down beside her. "What are you thinking, Tweetie Bird?"

She was caressing an old fashioned looking angel tree topper that she had insisted on buying. "This reminds me of my grandma. That's why I wanted it." She laid her head against his shoulder; "She always made Christmas special. She made all of the decorations; strings of paper links, snowflakes that she cut out, and I can remember stringing popcorn on thread and putting it on the branches. But she had an angel tree topper." She brought the angel to her cheek. "This one reminds me of it."

"So your family did celebrate Christmas when you were young."

She nodded. "Yes; especially when grandma was alive." She was thoughtful. "You know, we never had a lot of gifts. Mom and dad would give me winter boots, or a coat; always things that we needed. Grandma knitted socks and gloves and scarves. Grandma used to bake and she gave it away as gifts.

"But Christmas was about getting together with neighbours and having fun. She was Roman Catholic and we always went to mass on Christmas Eve. She was a happy person and she embraced everyone around her; she made me feel so loved and special."

"After your grandma died, did your mom and dad still celebrate Christmas?"

Shauna Lee sighed. "They went through the motions. But the spirit wasn't there. How do you celebrate love when it isn't there to celebrate?"

Brad stood up. He reached down to take her hand and helped her to her feet. He pulled her against him, brushing away a curl that fell over her eye. He smiled as he looked into her eyes. "There is plenty of love in this house, Tweetie Bird, and we are going to enjoy Christmas the way your grandmother did. We can even go to mass on Christmas Eve, if you want to."

She laughed. "What would your Baptist family think of that?"

"About as much as they'd think of you and I living together in sin. But I live my own life. I have since I left home."

Sunday morning they were up early. It was still snowing outside, but Brad had shaken the snow off the tree when he'd taken it out of the truck box the night before. He had stood it up in the garage so it would dry off. They worked together, deciding where to put the tree and then setting it up in the tree stand.

Karma ran around their feet as they threaded clear mini lights through the branches, then wove ribbons of glittering garland around the tree. Brad helped Shauna Lee put up the angel tree topper.

"Can we put on a few ornaments?" she asked.

He tapped her on the nose. "We were going to do that with the twins."

"We still can, but let's put up few; just you and I. It's our first Christmas tree."

"Let me get the camera first. We need pictures of this." While he went to his office to get it, Shauna Lee spread out the tree skirt they had bought. Brad was busy snapping pictures as she smoothed it out and sat back to admire it.

They took pictures of each other as they hung a few ornaments. Then Shauna placed candles and holly branches around the house. Brad left her to decorate the mantle with candles and fresh cedar boughs that they had bought the day before, while he prepared a big pork loin roast and put it in the oven for supper.

When he was finished he went out to the garage and opened a big box that he had hidden there a couple of weeks earlier. He took out a heavy plastic piece that looked like a red and white brick chimney top that had snow draping over the side. It stood about three feet high and was about two and a half feet square. He took it up and sat it on the step near the front door.

Then he went back and opened a second box. He took out a jolly looking Santa that was designed to sit on the edge of the chimney. It was three feet high. The suit was made of rich red fabric trimmed with white 'fur', and the traditional Santa's hat sat on his head.

He took the Santa outside and placed it on the edge of the chimney. Then he plugged it in and watched the face come to life; the jolly blue eyes lit up from within and pink flushed into its cheeks. The lips shone a natural red. Brad walked by it to check it out. He chuckled as it said, "Ho, Ho, Ho. Merry Christmas!"

He went back to the garage and brought out Santa's over-flowing gift bag and sat it on the step beside him. He stood back and smiled. *I can hardly wait to see Shauna's reaction.* He went inside. "It has quit snowing, Tweetie Bird. Do you think we could work at putting the lights up outside?"

She looked at him with raised eyebrows. "Won't the snow slip down off the roof and bury us?"

He grinned. "Probably; then we'll come in and have hot chocolate."

"You are crazy, but I'll go along with it. Is there anything that we should prep for supper first?"

Brad looked at his watch. "It's noon. They will be here around two o'clock. I guess we could get the potatoes ready to bake, and prepare the broccoli and carrots. Then everything will be simple to finish when they are here. We can sit around and visit and decorate the tree with the twins."

She nodded. "I like that idea."

When they were finished, they had a quick sandwich. Brad put his coat on and went out to get the ladder. Shauna Lee collected the strings of lights and put them in the entry. She grabbed her coat and gloves and slipped into her snow boots. She wrapped a scarf around her neck and pulled on one of Brad's toques. She didn't plan to get any snow down her neck.

Brad came inside to hurry her along. He laughed out loud when he saw her. "You're not taking any chances are you?"

"I hate getting snow down my neck!"

He pulled the camera out of his pocket. "I have to get a picture of this! I'll take it as you come down the steps so I get the snow too." He closed the door and went outside.

She frowned, as she looked at all the boxes of lights. "He could have taken some," she grumbled. She bent to pick up all ten of them and then decided to just take two. She pushed open the door and stepped out. As she turned to close it, she heard, "Ho Ho Ho, Merry Christmas."

She swung around, surprise and confusion showing on her face. She looked down the steps at Brad. He was busy taking pictures. She took a couple of steps and she heard it again, "Ho Ho Ho, Merry Christmas." She turned to look behind her. The boxes of lights fell to the ground as her hands flew to her face.

"Brad!" She looked at him, her blue eyes wide. "That is so adorable! But we didn't get this yesterday. When did you get it?" She flew down the steps to hug him. "I love it! The twins will love it too! Can't you just see them?"

Brad smiled as he dropped a kiss on the tip of her nose. "As long as my big kid likes it, that's all that matters."

She looked at him, a question in her eyes. "Were you serious about putting up the lights or was that just an excuse to get me to come outside?"

"Both! I should have gotten the lights up earlier, but I've been distracted."

They were putting the lights up when Frankie and Colt arrived. Colt offered to give Brad a hand, while Frankie and Shauna Lee watched them. The twins burned off their energy in the snow. When the lights were up across the front of the house, Brad declared the job done for this season. He gathered up the unopened boxes and took them into the garage.

Shauna Lee called the twins and told them to go ahead of them up the steps. When they saw the Santa on the chimney they burst into cries of excitement. When they heard the greeting they broke into howls of laughter. Brad was taking pictures one after the other. He would pick out the priceless ones later and print them off to share.

Once inside, Shauna Lee made hot chocolate for the children. Brad put the potatoes in the oven to bake and put the pork tenderloin in the warmer. Then he made rum and eggnog for the adults and they all sat around the kitchen table.

However, when the twins spied Karma, their hot chocolate was quickly forgotten and they were going crazy over the little dog. Colt got up and took them into the living room, so he could explain to them that they needed to treat her gently or they would hurt her.

Brad followed him, and sat down. Karma was at his feet immediately, clamouring to be lifted onto his lap. He smiled at the twins as he cradled her there.

Frankie asked Shauna Lee to show her the engagement ring, which she showed her with pride. Frankie admired it and asked her if they had set a wedding date.

Shauna Lee smiled. "Oh yes. In fact the planning is well under way already. We are getting married in the Baptist church at two o'clock on Saturday, February fourth." Shauna Lee reached out and rested her hand on Frankie's. "I want to ask you…would you be my maid of honour, Frankie?"

Frankie looked surprised, and then smiled tremulously. "I would be honoured to Shauna Lee. I am so touched that you would ask me."

"I wanted to ask you earlier, but it was after…"

"After the baby…"

Shauna Lee slipped her hand around Frankie's. "It's hard for me to feel right about being so happy, when I know how painful things are for you."

Frankie shook her head. "No…life has to go on."

"How are you doing, Frankie?"

Frankie tried to give her a bright smile. Shauna Lee shook her head. She took her hand and led her into the bedroom. "Frankie, I've never gone through what you have; you and Colt were so excited about the baby. He was so broken and worried about you the day…the day you found out."

Tears filled Frankie's eyes, "I feel so guilty…I blame myself. I don't understand how it could have happened…Maybe I shouldn't have gone riding…"

Shauna Lee hugged her. "Frankie, what happened is not your fault. It's nobody's fault." She led her to the bed and sat down. She pulled Frankie down beside her.

Frankie covered her face. "That's what Colt tells me. He's been so wonderful." Tears slid down her cheeks, "but....I feel so alone, so empty. I am angry. I am angry at myself. I am angry at God. I'm angry at everything; sometimes I'm even mad at Colt; and that is so unfair."

Shauna Lee brushed the tears away, "I think that is pretty normal. Frankie, nobody around here knows this, except Brad, but I know how devastating it is to lose a child. I lost my little boy when he was fourteen months old. I...I totally lost myself. It took me years to get over it. In some ways I never have. Brad has helped me to move on in many ways, but I'm certain no one ever forgets *that* child. It is always a part of you."

Frankie looked shocked. "I had no idea, Shauna Lee."

"I found my own way to cope Frankie. I wanted to die with him, but I didn't, so I shut myself off from that part of my life and built a new one. You don't want to go there Frankie. You have the twins, and Colt loves you so much. He would do anything for you. Hold on to what you have..."

"I know all that Shauna Lee, but I have to make my way through this...in my own time. I am feeling better physically. Now I just try to keep busy and not think about it. But at night...Sometimes I just can't escape..."

"If it ever helps to talk, I am here for you, Frankie."

"Thank you. Sometimes it's easier to talk to another woman. I've just never cultivated any women friends since I got married. You are probably the closest thing to a girl friend that I have here."

"It's the same for me, but you will get to know my secretary, Christina Holmes. She's going to be my bridesmaid. She's worked for me for ten years. I'm ashamed to say I've never taken time to get to know her until now, but she is nice. I hope you will like her." Shauna Lee grinned. "Maybe we will form a girls club; just for the three of us."

Frankie smiled wanly. "Maybe we should go check on the others and see if the twins have terrorized your puppy."

Colt and Brad were in the kitchen. Brad had put the carrots and vegetables on to cook, and he was making a salad. Colt was carving the pork.

"Brad, you should have called me," Shauna Lee protested.

"We can handle this; we figured you girls must be talking girl stuff. Did you ask Frankie to be your matron of honour?"

"Yes, did you talk to Colt?"

Colt was grinning. He reached for Frankie and pulled her close. "So, I guess we are going to walk down the aisle together, again."

She nodded and laid her head on his shoulder. "What are the twins doing?"

Brad laughed. "They are sitting in the living room, looking at the Christmas tree." He looked at Shauna Lee. "We finished decorating the tree. They had a ball. Colt and I kept an eye on them and we lent a hand once in a while. Then I plugged the lights in and they are sitting there, fascinated."

Frankie laughed, "What did you do? Tie them up?"

December passed quickly. Shauna Lee and Brad made dinner for her staff and their families at the house. She was amazed at how warm and friendly they were and how appreciative they were for having been invited.

For the first time since they had worked for her, Shauna Lee had seen her staff as people with families, rather than simply as employees. She had seen different members of their families before, when they had stopped in occasionally, but she realized that she had never seen each family together as a unit. And she was surprised to learn that Christina did not have anyone in her life.

Shauna Lee sent out an invitation to her clients, asking them to join the staff for coffee and goodies; most of them stopped by, including Colt and Tim. Everyone expressed appreciation for getting to meet the staff that worked behind the scenes and the staff members felt appreciated and happy, too. Each client was sent home with a box of chocolates.

Christina shook her head as Tim walked out. "That man would need ten boxes of chocolates to sweeten up the pucker that the lemon he sucks every morning puts in his personality."

On December twenty first, Shauna Lee spent the afternoon at Brad's office, helping him host an afternoon of coffee and donuts for his clients and people who had expressed interest in the wind turbines. They had sent out invitations and advertised in the paper and the turnout was gratifying. Shauna Lee was chatting with James Turner from East End, when a hand touched her shoulder.

She turned her head and looked into Bob Matzlan's blue eyes. Hers widened with shock.

Bob smiled. "I wondered if you would be here. I haven't been able to get you out of my mind since you were in Glaslyn with Brad."

"Oh…"

James Turner looked at them closely. "Are you two related?"

Shauna Lee swallowed a gasp. "No."

Bob Matzlan looked at him with a cautious smile. "Why would you think that?"

"Your eyes; they are almost identical. It's very noticeable."

Shauna Lee swallowed hard as she turned to look for Brad. He happened to glance her way and caught the stress in her expression. His eye slid to the person she was talking to. *Jim Turner; he shouldn't be a problem. Who is the other guy? Oh shit…*

Brad excused himself and strode to her side. "Bob! What a nice surprise. I wasn't sure you would make it." He turned to Shauna Lee. "Sweetheart, would you bring a coffee for Bob?"

She nodded. "Do you take cream or sugar or both?"

He smiled, his eyes drinking in her face. "Neither. I drink it black."

Shauna Lee turned away: anxious to escape his scrutiny. *Those eyes; they are like a lot like mine.* A knot tightened in her belly. *But why is he here? I know Brad invited him, but he must have looked me up first, because Brad hadn't seen him.*

When she came back with Bob's coffee, Brad and he were deep in conversation. Bob reached to take the cup from her trembling fingers. He looked directly at her. "I have just invited Brad and you to have supper with me after you are finished here."

Her eyes flew to Brad's. He reached out and touched her arm. "I told Bob we'd be happy to join him, Shauna."

Bob sensed her anxiety. "Shauna Lee, I don't want to disrupt your life. I just need some answers. This thing won't let me go."

Brad slid his arm around her shoulder. "It's all right, Tweetie Bird. I'll be there with you." He looked around the room. The crowd had thinned to just two people, and they had put their cups down.

"I should go say goodbye to them." He glanced at his watch. "It's after five. We can close up any time after they leave. We'll go for supper right away. I'll come back tomorrow and clean up."

Shauna Lee bit her lip as she looked at Bob. "How does your wife feel about this?"

He eyes saddened. "My wife died five years ago. She had cancer."

Shauna Lee reached out to him, her hand touching his arm. "I'm so sorry."

"She was a wonderful woman and I loved her. We raised a good family and I've lived a happy life. This…" he motioned between Shauna Lee and himself. "This has nothing to do with how I felt about her."

"Then maybe you should leave it in the past."

He smiled sadly. "I wish I could, but it won't let me go."

Shauna Lee turned away and moved to join Brad. Bob followed her. Brad scanned Shauna Lee's face with concern. Her discomfort reached out to him. He took her hand and turned to Bob. "We can go now. What do you like; Chinese, Steak, Seafood?"

Bob chuckled. "I like to support the beef industry, so let's make it steak; but more than anything, I'd like a quiet spot so we can talk."

Brad looked at Shauna Lee, but she wasn't looking at either of them. He sighed. "Let's go to the Steakhouse then. We can pick one of the back booths. It's still early. The crowd won't be coming in yet."

Brad helped her up into the truck. He rested his hand on her thigh and nudged her close to him. "I know you don't want to do this, sweetheart. But he's determined, so we may as well put this behind us so we can more on. I'll be right there with you, sweetheart. You already know what your dad told you. Bob can't hurt you."

She gritted her teeth. "I've done everything I can to leave my past in the past, where it should be; but it just keeps coming back to haunt me."

"This is not going to haunt you. You already know where he is coming from. He can't hurt you."

When they arrived at the restaurant Brad took her hand and led them inside. He looked around the room and walked to a booth at the back. He asked the waitress to wait until he asked her to come to the table, explaining that it would probably be half an hour or more before they would order.

When they sat down, Bob Matzlan placed a brown envelope on the table and slid it over in front of Shauna Lee.

Shawna Lee recoiled like she'd seen a snake.

"Don't be afraid, Shauna Lee. I don't want to hurt you. Please open it."

Shauna stared at the envelope but did not pick it up. Finally Brad picked it up.

"Do you want me to open it?"

"I don't want to see it."

"Do you mind if I look?"

She shook her head and looked away. Brad opened the envelope and took out the contents. There were three pictures. Brad picked up one and looked at it. A corner was torn and the picture was faded. It was a close up of two people; a blonde haired teenage boy with distinctive blue eyes and a dark haired girl with eyes so dark they were almost black. He was hugging her and they were both laughing.

Brad looked at Bob, knowing he was that young man. He picked up the second one and looked at it. The same couple were sitting on the hood of a car looking happy and in love. The third one showed the young woman looking back over her shoulder, as she stood in front of the boy with her arms wrapped around his waist. They both were smiling and vibrantly happy.

Brad's breath caught in his throat. *That has to be Shauna Lee's mother*, he thought. *That expression is hers, except for the eyes. And that is a young Bob; without a doubt.*

He looked at Bob. He nodded and turned to Shawna. "Sweetheart." He put his arm around her and pulled her head into the curve of his shoulder. "You need to look at these." He held one up in front of her. Shawna Lee squeezed her eyes shut. Brad nudged her. "They are happy pictures, Shauna. Look at them."

She sighed and opened her eyes. Her eyes widened as she looked at the picture. Then she reached for it. Tears filled her eyes as she studied it. She looked at Bob. "This is you?"

He nodded. "And Marie Holt."

"I never saw her look so happy. She was beautiful here." She caressed the picture with her thumb. "Were you really in love with her?"

"I always loved her, Shauna Lee."

"But you told me you loved your wife."

He smiled. "I did. She was wonderful and we raised three terrific boys."

"What do your sons think about this?"

"I haven't said anything to them, yet. But I will if what I believe is true. I think that you are my biological daughter."

"That could only hurt them. Why would you do that?"

Bob leaned his elbows on the table and looked at her. "Did you take a good look at my sons?"

"I only saw them briefly when we were there that day. What are you getting at?"

"When we got married my wife was a widow. Her husband had died in an accident. He had been my best friend; the three of us had been extremely close.

The three boys are their children. After Randy was born Suzanne had a tubal ligation, so she and I never had any children.

"I adopted the boys and raised them as my own. I love them like they are my own and the boys know that. They would be happy for me if I found out that I had a biological child; a daughter of my own. I'm sure they would welcome you as their sister."

"You raised another man's children and you loved them?"

His look was puzzled. "Their dad was my best friend. They had been part of my life from the time they were born. I was part of their household. I loved them before I married their mother. Being a father goes beyond dropping the sperm, Shauna Lee."

Her tears threatened to spill over, but she managed to push them away. She looked at Brad.

"It's your call Shauna, but I think you need to get it all out in the open."

Her tear filled eyes met Bob's. "I'm sure you are my biological father. It's hard to ignore our eyes, but…" She pleated the paper napkin on the table in front of her. "I saw my dad for the first time in twenty years a few weeks ago. I didn't want to talk to him, but eventually he insisted; just like you have tonight." Pain filled her eyes as she looked at Bob.

"There were so many things about my childhood that I couldn't understand. My dad and mom…" She shrugged. Brad took her hand again, and gave it a gentle squeeze of encouragement. "As long as could remember, they didn't seem to like each other. And Dad didn't have anything to do with me.

"I didn't know any better. I just thought that was how parents were. When I was eleven my mother had another baby. It was a boy. Dad was so happy. But that baby died when he was four. In the end, dad left mom and I.

Bob sat up straight, his face tight, his hand flexing open and closed.

"When dad came to see me, he told me that he had loved mom with all his heart when he married her. Sometime later, when they were fighting she told him that she didn't love him. That she had always loved someone else.

295

"He doesn't know who you are, but he told me about you being at the house party at Junor. He was thrilled when mom got pregnant, but after I was born he began to realize that he wasn't my father; because of my hair and my eyes."

"Oh, no," Bob said softly.

"Eventually he remembered the man at the party and he put it all together. He confronted mom about it. Of course she didn't want to admit what had happened, but I guess he wouldn't let it go. She finally told him the truth. He said that every time he looked at me, it reminded him of her betrayal and he came to detest me and her."

"Why didn't he divorce her?"

"He should have, but he said part of him still loved her and another part wanted to hurt her like she had hurt him." She sighed. "So they destroyed each other. Dad was bitter and drank all the time. Mom lost herself in depression."

Bob eyes shone with unshed tears. "And you? What happened to you?"

"It made me a survivor."

Bob bowed his head. "I'm sorry Shauna Lee."

"You know Bob, I hated my dad for years but once he told me what had happened, as much as he hurt me when I was a child, I can't hold it against him now. And mom and you...I can't hold it against you either." She picked up a picture and looked at it. "You were so happy then. I'm glad to know mom had some happiness in her life."

She laid her head against Brad's shoulder. "Life is hard sometimes, but once in awhile we get lucky. Brad has changed my life. He has changed me. He loves me for who I am."

Brad got up to get the waitresses attention. Bob reached across the table and touched Shauna Lee's hand. "I want you to keep the pictures and I hope you'll let me be a part of your life."

"Can you imagine? For thirty five years I didn't have a father who would acknowledge me. Now I have two of them.

It was Christmas Eve! Shauna Lee cradled Karma in her arms as she stood on the front porch and watched the huge snowflakes float down with the softness of goose down. Halos formed where the street lights shone through it. The coloured lights that Brad had threaded around the big Spruce tree at the edge of the parking area shimmered like twinkling ghosts. The snow edged down the roof and slid off to dollop on the bottom step.

She couldn't help herself. She stepped back and forth in front of Santa's sack of presents just to listen to the "Ho, ho, ho, Merry Christmas."

Brad opened the door and stepped out behind her in his socking feet. He threaded his arms around her waist and pulled her back against his chest. "It's beautiful, isn't it?"

She nodded. "It is. I'm so excited. I feel like I am ten years old! I can't believe that I never noticed all this beauty before. How could I have been so blind?"

"Most things are better when they are shared; especially times like this. But you know there are a lot of people that feel the same way about Christmas that you did."

She was thoughtful. "I wonder how my dad feels about it. Probably the same; I think he regrets the way he reacted when I was a kid. He has to feel lonely."

"Shauna, do you want to phone and see what he is doing? You could invite him for dinner tomorrow if you want."

"I don't know. You don't like him; how would you feel about it if we did that?"

"Sweetheart, I hate what he did to you. I hate how what he did affected your whole life. But in a way, he was a victim too." He turned her around and led her inside. "And if you want to go back further, then we could blame Bob and your mom."

"And then we could blame Bob's family for moving away," Shauna

Lee continued. "But really, it's just circumstances and life. Maybe it's time to let go of all the blame and anger and move on."

Brad wrapped his arms around her. "It would be a healing thing for all of us. Are you ready to do that?"

"You'll have to help me. Can you stop calling him an asshole?"

"Tweetie Bird; I will do anything to help you heal and move on with your life."

"It's kind of late now to call now isn't it? Tomorrow is Christmas."

"Who knows sweetheart? Some people would hitch hike through a blizzard to get here, if they got that call."

"I don't have a gift for him."

"What would you give him; a sweater or a tie that he probably wouldn't use? I'll bet he would be happier if you gave him a second chance. You could wrap up an invitation to the wedding and give it to him. Have you thought about asking him to walk you down the aisle?"

She smiled at him. "You are so wise. Do you have phone number for the ranch?"

"Come with me. It's in my office."

Shauna Lee dialed the ranch, but didn't reach anyone. She was deep in thought when she came back to the kitchen. "There was no answer there. They must be out feeding or something."

"Let's eat and then you can try to call again."

Brad took the small beef roast from the oven, while Shauna Lee took a salad out of the fridge and mixed the dressing. Brad was setting the table when the doorbell rang.

They looked at each other. Brad shrugged. "It could be Tim. I don't think he was going home for Christmas. I told him to stop by if he wanted to."

Shauna Lee nodded. "I'll get it."

She opened the door. The man at the door stood staring out at the snow, in much the same way as she had done earlier.

He turned to face her as she opened the door. Shauna Lee's jaw sagged.

"I didn't come to stay. I just wanted to give you this and I'll go." He held out a thin package.

Shauna Lee was momentarily stunned. He leaned down and laid the package on the Santa's sack, then mumbling that he was sorry, turned and walked down the step.

She reached out and grabbed his coat. "Dad, please don't go."

He turned to face her. Her eyes filled with tears. "I just tried to call you. There was no answer at the ranch."

He hesitated. "Ollie and I fed late. We fed enough so I don't have to feed tomorrow until the afternoon. I knew I would be late getting home tonight. Ollie went to Thompsons for Christmas. Ellie is having him over for supper tonight."

"Come in," Shauna Lee said, standing aside for him to enter.

Patch stepped up beside her. He looked into her eyes solemnly. "Thank you," he said softly. "I didn't expect you to ask me in. I...I just wanted to do something now that I never did when you were a child."

Shauna Lee hugged him. He hesitated then hugged her back. Brad stood back and watched as the tears seeped down the older man's cheeks. Shauna Lee released her hold and gently nudged Patch inside, closing the door behind them.

Brads eyes met Patch's. They measured each other for a moment. *He was a victim too,* he thought. *No matter how hard it is to understand the way he treated her. If she can try, so can I.*

Brad stepped toward the man who had been Shauna Lee's unwilling parent and extended his hand. "Welcome, Patch; and Merry Christmas." He looked at Shauna Lee. "I'll put another plate on the table."

Shauna Lee's look was grateful. She nodded as she took Patch's coat and hung it up.

Supper was quiet...and awkward. No one knew exactly what to say. When they finished eating Brad poured coffee for the three of them. Brad sat down and looked at Shauna Lee. "Did you show your dad your ring?"

She looked at her hand and then held it out for Patch to see. "Brad and I are engaged. We are getting married on the first weekend in February."

Patch studied the ring and then turned to Brad. "I'm glad Shauna Lee met you. I think you are a good man. It's time someone loved her and looked after her, and I think you will do that."

"Thank you, sir. I love your daughter with all my heart."

Patch looked from one to the other. "Always be honest with each other and don't keep secrets. They destroy love."

Shauna Lee swallowed hard as she looked at Brad. She gathered up the dishes and put them in the dish washer. Brad wished he could have a drink, but decided against it because he knew Patch was an alcoholic. He invited him to join him in the living room. The conversation relaxed as Brad turned it to the ranch and Patch happily talked about what was happening there.

Shauna Lee slipped into the spare room. She opened the box on the bed and took out an invitation and a reply card and envelope. She went to the cupboard and took out a small, thin gift box that she had purchased earlier.

She got a sheet of paper from Brad's desk and quickly wrote a note, then folded the paper and placed it under the invitation which she nestled in a froth of tissue in the box. She took a tag and inscribed it: "To Dad."

She took the gift out and slipped it under the tree with the other gifts. She and Brad had agreed to not go over board; even so, twelve packages were nestled under it. Neither one of them intended to get carried away but one thing had led to another.

Still, she acknowledged, one of the gifts was for Christina who would be over for Christmas dinner and another had Tim's name on it. Shauna Lee felt guilty when she looked at the small package she had placed there for the only man she had known as Dad.

Brad and Patch found they had experiences to share and other things to talk about. Patch had become a hunter after he went to the Gang Ranch. He was a fly fisherman too. Brad and he were soon swapping stories.

Shauna Lee sat back and listened, observing them both. In Brad she saw a passion for things that she and he didn't share. In Patch she got a glimpse of a side of the man that she had never known. They had things in common.

She loved Brad: she didn't know if she would ever be able say she loved Patch. She hadn't forgotten how he had treated her; but he was the only dad she had ever known. She knew he regretted their past. Could she give him a second chance in her heart?

The evening went quickly. Finally Brad looked at his watch and then looked at Shauna Lee. The look held a question. She nodded, and stood up. "Will you stay the night and have Christmas dinner with us tomorrow?"she asked.

"Thank you, but I hadn't planned to do that."

Brad leaned forward. "We'd like to have you stay."

"I don't want to impose on you two. I just wanted to give something to Shauna Lee." He looked around. Panic registered in his voice. "Where did I put it? Did I leave it outside? I don't want it to get wet." He got up and went to the door. Relief showed in his face when he saw it resting on Santa's pack, cold but sheltered from the snow.

When he handed the package to Shauna Lee, Brad intercepted it and carried it to the tree.

"We want you to stay Patch. We talked about this earlier and Shauna Lee phoned the ranch to ask you to come for Christmas dinner. But of course you weren't there."

Patch hesitated. "I should run it by Ollie. The cattle have plenty of hay, but it is snowing. He thought I was going back there tonight."

Brad reached for his cell phone. "I'll call Colt. You can talk to Ollie. But you should stay the night. You'd have a long drive to the ranch and it is still snowing hard." Brad dialed Colt's number.

When he answered Colt told him that Ollie wasn't there. "He's over at Ellie's place." Colt chuckled. "He's probably getting his Christmas present, if you get my drift." Brad heard Frankie scolding him in the back ground. He laughed. "It's true. Why did you want to talk to him?"

"Patch stopped in earlier and we'd like him to stay overnight. It's a long drive home and it's snowing like crazy."

"You know, Ollie and I talked about that earlier. Ollie said they fed plenty late today. He said Patch shouldn't even have to feed tomorrow, so tell him to spend the night. He can spend most of tomorrow as long as he gets home so he can feed the next day."

"Thanks Colt. Did all the parents arrive? It sounds like you have a house full."

"Everyone is here. The place is overflowing. The kids are going crazy with excitement. We had to let them open a few gifts this evening."

"How is Frankie doing?"

"She seems to be doing all right. She is busy and that helps. We just take one day at a time. She has good days and tough days."

"Well, Merry Christmas, Colt."

"Same to you, Brad. I'm glad you guys have invited Patch for Christmas dinner. He is a tormented man, and everyone should be with family for the holiday."

"Yes. We considered that earlier and Shauna Lee phoned the ranch but they were already gone."

Shauna Lee showed Patch to the spare room. She took the box of invitations into the office and then showed him where the towels were in the bathroom.

Patch looked at his clothes. "I didn't exactly come prepared for Christmas dinner. I don't have a change of clothes."

"If you give me your clothes I will put them in the washer and I can have them ready for you in the morning."

"Would you do that for me?"

"Of course I would. Just a minute; there is a house coat that will fit you in the closet." She slid the door open and took out a heavy forest green velour garment that Brad had left in there.

Patch looked at it. He smiled at her. "It's nice. I've never owned one."

Shauna Lee told him to leave his clothes on the floor by his door. She went out to the kitchen where Brad had taken the turkey out of the refrigerator to finish thawing. "I'm going to wash his clothes, so he has clean ones for tomorrow. I let him use the housecoat that was in the closet. He said he's never owned one."

"You know, I just put that in there in case my parents came. No one has worn it yet. We could give it to him."

Shauna Lee reached up to kiss him. "He's right, you are a good man."

She picked up Patch's clothes and threw them in the washer. She and Brad worked in the kitchen doing preparation for the turkey dressing and the vegetables for the next day. By the time they were finished everything was ready to put in saucepans to cook the next day and minimal time would be needed to put the dressing together and have the turkey in the oven.

The next morning Brad finished the turkey and put it in the oven. Shauna Lee pressed Patch's clothes and hung them on his door handle. Then she made coffee and heated cinnamon buns in the warmer.

She and Brad were as giddy as kids. She was anxious to show see him open his gifts and he was just as anxious for her to open hers, but they both agreed that they would only open one gift until every one left that night.

When Patch appeared they each grabbed a coffee and a cinnamon bun and went into the living room. Brad selected the gift he wanted to give her and handed it to her. She picked out the one she wanted to give him. Then she gave Patch her gift.

Patched looked at her in surprise. "I didn't expect a gift."

"Dad, this isn't much."

He opened the box and pushed back the tissue paper. He lifted out the invitation and his eyes filled with tears. "Are you inviting me to the wedding?"

"Yes," she said softly. "There is folded sheet in there too. You should read it."

He moved the invitation and the reply card. He picked up the folded sheet and opened it. The words blurred through his tears as he read them; "Dad, will you please walk me down the aisle at my wedding?"

He put the box down on the end table beside him and stood up. He walked toward Shauna Lee, tears streaming down his cheeks. "This is the most incredible gift you could have ever given me. I'll be honoured to walk you down the aisle. You cannot know what this means to me."

He turned to the tree and picked up his gift for her. "This is all I had to give you."

Shauna Lee's finger trembled as she opened the package. "Oh," she cried softly. In her hands she held a picture taken on her mom and dad's wedding day. They were both smiling and looked very much in love. "Where did you find these?"

"I took them with me when I left. Your mother had hidden them away years before. I knew she would never miss them. She was too deep in her sadness and depression. But I wanted to remember that we loved each other once."

Shauna Lee studied the picture. She looked at Patch. "She looks happy. She looks like she is in love with you here."

"I think she was. I've thought it about it since I talked to you. That's when I got those pictures out and looked at them again. Your mom had a sharp tongue. She was mad at me when she said that she'd always loved someone else. Now I wonder if she was just lashing out at me. She was so scornful when she said it and it hit me where it hurt the most.

"She was so beautiful and I was always insecure; always amazed that she had married me. I loved her so much and I was devastated when she threw that at me. I couldn't let it go."

Shauna Lee looked at him sadly.

"There's another picture there, Shauna Lee."

She started with surprise. "I didn't notice. I was so amazed to see this one." Her fingers slipped under it and pulled out another one. Tears flooded her eyes.

"That's your mom and me when you were born."

Patch was holding her in his arms; her mother was standing behind him with her hand on his shoulder. Patch was a proud father.

304

"I wanted you to know that I did love you when you were born. It just became too painful when I realized that you weren't mine." He looked away. "I let my foolish pride destroy our lives, our family. I'd do it differently now, but it's too late."

Shauna Lee hugged the pictures to her breast. "Thank you, dad. These are so special; I'm grateful that you gave them to me. We can't change what happened in the past. You and I can only move on from here.

She looked at Brad. "Open your gift, sweetheart."

He shook the box, puzzled. He took the wrapping off the package and chuckled when he opened it. "What's this?"

"We are going to learn to speak Mandarin, together. If you are going to do business in China, you need to be able to speak the language. And I want to learn it too, because I want to go there with you one day. China fascinates me."

"Open your gift," he said with a smug smile.

She opened the shallow gift box. When she pulled out the sheaf of papers inside it she realized that it was an itinerary. She read through it carefully and then jumped to her feet, letting the box fall to the floor. She threw her arms around his neck. "You know me too well! Three weeks in China next November? I love it and we have eleven months to dream and plan!"

"I hope the timing is right. It'll be our official honeymoon. You can't go now because of tax season. In the summer and fall I can't go very far because I need to be around to install turbines."

Patch smiled as he watched them. His heart warmed to see how happy they were.

Brad went to check on the turkey and Patch and Shauna Lee chatted about the past. She hesitated and took a deep breath. "Dad, I recently met my biological father."

Patches eyes widened in surprise. "How..."

"I'm starting to believe everything unfolds the way it is supposed to in spite of us. When I met Brad I wasn't a very nice person, Dad. He should have run like hell, but he looked beyond the surface and fell in love with me. I tried to push him away but he wouldn't go.

"And then everything started to happen. I started to recall things I had buried deep in my consciousness. Then, I saw you again.

"After that, Brad and I went to check on some of his installations. The first place we went, the man challenged me, asking about my back ground. He…he sensed something about me. It was bizarre, but he ended up telling me about himself and mom. But he didn't know who I was and I didn't tell him.

"We went to the second place and it turned out to be people who had supported me when…" She shook her head.

"When that no-good man…"

"Yes." She bit her lip and fought back tears. "I blamed you for that, you know. I felt that if you had stayed; if you had loved me; none of that would have happened. I realize now that that wasn't fair, but it took Brad to make me see that."

"But it was my fault."

"No dad. We were all victims. After we got back, Brad went to China and you came and saw me. You told me about you and mom and me and him. I realized then that he had to be my biological father, because your stories were the same."

She looked at him imploring. "I'm not trying to hurt you dad, but I want you to know everything. Last week he came to Brad's open house. He wasn't really looking for Brad. He wanted to talk to me.

"Actually he did what you did. He insisted on talking to me. He took Brad and me out to dinner and he gave me some pictures. They were of him and mom when they were teenagers; a couple of kids and their first love. He was blonde and his eyes are blue just like mine."

Patch got stood up and paced across the room.

"He and mom did…I was conceived the night of that party. He said she was mad at you because you were drinking and you passed out and one thing led to another and they…"

"Your mom admitted that."

"Later, he married the widow of his best friend. She had three boys. He adopted them, but they never had any children. He told me that he loved her with his whole heart and he loves those boys like his own.

"But he wondered if...I don't think he was ever with anyone else other than mom, before he married. When he saw me...the blonde hair and the eyes; our eyes are the same. He wanted to know if he had a biological child...he said once he saw me he had to know."

"I guess he wants to be your father now."

"He is my father and yes he did ask if he could be part of my life and I will be honest, I think I want to get to know him and his children."

Patch looked out the window. "So why did you give me that note, asking me to walk you down the aisle?" She could hear the dejection in his voice.

Shauna Lee stood up and walked over to him. "Because I want you to; he fathered me, you were my dad."

"You want that, even though I was such a poor one?"

"Dad, we all need to heal and move forward. It's time for honesty and forgiveness, not anger and blame."

"Is that why you asked me to be in your wedding?"

"Partly; but mostly I asked you because I *want* you there."

Tears glinted in his eyes. "I'm amazed that you can be so forgiving."

"Dad, to be honest this hasn't been an easy decision for me. Six months ago I wouldn't have asked you; I couldn't have. But thanks to Brad, I have learned that love can change our lives and I want to move forward and heal.

"I can feel that you have changed. My biological father is part of who I am, but he can never replace the fact that you were in my life from birth."

"Will he be at the wedding?" Patch asked.

"I haven't asked him. I'm sure he would like to be, but I wouldn't ask him without giving you a chance to think about it. And I won't ask him to come if you say you don't want me to. I can see where it might make you uncomfortable, but all of that happened a long time ago. We are all different people now."

Patch looked out the window.

"Dad, I don't want your answer now. You have a week or so to think about it. Brad and I are flying to Dawson Creek to meet his family at New Years. When we come home it will be only five weeks until the wedding so I'll have to make some decisions then.

# CHAPTER NINETEEN

*I*t was almost Christmas and the Thompson household bubbled with excitement.

Bob and Serena Thompson had arrived on the twenty second. They were loaded down with gifts. The twins were wild with excitement and constantly on the go.

Frankie was drowning in the confusion. *I love Colt's mom and dad,* she thought. *But right now I could do without all this madness. It is driving me crazy.* She put on her coat and slipped out to sit to sit on the veranda and soak up the tranquility, oblivious of the cold. *Tomorrow Mom and Dad will come, and everything will ramp up another notch.*

Five minutes later Colt came out to check on her. "It's pretty crazy in there isn't it?" He sat down beside her and reached to slip his arm around her. He felt her stiffen and withdraw. "Are you all right?"

"Of course I am," she snapped. "I just came out here to be alone for a few minutes. Is that too much to ask?"

Colt's heart sank. Frankie hadn't been herself since the miscarriage. *She just needs more time,* he thought. He sat beside her for a few minutes. The uncomfortable feeling grew between them. She did not respond when he put his hand on her thigh. She would not look at him and her face remained tight. Finally he stood up and went inside, leaving her there alone.

When he went inside his mother was quick to ask about her. Colt smiled, hiding his pain. "She just needs some quiet time. It's pretty chaotic in here."

Cameron and Rayelle Lamonte arrived early on the twenty fourth. They brought even more gifts and Rayelle had baked a lot of goodies. She and Serena took over the kitchen and Ellie looked after the twins.

Frankie distanced herself from everything. She wandered

through the house, tidying here and there. She put in enough of an appearance to be seen, but kept herself emotionally shuttered. She went upstairs to lie on the bed. *Just three more days; then everyone will go home. I just have to hang on that long.* She sighed and closed her eyes; *Just three more days.*

Colt came upstairs an hour later. She heard his steps and feigned sleep. *He hovers over me all the time. Sometimes I just want to scream. Can't he see that I just need time alone?*

Colt sat on the bed and took her hand in his. She couldn't jerk it away and still pretend she was asleep. She felt him caress it gently. She looked up at him and saw the pain in his eyes. Her heart warmed and she inched over and tugged him to her.

He smiled softly and lay beside her. He wrapped her in his arms and held her close. She relaxed against him, her cheek against his chest. He kissed her forehead and she heard him sigh. Frankie let herself slip into the comfort of his warmth and strength.

She lingered there until Colt stirred. "I worry about you Fran. I want to help you but I don't know how."

"I'll be all right. I'm just tired and there is so much going on all the time. I need to get away once in awhile." She leaned back so she could look into his eyes. "I'm sorry I'm so miserable. I don't mean to hurt you. But I just…I feel so empty. I know I should be happy. It is Christmas time. I should be down there with the twins but the truth is I just wish it would all go away. I could care less about Christmas this year."

"I can see that, hon. Ellie and our mother's are looking after the cooking. And the kids are enjoying themselves with everyone else." He eased her close to him. "It feels so good to hold you like this. I know it's early, but I miss having my friend and companion here with me."

She reached up and touched his face. Her eyes swam with tears. "It feels good to me too. I'm sorry. I don't know what to do. I wish I could just flip the happy switch and be there. But I can't."

"It's all right hon; but please don't shut me out. I want to be there for you but I can't if you won't let me." He dropped a kiss on her forehead. "I guess I should go back down and see what everyone is doing."

Frankie sat up. "I'll come with you." He smiled and took her hand and pulled her up to join him.

Christmas Eve! The kids were hyper, looking forward to opening their gifts. Finally Colt relented and said they could each open two. Eager hands ripped wrapping and tossed it aside. Then they lost then selves in the excitement of their new toys. The adults looked on indulgently.

Frankie was quiet. She looked at all the gifts under the tree. *This is ridiculous,* she thought. *They have so many presents; too many. I'm almost ashamed. There are so many people who can't even afford one and our children have enough presents for ten kids.*

Colt put his arm around Frankie. "If you keep frowning like that you are going to get wrinkles."

She looked up at him and then gave him a broad, fake smile. "I'm being Scrooge. It's almost embarrassing to see that big pile of loot for just two children."

"It is overboard. But remember those gifts are for more than the twins. There is one or two each for everyone else too."

She nodded. "I guess it's another symptom of my frame of mind right now."

"You are not wrong. We will talk to their grandparents and make sure they don't go over the top like this again. In fact they have birthdays coming up; that could be a good time to start."

"Thank you."

Christmas day was a melee of gift opening and excitement and noise. Frankie slipped away to the bedroom and shut the door. Her emotions overwhelmed her; sadness for the little girl she had lost; the huge ball of loneliness in her heart and the desperate emptiness she felt in her arms.

Heart wrenching sobs wracked her body and tears drenched her pillow. Colt slipped into the room. He lay on the bed and pulled her against him. He didn't speak. Instead he let her exhaust her tears and fall asleep.

His own tears dried on his cheeks. *I am totally useless here. Nothing I do helps her.*

Bob and Serena left for home the next day.

Rayelle Lamonte wanted to talk to her daughter and comfort her. She had experienced four miscarriages herself. She truly understood what Frankie was going through, but she didn't get a chance to talk to her. Frankie had erected an emotional wall around herself and she gave nobody opportunity to intrude into the space behind it. Rayelle and Cameron left the next day. Rayelle was frustrated; her heart troubled.

Colt was just as troubled, when he took Frankie for her check up just before New Years. She had developed a sharp tongue, lashing out at everyone; himself, even Ellie and on occasion even the twins.

She spent little time with the children now and Ellie had taken over in the house when his mom and Rayelle had gone home. She seemed to be tired all the time and all through Christmas she had sought to escape company of others.

Dr Wilfred said that Frankie was physically healed and they could resume having sex, but he warned them to take precautions so she wouldn't get pregnant immediately. Then he asked her how she was healing emotionally.

Colt looked at the Doctor intently, hoping that he would intuitively pick up on the anguish he knew that she was trying to suppress. When Frankie gave him a bright smile assuring him that she was doing well, Dr. Wilfred sat back in his chair and smiled at her kindly.

"Frankie, I know that isn't true; no one who wanted their child as much as you two did gets over it in one month. I hope you discuss your feelings honestly with each other."

"We do. Colt is doing fine and so am I."

Colt shook his head. "No honey, I'm not doing fine and neither are you. I'm hurting like hell for what we've lost and so are you. When I try to talk to you about it you shut down and refuse to talk.

"But when I hear you crying at night, when you go for a nap during the day and I peek in and see tears on your cheeks, and when you come down from the bathroom, your eyes red from the tears you have tried to hide; it tears me up inside."

She stared at him. "But you are moving on. I'll get there in time."

"No, I'm stuck in this spot, just like you are. I am trying to be strong for you Frankie. Neither one of us can move on until we deal with this."

Dr Wilfred cleared his throat. "Frankie and Colt; we have counsellors who help people deal with what you've been through. If you try to ignore your pain it will eat at you and it will probably eat at your relationship too. Colt you do not have to be so strong for Frankie that you deny you own feelings; with proper guidance you can help each other heal and face the future together."

Colt looked at Frankie. She looked away from both of them as her eyes filled with tears. Anger surged through her. "Can't I grieve for my baby? What is wrong with that! She was real to me."

Dr Wilfred reached across his desk to her. "Frankie," he said gently. "Of course, you have to grieve. And so does Colt. But there is more involved here for you. You are still flushed with pregnancy hormones. On top of that, your file shows that you have suffered from depression before and we don't want you to slip into it again. I would like to you to see a psychiatrist."

Frankie jumped up. "No! I'm not crazy."

"Frankie no one thinks you are. He is not going to have you lie on a couch like they do in the movies. Colt can go with you."

"We don't need a marriage counsellor either."

"Believe me. He doesn't have time to be a marriage counsellor. He will assess you and offer advice to help you cope. He may prescribe a medication, but that is his expertise. He has more knowledge about the treatments available for the best results."

"Give me a break. I just lost a baby. I cry. I didn't feel like celebrating Christmas. I need some time and space, but you have got me headed for the Loony bin already." She glared at Colt as she turned to the door. "I'm leaving here. Are you coming or are you going to plot with him to put me away?" She slammed the door as she went out.

Colt jumped up to follow her. As he opened the door, Dr. Wilfred said "Keep an eye on her, Colt. Call me any time."

She was at the truck door waiting for him to open it when he came out. She was fuming mad. They both got inside. Colt turned to her. "What would you like to do now?"

She glared at him. "Get away from you."

"Fran…" He reached out to touch her.

"Leave me alone. You went in there and made it sound like there is something wrong with me."

"Honey, you are not yourself."

"You have got to be kidding. What do you expect of me?"

They drove home in silence. Colt felt sick. Frankie's anger burned stronger with every kilometre. When they got home she slammed the house door in his face and rushed passed the twins when they ran to meet her. She strode upstairs into their bedroom and locked the door. Then she lay down on the bed and cried.

Colt hugged the twins, explaining that mommy wasn't feeling good. He looked at Ellie helplessly and then went up the stairs to their bedroom. The door was locked, but he could hear her sobbing. He stood there, helpless; not knowing what to do. Reluctantly he turned and went back down the stairs.

Ellie looked at him with concern in her eyes. He shook his head as his eyes met hers. "I don't know what to do."

"Give her time, Colt."

"She is shutting me out. I'd like to hold her and comfort her. I wish we could talk about losing the baby, but she won't."

"Can I get you a cup of coffee, Colt?"

Frankie stayed in the bedroom for the rest of the day. That night the door was still locked and Colt slept in the spare room.

The next morning Colt had breakfast with Ellie and the twins. Frankie was still barricaded in the bedroom. When he had knocked repeatedly on the door, she had finally told him to go away.

Colt felt like his world was falling apart. His wonderful, loving wife had morphed into a cold stranger in such a short period of time.

He wandered through the house aimlessly, trying to get himself grounded. He went into the office and sat down. *She will come around. We lost Cherish, but we still have the twins. And she loves them. She loves me. I just have to give her space and more time.*

He pushed a pen around on his desk. "I don't expect her to be done grieving yet; I want her to be able to cry and talk about how she feels," he murmured to himself. *But I didn't expect her to shut everyone out. It's not like her. She didn't talk to her mom about what happened; she was barely here emotionally the whole time when everyone was here at Christmas. She doesn't spend time with the twins.* "She doesn't want anything to do with me. It is scary."

The phone rang. It was Mona with questions about the house plans. Colt hesitated and then told her he would come in to her office. He went to the bedroom door and called to Frankie. "Hon, Mona called. She wants us to check out what she has done on the blueprints."

He heard her moving around. Finally she opened the door. She had changed into pyjamas, but her skin was pale and her hair dishevelled. She leaned against the door frame. "You can go in and see what she wants. I'm not into it now."

He reached out to touch her shoulder. "Fran, it might make you feel better if you got out."

She glared at him and pulled away. "As if you would know how I feel." She closed the door against him and locked it.

Colt felt like she had gut punched him. He went down to the kitchen. Ellie was bustling around. The twins were playing in the family room. "I have to go see the architect. I'll take the twins with me and give you some time off Ellie."

"They haven't had their afternoon nap. They could get tired and whiny."

"I'll manage. You go have a rest and take some time for yourself."

"What about Frankie?"

"I talked to her, but she said to go without her. It'll be good for me to get out and do something positive. Don't worry about supper. The kids and I will go out for chicken nuggets. They will love it."

Colt took the twins with him to Mona's office. The changes Mona had made were small and he approved them and told her to go ahead as planned. As Ellie had predicted the twins were getting tired and cranky.

When they got back into the truck Colt buckled them into their child seats, then he got in behind the steering wheel. "I don't want to go home yet," he said softly. "Besides, I told Ellie I would take the twins out to eat so she didn't have to make supper."

He sat for a few minutes then decided to drive over to Tim's place. If Tim was at home he could let the twins nap and the two of them could talk. Tim was just hanging out, watching TV when he arrived. He was surprised to see Colt at his door, but readily agreed to let the twins have a nap on his bed.

They were both asleep in their car seats. Colt brought them in one at a time and laid them on Tim's bed. He took off their boots and un-zipped their jackets and covered them with a light blanket that Tim handed him.

Tim offered him a beer but he declined, knowing he had to drive home and he had the children with him. Tim was watching boxing and Colt settled on the couch beside him. It wasn't his favourite sport, but it was a diversion.

Tim made coffee and brought a box of donuts from the counter and sat it on the coffee table. Colt picked up a new farm publication that lay there and leafed through it. He and Tim talked about a couple of articles in it, and passed two hours in comfortable companionship.

Sam woke up first and quietly wandered out to join them. Colt took off his coat and sat him on his knee. He looked at Tim and smiled shyly. Then he pointed to the donuts, indicating that he wanted one. Tim chuckled and gave him one and then went to get him a glass of milk.

Half an hour later Selena woke up with a wail. Colt looked at Tim and grinned. "The princess calls." He sat Sam down beside Tim and went to the bedroom to get her. He picked her up and carried her into the sitting room and sat down by Tim. She cried as he took off her coat. "I want mommy."

"Mommy is at home, honey."

Tim handed her a donut, which she took and her cries became a whimper. Tim looked at Colt. "How is Frankie doing?"

Colt looked down at Selena before he answered. When he looked at Tim, the strain he felt showed in his eyes. "She's having a tough time."

Tim nodded. "My sister miscarried and she was a mess. But her husband was a jerk. His attitude was to just move on, and they'd have another kid."

"But I don't feel that way, Tim. I understand that she needs to mourn. I do too." He shook his head. "But she has just closed down on everyone. It's hard to know what to do."

"I can't help you, bud. My ex was too busy to have kids, so I have no experience with births or miscarriages."

"I told Ellie to take the evening off. She is a god send! She has just taken over and takes care of everything. I'm going to take the kids for chicken nuggets at Smitty's. Then I can get something to eat too. Do you want to join us?"

Tim looked at his watch. "It sure beats eating alone."

Colt and the twins arrived home at a few minutes before seven o'clock. The outside light was on and Colt thought Ellie must have come over. He guided the twins up the steps onto the veranda and opened the door for them to go inside. He helped them take off their coats and he hung them up. Then he helped them take their boots off and reminded them to put them on the boot mat. "OK, kids. It's time to go upstairs and get ready for bed."

"I want to see Mommy," Selena complained.

"Honey, mommy's not feeling very good right now; she is probably sleeping."

He heard footsteps in the family room, and Frankie came around the corner. "Mommy is here, Selena."

"Mommy, mommy." Selena ran to her and Sam followed on her heels. Frankie pulled them close and hugged them to her.

She looked at Colt, tears shimmering in her eyes. "It was terribly quiet here, with everyone gone."

Colt smiled at her, his love reaching out to her. "I told Ellie to take the afternoon off and the twins and I went to Smitty's for chicken nuggets."

"Annn Tim too," Sam said.

"Yes son, Tim went with us too." He looked at Frankie. "They needed to have a sleep so we went over to Tim's after I went to Mona's office and they slept for a couple of hours. Then I asked Tim if he wanted to go to Smitty's with us. Did you have something to eat?"

"I had a cup of coffee and some toast."

"It is good to see you up."

She nodded, her eyes brimming with tears. She stood up and took the children's hands. "Let's get you ready for bed." She led them upstairs.

Colt hesitated, not sure that he should follow. She looked back at him from the top step and smiled wanly. He bounded up the steps to join them.

After the children were settled in bed she motioned for Colt to go ahead and she closed the door to their room. He wanted to take her into his arms and hold her but he wasn't sure how she would react. She looked at him and then stepped toward him, hesitantly.

He reached for her and enfolded her in his arms. "I've missed you," he whispered.

"I'm sorry Colt. I haven't been fair to you. I can't explain how I feel. Sometimes I'm just overwhelmed."

He bent down tentatively to kiss her. She lifted her lips to meet his and he kissed her gently. "I love you, Fran."

She nodded. "I love you too Colt. I honestly do."

"Do you want something more to eat? Toast isn't very much."

"I'm just not hungry. Will you come to bed with me and just hold me? I...I need to know that you are here with me."

"Honey, I've always been here for you."

"Just come and hold me please?"

He led her to the bed and helped her get into it. Then he stripped down to his tee-shirt and shorts and crawled in beside her. He pulled her close and held her against his chest. She was tense. He ran his hand up and down her back and she gradually relaxed, letting her cheek rest against his tee-shirt.

"I'm sorry," she whispered."

"Honey, you have nothing to be sorry about."

"I meant I'm sorry for locking the door last night. I was so mad at you. I felt like you had betrayed me."

"Honey, that's not what I did. We both have to work our way through this but we have not been communicating."

"I understand that." She pushed away from him. "But a psychiatrist? That was insulting."

"Hon, please let's not do this. I don't want to argue. I want to hold you. I need to feel your warmth. It's been so long."

"But you said we haven't been communicating. I'm trying to communicate."

"Not now. Not this way. Please."

Frankie pushed him away. "You only want to communicate if we do it your way."

Colt stared at her in dismay. "Fran, you are looking for a fight. I don't want to do that." He rolled out of the bed. "I can't do this. I won't do this. I'm going to the spare room."

He walked out of the room. Frankie stared after him, tears running down her cheeks. She jumped out of bed and slammed the bedroom door, locking it behind him.

Colt strode to the spare room. His heart was pounding; his mind in a whirl. "What the hell happened?" he murmured. "One minute she wanted me to hold her; the next she wanted to pick a fight. I can't seem to win." He lay on the bed, trying to think. His mind wouldn't settle and he knew he would never fall asleep.

He got up and went down stairs. He turned on the corner light and sat on the couch. Anxiety filled him, chased by fear. His eyes settled on their wedding album. He reached down to pick it up. He turned the pages looking at the pictures one by one.

"We love each other," he whispered. "How could loosing the baby tear us apart like this? We were the happiest people anyone could know."

His eyes rested on the picture of Frankie and her friend Becky Freemont. Becky… He remembered that Frankie said Becky was her closest confident. "I wonder if she has talked to Becky about the miscarriage; probably not." He looked at the picture for several seconds. *"What was her husband's name? Ron? No…Russ. That was it. Russ was his name."*

He stood up and went to the office. He called information and got the phone number and called without taking time to think it over. When a man answered the phone he asked for Becky, without explaining who was calling.

"Who is this?"

"Colt Thompson; I am married to Frankie Lamonte. Becky was her bridesmaid."

"Oh yeah, Colt; now I remember you. I was there too. How are you guys doing?"

"I need Becky's help. Fran had a miscarriage in November and things have been pretty rough around here…"

"Just a minute; Becky is the one you want to talk to. Here she is."

Becky came on the line. "What's up Colt?"

"Fran miscarried in November; on the twenty fifth. I know it hasn't been that long and she needs to grieve. But I'm worried Becky. Christmas was hard on her. Of course both of our parents came because it was Christmas and because they wanted to support her…us. But she just closed every one out. She's closing me out too.

"Her doctor suggested we get help because she has had depression before. He mentioned a psychiatrist and she hit the roof. I'm worried and I don't know what to do. Tonight…shit, I shouldn't be telling you all this…" He cleared his throat. "Do you have big plans for New Years?"

"We were going to go skiing tomorrow and then just stay at home on New Year's Eve. Do you want me to come out there and talk to her Colt? Because if you do I'll be there; just say the word."

"Becky, I don't want to mess up your New Years plans. But I don't know what to do. We've always been so happy and now…she just gets farther and farther away. Neither one of us can share how we feel. And one minute it looks like there might be a breakthrough and ten minutes later she's looking for a fight."

"I'll be there tomorrow."

"Look, discuss it with Russ before you decide."

"She is my oldest and dearest friend. Russ will understand. I'll go skiing with him another weekend."

"Becky. Let me see if I can get you a flight out here first. Maybe you could be home by New Years Eve. Or maybe Russ would come with you and we'll work something out. Talk it over and I'll check for a flight."

No commercial flights were available. Colt pondered the situation. Then he phoned a local cattle buyer.

"Thompson, what the hell do you want at this time of the night?" Bart Anderson barked.

"Have you got anything lined up for tomorrow morning?"

"Well it is New Year's Eve tomorrow night, but what have you got in mind?"

"Is your plane at the airport?"

"Yes, I went flying today. What's up?"

"My wife just had a miscarriage. She's having a pretty rough time, so I'd like to fly her best friend in from Calgary tomorrow. I tried the airlines but the flights are full. You are my last resort. I don't care how much you charge to fly them here; I'll pay it, if you'll do it for me."

Bart chuckled. "How deep are your pockets, man?"

"I know you'll be fair and this is very important to me."

"Damn it man, you're asking a lot. It's a long weekend and all," he groused. "But, I like that pretty little wife of yours, so I guess I'll do it for you. What time do you want to leave?"

"Bart, I owe you big time for this. How early can we be in Calgary?"

"I fuelled up this afternoon when I got in, so we can leave here at six o'clock in the morning if you want. That will put us in Calgary by eight thirty. We'll stop over to stretch our legs and have breakfast. We can be back in Swift Current by twelve thirty or one."

"Can I phone Becky…and is it all right if her husband decides to come along?"

"It's a six passenger, so there's lots of room."

"One more thing Bart; will you fly them home after the weekend?"

"Shit! Next you'll be asking for my wallet too. This is going to cost you big time man."

"I'm hoping that bringing in her best friend will help Fran. The money is secondary."

"Phone your wife's friend and set it up. We'll be there."

Becky called just as he put the phone down. "We are both coming, Colt. We'll leave here early tomorrow morning."

"Just a minute Becky; can you be at the airport by eight in the morning? A cattle buyer that I deal with has a Beechcraft Bonanza. He's willing to fly out of here at six and I'll come with him.

"He says we should be there by eight. If you meet us there, we'll grab breakfast and head back to Swift Current. We should be back here no later than one o'clock. And he'll fly you home on the second."

"Wow! You know people in high places, Colt!"

"He likes my wife!"

"Is he a good pilot?"

"He flies all the time. I trust him or I wouldn't have called him. He was in the air today."

"Let me check with Russ. I'm sure he will like the idea." She was gone for a couple of minutes and then came back on the line. "That sounds great. Do you have a spare bedroom?"

"Yes. But there's nothing very exciting going on at our house for New Year's. I can get you a good hotel room in town and give you an all expenses paid evening."

"Colt, don't be ridiculous. I am so excited about this. I haven't seen Frankie since you got married and I've never seen the twins!"

"I can't thank you enough, Becky. I hope you can get through to Frankie."

"We'll meet you at the airport at eight in the morning. Thank you, Colt." She gave him her cell number so they could contact each other when the plane landed."

Colt phoned Bart and completed their arrangements. Then he walked over to Ellie's place. To his surprise Ollie was there. They were playing a game of cards and enjoying a drink.

Colt felt guilty when he asked her if she could come to the house by five o'clock in the morning, because he would be gone until mid afternoon. He asked her to change the sheets in the spare room and he asked her if she would make a special New Year's Eve supper. He thought there was a ham in the freezer.

Her eyes were full of questions, but he didn't answer them. He went back to the house and upstairs to the spare room.

The alarm in his mind went off half an hour early. He looked at the clothes that he'd worn the day before and decided to check the laundry room. He smiled when he went inside. "Bless you Ellie! What would we do without you?"

He slipped a shirt off a hanger and a clean pair of jeans that she had creased and hung up. He ran upstairs and dressed, then checked on the twins. He dropped a kiss of each one of them and then carried his dirty clothes down to the laundry room. He set up a pot of coffee to brew and waited for Ellie. He was sipping a cup of coffee when Ellie and Ollie came in.

He hugged Ellie. "I don't know what we would do without you. I will make all this up to you, once our life gets straightened out. One other thing; should Fran happen to ask about me or what I am doing, please don't tell her anything.

"Not about changing the sheets in the spare room or anything. We had another disagreement last night. I slept in the spare room again. She may not get up before I'm back. Maybe that would be best in the long run. But she's not eating enough either and I don't like to see that happening."

Ollie cleared his throat. "Well, maybe Ellie can't ask you what you are doing, but I can. What are you up to, Colt?"

"Ollie, you have nothing to worry about from me. I love that woman upstairs. That is all I'm going to tell you now. I assume you'll be here for supper?"

Ollie nodded.

"I'll see you them. I have to get out of here now."

The weather was beautiful that morning and when the sun rose it was a spectacular day. The flight to Calgary was a beautiful ride. Colt phoned Becky when they landed and they met at a restaurant in the airport.

After they had breakfast, they made their way through the airport and back to Bart's plane. While he made his pre-flight check, Becky, Russ and Colt settled inside. Colt suggested Russ ride up front with Bart so he could get the full view of the trip. Becky and he talked about Frankie and the twins and the miscarriage as they flew to Swift Current.

It was a few minutes after one o'clock when they arrived at the farm. Frankie had not come down stairs yet. Becky looked at Colt, and then took off her coat. "I'm going to go up and get her out of bed."

"Becky, don't be surprised if she won't see you."

"I won't let her get away with that. I'll pick the lock or I'll get you and Russ to help me break the door down. She won't hide from me." She touched Colt's cheek. "She is so lucky to have you Colt. Which door is the one to your bedroom?"

Colt took her up the stairs to the bedroom door and then left her there. *This has to work! Fran has always turned to Becky. Hopefully she can get through to her now.*

Becky knocked on the door. "Get up lazy bones."

There was no response. She pounded on the door. "Frankie let me in! It's Becky and I didn't come all the way from Calgary to have you sleep all the time."

She heard footsteps. Frankie opened the door cautiously. Her hair was a mess, her eyes were red and swollen. She stared at her friend, uncomprehending. "Becky? What are you doing here?"

Becky pushed in and threw her arms around Frankie. "It's New

Years Eve, silly girl. Russ came with me. We came to see you, and those beautiful twins of yours and that wonderful husband of yours. We here for the weekend, so get up you sleepy head. I don't want to miss a moment of this visit."

Frankie clung to her and started to cry. Becky reached back and slammed the door shut, then held her close. "OK girl, tell Becky all about it. What is going on with you?"

The two friends sank onto the bed. Frankie sobbed. Becky probed with gentle questions and gradually Frankie poured out her heart, expressing her anger, her fears and her devastation over her loss.

Four hours later Becky persuaded Frankie to have a shower, fix her hair and get dressed. Frankie was exhausted when she came down stairs with Becky, but her heart was lighter than it had been for the last month.

Ollie and Ellie were in the kitchen putting the finishing touches on the New Years Eve feast. The aroma of roasting ham filled the kitchen.

Frankie looked around the room. "Where are the twins and Colt?"

Ellie smiled at her. "Colt and Russ went to Swift Current to get snacks and replenish the 'happy cupboard'. They took the twins along with them. They will be back soon."

Frankie looked at Becky. "Did you meet Ellie and Ollie?"

Becky grinned. "I met Ollie at the wedding. And Colt told me all about Ellie on the flight back here."

Frankie looked puzzled. "Colt flew with you?"

Becky covered her mouth. "Crap…I shouldn't have opened my big yap."

Frankie looked at her expectantly. "Well…"

"He phoned last night and asked if we would come. He's worried about you, Frankie and he knows how close you and I are. That man is crazy about you. He moved heaven and earth to get us here. He hired a private plane and they were at the Calgary airport at eight o'clock this morning to pick us up."

She grabbed both of Frankie's arms and looked into her eyes. "And here we are! I am so excited to be here! I haven't seen you since the wedding."

Frankie leaned forward and put her head against Becky's breasts. "I was so nasty to him last night. Now, I'm so sorry."

"He didn't say anything about that. He just said you won't talk to anyone. He hoped you will talk to me."

Frankie turned around and went up the stairs again. Becky followed her. Frankie sat on the bed. She covered her face and tears trickled through her fingers. "I'm such a mess, Becky. I feel so empty and so lonely. We wanted her so much. And I lost her."

"Frankie, you are not responsible for what happened. That was out of your hands."

"I'm so tired. I hated Christmas."

"Frankie, this is not you. You have been through a lot. Have you talked to the doctor about depression?"

"He wanted me to go to a Psychiatrist! I am not crazy. I just lost a baby."

"Did the doctor say he thought you were 'crazy'?"

"No. But that's why you go to a psychiatrist."

"Frankie, you need to do some research. That is not why people go to a psychiatrist. They go because they are ill; just like they go to a surgeon if they have gall bladder trouble or cancer or anything like that. Crazy is an uneducated term. People are ill. The psychiatrist diagnoses and prescribes medication to heal the illness. You have suffered from depression twice in the past six years. It could be a very real problem for you now."

Frankie's anger flared. "I didn't go to a psychiatrist. I got over it."

"You did get over it, but each time you left the problem that was the root of your depression, and you healed in a new environment. You can't leave this problem behind and start over. This time, you lost something that was inside of you and no matter where you go that pain is going to go with you.

"You cannot leave the twins. They need you and you need them. And Colt will do anything for you. You are the center of his world. I hope you know how much you have been blessed with Frankie."

She forced Frankie to look at her. "You need to listen to your doctor,

Frankie. Get help. Don't ruin your life and the lives of those who are a part of it."

Tears slipped down Frankie's cheeks. "I...I don't want to. I just...."

"Go wash your face. The guys will be here soon. I want you to see Colt through the eyes of love, not the guilt you feel. And love those babies that I haven't had a chance to meet yet. Go!"

Frankie washed her face and pressed a cold facecloth to her eyes. Finally she came out of the bathroom and looked at Becky. "Let's go downstairs and see if we can do something."

"How about a smile, first?"

Frankie gave her a wan smile.

"I want to see a real smile. Try again."

Frankie smiled. Becky gave her a hug and they went down to meet the others.

New Years Eve was fun at the Thompson household. By the end of the evening, Frankie was smiling and when it was time to go to bed she reached for Colt's hand and led him to the bedroom door.

He tugged her with him to look in on the twins. Then they went into the bedroom and Frankie locked the door behind them.

Frankie threaded her arms around Colt's neck. "Thank you for bringing Becky here. She always makes me see things in a different light. I've been such a mess and I've taken everything out on you. I'm so sorry."

Colt held her close. "I love you. I love the twins. I loved Cherish. But we have to heal and get on with our lives. I know it's only been a month, but I hope we can talk about how we feel and do this together. It's going to take some time for both of us."

"Colt," she whispered. "Will you make love to me tonight? And then will you hold me in your arms and fall asleep with me."

Colt kissed her gently. Then he lowered her to the bed. He went to his night table and took out a condom. She helped him put it on and they made gentle, healing love that soothed both of their souls.

When they were finished Colt slid off the condom and wrapped it in a hand full of Kleenex. He wrapped Frankie in his arms, pulling her cheek against his chest. "I have missed you so much hon. I love you more than you know."

"Do you realise that it was four years ago tonight that we got engaged?" she whispered.

"Yes, it is." He smiled softly and dropped a kiss on her forehead. Then they both drifted off to sleep.

January first, was a fun filled day. The six of them drove out to the ranch to show Becky and Russ where they were going to build their new home. Two car seats made the seating close, but Frankie rode in the back seat between the twins. Becky and Russ rode in front with Colt.

The sun danced on the snow and it was a winter wonderland. It was late when they got home that night, but everyone treasured the memory of the day.

Colt touched base with Bart and confirmed the arrangement for him to fly Becky and Russ back to Calgary. Frankie and Becky hugged before they left the next morning.

Frankie cradled Becky's face in her hands. "Thank you for coming. I needed to see you and get a shot of reality. I've been wallowing in my pain and pushing Colt away. He has tried so hard to support me, but most of the time I haven't let him. You are right. I have so much to be thankful for and I don't want to lose that. I will go to see my doctor and do what he suggests."

Becky grinned. "I have enjoyed this New Years immensely and I'm glad you feel better. Believe me; you will be seeing more of us. I can't wait to visit you in your new house at the ranch. We'll go riding. I love it."

Colt and Frankie waved as the plane took off. They locked hands and walked back to the truck. Colt wrapped his arms around her and pushed her back against the door. "It is so wonderful to see you smile again." He kissed her hungrily arousing passion in both of them.

Frankie pulled back and looked into his eyes. "I will phone Doctor Wilfred tomorrow and ask him to make an appointment with the psychiatrist for me. I can't promise you that I won't ever be horrible again. It may happen, but I'll try to recognize what I'm doing."

# CHAPTER TWENTY

On January first, Brad and Shauna Lee stood in line at the Grande Prairie Airport. Brad's brother and sister-in-law had driven them there from Dawson Creek. Their luggage stood on the floor beside their feet as they said their goodbyes. Everyone was excited about the upcoming wedding and they were engaged in animated conversation.

Once they were on board, Brad took her hand in his and kissed it. "So was meeting the family too traumatic?"

She smiled at him. "They are wonderful and they made me feel very welcome. Your mom and dad were great."

He chuckled. "I asked mom if I could sleep with you."

"You didn't!"

"I did, and she said it would set a bad example for the others."

"You are so bad. You knew she would say no."

"Yes, but it killed me to be around you all day and not be able to touch you like this." He slid his hand to her crotch.

She pushed it away. "Someone will see you." she whispered hoarsely.

"There's a blanket up there. Shall we join the mile-high club?"

Shauna Lee blushed furiously. "Stop it," she whispered.

He laughed, but kept her hand clasped in his, cradled against his thigh.

They changed planes in Edmonton and then flew on to Regina. It was seven o'clock in the evening when they exited the terminal and walked to the pickup. It was a pleasant evening, and Brad noted with satisfaction that it hadn't snowed any more while they were gone, so he didn't have to sweep off the truck.

He opened the door on the driver's side and tossed their luggage inside. Then he turned to Shauna Lee. Instead of boosting her up onto the seat he pulled her hard against him and ravaged her mouth, groaning as he slid his tongue inside. His arousal could be felt through the thickness of her winter coat.

"We could get a motel," she whispered, "But no King sized bed! Every time we get a room with one of them in it, something goes wrong."

He helped her up into the truck and then slid in beside her. The motor started and he put it in gear. After he eased out of the parking lot his hand fell to her inner thigh, stroking gently, stoking the fire within.

He pulled into the Sandman Hotel and parked. He kissed her hungrily again and helped her out of the truck. They went inside and booked a room. There were no queen sized beds available, so Brad took a room with a King sized. They stepped into the elevator and rode up to the second floor.

Shauna Lee looked at the King sized bed and chuckled. "Do you think the third time will be lucky?" she asked motioning to the bed.

"There weren't any queens left. Only doubles. I want room to make love to you."

They took off their clothes and tumbled onto the bed.

"I've missed you and this."

She stroked his erection. "Uhmm. So I see!

They made fast, hard, passionate love. When they were drained and satisfied, they cuddled on the bed. Eventually Brad propped himself up on his elbow. "You know what? I'm hungry. Shall we go eat?

The next morning they slept in until nine o'clock. They showered; pulled on the clothes they had worn the day before and went down to have breakfast. When they arrived home in the mid afternoon they looked at each other and smiled with contentment.

Shauna Lee's blue eyes shone. "It feels good to be home."

He clasped her hands and nodded. "Our home."

January flew by. Wedding plans took up most of the month.

Shauna Lee, Christina, Frankie and Selena drove to Regina the first weekend in the month and bought their dresses.

Shauna Lee had her heart set on a simple satin dress and she found exactly what she was looking for. It was a strapless floor length sheath with a sweetheart neckline. She was delighted with the simple elegance of it and she felt beautiful in it. Instead of a veil, she chose a wide brimmed bridal hat that featured accents of seed pearls, tulle and netting.

Frankie and Christina's dresses were floor length royal blue satin sheaths that complemented both of them. Simple satin high heels were sent to be dyed to match them. Selena was darling in a full skirted white dress that featured layer of organza and a royal blue sash. The girls were bubbling with excitement when they came home.

When Frankie called Patch and asked him how he felt about her inviting her biological father to the wedding he said he wasn't comfortable with the idea. With a twinge of regret, Frankie assured him that she would respect his feelings.

Patch came to Swift Current the following Tuesday and Brad, Colt, Tim, Patch and little Sam went to be fitted for tuxedos. Brad groused about having to wear 'penguin' suits. Frankie and Shauna Lee chuckled and told him what a handsome penguin he was.

Brad came up to Shauna Lee and shook his finger at her. "Why is it all right for you to see me in my tux, but it is bad luck for me to see you in your bridal gown?"

"I don't know. That's just how it is. Ask Frankie."

Frankie and Colt were looking at royal blue shirts. Frankie was giggling when Shauna Lee walked up to her. "This is the colour of our dresses isn't it?" Shauna Lee looked at it closely. "It is," she agreed. "I love that colour." She missed Frankie's wink at Colt."

That afternoon, when Brad and Shauna Lee were going home he looked at her with a grin. "Tell me Tweetie bird; is there any reason why we have to wear those 'penguin' suits for the wedding?"

"I...I guess not. It is just what people do."

"But there is no hard and fast rule that says you have to have a bunch of penguins standing up there at the altar?"

She smiled. "What would you rather do? Wear blue jeans?"

"Why not?"

"So are you telling me you would like to wear blue jeans and cowboy hats?"

"It's just a thought. None of us are penguin suit type of guys."

"Brad this is your wedding too. My dress is very simple; no frills and lace…"

He laid a finger across her lips. "Don't tell me too much. We don't want any bad luck. And honestly, I don't think you should see what I'm going to wear either. What if it brings bad luck?"

"There is no such thing…"

"Can you guarantee that?"

She shook her head and looked at him. "Brad, I'd marry you in your work pants. I would have eloped. This big wedding is your idea. If you don't want to wear a tux, cancel the order. Just one thing; please don't wear blue jeans and chartreuse cowboy shirts. It would look pretty wild in the pictures."

Brad grinned. "And you won't see me until you come up the aisle, right?"

"I'll trust you. But you'll have to co-ordinate the rest of the guys too."

He smiled with a devilish twinkle in his eye.

"You already have this all figured out, don't you?"

Patch came to Shauna Lee's firm on Friday of the third week in January. Christina motioned for him to go into her office.

Shauna Lee looked up with surprise when she saw him there. "Dad, what are you doing here?"

"I would like to take you to lunch. I need to talk to you."

"I can go with you. What do you want to talk to me about?"

"The wedding."

Shauna Lee groaned. "Dad, please tell me there are no more secrets. I can't deal with that now."

"No secrets Shauna Lee. It's just that I have been thinking. I feel kind of bad about not wanting you to invite your f..father."

"It's OK dad. It might be best."

"No, it was small of me. If it's not too late, I think you should invite him. Because of him you are here. I can't claim that right. I put a roof over your head, but it's only by happenstance that I can be called your dad. I wasn't even a good one."

"No more of that kind of talk. We are starting over; remember? I'm a woman who had no one I considered to be a friend and no family. Now I have a few precious friends and two men who want to be my parent. If you truly are comfortable with me asking him, I'd like to."

"Please do it. Now can I take you for lunch?"

She put on her coat and took his arm. "Can I ask Brad to join us?"

"I already did." His smile was pleased.

Christina held a bridal shower a week before the wedding. Frankie and the girls from the office made a surprise trip to the house on Friday night and showered her with gifts. They spent the evening drinking wine and eating snacks, laughing and talking until early in the morning. Shauna Lee was overwhelmed with emotion.

Cole invited Brad, Ollie, Tim and Patch to the farm for the evening. Brad volunteered to make pizza for them and they sat around and enjoyed a beer and talked the evening away. Patch hadn't come; he had stayed at the ranch to do the chores and Ollie spent the night at Ellie's place. Brad and Tim headed for home at midnight.

The night before the wedding they had the wedding rehearsal at the church. Then everyone went out for dinner at the steak house. Brad and Shauna Lee reluctantly parted.

Their wedding day dawned crisp and clear. She got out of bed and wandered into Christina's kitchen. Christina was up already. "So how is the bride this morning?" she asked.

"I'm as happy as a clam! By tonight I will be Mrs. Tweetie Bird Johnson! How does that sound to you?"

"Where does this 'Tweetie Bird' thing come from?"

"It's just a private joke between us. Brad's dad calls his place a bird house. He told Brad he just needed a bird to put in it. Thus I became Tweetie Bird."

Christina laughed. "That is cute."

The smell of coffee floated on the air. Shauna Lee laughed as she poured herself a cup of coffee. "It is endearing."

Frankie and Selena arrived by nine o'clock. From then on, the morning moved from one appointment to the other.

Shauna Lee gave Frankie and Christina a set of dangling earrings and a small pendant. They sparkled prettily against the royal blue of their dresses. She gave Selena a pendant that matched the others.

At one thirty Shauna Lee was dressed and ready to go. She wore a dangling set of diamond earrings and a diamond pendant. She knew she looked beautiful in her gown and now, she was impatient to walk down the aisle.

When they got to the church, Patch met them in the back room. He was wearing a soft grey pinstripe suit, with a royal blue shirt and a white tie. "Pretty snazzy," she commented. "So, what do the rest of them look like?"

Patch just shrugged and gave her a smile. Frankie smirked and Christina turned away.

"You both know! This isn't fair. It's my wedding..."

Christina turned to face her. "Uhuh; You and Brad's wedding. Not just yours. You'll see him when he sees you."

"Wait until you get married," Shauna Lee threatened.

"I hope you are not holding your breath," Christina replied.

The organ started playing. Frankie walked down the aisle, followed by Christina. Then Selena and Sam made their entrance.

Selena was charmingly precocious, looking at every one and stopping along the way to preen. She carried a basket of flowers and sprinkled white blossoms as she walked down the aisle.

Sam was adorable in his soft grey pinstripe pants and royal blue shirt with a white satin bow tie at his neck. A small top hat sat on his head and grey and white suspenders looped over his shoulders. He proudly carried the white satin ring pillow.

When the music changed to the wedding march, Patch looked at his daughter. "Are you ready? You are beautiful; your mom would be so proud of you."

As they stepped through the doors, someone perched a top hat on Patch's head. He barely broke stride as they moved and Shauna Lee was so busy looking ahead for Brad, that she didn't notice.

Then her eyes connected with Brad's and she forgot about what they were wearing until she stopped with Patch at the altar. Her eyes widened. Brad's eyes were twinkling. He was wearing a light grey pinstriped suit, with a royal blue shirt and a white satin tie. On his head he wore a light grey top hat. Pinned to his jacket was a Calla lily that matched the white tinged with pink ones in Shauna Lee's bouquet.

*He is so handsome*, she thought. Her eyes slid over Tim and Colt. They both wore light grey pinstriped pants and royal blue shirts with white satin ties. Grey and white suspenders were looped over their shoulders and they both wore top hats.

Her eyes shot to Frankie, who was trying hard to stifle her laughter. As Brad took her hand she said softly, "I love your outfit. High Society is a way more exciting than penguins." She pushed back his jacket to look for suspenders. She wasn't disappointed; they were there. She winked at Brad and he had to squash a chuckle.

The day went flawlessly. Everyone commented on the bridal party's outfits and Shauna Lee just smiled at Brad.

Before the reception, Shauna Lee and Brad introduced Patch and Bob Matzlan. She held both their hands and said, "Bob, this is my dad, Patch Bergeron. Dad, this is my father, Bob Matzlan." There was a moment of awkwardness as the two men looked at each other.

Brad put a hand on each of their shoulders. "We are happy to have you both here. You are both a part of Shauna Lee's life. The past is long gone. It would make us both happy if you could get to know each other and get along." Patch hesitated and then extended his hand to Bob. Bob let out his breath slowly and shook Patch's hand heartily.

It was late that evening when Brad and Shauna Lee went home. He tucked her into the car he had rented for the wedding. He smiled when he opened the passenger door for her. "I wanted to bring my bride home in style."

When they reached the house he insisted on carrying her from the car. "I have to carry the new bride over the threshold."

She smiled as she threaded her arms around his neck. "A little late don't you think? I've been over this threshold hundreds of time."

He fumbled to open the door. As he swung it open he shook his head. "No, you have never been over this threshold, Mrs. Brad Johnson." He let her slip down to stand on the floor. "Welcome home, Shauna Lee Johnson."

He pulled her against him with no regard for crumpling her dress and he kissed her; really kissed her. When they came up for breath he sighed. "I've wanted to do that all day. Those little pecks for the crowd drove me crazy."

She eased her hand under his suspenders and pulled them. "I like this look. Whose idea was it?"

"Don't you think I'm that imaginative?" he asked as he picked her up and carried her into the bedroom.

"You are very imaginative, but I saw Frankie and Colt looking at these shirts, and she was giggling. I have a feeling..."

"And I have a feeling it's time to initiate this bed, Tweetie Bird Johnson." He reached to undo the zipper of her dress. "Did I tell you how beautiful you looked today?"

"You did, but you can tell me again."

"Your dress is beautiful and I love it on you. But right now, I know I'll like you better without it."

They helped each other undress slowly and lovingly. Shauna Lee snapped his suspender playfully. "Who would have thought these could be sexy? But they are."

Brad unclasped her bra, kissing her neck, following down to her breasts as it fell away. She shivered as he slowly eased the lacy thong off her hips, kneeling to trail his lips down her legs as he slipped it down.

He lifted her onto the bed. They took turns touching, kissing, nibbling, and stroking each other until they could wait no more. When they took each other it was sensuous and gentle. Later they lay satiated and peaceful.

Shauna Lee giggled. "I guess you found a bird for the cage."

He chuckled. "Yes, my Tweetie Bird."

# CHAPTER TWENTY ONE

Frankie and Colt gathered up the twins and bundled them into the truck. Colt took Sam's top hat and nested it with his and handed them to Frankie.

He looked at her carefully. "How are you doing, hon?"

She smiled. "I'm tired now but it's been a fabulous day. Shauna Lee was so gorgeous."

"So were you. You are stunning in that dress."

She reached over and flicked his suspenders. "You guys looked sharp too. I loved your outfits! Shauna Lee did too. She said High Society was away more exciting than penguins."

"I think you have to take credit for getting rid of the penguins. This look was fun though. And Sam was such a little man in his top hat and pin-striped pants. I almost burst with pride!"

"And Selena, sprinkling the white petals down the aisle. She was so adorable." She smiled. "We have wonderful kids."

When they got home they undressed the twins and put them to bed. Colt took her hand and led her into the bedroom. He shut the door and reached for her. He held her gently and nuzzled his face in her hair.

"That's the first wedding we've been to since we got married. It brought back memories; how beautiful you were that day."

"How big I was."

"Sweetheart, you were beautiful! And yes, you were pregnant but look at the beautiful family we have."

"I know. And I would never change them. But if we had it to do over, I'd have the courtship, the wedding, and then the twins."

"Does it bother you that we didn't?"

"Not really, but we both got cheated in some ways. You and I never got to do fun things together before we had responsibility. And you missed all the special things in the pregnancy journey with them. That's why I wanted to have Cherish so badly."

He held her against him, his hand cradling the back of her head. She rested her cheek against his shirt. After a few moments he slid his hand to the zipper at the back of her dress. He slowly eased it down, then pushed the dress away from her breasts and slid it down off her body. He unclasped the strapless bra and let it slip to the floor. He teased her pantyhose down over her hips and peeled them down her legs. One by one she lifted her feet so he could slip them off. Then he eased her lace panties off of her.

She smiled at him as she reached for his suspenders. "My grandfather wore suspenders. I never thought of them as being sexy, but they are on you." She pushed them over his shoulders and unbuttoned his pin-striped pants. As she unzipped the fly she could feel his arousal. She stoked it gently as she slid the pants down.

When she reached to unbutton his shirt, his hands slid over her back. She reached up to kiss him as she undid the first button. He pulled her tight against him as she struggled to undo the rest of the buttons.

He kissed her eyes, her lips and down her neck to her breasts. She was squirming, trying to get his shirt off. Finally he pulled it off his shoulders and down his arms, letting it fall to the floor.

He pulled her against him again, savouring the feel of skin touching skin. She threaded her arms up and around his neck. He felt the softness of her breasts rise and strain against him. He ran his hands down to her buttocks and cupped them, lifting her into him.

She cradled his head and pulled it down so his lips met hers. Their kiss deepened until he swept her up in his arms and laid her on the bed. He grabbed a condom from the night table drawer and slid it on; then their bodies melded into one and they lost themselves in ecstasy.

Sunday morning they lay cuddled in their bed. Colt played with Frankie's hair, entwining it in his fingers. "Hon, how are you feeling this morning?"

Frankie stretched and sat up. She looked at him and smiled. "I feel good."

"You're not tired out from yesterday?"

"Not really."

"It's good to see you feeling better. I'm glad you went to get help."

"I have to thank you for bringing Becky here. She always gets through to me; I probably would have been too stubborn to see the psychiatrist otherwise. I could have sunk into a deep depression. I'm sorry I wouldn't listen to you."

He frowned. "You just weren't yourself. It really worried me. I didn't realize that you had been depressed before and I didn't understand what it could do to you."

"It never occurred to me to tell you. It was just part of my life. It happened twice, and it always was when really painful things happened. The first time was when Dad got hurt and Martin dumped me, both at the same time. That was when I came out to work at the ranch. It was the perfect place for me to heal in peace and quiet."

"And the second time?"

Frankie looked away. She hesitated.

"Hon, when was that?"

She swallowed hard. "When I realized that I was pregnant with the twins. And…and I knew I loved you and you didn't want to be with me," she whispered.

"Fran…"

"I was a mess. Becky made me see sense that time too."

"How did Becky help you?"

"Colt…" her eyes shone with tears. "You'll hate this…"

"No, I should know."

"I…I was so desperate…I was such a mess…I went to Calgary to see a doctor. I planned to have …." She covered her face. "I was going to have an abortion. But I just couldn't do it."

Colt jumped out of the bed. His face was white, his fists clenched.

"Please don't hate me, Colt," she sobbed. "It wasn't that I didn't want the baby, but I was such a wreck: I couldn't see how I could look after a child when I could hardly look after myself. I didn't know I was carrying twins then. I hadn't been to a doctor yet.

"I went to the clinic in Calgary, but I didn't see the doctor there either. I thought of you and I knew I loved you. Reason hit me; I just couldn't believe I had even considered an abortion. I ran out of the clinic and went back to Becky's place."

Tears filled his eyes. "I don't hate you Fran. But to think you were so desperate..."

"It still haunts me. I look at those precious children and think how awful it would have been if I had done that. I couldn't have lived with myself."

Tears slipped down his cheeks. "Why didn't you come to me?"

"I should have. I was going too, even though you had told me.... that you would never...love me. I was going to tell you at the barbecue, but then you announced your engagement to Shauna Lee."

He groaned. "I was such a fool. I nearly cost us everything. And the worst of it is that I had loved you all along."

"Colt, we both made mistakes; but we found our way. And the one good thing is that I knew you loved *me* when we got married. I couldn't have handled living with you and thinking you had only married me for the babies."

He walked to her side of the bed, sat down beside her and took her hands. "I've been so happy these past four years. I didn't have any idea how deeply I had hurt you." He wiped his eyes with his arm.

"Oh Colt, I've been happy too. But I've felt guilty about what I almost did. I think that is why I wanted Cherish so badly. I wanted to share everything about her with you."

"Fran, I have so much to make up to you for." He groaned. "A lifetime won't be enough."

She shook her head. "I don't want you to feel like you have to make up for anything. Please; let's just be happy."

He folded her in his arms and held her. He knew he would never see her in the same way again. In his eyes she was a saint.

Ollie and Ellie came in before they went down stairs. Colt could hear them laughing and chatting, and in moments he could smell coffee brewing. He got up and pulled Frankie to her feet. "I think we have to go down stairs."

She nodded and stood up. Colt pulled on a pair of jeans and a tee-shirt. He handed Frankie her housecoat when she came out of the bathroom. He took her hand and kissed it. "Let's go, love."

Ollie laughed when they came down the stairs. "Look who decided to relive the honeymoon this morning."

Frankie blushed. Colt stopped short. Then he looked at Frankie. "We didn't have a honeymoon."

"Then you damn well should," Ollie said.

Ellie poured two cups of coffee and set them on the table. "Come on you two."

They all sat around the table and talked about the wedding. Ollie chuckled. "It did my heart good to see Patch walk Shauna Lee down the aisle. He was so happy when he came back to the ranch after Christmas."

Colt chuckled. "And Brad isn't out to kill the man anymore. Something big must have happened."

"What did you think of the other guy? The one she introduced as her father, and she introduced Patch as her dad. What the hell was that about?"

"Ollie, I think Shauna Lee's life has been a way more complicated than any of us can imagine. I wouldn't even dare to guess what happened there but she and Brad were comfortable with it and Patch and Bob seemed to understand what was going on."

Frankie went upstairs to check on the children and Colt chatted with Ollie and Ellie.

"How is she doing?" Ollie asked, motioning upstairs.

"She's doing much better. But I am realizing some things that had totally escaped me. My life has been centered on work my whole life. Since we got married, I've been content with my family. It never occurred to me how much Fran and I had missed; we never had a courtship; not even a honeymoon.

"The past four years have been all about the children. It's late, but not too late. I want start spending more time with her, doing things together.

"I want to court her now like I would have before we got married if things had been different. I can't overload you, Ellie, but if we give you blocks of times off, say four or five days at a time, would you be comfortable with being here with the twins over a long weekend?"

"Colt, I can manage the children with no problem. I'm not sure what I would do with that many days off, though."

Ollie grinned, "Well you can come out to the ranch and spend a few days."

She gave him a light smack, "You just want me to clean that place up."

Ollie shook his head and looked at her with a grin. Ellie blushed.

Colt cleared his throat and gave Ollie a pointed look. "Listen here man. I found her first! Don't steal her out from under me."

Ellie chuckled. "Imagine, two men fighting over me at my age! But I've already got a boyfriend. He's upstairs with his mom."

She smiled at Colt, then looked at Ollie, "I think I would enjoy going out to the ranch for a few days. I can beat him at a game of Canasta again."

Colt looked up the stairs. "I want to surprise Fran and do something special for Valentine's Day. I haven't decided what, but if you want too you can take off today and come back on Wednesday. Fran and I will be fine with the kids."

Ellie surprise was obvious; she looked at Ollie.

Ollie was smiling from ear to ear. "So, what are you waiting for? Like I said, I want another chance to beat you at Canasta."

Ellie almost seemed uncertain.

Ollie sensed it. "You do want to come don't you?" he asked hesitantly.

"Oh yes, I do. I'm just thinking how much I'll miss the kids."

Colt laughed. "I promise you they will be here when you get back."

"You are right. I am being silly." She turned to Ollie. "Are you sure you want to put up with me for that long?"

Ollie smirked. "Pretty tough job, but I'm willing to give it a try."

Colt didn't miss the look that passed between them. "Just remember. We'll all be moving out to the ranch in the fall. So don't rush into anything you two." He chuckled. "And no twins; Ellie already has her hands full already."

Ellie turned scarlet. "*Colt!*" she sputtered.

When Frankie brought the twins downstairs she was surprised to find that Ellie and Ollie were gone. "Where did they go?" she asked.

"I told Ellie to take time off until Wednesday. She has worked a lot these past six weeks."

"I'm glad you did that. She deserves it. I don't know what we would have done without her. So what is she going to do?"

"She is going out to the ranch with Ollie."

"Ohhhh," Frankie said with a knowing smile, "I hope we don't lose our nanny."

"I told Ollie not to steal her because I found her first. I also reminded them not to do anything rash. No twins!"

"Colt! You didn't." His amused grin told her he had. "What did Ellie say?"

"She blushed like crazy."

"You are bad!"

"That's why you like me, isn't it?" he teased. He pulled her close and kissed her.

Selena was tired of waiting. "Mommy, I want some Cherrios."

Colt smiled at his daughter. "Just a minute,princess. Daddy was just giving mommy a hug."

"No you weren't. You were kissing her," Selena responded. "Just like Brad and Shauna Lee did at the wedding."

"You are too smart for you tiara, princess. Let's get you some Cheerios."

Sam was looking thoughtful. "Did u hav a weddin mommy?"

Frankie smiled at him. "Yes, daddy and I did have a wedding."

"Did you have a pretty dress too?" Selena chimed in.

"Your mom wore a beautiful dress, Selena. You guys eat your

Cherrios and then we will show you pictures of our wedding."

"Oh goodie," Selena said.

The children had eaten their breakfast and Colt had brought the wedding album to the table when Ollie and Ellie came to the house to say good bye.

Ellie said she was going away for a few days and Selena asked her where she was going. When Ellie told her she was going to the ranch with Ollie, Selena looked at her with big eyes. "Are you getting married too?"

Ellie blushed softly. "No Selena, I'm just going to visit at the ranch. I will be back here on Wednesday to be with you."

"See, Mommy and Daddy!" Sam exclaimed excitedly, pointing at their picture in the album. Ellie stepped over to the table to look at it. Selena pushed in beside her and got up on a chair. She turned the page and squealed. "There's Ollie! He's standing with Daddy and Mommy and that other lady!"

"Thas Becky," Sam said recognizing his mother's friend.

Ellie studied the picture, and then smiled at Ollie.

He almost looked embarrassed; then he nodded with a shy grin and said "Let's go."

Colt and Frankie walked them to the door and waved goodbye. When they came back the twins were still looking at the pictures.

"Mommy isss pretty," Sam exclaimed stabbing his finger at a picture.

Colt laid his arm across her shoulders. "I think so too, son."

Frankie & Colt dressed the children and took them out for a toboggan ride. They spent the morning playing in the snow and everyone came in tired and hungry. After lunch the children were bundled off to bed. Frankie and Colt went to their bedroom and lay on the bed, fully clothed.

Colt reached for her hand. "What kind of things do you think we would have done if I had courted you?"

She rolled over and propped her head on her hand. "I haven't thought about it. What would we have done? What would you have liked to do?"

"Honestly, after my divorce, I just lost myself in work. The only other thing I did was spend time with my race horses; and in a sense I made that my work too. I don't know. What would you have wanted to do?"

She eased onto her back and stared at the ceiling. "Well, I used to rope when I was younger. I wasn't doing that by the time I met you, but I still enjoyed rodeos; even the small ones. Sometimes they were the most fun. And I used to go fly fishing with my dad back home. I loved to ride horseback just for fun, but I loved riding on the range too."

"Did you like going to a show or swimming or hiking or anything like that?"

She sat up and looked at him. "When we were kids we went to shows. But now there is so much on TV that I don't know why anyone would go to the theatre." She giggled, "Unless they want to make out in a safe place."

"Did you go swimming?"

"Well, we used to go for picnics at Rochon Sands and we'd swim in Buffalo Lake. That was always fun. A friend of dad's had a small boat and he'd pull us around on a tube. Some of the kids would water ski, but I didn't."

"Why."

"I was afraid when I was in water over my head." She shook her head. "We used to hike down by the Red Deer River. That was fun; except if you fell on one of the little cactus plants that used to grow on the hills."

Colt chuckled. "I've forgotten some of the things I did. Dad was a farmer first and foremost, so our life was built around the farm. In the winter mom and dad curled, but I never did. When I went to high school I got into high school rodeo; bull dogging steers. And I always loved horses and cattle. Obviously I did some of the other kid stuff, but basically we were all workaholics."

"Hmmm. You still are, but you are a great father and a wonderful husband."

"You'll have to teach me how to play."

"I'm not sure that I know how to anymore."

Ollie brought Ellie back to the farm early on Wednesday afternoon. The twins were excited to see her. Later Colt went over to Ellie's place and told her about his plans for the weekend. She was delighted and assured him that everything would be fine while he and Frankie were away. He had filled Tim in on his plans that morning when they had been out in the machine shed. Tim had assured him that he would be around every day while they were away.

That evening he casually told Frankie that he needed to go to Regina the next day and he suggested that they could spend a night or two there. He smiled as he looked into her eyes. "It might be fun if we went to a show and made out."

Her eyes twinkled as she smiled at him. "Hmmm...do you think we can still do that?"

"I'll bet we could teach those young kids a thing or two! Bring a nice dress. We are a day late for Valentine's Day, but I want to take you out for dinner to some place nice and then maybe we'll go to a show."

"We celebrated Valentine's Day with the twins last night."

"Ahhh...but this will be a night for lovers. And please do me a favour?"

"What is that?"

"Take those sexy new jeans that I bought you for Christmas and your cowboy boots. You look hot in them!"

"Mmmm...hot eh?"

"Sizzling!"

They left for Regina early the next morning. On their way into the city, Colt looked at his watch. "I should slip out to the airport now. Tim ordered a part and it's coming in today."

Colt stopped in the parking lot. He grabbed the small carry-on luggage that Frankie had packed from the backseat, along with his leather jacket, which he draped over his arm to conceal the carry-on. He took Frankie's hand and walked casually into the terminal.

His heart was beating so hard he was certain that she would hear it. He suggested that she wait by the elevator for incoming passengers, while he went up to the wicket to check for Tim's part.

Frankie looked around at everything while she waited. Colt came back and told her had to run back to truck and get a piece of paper he had forgotten, and he had to put the parking stub on the dash so he wouldn't get a ticket.

Half way out the door he offered to put her winter jacket in the truck because she had taken it off. She gave it to him and watched him run across the parking lot. She saw him open the truck door and toss her jacket inside. He took something else out of the back and reached to put the parking stub on the dash.

When he came back to meet her, he took her hand. "We have to go up to the next level. We might as well grab something to eat while we wait for the plane to come in."

He guided her through the terminal, taking her through the security check. She looked at him puzzled, but he just emptied his pockets, took off his cowboy boots, watch, ring, belt & buckle and his coat and placed them in the plastic tub and went through the process without question, so she did the same.

When they were putting on their cowboy boots she whispered, "Why did we have to go through security?"

He smiled. "It's standard procedure now."

"Yes, but…"

"Hon, security is over the top everywhere now, even in these little places. There's a Tim Horton's. Let's stop and get something to eat." He looked at his watch. "We still have an hour and a half before the plane gets in."

They each had a coffee and muffin. Then they went to the waiting room for the flight that he told her they were waiting for.

When the arrival was announced Frankie looked at Colt. "Are you sure we are not in the wrong place?"

"This is where they told me to come." In a few minutes people began to arrive through the jet way and Frankie felt reassured. When no one else was coming through, Colt got up and went to talk to the lady at the travel desk. Frankie saw him take some papers out of his coat and show them to the attendant.

He engaged her in serious conversation for a couple of minutes and it looked like he signed a few papers. The woman looked at Frankie and smiled. She said something else to Colt and they both laughed. When Colt came back to sit down, he told her it wouldn't be much longer.

In about ten minutes children and elderly people started loading, then first class passengers. Colt took Frankie's hand and pulled her to her feet. She looked confused, but he tucked his arm around her waist and let her to the jet way. He nodded to the attendant and handed her two pieces of paper. Then he guided Frankie into the corridor.

"Colt, what are you doing?" she whispered, her eyes wide as saucers. "Where are we going?"

"To Kissimee, Florida."

"What...what are we going to do there?"

"Well, besides what all lovers do, we are going to go to the Silver Spurs Rodeo this weekend."

Colt's courtship had begun.

# CHAPTER TWENTY TWO

On Valentine's Day, Brad came to the office at lunch time and brought Shauna Lee a bouquet of red roses. He also brought a package that was wrapped in red and covered with ribbons and hearts.

Shauna Lee smiled as she took it. "This is so soon after the wedding. You are spoiling me too much."

"It is something simple, but I thought you would like it."

Shauna Lee opened the package. Her eyes misted as she looked at the framed pictures Brad had nestled in tissue and laid one on top of the other in the box. She lifted the top one out. He had scanned and enlarged the pictures Patch had given her at Christmas.

She ran her finger over the glass frame, touching the smiling faces of her mother and Patch as he cradled Shauna Lee proudly in his arms. She lifted out the second one. It was one of Patch and her mother when they were first married; happy and in love. She set the pictures on her desk and turned to him.

He drew her into his arms and looked into her eyes. "They are your family, sweetheart. They weren't the best example of parents, but they were your family."

She swallowed hard. "I know that; and now you are my family and you are teaching me to live life. We'll make sure our children are loved and learn to live life the way you have. They'll never be emotional cripples like me."

He smiled. "Our children?"

She blushed. "That just slipped out."

"Do you want to take it back?"

She looked at him thoughtfully for a moment. "No Brad, I want to have your child."

Brad's heart felt like it would burst with joy. He kissed her gently, almost reverently. "Thank you," he whispered. "I wasn't sure you could ever feel that way after everything you have been through. You never cease to amaze me, Tweetie Bird."

They went out for supper that evening. When they went home and were ready for bed, Shauna Lee took a small package out of her night table drawer. It was wrapped in white and tied with pink and blue ribbons threaded with tiny red hearts.

She sat down on the bed and motioned for him to sit beside her. She put the package in his hand. He smiled as he looked at it. The size and shape gave him no clue to its contents. "It's not much." she said softly.

He released the pink and blue ribbons and loosened the paper. It eased away to reveal a birth control prescription disk. He turned it in his hands, and then popped it open. There were five pills left. He looked at her, a question in his eyes. She closed the lid and pointed to the number of refills.

Brad looked closely. 'Refills:00.' He laid it on the bed beside him and turned to her. "What are you telling me Tweetie Bird?" he asked softly.

"I'm thinking that if it's all right with you, I won't get any refills for awhile. I'm thirty nine...my biological clock is winding down. I think we should make a baby as soon as possible. I will take these last five pills. I don't want to take the chance of messing up my cycle. It could take a while for me to conceive. I've taken birth control pills for twenty years."

"Two babies?; a boy and a girl?"

"I'm game for two. Even three if we don't get one of each in the first two tries."

He was smiling gleefully as he pushed her down onto the mattress. "We can't make a mistake with this. We need to start practicing right now."

As February passed, Shauna Lee felt like she was consumed by work. Swift Current Accounting and Bookkeeping Services became a hive of activity as income tax season started to gain momentum.

February slipped into March; March slipped into April. By the end of April Shauna Lee was exhausted. The April workload had required late work days, even weekends.

Brad's business was growing too, but he had kept the house tidy and cooked meals for them; still, they both missed having time together.

They both sighed with relief after April thirtieth. Self-employed people had until the first of June to file, but the biggest push was over.

The first weekend in May they slept in, luxuriating in the feel of their bodies touching each other, knowing that they didn't have to spring out of bed and rush off to work.

"What would you like to do today, Tweetie Bird?"

"Hmmm. I'd like waffles and strawberries and whipped cream for breakfast and a side of bacon. Do we have strawberries?"

"If we don't, I'll drive into town and get some."

Shauna Lee smiled. "I don't expect you to do that. We can have waffles and eggs and bacon. I just love your waffles; and it'll be so nice to sit at the table and sip coffee and just talk, instead of rushing."

"I agree. We cheated for time together so often before we got married that it's been a shock to have get back into our regular schedules again. I've missed cutting out and playing hooky with you."

"We couldn't have done that if we hadn't owned our own businesses. And realistically, we can't keep doing it or they will suffer."

"What are you going to do when you get pregnant?"

"I have to get pregnant first."

"You will. Its only two and a half months since you went off the pill."

"I know. I just want it to happen now. I hate waiting."

"You've been under a ton of stress at work."

"What if my body doesn't co-operate?"

"It will," Brad assured her.

There were no strawberries in the fridge, so they had waffles and bacon and eggs for breakfast. Then they went for a walk around the property. Spring was creeping over the land, green grass poking through and leaves ready to burst out. The sky was clear and the sun was shining.

"What a wonderful life we have," Shauna Lee breathed.

February and March and April flew by for Colt and Frankie too. Colt courted her tirelessly. She never knew what he would come up with next.

After the trip to Florida, he took her to a movie theatre in Regina so they could make out where no one would know them. At first it felt awkward, but he teased her until she relaxed and became a willing and eager participant. Before the show was over they left for the privacy of their hotel room and made love like a couple of horny teenagers.

In March they flew to Calgary and visited Becky and Russ. The four of them drove to Canmore and into the Kananaskis. The snow was deep along the road and the mountains were spectacular. They stopped at the Nakisa Ski Resort and watched the skiers come down the hill. It was a fun filled weekend and Colt and Russ had cemented their friendship.

In between trips they were busy working on plans for the house. They enjoyed fun filled days with the twins.

Their relationship took on a new dimension. They had always loved each other and their sexual chemistry had been undeniable. Colt had always loved her as his wife and Frankie had always cherished him as a husband and father; but now their world was expanding. They were learning to have fun together and make new memories as intimate friends, compounding the depth of their loving relationship.

In April they remembered the day Cherish would have been born. Colt comforted Frankie as she wept after they planted a flowering plum at the farm.

A couple of weeks later he surprised her by taking her to horse races in Kentucky. They watched with excitement as his horse ran and even though she placed third from last, it was fun.

In May the whole family went out to the ranch. To Ollie's delight Ellie joined them. Colt brought Ollie's mail and left it on the table for him.

Colt and Frankie took the quad up to the bench above the main building to inspect the site for the house. They sat on it and looked over the ranch buildings below.

She reached over and squeezed his hand. "I almost want to pinch myself to make sure this is real."

He leaned his head against hers. "It's real. By this fall there will be a house here. We'll sit out here in our lawn chairs and watch the twins play in the dirt with their Tonka toys. And we'll plant a flowering plum tree in memory of Cherish where we can watch it grow."

Shauna Lee nodded with a smile.

They went back to the ranch house for supper. Ollie and Ellie were working in the kitchen while the children entertained themselves with a cat that Patch had rescued.

Colt sat down at the table while Ellie poured him a cup of coffee.

Ollie pointed to an opened envelope on the table. "Look at that Colt." Colt picked up the envelope, noting that the return address was a legal firm in Vancouver.

"So what is it? Did a long lost relative leave you a fortune?"

"Well, apparently somebody left somebody with something. Read the letter inside the envelope. There has to be some mistake."

Colt drew the folded sheet of paper out of the envelope. He read it and then looked at Ollie."

"Did you sow many wild oats when you were young, old timer?"

Ollie snorted. "Forty four years ago…how the hell do I remember? For certain, no one told me if I did."

Colt smirked as he handed the letter to Frankie. "Your past is catching up with you. You've always said you were a rolling stone until you came here."

Frankie read the letter. "It's odd that a woman would leave a message in her will, telling you that she had given birth to a son that was yours." She studied the letter. "And it looks like she gave the child up for adoption." She frowned. "This is a cruel thing to do. How would you ever find out where he was or who he was?"

Ollie shook his head. "It says to contact the legal firm for more information." That boy would be forty four now; a grown man. "He probably has a family. I could be a grandpa and he doesn't even know I exist."

"You are going to call them, aren't you Ollie?"

"I don't remember a woman by that name: Wanda Ethridge."

"It could be her married name," Ellie said.

"But Wanda...it just doesn't ring a bell."

Frankie frowned. "I'm sure she didn't pick your name out of the hat Ollie. It seems like it took them a while a while to track you down. She died eight years ago."

"I'll phone them sometime and see what they have to say."

The next day Colt and Frankie went riding on horseback to check out the pastures. They made it a leisurely day, stopping to look over the hills, enjoying the ride up through the ravines. When they reached the top they swung out of the saddle and sat on a big rock. Colt took her hand and looked into her eyes.

"How are you doing hon?"

She knew he wasn't asking how she was enjoying the ride. They had stopped using condoms at the end of March, hoping to conceive again, but so far it had not happened.

"I...there were big blood clots again the day before yesterday. I talked to mom; she said that happened to her too; many times. Basically I miscarry every time it happens."

"You didn't tell me."

She nodded. "I needed to think. We have the twins. I don't want to ride this roller coaster of hope and despair every month. I planned to talk to you about this before I did anything, but I think I should go back on birth control pills. They worked well when I was with Martin."

"It's your body, hon. You have to do what works best for you, but I'm totally in favour of you going back on birth control pills. We have a busy summer ahead of us and the twins are getting older so we will be doing more with them."

"Are you saying you don't want another baby?"

"No, I'm saying that we have a lot going on this year and that is stressful for both of us; also, your body needs time to heal."

"I was sort of thinking the same thing. Now that we've talked about it, I'll make an appointment with Dr. Wilfred when we get home."

They let the horses pick their way down to the bottom of the field and rode along the Frenchman River. They stopped where they could sit on the bank and watch it flow past them. Frankie took a package of sandwiches out of her saddle bag. Colt took out a thermos of coffee and filled two plastic cups.

They sat in companionable silence, soaking up the warmth of the sun as they were serenaded by the birds and listened to the river rush by their feet.

When they were finished eating, Colt lay back on the grass and looked up at the sky. He chuckled. "Funny how you remember things sometimes. I remember lying in the grain field when it was about eight inches high and looking at the clouds."

Frankie lay back beside him. "I remember lying in the pasture and looking at the clouds too. I'd see horses and dragons and hearts."

"And eagles and flying saucers. All kinds of things! We'll have to do that with the twins!"

"This is nice isn't it?" she murmured. They found each other's hand and lay with their eyes closed. Frankie smiled, squinting at the sun through partially closed eyelids. "I'll have to teach you to fly fish. We could do that right here."

"I'll give it a try. You'll have to teach Selena and Sam too."

"I'll have to get my dad to come out here. I wonder if he still fishes."

Half an hour later, they got up and collected the sandwich bags, thermos and cups and put them back into the saddle bags. Then they swung up into the saddle and headed for home.

As they rode into the barn yard, Colt looked at Frankie. "Are you happy?"

"This has been a wonderful day. I'm totally contented."

When they went into the house the twins were excited to see them. The four of them sat on the floor and Frankie and Colt told them about their day. The twins didn't fully understand, but they knew that mom and dad had fun riding horses and that they had been at the river."

Ellie called them for supper and everyone sat at the table. Once the twin's plates were filled, Frankie looked at Ollie. "Did you phone those lawyers this afternoon?"

Ollie scooped mashed potatoes onto his plate, and then nodded. "Yes, I did."

"And?"

"It seems that Wanda's will also stipulated that I wasn't to be contacted about the child until the adoptive father died. He died three years ago. It pisses me off that I was kept in the dark for so many years. I have no idea who she is, but apparently they have a birth certificate. I asked them to send me a picture of her. They said they would. The crazy thing is I can't be sure I'd recognise her anyway. I never had any long term relationships."

Frankie looked at him. "Why didn't you, Ollie?"

He sputtered. "I just never was the settling down kind; especially when I was twenty years old."

By the middle of June the basement was poured and the contractor was starting to frame the house. Colt and Frankie were spending more time at the ranch with Ellie and the twins. The third week in June, Colt needed some supplies for the contractor.

Patch offered to go in and bring them back to the ranch if he could stay overnight with Brad and Shauna Lee. He had begun to spend the night at their place whenever he went to Swift Current. Patch liked to garden and he was planting a perennial bed in the back yard for Shauna Lee.

She worked with him when she could and she had discovered that she enjoyed working with plants. The shared project was strengthening their relationship; that was something that both of them treasured.

He left right after breakfast the next morning. Colt and Frankie worked at the house with the contractor all day. Frankie had learned to pound nails side by side with the men and she enjoyed watching the perimeter of the house go up.

That night they were eating supper when the phone rang. Ollie answered it and told Colt that Tim wanted to speak to him. Colt took it in the office, leaving the rest of them talking around the table.

# CHAPTER TWENTY THREE

*S*hauna Lee smiled when Patch came into her office. "What brings you to town today, Dad? You were just here last week."

Patch smiled. "Colt and Frankie and Ellie and the twins are staying out at the ranch right now. The contractor needs some supplies for the weekend, so I volunteered to come in if I could stay overnight with you. I want to finish up that perennial bed today. I'm excited to see the finished project. Would you like to go for lunch with me?"

Shauna Lee nodded and reached for her purse.

"Where shall we go?"

Shauna Lee thought for a moment then smiled. "We could go to A&W and get a hamburger and something to drink. Then we could go to the park and sit on the bench and eat there. It's a beautiful day. You can tell me how you plan to finish off the perennial bed."

"I'd like to do that Shauna Lee."

As they sat on the bench and ate their hamburger and drank a tall cup of root beer, Patch told her about the flowering plum tree that he planned to plant in the bed, along with two red Wiegela shrubs to round out the end of it.

Shauna Lee smiled. "It will always be a symbol of our renewed family relationship. I'm glad we have made peace and found our way back to each other dad." She reached out and squeezed his hand. "I love you, you know."

His eyes misted. "I love you too. I only wish your mom could have lived to know this."

"May be she does, dad. Maybe she has brought us together, finally. What are the odds of it happening on its own?"

Patch dropped her off at the office. She hugged him before she got out of the truck, promising to see him at the house later. When she got out of the truck she walked to the back and looked at the flowering tree in the box. The pink blossoms were already bursting into full bloom. She touched it gently and then waved to Patch as she went inside.

Shauna Lee's heart was happy. She had the pregnancy test that she had used that morning in her purse. She had slipped out and bought it after Christina had come to the office. When she came back, she had gone straight to the bathroom and used it.

She had carefully put it in her purse and took it back to her office. It was impossible to concentrate while she waited. Her heart had pounded as she waited the required five minutes to check it. She could hardly contain her joy when it tested positive.

Brad had to be the first to know. She was about to call him when Patch had come into her office. When she got back from lunch she called Brad's cell. It went to voice mail. She groaned and hung up.

Then she called again. Still no answer; she decided to leave a message. "Hi, daddy; the test was positive! Call me right away."

Brad hadn't called by four o'clock, so she called his cell again. Still no answer, so she told him that Patch was at the house and she was going home.

Brad was on his way home from a meeting with Tim at the farm. Shauna Lee had looked into federal grants for green energy and discovered that substantial aid could be received, so he and Colt had worked out a package deal for ten wind turbines. Three of them would be installed at the farm.

Tim had made a comment that bothered him. He said that a man had dropped by his place the night before looking for Shauna Lee. When Tim said she didn't live there the man had told him that he knew she did and had shown him a luggage tag that had her name and address on it. Tim had told him that he was wrong and the guy had left in a disgruntled mood.

Brad felt uneasy. "How did some guy get Shauna Lee's luggage tag?" he wondered out loud. He reached for his cell phone and cursed when he realized that he had shut it off. He had messages. They were from Shauna Lee. He listened to the first one. "Hi, daddy."

Happiness rushed through him. "Daddy! She is pregnant! We are pregnant!"

He stopped at the florist and bought the biggest bouquet he could find. He bought a crystal vase to put them in and hurried home.

Shauna Lee had hurried home from the office. She went inside and changed into an old pair of sweat pants and a tee shirt. She grabbed a pair of cotton gloves and slid her feet into her runners and then went out to join Patch. He had planted the tree and he was planting the last Weigela bush. Shauna Lee watched as he finished, then helped him shovel bark mulch over the surface of the entire bed.

They stood back to admire their work. "It looks great dad." Shauna Lee hugged him and kissed his cheek. "Let's go inside. I'll make us some coffee. Brad will be home pretty soon."

"You go in and make the coffee. I'll put away the tools and clean up here first. Then I'll be in."

Shauna Lee ran inside, tossed her gloves on the bench and slipped out of her shoes. She opened her purse on the counter and grabbed her cell phone, flipping it open it as she went to the coffee maker.

She was just about to dial when she heard the front door open. "Brad," she cried as she ran around the corner to meet him in the entry.

She stopped abruptly. A stranger stood in front of her. She couldn't think for a moment *How...oh, I left the door unlocked for Brad,* she thought.

"Can I help you?" she asked, puzzled.

"You fucking bitch," he snarled. She recoiled. "You didn't think I'd find you?"

She stepped backward. "Who...who are you? What are you talking about?" Her finger dialed 911. She left the phone on.

"You think you could fool me? Call yourself whoever you want; those eyes are a dead giveaway." Shauna Lee backed around the counter, putting it between them.

"What are you talking about? I...I don't know you."

"You lying bitch. You put me in jail for getting rid of that little freak. I spent twenty years of my life in that hell hole, while you've been running around having a good life."

Fear struck Shauna Lee's heart. Suddenly, she realised who he was. She couldn't let him know that she knew; her life might depend on it.

The phone was still on.

"Sir, I have no idea what you are talking about."

"*Sir*," he snarled. He came around the end of the counter. "You sold my farm you bitch. You stole my life. You built yourself a pretty cushy one here while I rotted in jail."

"You have got the wrong person."

He rushed at her and swung his fist. It hit her cheek. She sprawled on the floor. He lifted his leg to kick her in the belly.

"No! No!" she screamed. "I'm pregnant. You'll kill my baby."

Patch had just stepped in the back door. He heard Shauna Lee scream. *What the hell is going on?* Then, her words registered in his mind. *She is pregnant!*

Suddenly he heard a sick laugh. *Who is that?* As he ran down the hall, he saw Brad coming up the steps. He rounded the corner to see a stranger standing over Shauna Lee as she lay on the floor.

The man was laughing crazily. "You are pregnant! You are going to bring another freak into the world." He threw his head back and cackled. "You stupid bitch; you're going to pull the same shit on another sucker? No man will want your freaky spawn. I should let you live but I came to settle my score with you. The lucky bastard will never know what I saved him from." He reached into his pocket and in a flash he had an open blade in his hand.

Everything happened at once. Shauna Lee threw the phone at him as she rolled onto her side. Patch yelled as he launched himself at the man. The stranger turned slightly and drove the blade into Patch's chest.

Brad roared as he came over the counter, the crystal vase raised. He slammed it into the intruder's head. There was a sickening crunch and the man fell to the floor.

Brad reached for Shauna Lee but she pushed him away as she scrambled to reach Patch.

"Dad," she sobbed. "Noooo," she screamed. "Dad; please don't die. You can't leave me now."

Police were suddenly everywhere. Brad scrambled to reach Shauna Lee. He dropped down beside her, putting his arms around her. She cradled Patch's head on her knee. Blood seeped out of his mouth. His breathing was laboured and irregular; gasping. He opened his eyes and looked at Shauna Lee. "I love you," he gasped. "Take care of my grandch..."

The words faded away with a gurgle and his eyes glazed over.

Shauna Lee keened eerily, her grief unbearable. "He saved my life. He died protecting me and the baby."

A policeman lifted Brad away from her. "Is she pregnant?"

Brad nodded numbly. "We just found out today."

The policeman touched his shoulder with compassion as he asked him to make way for the EMT's.

Brad felt his world crumble as they gave her an injection in the arm and loaded a hysterical Shauna Lee onto a stretcher. He fought to go with the ambulance, but the police required his statement before he could leave the scene.

He cursed them roundly, telling them that he had walked into the house to witness a stranger threatening his wife. Her father had charged at the man and Brad had vaulted over the counter and hit him on the head with the vase.

Water and flowers were scattered all over the floor. Brad wept as he told them he had brought them home as a gift to celebrate the fact that they had just learned that they were going to have a baby.

The police asked who they could call that would come and stay with him. Brad looked at him blankly. "You can't stay here alone, sir."

"But, Shauna Lee?" Brad asked in confusion.

"She won't be home tonight. She has had an extremely traumatic experience."

"Then I'm going to her..."

"You need to have someone with you. Your emotional state is not such, that I can agree to letting you drive."

Brad gave the police officer Tim's number. Tim was there in fifteen minutes. He watched two bodies being carried out. He recognized them both. Patch and the stranger who had came to his house the night before.

He took out his cell and called the ranch. When Ollie answered he asked for Colt and told him what had happened.

Four months later.

Shauna Lee stood in front of the tree in the perennial bed behind the house. Tears ran down her cheeks as she looked at it. Her hand touched her belly. Patch had died to save her and the baby boy in her womb.

Brad had risked his freedom to save them. For a few weeks it was uncertain if he would be charged with manslaughter or not. He had hit Dave Trutcher from behind and the blow had resulted in the mad man's death.

By chance Shauna Lee had recorded the entire conflict with her cell phone. In the end that had provided the evidence that assured Brad's freedom.

They had determined that Trutcher had been released on parole six months earlier. He had been employed as a janitor at the Grande Prairie airport. Shauna Lee and Brad deducted that he had recognized Shauna Lee and had stolen her luggage tag. Shauna Lee vaguely remembered that a janitor who was cleaning the floor had bumped into her, but she had been involved in the conversation with Brad's brother and sister-in-law and hadn't really paid any attention to him.

The information on the old tag had led him to Tim's place. When Tim had told him Shauna Lee didn't live there he probably hadn't believed him.

When Tim had arrived home the next evening, he was surprised to find the back door open. At the time he hadn't noticed anything missing. Days later he checked the door and could tell it had been picked.

Later still, he remembered that he had left one of the cards from Swift Current Accounting and Bookkeeping Services on his table with miscellaneous other things. Shauna Lee's name was at the bottom of the card.

The police eventually determined that Trutcher had waited outside her office in a stolen car and followed her home. He had parked the car out of sight down the road and walked to the house. They had found it there later.

He had probably watched her working in the back yard with Patch. When she came into the house alone he had made his move.

Brad came out of the house to join his wife. Pain still clouded her eyes. She had been going to counselling for four months, and he knew she would have a long way to go. The shock of her dad's death had been devastating, but the therapy was reaching into other dark corners of her mind too. It would take time, but he was relieved to know that she was on a healing track.

Brad hugged her.

"You were right, you know." She said looking at him.

"I was right about what?"

"I did need help…therapy to help me deal with the past. Your love and support have done so much for me, but I need to deal with a lot of it myself; and I need guidance from someone impartial who can help me face reality."

She picked up Karma and cuddled her as she studied the tree in the perennial bed. "I am discovering that in many ways, emotionally, I am still that frightened, eighteen-year old that I thought I had buried. My whole life has been a facade that I have built to help me cope."

She squeezed his hand. "And you sensed that all along; I just wouldn't accept that I needed help."

"Tweetie Bird, I am just grateful that you are all right. You were sedated for three days. I was afraid I'd lost you. The trauma of what happened could have been the last straw. I was scared to death."

He touched her stomach. "And little Patrick in there; I was afraid for him. He was so new, but he's a survivor like his mother. He hung on tight and now he's strong and kicking. Patch will live on through him."

Shauna Lee sighed. "Life is strange. Dad and I came full circle. He loved me when I was born, then he couldn't stand me and I learned to hate him. He showed up here twenty years later and against all odds, we learned to accept and trust and love each other again. We gave each other a second chance."

Shauna Lee laid her head on his shoulder. "And we would never have done that if you hadn't come into my life and given me a second chance. You became my safe warm place even when my past came back to haunt me, and I have learned that *you can run.... but you can't hide.*"

# Authors Notes

I have fictitiously used the city of Swift Current, Saskatchewan, Canada and all of the other towns, cities, villages, hamlets or abandoned places on the map that I mentioned in this book. I have done all my research about the area on the internet. I have *fictionally* used the names of actual businesses that I found in my internet research; (restaurants, fast food places, grocery stores, big box stores, hotels, motels, churches, airports and tourist spots etc.) in fictitious situations in this book.

One day I would like to visit Coronach, the Big Muddy Badlands, Castle Butte and take a tour of Sam Kelly's outlaw caves. I have no idea if the area is as interesting in real life as it sounded on the internet, but it seems that there is some very fascinating history there.

The "Eliminators Show and Shine" is an actual event that I discovered on the internet. It looked like an interesting venue, so I incorporated it into the story in a fictional way. I set it at a different time of the year than it is held in real life because it worked to carry the story forward.

If you have any interest in the places in *"You Can Run...."* have fun exploring them on the internet. It could be a learning experience!

Watch for the Book III of the Thompson Family Trilogy in 2013. If you visit my website at **http://gloriaantypowich.com/ I will keep you posted.**

**If you enjoyed this book please leave a book review on Amazon, Barnes and Noble, Smashwords, WLC Readers Forum and/or my website. It would be appreciated so much. Thank you!**

CPSIA information can be obtained at www.ICGtesting.com
Printed in the USA
LVOW102320290413

331460LV00006B/23/P